HITTING HOME

MAKING IT PERSONAL

Book 3 in The Atrocities Series

by JOSEPH MITCHAM

Copyright © 2022 Joseph Mitcham

All rights reserved.

ISBN: 9798819505199

Joseph Mitcham

Acknowledgements

The text of this book is in better shape thanks to the inputs of Phil, Kev, José, Heather, Derek, Col Jamie and Colin. Support to the artistic elements of the project came from Jonathan, Kevin and Stephen. Thank you all.

The views and opinions expressed are those of the author alone and should not be taken to represent those of Her Majesty's Government, MOD, HM Armed Forces or any government agency.

Whilst some of the characters in this book are based on people I know; each is a creative work of fiction retaining little by way of fact from the life or career of the person in mind and is not intended to be representative of them.

Prologue

Sami thanks the old Nepalese shopkeeper and stows his purchase in his otherwise empty holdall. He takes a final look around the neat, polished and fairly sparse room of antiquities. He realises that it is the hygiene and tidiness that has made this shop stand out from others that he has visited – maybe a giveaway to the proprietor's former life.

The vast majority of items on display are relics, trinkets and heirlooms that have been sold on or donated by the soldiers of the locally barracked Royal Gurkha Rifles. Sami has seen the serving and retired members of the Regiment, and members of their families, walking the streets over the past few days since returning to Folkestone, having only recently retreated back from the bustle of London, back the only way he had known, south, almost to the point where he had arrived on these shores.

He sets off down the hill, following the street as it winds, twist after twist between the colourful shopfronts and semi-permanent market stalls. He tips a nod and a smile to a pair of smartly dressed young Gurkhas, their regimental polo shirts and blazers buoying their profiles with an edge of humble pride. Sami feels a sense of kindred spirit with the young warriors, and the reciprocal body language that they reflect at him brings him a warm glow. This is an unexpected change from the stares of respectful disdain that he might have received prior to his recent excursion to the barbers and trawl through the charity shops.

Joseph Mitcham

Having received an additional allowance in order to be well presented for his role, he has traded his unkempt trusses and wispy black whiskers, for a slick and trim, jet-black crew cut. Foregoing a tie for practical reasons, he has kept the neck of the crisp white shirt open, giving him a modern, smart-casual look with the navy-blue summer jacket contrasting perfectly with khaki chinos. Feeling guilt for every penny that he spends, he has been efficient, and squirrelled a little extra to add to what he has sent home to Egypt this month.

He catches sight of himself in the window of one of the back-street jewellers, the backdrop of diamonds and gold adding effect; he feels a pride in himself that he has not felt since leaving his homeland - I am worth so much more than this.

*

It is a lovely bright Friday morning, beautiful for a walk through the coastal park. Sami smiles at the children and their families as he heads west along the broad path under the lush foliage of the giant oaks. After enjoying nearly two kilometres of the well-maintained narrow woodland walk, set perfectly under the cliffs, he drops down onto the seafront footpath and continues for another ten minutes before crossing the road and heading north through a car park and onto Military Road. He is now feeling a little nervous anticipation as he runs through his patter; what will he say to gain the trust of his customers? How will he get what he needs from them? He has done his research; he knows that the residents of the area are almost exclusively elderly, and mostly single occupants – as would be expected with such a coastal residential area of bungalows remote from the commercial centres. He smiles and bows his head to one such lady as she pushes her wheeled shopping bag. She returns a kind smile, but her cautiousness is given away as she grasps the lapels of her light summer jacket together and looks to the ground as she passes him.

Sami turns left into the Birdbrook Fields cul-de-sac and takes a deep breath as he approaches the first house. He opens the decorative wooden gate at the end of the garden path and admires the flourishing beds and manicured edges of the perfectly trimmed lawn. He knocks firmly enough to be heard by the slightly hard of hearing, but with a friendly rhythmical beat; he rings the doorbell for good measure, then steps back a respectful distance from the porchway.

Clutching his holdall, he begins to doubt that there is anyone home, but then he sees someone moving through the frosted glass. The door opens and he is greeted by the friendly, but curious face of a lady looking to be in her seventies. "Hello?" she says, tilting her loosely curled white locks over to the left inquisitively.

"Good morning, Madam. My name is Sami, I am collecting for the community food bank, I wondered if you might be kind enough to spare some unwanted groceries from your cupboard? Maybe some things that you have not used, that would otherwise go to waste?" He smiles a submissive smile, bending at his knees, almost curtseying.

She returns a smile, but Sami senses her lack of conviction with more than a hint of fear. He pulls on the lanyard around his neck and the laminated identification card attached to the end of it slides out from under his jacket. "I'm from the Moreham Ford Action Group." He pushes the card towards her, but makes no effort to move forward, maintaining his distance. She looks at the card but doesn't really interrogate it. After a brief pause, it is clear that he has done enough to appease her fears.

"Good for you, young man." she says, the smile returning to her face. "I'm sure I'll have something in here." She looks at his empty holdall; "Won't you come in a minute?" She allows the door to gently glide open invitingly and beckons him in as she turns and heads gingerly along the hallway towards the kitchen.

Sami steps into the bungalow and pulls the door closed behind him. He reaches into his bag and pulls out the razor-sharp kukri.

Joseph Mitcham

1

New office

Lucy has taken to the new office on the second floor of 12 Millbank like a duck to water. She is enjoying the associated privileges and additional levels of access that her new Security Service attachment brings with it.

Having bounced from a lowly Corporal at the Army's Main Server Building in Whitehall, up to Sergeant attached to the West Midlands Police Counter Terror Unit, she is now, just weeks later, an Acting Staff-Sergeant. Returning to London; the old MI-5 building and hot on the trail of the most dangerous terror network to have ever emerged on the UK mainland. As yet to announce itself, it has been locally dubbed 'the Interest Group'.

This is no easy ride though; she has barely stopped since the fifteenth of July. Over 700 people have so far been confirmed dead from the double train derailment and explosion - the 'Belton Tunnel attack'. Her only live leads are nine members of the UK Terror Watch List, thought to be a part of the same mysterious emerging terror organisation. The nine disappeared in the hours before they should have met their ends at the hands of a highly professional vigilante group of ex-soldiers, along with the 159 targets that were hit simultaneously.

Lucy knows this because it was her, now, boyfriend Alex who stole the list – he had taken it from the Security Service network whilst working at the Main Server Building - under her supervision and without her knowledge. As they had become close; Alex had let this slip to her and appealed to her aggressive nature, persuading her to join his team. She willingly crossed the line, risking her career and liberty.

*

"Are you okay?" Dev asks as he walks into the room, not having seen her frown like this since Belton Tunnel.

A smile breaks across her face as she looks up. "Argh, Detective 'Sergeant' Jackson. Congratulations." She jumps from her seat to give him a hug.

Dev made little real tangible contribution towards tracking down the perpetrator of the Belton Tunnel incident, but he had been credited with tackling an armed suspect during the investigation leading to him getting shot in the arm for his troubles; this had been enough to push him over the line for what is an impressively early promotion.

"Were you told to smarten up for your new rank?" she asks, stroking the sleeve of his new, fashionably cut, light brown blazer and reaching up to wave her hand around over his neatly braided-down black hair, a big improvement from the previously shapeless fuzz that had engulfed his head.

"No luck yet, then?" he asks, ignoring her question.

The frustration returns to Lucy's face. "Nothing. It's like they've just disappeared." she says plonking herself back at her desk. Lucy has searched and scoured every possible means, even following leads into Europe and across the Middle East trying to find anything on the potential members of the illusive Interest Group. Dev walks around the back-to-back desks and takes his seat opposite her in their new open-plan team office. Their new Security Service colleagues seem to be quite aloof, preferring to work in isolation and away from the hub, the other desks in the room seem to be rarely used hot-desks, home to laptop docking stations and black screens.

"These people are clever." Dev says, somewhat redundantly, "They clearly have entirely new identities in place and have ditched their previous lives. With the work you've put in; you'd have found them by now otherwise. We've got nothing from their finances, properties, family members, or social links."

"I'm beginning to think you're right." Lucy pauses, gazing at a spot on the wall. Staring so hard into the off-white paint that it makes a myriad of colours stream across it like a whirlpool of rainbows in her mind's eye. She finds herself in the same soup of thoughts that she has time and again over the past six weeks. We can't find them, maybe we can find where they want to be or what they want to get. She thinks back to her encounters with their operatives, when they attacked her and Alex, when they stole Alex's copy of the Watch List.

"Lucy, are you okay?"

"Hmmm." Her eyes flash back to her computer screen and she moves the mouse to open a file. "Maybe we can't find the members of their organisation, but maybe we can find some of their recruiting targets."

One of the foot-soldiers of the group had let slip to Alex that they were more concerned about securing a copy of the Watch List, than they were about saving any of the listed extremists from the team of British Forces' veterans who had each vowed to neutralise the top 179 list members. With the names and full contact details of in excess of 23,000 individuals who had been noted for terror offences or for having close links to those who had; the list is virtually a phone book of ideal candidates to join their group.

"You're on about the Watch List again, aren't you?" Dev says with irritation, having seen nothing tangible come out of her theory about the missing members of the top tier. "What are we going to do? Actually watch some of the Watch List members and see if anyone approaches them to join a group of terrorists? Monitor their mail in case they get an invite for an insight day?" he says mockingly.

Unable to confess to Dev her confirmed knowledge of how the list was filtered, and that Alex's ordered version of the list is in the hands of the Interest Group, Lucy has to be careful how she broaches this conversation. "You know how I filtered the list to get the same names in the top 179 as the group of unknowns did for their killing spree?" she asks, but doesn't await Dev's confirmation, "Well if I take the least dangerous of the filters off that streaming; let's say, 'refusing to attend an anti-extremist course', it adds another 54 names to the bottom of the list." She looks over her screen to gauge Dev's reaction; he shows no signs of being impressed. "That 54 might be the first batch of potential recruits that the Interest Group might approach."

Dev looks back at Lucy, ideas of how that intelligence might be used to best effect, if at all, stream through his mind. "These aren't going to be the kind of people we can walk up to and ask; 'excuse me, have you been approached to join your local terror outfit?', I don't think that's got legs. The alternative is putting large numbers of the candidates under surveillance and waiting for God knows how long."

Lucy works on in silence, knowing that further discussion about the Watch List comes with the risk of igniting Dev's interest in what had happened to the unfortunate 159 entrants from the list.

*

The slightly tense atmosphere in the office is shattered as the door flings open. "Fooking bollocks." Charlie seethes, hot from Desk Heads' meeting. Dev and Lucy both know better than to try and get into the detail while she is still so angry and allow her to pass them by uninterrupted, both watch on in silence as she steams across the room. She slams the door of her partitioned office behind her violently.

"Another week without results will do that." Dev says with no hint of insincerity. From the three major terror incidents in the past four months, other than the two perpetrators arrested at the scenes, there have only been three individuals investigated, and all three are dead. Mr Sayeedi and his son – one or both thought to be members of the organisational hierarchy of the Interest Group, were both shot when what should have been a routine house search went pear-shaped; Dev sustaining a superficial wound to the arm. The third was Tony Blunt, a firm lead connected to the Pavilion Gardens, had been killed at the Belton Tunnel attack.

Despite the weight of The Security Services' finest, with the nucleus of the team being led by Charlie, none of the forty or so members of the Interest Group that are thought to exist have been traced.

As well as the internal resources Charlie commands, she has Lucy and Dev attached indefinitely, and has agency over a loose band of veterans, led by John Gallagher, a fearsome ex-SAS Staff-Sergeant, and now seemingly well-established as her boyfriend. The only member of their core team currently missing is Alex.

After a pertinent pause to allow Charlie to calm down, Lucy gets to her feet. "Would you like a brew?" she asks Dev, in her polished, but not posh, home counties accent.

Dev smirks, "No thanks." having learned from experience.

She sneers at him and walks over to Charlie's door, knocking gently and opening it. "You okay? Would you like a drink?"

Charlie's angry face breaks into a relieved grin. "Who's making?"

"Me."

"You're all right, Hun." Charlie replies, relishing the nugget of humour that is Lucy's rubbish brew-making abilities. Lucy hangs in the doorway, lingering, offering herself as further release for Charlie to unload her frustrations on. "Eeee." Charlie's adorable Mak'em twang always seems enhanced when she is angry or emotional. "We need to find something, and soon." she sighs.

Lucy sees her opportunity to get moving on her latest idea. "How about putting 54 members of the UK Terror Watch List under some proper surveillance?"

"54?" Charlie asks, intrigued.

"I've made some calculations; I think I've identified who they're going to go after as their next batch of activists."

"54, though?" Charlie's expression is pained. The shadowy little office is silent as they both permutate the possibilities and implications of putting such a large number of individuals under watch. "How technical does the surveillance need to be?"

"Not very, but it would be useful to have phone and email taps." Lucy says, not entirely sure what Charlie can legally authorise.

Again, Charlie pauses for thought.

"How's that young man of yours?"

Lucy's face tells Charlie that Alex still isn't in the right place to be getting involved.

"Maybe this is something him and John could take on together?" Charlie says with an overtly manipulative grin edging across her face. "Well, see what he reckons. I know John will be up for it; he's got hundreds of his other little Army pals buzzing about the place wanting to get involved. They could do with something constructive to do."

2

Generous souls

"Hello? Please, I need the Police and Ambulance, someone's been murdered."

"Okay, calm down. Have you checked the victim for a pulse?"

"NO, No, they're definitely dead; there's so much blood."

"Okay, what's your name?"

"Mark. Sorry - I'm all over the place - sorry."

"I'm with you, Mark. You're doing really well, but we just need to know exactly what's going on so that I can help you the best I can. You got that?"

"Yes, okay, I'm sorry. I'm a carer – I'm her carer. I've seen dead bodies before, but nothing like this."

*

Dropping his empty bag to the floor in the hallway of his seventeenth victim, Sami races to catch up with her as she heads into the kitchen. He reaches over her shoulder with the angled Nepalese knife and places the palm of his other hand firmly on the back of her neck. Before she has a chance to properly react; Sami drags the kukri hard across her throat, he feels the steel sink through the layers of soft tissue and carve easily through the tough, but thin cartilage of her windpipe. As the blade slides free from under the jawline of the dying woman, Sami flicks his wrist outwards, jetting blood at the wall, leaving the cutting edge almost clean. He shoves the gasping old woman forward onto the kitchen floor, clutching in vain at the wound, trying desperately to contain the spewing blood. In a few seconds she is lifeless, seemingly floating in the red pool that surrounds her.

Mindfully trying to calm his breathing, Sami looks himself up and down to check for any blood splats; he is clean. He bends down and wipes the kukri blade clean on the back of the dead woman's dress and retreats from the growing pool of blood, which is oozing across the ivory porcelain tiles, back to where his bag lies. He squats down, picks up the ornate, black leather sheath from where he had dropped it and slides the blade back into it.

As he is about to stand up, he notices the light from the mottled glass of the door's window change slightly - there is someone outside. The doorbell rings. Sami's mind is flooded in panic, unsure of what to do – he freezes. A sense of fight or flight has never been so acute or relevant to him. He refocuses, pulling together his inner strength and conviction - he draws the kukri back out of the sheath.

"MUM, ARE YOU OKAY? IT'S CAZ." A round, pink face presses up against the contorted glass. "HELLO, MUM IS THAT YOU?" The daughter of his victim steps back, Sami hears the fumbling of keys. He moves quickly to his left, ducking into the living room and nudges the door to. He inverts his grip on the knife, changing from an upward, slicing grip to an over-hand, dagger grip. He raises the weapon above his head and rests his forearm against the top of the doorframe.

The key rattles into the barrel of the lock. Sami's senses are accentuated by anticipation; he hears an unsuccessful attempt to turn the lock. The door handle turns with a crunch as the bolts dislocate. "Oh, Mum, I've told you to keep the door locked." the portly woman says as she crosses the threshold into the hall. Sami peeks through the crack of the living room door in time to catch her reaction to the sight of her murdered mother.

"MUM!" she screams, lurching forward and falling down to her knees over the body.

Almost casually, Sami slips back into the sparse, dull hall and stalks up behind her, knowing that her attention is consumed entirely; her brain overloaded, attempting to process the fact that her beloved mum has gone forever. He aims high on the back, knowing that he will not be able to reach around her huge mass to get a clean swipe at her throat. He makes a direct line to her, approaching from her 4 o'clock, enabling him to get a better reach, and so prepares himself for a potentially more enduring ordeal than the easy series of kills that he has made over the course of the morning.

A glimmer of guilt passes through Sami's mind as Caz wails, her intense sobs full of tortured love, but any sense of reticence is short lived. He thrusts down hard and mercilessly. The tip of the kukri blade pierces through the thick pink cardigan, into the layer of soft fat, through the tough flesh of the trapezius, finding its way between her top two ribs. A sharp yelp halts her cries. Caz's posture slumps immediately; she drops down onto her dead mother.

Over-shooting the spine, the knife lodges deep into the top of Caz's left lung. Sami takes a knee in the centre of Caz's back, using her as a stepping stone into the pool of her mother's blood. He fixes the squirming, groaning woman with all his weight as he clasps his right hand over his left to get the strongest possible grip, crossing his thumbs under the ivory handle. Sami yanks the kukri hard, forcing it into the gap between the eighth and ninth vertebrae. A second, harder yank tears into her spinal column, paralysing her from the chest down. Her arms flail, slipping and splashing in the congealing pool of blood. Sami pushes hard off his resting knee and wrenches the blade from its fleshy sheath.

"WHAT THE FUCK…" screams a voice from nowhere. Shocked, Sami turns around to see the open front door and a man standing on the step holding two full shopping bags.

"Caz?" he says desperately, looking on at his wife, lying on the floor, coughing and spluttering blood, helpless to move and quietly dying. "WHAT HAVE YOU DONE?" he bellows madly.

In the briefest of pauses, Sami hears a siren, an ambulance maybe. The shopping drops to the ground, and an angry, determined look replaces the shock on the husband's face. He is a strong looking man, tall, heavy set with muscle and, in his distraught state, clearly not scared of confronting someone holding a knife. He launches himself into the house, placing a deliberately wide step to power a sweeping haymaker at Sami.

The punch is lumbering, giving Sami the time he needs to plan his counter; he steps clear of the incoming fist. The husband, too heavy and lacking the agility to alter his direction, manages to abort the shot just before impacting into the wall - he stops himself against it with his open hand.

Sami has already switched his stance and delivers an upward stab with the knife into the husband's gut. This is painful and devastating, taking all of his opponent's strength and will. Sami slices the blade sideways out of the man's torso, causing blood to run freely out onto the floor. The husband drops to his knees, his hands reaching up to Sami, no longer fighting, almost submissively begging for help and mercy. Sami looks him in the eyes as the remnants of his strength drains. As his head drops, Sami again rotates the grip of the kukri and swings it point down, hard into the back of his victim's head.

*

Sami knows that his door-to-door routine has come to an end. With blood splashed on his sleeves and all over his trousers, and with the emergency services on the scene, he thinks through the transition of his operations. The kukri has served him well, but he is not comfortable with it as a weapon in combat. Primarily designed for slashing at vegetation in the tropics, its angled blade makes delivering powerful stabs awkward, as it is difficult to direct force through its point. He retrieves the sheath, replaces the knife and puts it into the deep inside pocket of his jacket.

Stepping over the bodies, being careful not to slip in the blood pools, he makes his way into the kitchen. Opening the drawers in turn, he finds what he is looking for at the third attempt – a large carving knife. He recognises, from the pattern of wear on the cutting blade, that it must have been frequently sharpened, so rummages further through the drawers' contents and finds an old-style sharpening steel. Gliding the cutting edge slowly at a low angle, Sami focusses his attention on the end of the knife, the part of the blade that will need to be the sharpest.

Looking out from the front door, Sami sees the back end of the ambulance across the corner of the garden of number nine. Stopped outside number six, he cannot see any members of the crew, but a couple of people stood on the pavement, just in view behind the vehicle, which has its strobes still flashing. The people look panicked and are gesticulating - pointing in all directions.

Sami takes the sharpened kitchen knife in an inverted grip and cocks his wrist, forcing the blade close against his forearm, offering perfect concealment within the fold of his sleeve. Stepping out of the house, leaving the pile of bodies in his wake, he strides out of the garden and takes a direct route, cutting across the corner of the road. More sirens wail in the distance, but Sami doesn't hear them, he is oblivious, now high on adrenalin as he breaks into a jog towards the bystanders on the path next to the ambulance.

"I don't know Jeff, maybe he came in from the back garden?" one of them says, but Jeff is distracted, looking around to Sami, and greets him with an expression that looks as though he is excited to have someone else to pass on the gossip to, but that look is instantaneously replaced by one of terror as Sami raises his arm and straightens his wrist to expose the blade high in the air.

Jeff, in his seventies, stumbles backwards with fragility, away from Sami and trips over the lead of the other man's dog, and falls onto his back. This tugs his friend forward into Sami's path.

Yet to notice the knifeman's approach the second man barely sees the blade before it plunges down deep, directly into his right eye socket. His legs buckle beneath him, and he falls awkwardly, hyper-extending his knees behind him, but he is dead already.

"HARRY!" Jeff cries.

The small terrier barks viciously, but he is pinned by his lead under the weight of Jeff's body. He is rapidly descending into a deep and hopeless level of shock. Sami yanks the blade from the skull of the dead man, most of the jet of blood that squirts from the socket hits Jeff in the face, further exacerbating his state of despair.

Jeff frantically tries to shuffle away from Sami, half crabbing backwards on his hands and feet, but the yapping dog is directly behind him and now being squashed under him halting his pathetic attempt to retreat. Sami swipes down with the knife, piercing the side of Jeff's neck just below the jaw line. The old man slumps back, further crushing the dog. Sami mercilessly plants a foot on Jeff's contorted face and goes to work sawing the blade up through the muscle and vital blood vessels, contouring around the windpipe, using it for leverage to get through the softer tissues.

"STEVE, STEVE, STEVE!" The ambulance driver stands frozen in the road having dismounted from the cab to investigate the commotion. Sami glares at her over his shoulder, she edges backwards further into the road. Wiping the blood that soaks his hands on his clothes, seemingly smearing himself deliberately to make him appear more fearsome, he walks towards her.

The tacky dryness of the remaining blood makes his grip on the knife feel absolute, almost as though it is melding into the palm of his hand. Through the fog of emotion and powering rage, he is aware that the arrival of the Police is imminent, the sirens scream, he knows he still has time for one last kill.

"Please, no, I've got children." she cries. Sami advances steadily, raising his stained weapon. The Police car doors slam, but the officers are too far away to help her. Sami picks his spot, just above where 'NHS' is embroidered into her deep green polo shirt. He breathes in sharply and channels every ounce of his strength into his arm. As he is about to deal the killer strike, he sees his victim's eyes flicker to his right. He is smashed in the side, a burly shoulder crashes into his ribs and kidney, taking him clean off his feet.

Sami's wind is lost as the weight of the Ambulance crewman lands, with aggravated force, on his side, but he still manages to maintain a firm grasp of the knife handle. He flails his legs and free arm to roll himself into an attack position, but Steve is strong and has the advantage of gravity over him.

Steve pushes down with all his weight onto the inside of Sami's elbow, preventing any attempt to use the knife, the resulting twist through his shoulders primes his left, and he wastes no time in launching his fist into Sami's face. The first blow slides off Sami's cheek, causing him to squirm further. Steve shifts up to a better position for the second and puts the knifeman's lights out.

3

Veteran army

Walking the few hundred metres north-east along Rampayne Street from Lucy's flat, Alex wonders what it is that John really wants to talk about. He doubt's it's going to be the simple friendly catch-up that it's billed to be.

Alex's understanding of communication systems and security have made him a valuable commodity in the fight against the growing national terror threat. He has had Lucy trying to persuade him to get back on board under the Security Service blanket, and now it would seem that John is trying to pull him back in too.

John's network of hard-core veterans is very much from Special and Elite Forces' backgrounds. His arrogant ego and extreme esprit de corps focussing purely on the warrior elements of the fighting forces that he's been a part of. This professional snobbery had meant that he never allowed himself to properly bond with members of the combat support elements, such as the lowly signallers, even those who had passed the milder form of SF selection as members of 18 (UKSF) Signal Regiment. His bond with Alex is unique to him, and the skills that Alex has are now vital to him.

"Oye-oye, knob 'ed." John's standard, affectionate greeting that he has no qualms shouting across a cafe full of strangers. This brings a grin to Alex's face; he cannot help but feel elated to be in the grateful presence of this most bright and powerful of characters.

Joseph Mitcham

The other diners turn back to their sandwiches and coffees as Alex joins John at his secluded corner table. Staying on his feet, John embraces Alex and gives him a firm pat on the back.

"That's fading well." Alex says almost convincingly, tipping a nod to the angry red scar that covers most of the right side of John's forehead.

John raises a hand to touch the painfully thin skin. With his shaved head and buzzard-like features, it has enhanced his menacing look. Alex has only ever seen John wear black clothes; he seems to revel in presenting himself as some sort of prince of darkness. "Still a good-looking bar-steward." he smiles with a deliberate sneer.

Having gone through parallel ordeals at opposing ends of Belton Tunnel, the two have been in frequent contact in the intervening period, mostly filling conversation with talk of their respective developing relationships. Everything has been sweetness and roses for Alex and Lucy, them both being distracted enough with work to keep them from over-fixating on one another but needing the relaxation so much that they make sure to enjoy their time together.

Charlie and John, however, has been a much more volatile affair so far and shows no sign of settling. The level of intensity that they both run at has made for some explosive comings together. The strength of their combined passion has been enough to keep them together, like some sort of nuclear fusion. The lack of stability and hap-hazard balance has kept it exciting, further stoking the fire.

"How's work?" John asks, knowing that Alex is being run ragged by Dickie, the contracts manager who is making the most of Alex while he has him.

Alex laughs. "Plenty to do. I'm getting some good exposure to stuff that's keeping me challenged." The stella work that he executed on the Military's new Skynet system has enhanced his and Dickie's reputations; many other Government departments now have them on the radar and the work has been coming thick and fast. "Most of it is in and around London, so I get to stay near to Lucy." Having sold his house and with no fixed bills; he is practically off grid. This is not by design, but since coming to the attention of the Interest Group it is the way things need to be for now.

"So, Lucy's not persuaded you to get back on the horse and take up Charlie's offer?" John knows a direct appeal is not the way to go.

"No." he replies dismissively in a firm tone. "How are you and Cliff getting on? Still trying to raise your private Army?"

John cannot hide his glee. The flood of interest from ex-colleagues of his, and others in his immediate network has brought forth a legion of highly trained and battle-hardened men, numbering into the hundreds. "Mike's back from Iraq, brought a load more blokes with him onto the books. He's become my sort of ops manager."

Mike is John's partner in crime. Having been moved from 1 Para to the Second Battalion after some nasty bullying allegations, Mike had joined John's rifle company as a fellow section commander, and they had gone forward to SAS selection together. Alex had met him during the Watch List mission, where Mike and John had carved up responsibility for Birmingham as operator handlers, overseeing the demise of around 20 targets each.

"We've attracted some serious sponsorship now, enough to pay a decent retainer to the blokes that we want to be able to call on." John sounds excited and enthused. Alex isn't sure where to start.

"An ops manager? Operatives on retainers?" Alex's jaw hangs open with the questions. "What ops are there to be managed?" The bustle of the café seems distant around their little corner as Alex awaits enlightenment.

John's lingering, staring smile attempts to placate Alex. "Nothing hard-core. Just background stuff, maybe we'll turn up some leads to throw at Charlie."

All too aware of how dangerous the Interest Group has become; Alex has mixed feelings about John's efforts becoming sustained.

"There might be a retainer going for you too?" John dips his head to try and achieve eye contact. "You know we struggle for a decent comms bloke."

Alex is impressed that John has had the patience and made the offer so subtly. Is his anticipation of the approach, and his gnawing impatience for it to come, a sign of his subconscious desire to be involved again? He thinks through the options. Is John's retainer compatible with Charlie's similar standing offer of full London expenses? Might he still work full time for Dickie while on both? The potentially lucrative scenario weighs heavy in the balance against his aversion to putting himself in the line of fire of the Interest Group.

"We won't be needing you on the ground, you'd be completely hands-off." John appeals to Alex's need for more physical security than he's had lately.

"It's tempting. I'll talk to Lucy."

4

21 dead

From the comfort of the sofa, Alex's eyes flash to the apartment door. Lucy lethargically drops her laptop case in the hall and staggers wearily into the lounge and slumps down next to Alex, turning to him for a hug as the 10 o'clock news headlines are read.

"The nation in shock. 21 confirmed dead as a knifeman destroys an elderly community in Folkestone. With one suspect in custody, we bring you pictures as Police continue to investigate the scene."

"Has this been keeping you busy?" Alex asks. Lucy is never one to stick to a nine-to-five routine, but this is late, even by her standards.

"Oh, Alex, it's so awful." She clutches onto his arm. "It happened right on my nan's street. He might have knocked on her door."

"Oh my god, seriously? Is she okay?"

"Yeah, she's fine, she'd been out shopping all morning. She got home and the whole area was swarmed with blue lights."

They watch on as the reporter describes the likely movements of the killer as an animated pictorial overlay traces his route. A red line trails between the boxes, symbolising houses, moving systematically clockwise around the loop of Birdbrook Fields' properties.

"I can't get my head around why someone would do something like this?" she asks in vain. "He went door-to-door, somehow gaining the trust of the residents, followed them into their houses and sliced their throats open with a Nepalese kukri. Alex is familiar with the weapon, having served in units incorporating Queen's Gurkha Signal Squadrons.

The schematic rotates and zooms in to show where the attack had culminated by the ambulance.

"The suspect was eventually tackled and brought under control by a member of the ambulance crew."

"The guy didn't mess about. By all accounts he hit him like a steam train, taking him down with a Rugby tackle, breaking several ribs, then punched him in the face until he stopped moving. A proper hero."

Alex says nothing, but feels his paranoia boiling. What did she mean 'proper hero', haven't I done enough?

Having followed the coverage since the news broke just after lunch, today's attack has further steered his thoughts in favour of re-joining the team, he is just not quite sure where he could have greatest effect – working with Lucy for the Security Service, or with a bit more freedom of movement with John.

"Would I be out of order to take a retainer from John and expenses from Charlie?" he says.

Lucy is surprised by the 'out of the blue' question. "What? To help out tracking down the group?"

"Yes. That and help manage John's information and communications for his growing gang."

"Well, that's two separate work streams, there's no reason why you shouldn't be compensated for both. Neither are going to take up a lot of your time, even with working for Dickie." Lucy snuggles deeper into his side. "It would be great to have your help. Professor Banbury and his DSTL team have started talking to GCHQ, and his reports aren't making a lot of sense to me… or anyone in the office for that matter."

Professor Banbury leads the team of scientists and researchers at the Defence, Science and Technology Laboratories based at the infamous MoD Porton Down, and until today's attack, they had been their best hope of identifying leads to the illusive terror organisation.

"GCHQ? Really?" The enigmatic organisation has long been a source of intrigue for Alex. Cheltenham being the Mecca of SIGINT – signals intelligence, and COMINT – communications intelligence, he would jump at the chance to see what goes on there.

"Can you sort me out a chat with Charlie? I'd need to nail down some terms of reference if I'm going to get back amongst it. I'll give John a call in the morning."

5

The way forward

"So, produce the receipts for pretty much anything and I'll have it paid out." Charlie says with candid benevolence from behind her desk.

"That sounds grand – I fancy some new wheels; maybe a Porsche?" Alex smirks, not wanting to appear over-grateful.

"Don't be takin' the piss out o' me, yer little sod." Charlie manages to hold her scowl briefly before breaking into a smile. Having got to know each other intimately well at their first ever meet, she is well attuned to his sense of humour and there is no awkwardness between them.

"I'm counting on you for close support to Lucy, Dev and the rest of the core team to help provide some second order analysis of the Prof's intelligence. I want you to come up with some of your 'out of the box' magic to develop leads that'll help track these animals down."

"No problem. And you're happy that I carry on working contracts for Dickie, and help John and the boys out?"

"As long as you're around when I need you. Anyway, John might have a bit more of a call on you in the near future; Lucy's working up a plan now."

Just as Alex thinks that the conversation is over, she looks at him hard. "You know I've got people that could do what I'm asking you to do?" Alex doesn't answer. "What you know about this Group, and what went down with the 159, Craig Medhurst, and all that – that's why I need you on this team, but that is purely between you, me, Lucy and John. Got it?" Alex gives a simple, unpunctuated nod.

"How are you doing?" she asks, changing her tone, only too aware of how deep an impact recent events have had on him. Alex tries to give an upbeat smile but fails to convince. "It was a shame about Blakey and Spence." The two had died in a flat raid in the search for Tony Blunt. Their bodies remain on slabs while the investigation into the explosion and their deaths gets slowly buried by Charlie's colleagues who work to assure the Police that there is no bigger conspiracy involving John, Cliff and Alex, who had been arrested at the scene.

Alex gulps back his emotion thinking about them, both fantastic characters in their own, very different, ways. "They're part of the reason I'm here. I want to help finish this for them, and the other thousand or so people that this bastard group have murdered."

Charlie nods solemnly. She gets up and walks past him, beckoning him with a tilt of her head towards the door.

She whisks through the office. "Lucy, you got a minute, please." She doesn't break stride.

"Do you need me, Boss?" Dev asks, spinning on his chair to track her on the way to the exit.

"No, thanks."

Alex gives Lucy a broad grin as she stands, and motions with his hands for her to follow Charlie ahead of him.

*

The white-walled meeting suite has no windows and is starkly lit with spotlights. This is the first time that Alex has been in a room together with just these two phenomenal women. He wonders if Lucy knows about what he got up to with Charlie. Seeing them side by side in isolation, he finds himself comparing them in a way he'd resisted doing before. Charlie is older, but every bit as attractive as Lucy, and far wilder.

"As you know, so far we've got nothing," Charlie's face wrinkles with the frustration at their lack of progress, "but Lucy's come up with an idea to pre-empt likely recruitment targets from the stolen copy of your Watch List. We might not be able to find the established members directly, but we may be able to intercept them."

"I get the idea." Alex says, already having heard Lucy's thoughts.

"I've had our analysts looking at the prioritisation, we've come up with a list of the top 20 most likely candidates."

"What the hell, Charlie?" Lucy bites, she cannot hide her anger. "You know I've been working on this. I've got it down to 45 real good prospects."

Charlie has a look of pained realisation. "I'm sorry, Lucy. I briefed your idea up last week at the Department Leads' meeting and I got an offer from the head of JTAC for some expert advice."

Alex senses Lucy's anger intensifying. "Well, how do the lists compare?" Alex asks, breaking the awkward pause. Lucy gets up and heads for the door. "I'll be back in a minute."

Charlie takes her ever-present palm-top from her bag and opens the lid. "I can't believe I've done that; she's been working so hard. I've been so busy, I forgot."

"What's JTAC?" Alex asks.

"Joint Terror Analysis Centre, a big part of the Security Service family, they're on the third floor. They were set up in 2003 to do the holistic deep analysis on the terror data our investigations had started kicking up; a bit of a reaction to the post 9/11 developments."

Lucy re-joins them, having cooled off a little, she places her laptop next to Charlie's and sits down. Not content with looking at the backs of the screens, Alex stands to move behind Lucy and looks in between their shoulders.

The primary focus is on Charlie's list. They go through it, comparing where each of the candidates rates on Lucy's formulation. Lucy makes notes of any that appear on her list by highlighting the names in red on her spreadsheet.

"I've got budgetary approval to put full digital and physical surveillance on 20, that's why JTAC's list is so short."

The pause is pertinent, and Alex can see exactly where this is going. He begins to think that Charlie allowing two priority lists to evolve was no accident. Is there more to the timing of John's catch-up? He decides not to call it out.

"Three of your 20 don't even make my list, leaving me with 37 who have just as much, if not more potential." Lucy says with a hint of what sounds to be insincere exasperation. Alex is now wondering if she is in on the play.

Charlie has let it hang as long as she is willing to without a bite, knowing taking it any further risks making mugs of them all. "All right, this additional 37, I want them tracked, but off the books. I want you," she nods over her shoulder at Alex, "and John to put a network of tracking teams together, and mirror what we're doing with the other 20."

Alex is stunned that things have developed so quickly; he tries to picture the scenario in his head. "I get the physical surveillance, but what do you want us to do in terms of communications monitoring?"

"I've not got the capacity to do anything else apart from ask for flags on their call content, that can be automated." Charlie offers, knowing it's not much. She can see that Alex is disappointed.

Alex has some ideas. He goes back to his seat. "If the approaches from IG are made through social media, email or even encrypted messaging apps, I might have some methods of getting access to some or all of those." Charlie doesn't need to look up to see his questioning expression; his coy tone tells her that he is waiting for her opinion on the use of such techniques.

"I can't sign that off, Alex. I'm very happy that you do what you need to do, but don't be getting caught."

Charlie's lack of will to provide 'top cover' gets Alex thinking about what his late friend Spence had told him about MI-5; they'll give you the rope you need to hang yourself, then let you hang, or even hang you out themselves. Alex knows the risks, he's taken worse so far in this mission, and he knows how to cover his tracks. "You got it."

6

Parallel planning

Charlie looks up to the images that Lucy has projected onto the white rectangle of paint on the wall as she launches into the meat of the meeting. "Based on Samir 'Sami' Alfredi's unique MO, failure to claim allegiance to a named organisation, and his placing on the UK Terror Watch List, we think that he is affiliated to the Interest Group.

"We believe that they are using a stolen copy of the Watch List to recruit from, and anticipate others, like him, to be approached. We have a list of 20 Watch List members that we have identified as the most likely targets. I have Security Service and Police resources in place to surveil these individuals."

"So, where do we come into it then?" Cliff asks impatiently.

"We have a secondary list of a further 37 potential candidates that we also need monitoring. Can you handle that?"

"37? Not a problem. Haven't you got any more?" John asks arrogantly. He looks left and right at Mike and Cliff; they chuckle eagerly.

Charlie smiles at her lover-man. "37 is all we need for now. Along with the 20 we'll be tracking, we should get lucky and find ourselves an Interest Group recruiter.

"Alex has some ideas on how you can keep tabs on their communications, I'll leave him to go through that with you. I just want to get us on the same page with what's going to happen on the ground."

Joseph Mitcham

"You can trust us with that, that's what we do." John says, looking from Charlie, over to Dev and Lucy. They don't seem impressed.

"I know what you're good at," Charlie raises her eyebrows provocatively, "I just want to establish some ground rules for your fellas, make sure that no lines are crossed."

"There's no come back on you, Darlin'," Mike snaps across John. "If you're not offering us any protection if it should go pear-shaped; you're not calling the shots on how we do our business, alright?"

John winces, knowing he is in a difficult position; his operational independence and integrity being potentially compromised by his loyalties to Charlie - he has to play peacemaker. He turns to his best friend and places a soft hand on his shoulder. "Mike, don't fret, pal. We've worked together before, this is nothing to worry about, we're all pointing in the same direction, this is just making sure our control measures are set to the right level.

"It's my intention to keep this as purely surveillance. We're not looking to get involved." John says across the table to Charlie's team. Alex sits alone at the head of the table feeling like a silent arbitrator, his default position between the teams could get uncomfortable – he is thankful that John's relationship with Charlie is taking the sting out of what could be an exceedingly difficult scenario for him - he hopes that it endures.

"Good, so we are clear that this is a 'hands-off' operation?" Charlie says like an irritated school teacher, "Cos if these fuckers get a sniff that we're on to them; they'll be gone." She takes a deep sigh, her eyes flicking between John, Cliff and Mike. Eventually she moves on. "Like I said, Alex has the comms plan. I've got some commercial listening kits you can have. I can probably get some optics for you too – just ask Alex if you need anything else.

"It's imperative, particularly if any nefarious activity is detected, we don't allow ourselves to become compromised. We need to be able to trace the contact as far back into their operation as is possible."

Charlie stares hard at Mike. "The first sign of any interaction with a member of the Interest Group; you inform me directly, switch covert surveillance to them if possible, but otherwise keep your dicks in your pockets, alright?

"We're aiming to start our watch pattern from midnight tomorrow, it would be good if you could match or better that."

"No problem sweetheart." Mike says confidently. Charlie's eyes roll, but she restrains herself from biting.

"Is there anything else you need from me?" Her eyes scout across the faces of the formidable three. "No?" She looks across to Alex with marked separation, signifying the end to her chat. "Feel free to use the room for as long as you like. Lucy is your link-woman." With that, she stands.

"I'll see you gents later." Dev says getting to his feet and following Charlie out of the room.

*

"We've got plenty of men to put two or three on each target." Mike says, eager to get on with the detailed planning for the operation.

"What's the distribution like?" John asks.

Lucy lifts the lid of her laptop. "It reflects the Watch List mission targets, clusters in Birmingham, Manchester and London, with a sparse smattering across the rest of the country.

"We won't bother with handlers for this one. We'll issue command and control from a headquarters-type hub – we'll get better oversight." says Mike. "We can base ourselves out of the Contingency Group building in Solihull."

"Roger," John acknowledges, "You get the personnel boxed off and work with Alex on getting them onto a common communications network." he says to Mike, giving a nod to Alex, seeming pleased to have him around again. "What are these ideas you've got, Alex?"

Alex takes a deep breath, sensing that a lot of explaining is going to be needed. "I'm thinking that with a combination of cloning, ghosting and proximity, we should be able to see and hear everything, voice and data, that goes through their phone handsets."

"What about emails and chatrooms?" Cliff asks. "Isn't it online forums and stuff where a lot of these connections are made?"

"Fair one." says John.

"I can probably crack their listed email addresses from the Watch List information and check for anything suspicious." says Alex.

"I have an agency list of chatrooms and platforms that would be likely hosts for the conversations that we're looking for." Lucy chips in. "I can run the email addresses against them and see if we have any logins for any of them."

"Great." John seems satisfied with what he's heard so far. "This cloning and ghosting, Alex, how hard's that to do?"

"I'm not a hundred percent sure; I've never done it." he replies honestly. "I think it's just a case of getting the right spyware program and sending a link for it concealed in a text message. It should just need the address or phone number of the recipient device inserting into the coding, and bingo; the image from the phone screen should appear on the operative's phone. I'll look into it, but I think with the right software; we'll be able to get a full rip, getting us access to encrypted messages – the whole shebang. We can do similar through email to their computers too if necessary."

"So, nothing our men need extensive training for then?" Cliff asks.

"No, I can do it all centrally. They just need to know not to give themselves away by playing with their shit on the handsets, as it'll replicate back on the subject's phone." The explanation has been received well with minimal, sensible questions. Alex is once again guilty of underestimating these characters; their rough and ready exteriors masking the technical knowledge and understanding that years of Special Forces service has given them.

"There were a few of Charlie's names on my original list, I've taken them off. I've put the remaining 37 into a priority order, so allocate your guys accordingly." Lucy hands a neatly printed and bound booklet over to Mike. "I'll send you all copies of that digitally too."

"I'll get cracking on the spyware tonight." says Alex, "I'll try and have it ready to go for when you're about to hit the ground. I'll need the phone numbers of the recipient handsets that each operative is using. As before, I don't need their names, just the codename of the target they're monitoring."

"Will they need separate handsets from the ones they're communicating on?" John asks.

"Technically speaking; no, but it's probably best that they do, so that a designated device can remain on the watch position at all times. It will also reduce the likelihood of the operatives doing something on the wrong device and giving themselves away." Alex replies.

"Makes sense." John says. "We've been setting the blokes up with comms the same way you had us for the Watch List mission, same phones, same comms app, we can just issue an extra handset for each target." Cliff and Mike nod in agreement.

"Great." says Alex, knowing that the complex work is for him to do, and that even this should be well within his capabilities.

After playing an active role in the Watch List mission, he finds himself curious as to what will be going on out on the ground. "Any approaches made over the phone or by email should be pretty self-evident, but how are your operatives going to know if an approach is being made in person?"

"We have a range of techniques." says Cliff. "We can use bugs in their accommodation, hopefully Charlie's got some decent kit for us, otherwise; it's not that expensive to buy adequate listening devices that will transmit straight to mobile over the phone network."

The idea of bugging gets Alex thinking; "I'll see what I can do with this spyware, it shouldn't be too difficult to activate the host phone's microphone and transmit on permanent send in the same way."

"That would be very handy." says Mike. "Being able to hear them in any environment would be mega."

Cliff goes on, "Outside of their accommodation, our teams will mobilise and track as best they can from a distance. Based on the information that is contained in the Watch List; I'd say that this will be low priority. It's highly likely that contact will be established digitally, by social media, email or phone, so our boys won't be risking compromise with overly ambitious physical surveillance."

"Any thoughts on likely hit rate?" Mike asks looking in at John.

"Not quite fishing with dynamite, but I'd say it's fairly dead on, knowing the trouble they went to for that list."

7

Online approach

"So much for this being a buckshee load of free stuff for doing nothing." Alex says as Lucy slumps onto the sofa next to him. "I haven't stopped since I got back." Alex has busied himself with attacking the email accounts of the 37 candidates. He has been largely successful at hacking into the accounts and is just beginning the process of interrogating the traffic that has been passed and received. "It looks like a few of them haven't been logged into for a while." Lucy says nothing. "Are you okay?" He puts the laptop down on the coffee table and turns to her for a hug.

"It's been another long day. We've cracked on with the other list, so much the same as you and the guys. I've been working with JTAC and Digital on their emails and phones, while Dev's coordinating with the Police and the ground agents to start the physical surveillance.

"We'd got most of it done when we got word from the team working on Birdbrook Fields – they'd dug into Alfredi's online profile and found a message inviting him to become 'a servant to the cause'. It told him to meet at a local park later that day. He replied that he would be there, and that was the last email sent from the account."

A kaleidoscope of interrelated questions fire through Alex's head; "When was that?"

"19th of July. The Wednesday, in the week after Belton Tunnel."

"Originating email address?"

"Just a generic, meaningless set of numbers and letters from the Notmail domain. We're having it checked out, but we're not expecting to find anything."

"Any CCTV between his address and the park?"

"No. The address is out of town and the park is close by, so nothing on the streets. There is a camera monitoring the park - Alfredi can be seen walking through its arcs just before 1200 hours on the day, but he goes behind an amenity block and never comes back into shot."

"What about his phone?"

"The number that he had been using died off the network on the afternoon that contact was established. The one he had on him when he was arrested was a classic 'burner', only messages and calls on an encrypted application to one other number, and you've guessed it…"

"It's dead?" Alex replies. Lucy nods. "What about geo-data? Can we see where their handler was?"

"Yes. The phone was only ever switched on once a day at the most over the period between first contact and a few hours before the Birdbrook Fields attack; almost every appearance of it on the network was triangulated to one part or another of Peckham Rye Park in South London. The only exception being one transmission on the 27th of July – that was made from Bordesley Green, a recreation ground just east of Birmingham."

"Hodgehill?" Alex says instinctively. This small hamlet in the West Midlands is becoming synonymous with Interest Group activities. The home of the Millbank bomber; Zafir Abdulaziz, the venue of the team's orders group that was infiltrated by Tony Blunt; now known primarily as the now deceased Belton Tunnel attacker.

"We're looking into CCTV and have officers deployed, speaking to staff and regular visitors to Rye Park to see if they remember seeing anyone loitering or making phone calls." Lucy shrugs her shoulders, not seeming to be enthralled by the prospects of getting a result.

"We've hit longer long shots." Alex says with a wink. "Fish finger sandwich and a glass of wine?"

*

After their late supper, Alex and Lucy return to the sofa clutching glasses of Malbec. Alex psyches himself up for the task of trawling through the candidates' email accounts to try and identify any possible approaches, or any other illicit activity. He logs into the first of the accounts, belonging to Yusr Amir. "How are Charlie's team getting on with their 20?" he asks.

"Not as well as you I shouldn't think. This is just another job for them, they don't have the focus that you have." Alex doesn't respond, unironically lapsing into the same consumed, transfixed state he always falls into when on task.

*

It is a little after midnight as Alex completes the analysis. "11 of them already contacted." he says loud enough to stir Lucy, who hasn't moved for the past three hours.

"Huh? 11?" she says, attempting to appear alert.

"Yeah, seven of them went the same way as Alfredi, and ceased all conversations after a brief exchange of emails."

"Bloody hell. What about the other four?" Lucy says, sitting up and rubbing her eyes as she tries to focus on Alex's screen.

"No response at all from three of them, and two of those hadn't even opened the message. The fourth had opened the email but has moved it straight to the recycle bin.

"We can strike that one off our list then," she says rhetorically. "but we have seven to add to the search list, three to put on the 'urgent tracking list', and I guess we'll just have to wait and see if any of the others are approached. What timelines are we talking about here?"

"All 11 approaches were made on different days, no two within three days of each other; the earliest made on the 17th of July."

"Before Alfredi?"

"By a few days. The latest was just a couple of days ago – that was one of the ones that hasn't been opened yet."

"Alfredi would have been inside my draft of top candidates if he'd not already been accounted for." Lucy reveals. The stark reality of what these individuals are capable of is put into context.

The level of detail and intimate level of knowledge that they are exposed to make the situation feel very real, Alex shudders with a sudden chill. "This is a nightmare. As well as the 40 that Zafir alluded to, they look to have recruited another seven. That's just from the 37 I've looked at. We have no idea if they've kept the list filtered the same way I left it; we might only have a tiny fraction of who they're eyeing up."

8

Not again

Veronica sighs at the sight of the queuing cars on the forecourt as she drives past them on the outside of the hardstanding. A few minutes before eight in the morning, she pulls into the small yard at the rear of the petrol station just next to the exit back out onto Bourges Boulevard. She parks, releases her seatbelt and pulls her jumper up over her head, revealing her branded green polo shirt. The morning sun makes it just warm enough for her to do without her awful work cardigan. She hurries in through the rear entrance of the building, trying not to slip on the smooth, terracotta tiles that the night shift have managed to find time to mop for once. She notes the gaps on the rows of shelves that had been fully stacked with boxes of confectionary when she'd left yesterday evening.

"The night shift's been busy then?" she says, expressing her surprise to Karen, her shift-mate and best friend. "You're in early too – what's got into everyone? Are there redundancies in the offing that I don't know about?" she laughs, knowing that it would be a happy release from the Groundhog Day purgatory that her life has become. This job was only ever supposed to be a stopgap until she found her dream job, whatever that might have been, but it had never happened – she never made it happen.

"I just wanted out of the house this morning," Karen replies, giving her a kiss on the cheek, "the kids were creating merry hell."

There is a loud thud as a twine-bound stack of newspapers hits the tiles by their feet. "Come on ladies, no time for gas-bagging, it's rush-hour and we've got to get the nightshift off." Keith, the manager, is sweating profusely from sorting yesterday's returns, a droplet runs through his thinning hair and down his cheek, splashing off his pale-green polyester shirt, which has damp patches emanating, further than usual, from his armpits.

"Coffee before we get settled in, Ronnie?" Karen asks as Keith shuffles the old newspapers to the back of the stock cupboard.

"No, I need to get down to 'bikini size' before the holiday." says Veronica.

"Fat chance!"

"Exactly." she laughs, "Oh, go on then – honestly, I've got the breaking strain of a wet Kit-Kat - I'm never going to shift this in a fortnight anyway, am I?" Veronica grabs on to her midriff, taking hold of nothing much at all.

"There's nothing of you." Karen says, heading through the open door into the public area of the shop to get the brews.

*

As the girls settle into their shift, the queues persist. "They're going to need to put in a slip road if we get any busier." Veronica says between customers, looking out at the line of cars spilling out onto the dual carriageway.

"Do you know what the only thing that really worries me is?" Karen replies. Veronica looks at her with interest. "Whiling away the next seven hours and 45 minutes, that's all I care about."

Veronica wishes that she could empty her mind of the things that bother her and be more like her friend – ambivalent and carefree, taking each day as it comes. She sometimes finds herself angry at Karen's lack of interest and will to take things more seriously, but on days like today she is just jealous of the sense of liberation and freedom that she must feel.

"That's not the attitude, Karen. Don't be wishing your life away." says the next customer up to the till. The smooth looking gent in his sixties is well-tanned and looks dressed to enjoy the sunshine.

"Hi Tom, how's Kathy?" says Karen.

"Planning yet more holidays, bless her." he says nodding out towards the car. They can see her tapping away on her phone.

Tom makes his payment, puts his wallet away, then leans forward onto the kiosk. "You know, it wouldn't surprise me if she's planning on us visiting all of the Greek islands - there's hundreds of them."

Veronica smiles trying to be patient – she likes Tom, he's one of her favourite regulars, but he is blissfully unaware of the growing queue behind him, and unable to hear the tuts, having forgotten to put his hearing aids in - again. Veronica smiles as she subtly tilts her head to look beyond him. Tom looks over his shoulder to as far as the exasperated white van man frowning behind him. "Sorry, I'm gabbling, I best be off."

"Lovely to see you Tom, give our love to Kathy." Veronica says kindly as he turns and walks away.

"I wonder how their lad is getting on?" says Karen.

"Dunno, I haven't seen him since school. I think he joined the Army. Veronica replies.

"What the hell is that dick head doing on four?" Looking beyond Tom's car as he opens the driver's door. She notices splashes of fuel hitting the ground at the back right of the centre column of pumps. As she grabs the Tannoy microphone from the back shelf, she sees a huge jet of fuel spray over Tom's car, splashing into his face, causing him to throw his arms up, spin and fall back towards the shop. Veronica freezes in panic. The arc of petrol quickly flicks to the left and then back over to the right, dousing cars and pumps all over the forecourt.

"HOLY SHIT." shouts Keith, "HIT THE CUT-OFF."

Both the girls fumble to kill the pump. After the initial gasps, there is a moment of stunned silence in the shop, as a sense of what is unfolding envelops everyone. The man at pump four drops the impotent pump nozzle and pulls a tube from his back pocket. He appears to move in slow motion, but no one else seems to be able to move any quicker. He strikes at the top of the tube with something in his other hand. Shockingly bright pink sparks fly and ignite the thick petrol fumes immediately, seeming to catch the assailant by surprise. Having only gotten as far as cocking back the tube, ready to throw, he drops it as he is consumed in flames.

That is all that Veronica sees as she drops to her knees behind the counter as the pressure from the fireball whooshes, flexing the toughened glass of the window inwards.

*

"EVERYBODY - OUT THE BACKDOOR." Keith shouts from the entrance to the stock room. Karen wastes no time in scrambling from her hands and knees past the station manager. There are screams and wails from the shop floor as the stark reality hits some of the customers with family members outside in their cars.

The roar from the flames intensifies as they take hold of solid fuel, the windows of the shop front look like some sort of video image of the surface of the sun. As she gets to her feet, Veronica is horrified to see people writhing in agony and falling to the ground trapped in the inferno. She staggers backwards, "COME ON RONNIE, GET OUT OF THERE." Keith beckons her towards the exit waving at her impotently. She looks at him with a mild defiance and makes her way out onto the shop floor where customers are cowering in the aisles, frightened for their lives.

"GET UP, PLEASE, EVERYONE, GET UP AND GO WITH KEITH." She directs them to the back corner of the shop from where she had emerged. Most are on their feet and helping one another to the door. Veronica sees 'old Rose', the lovely lady who has walked round for her papers every day since long before Veronica's time at the shop. "Rose, come on love, up you get." Veronica runs to help her, taking her stick and leaning it up against the crisps basket and then hauling her gently to her feet. She hands her the stick, holds her hand and puts her other arm around her. "Come on, let's get out of here."

As they slowly begin to move towards the innermost aisle, away from the intensifying heat, one of the huge panes of glass splits across its diagonal with an ear-piercing crack. The old lady yelps quietly like a startled lapdog. As they make it through the doorway and round into the stock room, another of the windows shatters completely; the wave of heat wafts over them but they are safe.

*

As luck would have it, the Peterborough Fire Station is a mere 350 metres south down the boulevard and Veronica hears the sirens as she aids Rose to the far side of the car park.

"Have you killed the fuel, Keith?" She demands an answer, knowing more than most cashiers might about the engineering of the fuel reservoir isolation system. Keith is in mild shock, unable to come up with an answer, a mixture of reasons and excuses log-jamming in his throat; he stammers and stutters. Veronica already knows the answer, she doesn't need to wait.

"Where are you going?" Karen asks, her voice full of concern for her friend.

"The whole place will go up unless we kill the fuel supply to all the pumps." she says without looking back. She runs to the corner of the building and checks around it to see that it's safe. The narrow passage is smoke-filled, but free from flames at least up as far as the end of the wall – the corner of the shop front. She knows that the fuel cut-off switch is just two metres around that next corner, but she can feel

Joseph Mitcham

the heat of the fire from here, what is it going to be like at the other end of the passage, let alone around that corner?

Veronica walks as quickly as she can being careful not to trip or get caught on the untidily abandoned stock trolleys and boxes. As she nears the corner the heat becomes uncomfortable, she wishes that she had put her cardigan on now. She can see the burning cars and knows that some of them still have their occupants in or around them, she winces as a wave of intense sadness hits her like another wave of heat, but she knows she must be strong.

The air is searing as she reaches the corner; too hot to breathe, she can barely open her eyes for more than a split second as they dry in an instant, she feels skin on her face desiccating and the soft, delicate skin of her lips cracking. Taking the deepest breath she can with her hands covering her mouth, she launches herself around the corner. Taking two quick steps with her eyes tightly closed, she allows herself the briefest of peeks up the glowing orange wall, she cranes her neck to get sight of her target mounted two metres up on the wall. Hitting out with the palm of her hand; she feels the satisfying click of the switch, but doesn't wait around to savour her success, and darts back into the relative cover offered by the corner, screaming in pain as the super-heated polyester of her shirt melts onto her back.

9

Devastation

"Jesus, have you seen the news?" Alex says as Lucy and Charlie walk back into the office.

"What's wrong?" Dev says, picking up instantly on the vibe coming from the two women.

"Lucy? What's the matter, Sweetie?" Alex says, catching on quickly as he sees her tears and puffed-up eyes.

"Alex," Charlie says sternly, "Come in me office for a sec, Luv." Alex's skin chills all over, he feels a deep sinking feeling in his chest; he knows something is badly wrong. He stands nervously, looking to Lucy for a clue, she rushes to him and holds him tight. "Come in." Charlie says already at the doorway to her room. Lucy urges him in, seeming to need him to know whatever it is as a matter of urgency. They sit down together opposite Charlie.

"There's no way to sugar-coat this, Darlin', I take it you've seen the news about the petrol station attack in Peterborough?" Alex nods, unable to muster any form of noise. "Honey, your mum and Tom were there. I'm afraid they were both killed, Luv."

Alex shivers with spine-tingling cold, he feels completely empty. His mind dithers, unable to put anything together that makes any sense. "I, I, I tried calling Mum when I saw the news. It went straight to voicemail. It was so close, so close to their place, it was their garage, they go there all the time – I thought they'd know what had happened."

Lucy puts a loving hand on his back as he slumps in despair. "I'm so sorry, Alex."

His head jerks up from the desk suddenly. "Well, let's hang on a minute, are we sure it's them? From what I've seen, the bodies aren't likely to be easily identifiable." He cringes at the self-induced thought of what the victims had gone through.

"I'm sorry, Alex. An eye witness says they spoke to Tom in the shop and saw him getting into his car just as the fuel ignited."

The image of Tom, smiling in his usual way, getting into the ageing, but pristine Ford Mondeo alongside his mum, as they are engulfed in flames is too much for Alex; he breaks down into sobs.

"Go home with Lucy. Take some time." Charlie says with a kind empathy. "Get in touch with your sister – she'll be needing you now."

Protective instinct brings Alex's thoughts some clarity. "Were they targeted?" he asks. The question has come too soon for Charlie, she doesn't have enough information to answer it right now, but the look on her face tells Alex that she hasn't ruled it out. "If they've gone after my parents; they might go after Sara?"

He snatches his phone from his pocket and swipes through his recent call list and dials his little sister. "Hi, Sara, where are you?"

"Hi, I'm just driving back from Morgan's. I'm hoping Mum's got something in for lunch, I can't get through to her."

"Sis, listen, don't go home. Go to the nearest Police station and call me once you get there, okay?"

"Alex? What's the matter? Is everything okay?"

Alex feels himself losing control of his emotions; he raises his voice to give it the strength it needs to get the message across without faltering, "Sara, please, just get to a Police station and ring me back as soon as you can."

Sara gasps in shock and there is a loud bang and smashing of glass on the line, quickly followed by the screeching of tyres on smooth tarmac.

"SARA!" Alex jumps to his feet with his phone pressed hard to his ear. He can hear her moaning; she only sounds semi-conscious. "SARA." he bellows again. Lucy and Charlie reel back in their seats, helpless to do anything.

Alex listens intently for any clues as to what is going on at the other end of the line. There is a click of the door lock mechanism and a screech as a buckled car door is opened. Has someone come to her rescue? After a moment of silence Alex hears a few words quietly spoken, "Alan hu waqtak."

"LEAVE MY SISTER ALONE." Alex screams down the line, but his words are futile, he hears a slick swipe of a blade through flesh.

10

Unpicking the firestorm

"How's Alex doing?" John asks Lucy, walking alongside her, with Mike in tow, down the magnificently tall corridor that seems to glow in a subtle pearlescent cream.

"Not great." she says, still barely able to contain her own emotions. Though only having met Kathy, Tom and Sara on two brief occasions over the past couple of months, she has been made to feel like one of the family. Not only is she feeling Alex's heartbreak and turmoil, she is equally fearful for the security of her own family.

They walk into the ground floor briefing room at Thames House, which is beginning to feel like a second office to Lucy, as one of the only completely private places in the headquarters where visitors are cleared to go. The three of them join Charlie and Dev at the table in their usual spots.

"So, these hits on Alex's family - no coincidence, I take it?" Mike asks, wanting to make sure that he is on the same page as everyone else in the room.

"It's almost too raw to take in; that they could be so flagrant, but no, this is no coincidence." Charlie says.

"We should have seen something like this coming." says Mike. "Alex is the man with the plan, he's done them a lot of damage." Charlie and Lucy's heckles go up instantly. Lucy buts in; "Dev, do you want to come and help me get some drinks?"

Dev seems a little aggrieved to be taken away just as the discussion begins. He gets up and walks in silence out of the room with Lucy.

*

"I'm no mug, Lucy." Dev says aggressively turning in the centre of the corridor to face her at point-blank range. "I'm a detective, not a dip-shit." Lucy's face breaks into a laugh despite her best efforts to stifle it. The tension broken; Dev rests his head on his forearm against the wall. "Alex, John and their posse, they're in this up to their necks?" He thinks through the implications of their ties with Charlie and Lucy, "The Watch List killings were Security Service sponsored?" he asks.

Lucy's brain is in over-drive; trying to find the right words. "There was an understanding." she says, bending her interpretation of her early relationship with Charlie as much as she can within the bounds of her moral integrity – just.

"And Alex planned it all?"

"Alex came into possession of the list. He got hooked up with Craig Medhurst, it just kind of grew arms and legs from there."

"How do you fit into this little puzzle?" Dev pushes.

"Alex asked me out as it was all coming about. He let slip what was being considered. I was outraged to begin with, but when I looked at it as part of the bigger picture, it made sense."

"Take the perps out of the game before they're perps?" he says.

"Exactly."

"For fuck's sake, that's not how it works. That's rough justice at its worst."

"I know. It doesn't sit well with me either," she leans back against the opposite wall, "but with the frequency of terror attacks recently; it seemed like a dirty battle was the only way of winning the war."

"How's that working out for you?" his words sullied with disgust.

"I hadn't factored the Interest Group materialising into the equation." Lucy says sheepishly. Dev cannot help but laugh. Lucy takes a serious tone, "This is not the usual kind of threat, you know?"

Dev stares back at her sternly; "I know."

*

Lucy makes sure that she leads back into the room. With a drink in each hand, she gives Charlie a clear nod, then smiles at John and Mike as Dev struggles in behind her balancing three paper cups and trying to shut the door.

"What do we know, then?" John leans back in his seat and waves the upturned palm of his hand in the air.

"We're having trouble identifying the fella from the petrol station, he was burnt beyond recognition, nothing yet from DNA or dental. We got a registration from the station's CCTV, but the plates came up false. The CCTV quality ain't good enough for facial recognition software, but Dev's working through mug shots from what's left of the top end of the Watch List to see if he can find anyone with a resemblance."

"If they're using the Watch List the way Lucy thinks; I shouldn't have to look too far." Dev chips in.

Charlie touches the screen of her palmtop. "Sara's killer, and attempted murderer of another four members of the public, Heydar Makasi, was taken into custody at the scene after receiving a hell of a kicking from a group of lads."

"You can always rely on the Posh." Dev says, referencing the less desirable minority of Peterborough United's fan base.

Charlie continues, "Makasi was amongst the 37 suspects on Lucy's list of candidates for Interest Group recruitment, ironically, Alex had already highlighted his likely recruitment in his early research."

"We might have prevented her death if we could have got our operatives out on the ground a day quicker." John says angrily.

"Well, he effectively disappeared over two weeks ago." Lucy says, hoping to quell John's anger, but seems to agitate him more.

"Let's not dwell on that." Charlie says, moving on. "He's Somalian and got quite an impressive record back home in Berbera for violent crime. A prominent religious activist too. He is here supposedly seeking asylum, but it looks more like he's running away from being locked up for crimes that he'd not yet been charged with when he arrived here. He was added to the UK Watch List two years ago for a fairly minor public order offence committed in Glenfield - Leicester is his immediate neighbourhood. When his history caught up with his UK profile; he was elevated up the rankings. He had been under infrequent monitoring for a period of months but was soon reduced to triggers."

"Triggers?" Mike asks.

Charlie's eyes roll subtly, but she decides that it is worth a few moments of her time to clarify how things actually work in layman's terms. "The Watch List is two parallel lists, the first, which is the one you imagine, a big database of names, addresses, complete histories of everything we know about all suspects." There are eager nods of understanding around the table. "The other part is a duplicate of the names but it's an active programme linked to all sorts of government systems. This is where the triggers come in – any number of activities recorded on state systems can activate a trigger, which will notify one of our analysts.

"When we say, 'reduced to triggers', that means any level of physical surveillance has ended and they are only being monitored by this automated computer system." Charlie can tell that this has been a few seconds well spent from the looks on John and Mike's enlightened faces.

"Makasi's digital footprint shows that he was approached in the same manner as Alfredi. We're working with Leicestershire Police to build a picture of his activity over recent months, maybe we'll get lucky with a sighting of his meeting with his recruiter this time."

"The horse has bolted with this one. We're not going to get anything of value looking backwards, not with the way they're operating." John seems riled. "You're on the right track with the plan to wait for them to pick up new candidates. We're wasting time here; we need to get our blokes out on the ground."

Charlie is not put out, she agrees entirely with her no-nonsense man, but her reservations about being able to maintain control over his operatives are stretched further by the emotions stirred by the attacks on Alex's family. She knows how well thought of Alex is by the fellas and can see things getting out of hand should they identify a member of the Interest Group.

"What we need to be clear on is how we proceed should we turn up one of these characters." she asserts. John and Mike's brows go down as they feel another gypsy's warning coming. "It is a complete waste of our fookin' time to track these guys down, to then go and spook them, or worse," she pulls a face at John, knowing what he is capable of, "before we find out who they're connected to."

"We know how sensitive these people are," John rebuts, "we know that as soon as they get the idea they've been compromised; they'll disappear, and we'll be back to square one."

"What square are we on at the moment?" Mike asks sarcastically.

John grins, giving Mike a virtual high five with his facial expression, which drops immediately as he makes eye contact with Charlie. "Shut up, Mike." he says, smiling at her, trying to make a regain. "Seriously, though, we know the score; maintaining covert status will be our main effort, you don't need to worry about that. We've got some top-notch fellas ready to go; men who this is bread and butter stuff for. They understand the bigger picture; we need to keep our powder dry."

"Good." says Charlie, gently relaxing her tense body posture, sitting back into her chair.

"What other eggs do we have in other baskets?" John asks.

"Our interrogators have got Alfredi and Makasi to work on, and it may be worth a revisit to Majid Jaleel and Zafir Abdulaziz. Zafir might have had a change in perspective since his conviction for Millbank." Abdulaziz had not only planted and detonated the bomb that destroyed the Millbank Conferencing Suite, just yards down the road from the building that they are sat in, but had also been found guilty for his part in masterminding and building the vehicle-borne device used in the Pavilion Gardens attack. Just talking about these individuals has John and Mike trembling with fury.

"Any chance of me getting ten minutes in the interview room?" John asks, grasping his knuckles. The red scar on his forehead seems to glow and throb with as much anger as the expressions of hatred on his and Mike's faces.

Charlie frowns, almost wishing that she could set her man on the prisoners. "Just you boys get focused on tracking these candidates."

# 11

Candidate L23 - Hamza

"Hey, Jambo. Bloody good to see you mate." Spider says, wrapping his arms around his old friend. "It's been a while since C Company." The pair were best mates in Nine Platoon of the First Battalion of the Parachute Regiment.

Spider had remained with the Regiment for the entirety of his military career, only leaving the First Battalion for two years to instruct recruits at Catterick, and for five years with the Pathfinder Platoon in Colchester. 1 Para had transitioned from a standard Airborne infantry unit to form the basis for the Special Forces Support Group, moving from Connaught Barracks in Dover to RAF St Athan in South Wales during his time with them. The reconstruction of the unit had been ideal for Spider; his preferred methods of operation became the standard operating procedure of SFSG, and his skillset was well-suited to the way that the newly formed unit employed its soldiers.

"You seem to have filled out a bit from the SF lifestyle?" Spider says, patting Jambo on his muscular upper arm.

"I've probably spent a bit too much time with the Delta lads; can't get them sods out of the gym." He rests back against the only car in the yard; a battered old Nissan Almera; its suspension flexes latterly as it takes his weight.

A 12-month attachment to a US Delta Force team in Baghdad as the UK Special Forces Liaison Officer had been the culmination of his distinguished military service. It had also been a useful introduction to some heavy-weight contractor organisations – one of which had offered him gainful employment - an opportunity for which he had decided to take his immediate Army pension for.

Having embarked on Selection from 1 Para and graduating to B Squadron, Jambo had excelled in the 'small team environment', his sharp fieldcraft skills and ability to think on his feet, to 'improvise, adapt and overcome', set him apart from others within his cadre, putting him on a swift run of promotions once established at Hereford. This took him to a prestigious post as a Sabre Squadron Sergeant-Major in the shortest of timeframes, and he had been the first black soldier to achieve this.

"What have you been up to? Last time I saw you was on the back of a Herc in Kandahar, wasn't it?" Jambo asks.

"Yeah, heading back to Lashkar Gar, doing a bit of Terry hunting. What was that? Herrick 16? What would it have been? 2012?" The six-month Herrick tours of Afghanistan had ticked by since the twin towers had come down in 2001, offering almost every Service person of a generation an opportunity to test their metal.

"Something like that. I can't even remember what I was doing, the turnarounds were so quick." Jambo had seen so much over his 22 years, most of it overseas, Iraq blurring into Afghanistan, Syria and countless other places where his efforts would never make the news.

"What's the relevance of this place?" Spider says, looking around the deserted building site.

"Nice and quiet, and walking distance, but not in line of sight of the target property." Jambo pops open the boot of the tired old car. He grabs the handles of a large trekking rucksack and swings it over his shoulder. Spider follows Jambo across the roughly tarmacked temporary surface to a single unit portacabin. Inside is sparse, just a collapsible table, three poly-prop chairs, and a fridge with a kettle and brew kit laid out on top of it.

"Get the brews on will you, mate." Jambo says as he opens his kitbag and takes out a new, compact laptop. "We've got a video call with the comms guy in ten."

*

With the coffee made and a selection of Charlie's listening devices laid out on the table, Jambo dials up Alex on the encrypted communications app on his laptop.

"Hi, Alex, can you hear us?" Spider says, tilting the screen back a touch to show him and Jambo sat side by side.

Alex looks to be sat hunched over his computer, it might be the bad light in the room, but he appears hallowed and miserable. "Hi, gents." His voice is devoid of enthusiasm and energy.

"Mate, we were sorry to hear about what happened yesterday. If we could do this at another time, we would, but we need to get after these fuckers." Spiders says with sincere empathy.

Even over the poor-quality video feed, Alex looks close to tears. "Thanks, guys." Still raw with emotion, he doesn't want to talk about it, especially not with two men he's never met and doesn't even know the names of. As far as he's concerned these two are Lima Two-three Alpha and Lima Two-three Bravo, the round-featured black man on the left is the former, the slimmer white guy on the right with the whiskery beard is the latter. Alex can get through this by treating the meeting in a business-like manner, keeping his eyes on the goal of tracking down the group that sanctioned the murder of his mum, stepdad and sister. "Have you had eyes on the target property yet?"

"No." Spider says.

"Only on Google Maps." Jambo cuts across his friend. "Number 42 - looks to be a pretty shitty bedsit-type terraced house, very narrow, a fully enclosed back garden – that'd make a hide location to the rear secure, with little chance of compromise, but very difficult to access, and destroys any chance of a hasty covert pursuit."

"What about the front?"

"Flat-faced front wall, straight out onto the street; no garden."

"Shit."

"It's not so bad; there are a couple of large, thick trees in a yard across the street that might lend themselves to an off-the-ground OP." Jambo sounds excited at the opportunity to build what would effectively be a treehouse for his observation post. "That'd have the added benefit of a better view in through the first-floor windows."

Building OPs not being Alex's area of expertise; he moves on. "You've got the kit you collected from Mike?" Over the past 24 hours John and Mike had rendezvoused with one member from each of the 30 pairs of operatives deploying across the country, passing on secondary phones and monitoring equipment.

"Yeah, I'm familiar with most of it." Spider says, having conducted similarly complex commercial surveillance tasks in his post-Army career.

"Great, one less thing to worry about. The devices are prepped and will automatically connect to the phone. There's a booster that you'll have to stash in the property if your OP is out of Bluetooth range of any of the devices. Again, that's all set up – you just need to turn the devices and booster on, place them and that should be it – sound and vision on the phone, which you've got wireless ear-buds for."

Alex has perked up now that he is in his stride and immersed in work. The challenge of getting these men set up with what they need to do a good job is an effective use of his energy and anger, channelling both into what might become his pathway to vengeance.

He goes on, "The phone handset will double as a device receiver and as a ghost of the target's phone; you will see his screen and hear his audio. I've worked a clever little patch from the microphone, so you'll be able to hear what he's saying, as well as what he's hearing. The only thing is that you will only be able to see and hear the ghost phone or monitor your devices, you can't do both simultaneously."

"Roger." Jambo and Spider say together.

"What if we type stuff on the ghost, or speak when he's on a call – he won't see or hear that?" Spider asks with concern.

"No. There could be a risk of that on some apps if it were a clone, but this is a simple ghosting – think of it like a projection of the target's phone – it's strictly one way." Spider nods his understanding.

"I'm on the case with cloning all the targets' phones from here, I'm expecting a crate of handsets this afternoon and the spyware is already embedded on most of their phones, just a few left to take the bait. Your fella has fallen for it."

Alex had spent last night creating a package of software that would infect the recipients' phones with the simple click of an internet link. He had neatly disguised the URL as a link to an extremist video. The text message would appear to have originated from a mobile number that had no useful identity behind it. Of the 30 candidates remaining of Lucy's 37, only five are yet to click it.

"Have you had a look through the rest of the target pack?" Alex asks.

"Yes, Hamza Mohammadin, Iranian, been in the UK since 2005 on successive student visas." Jambo says, reviewing the file in another window.

"He must be very well educated by now." Spider says in a mocking tone.

"You sound like you're squared away – I'll leave you to it."

"Thanks, Alex. We'll be in touch if we need you. Let us know if you get any new information from the clone." Jambo tilts a nod to the camera and closes the window.

12

In pieces

Alex closes his laptop and places it on the plush, brown, velvety arm of the sofa and decides to give himself five minutes. He turns on the television, the Sky news hourly fanfare sounds as the anchor delivers the headlines.

"Further arrests are made as Police search properties connected to the horrific incidents in Peterborough yesterday.

An historic day for Kenya as it's Supreme Court…"

Alex isn't listening anymore. The glimpse of the image of his sister's smashed car behind the big old Volvo, that had clearly been selected for the task of bringing her to her death, overloads Alex with desperate pain and sadness. His active role in trying to hunt down members of the Interest Group is a worthy distraction, but it is doing little to allay his feelings of guilt. His part in the plan to strike out at those who would damage his society has caused the deaths of the ones he loved the most, the ones he needed the most. He feels his inner self trembling, his very being stressed to breaking point. He has never felt anything like this. The self-induced pressure he felt when planning the Watch List mission pales into insignificance against it, he just wants to curl up and die – what is the point of going on?

His phone buzzes with a message on the secure app, "Lucy's just leaving work."

Hitting Home

John has assigned Alex and Lucy each a close protection detail. Not just for their personal security, but maybe they'll get lucky and catch themselves an active IG operative.

Before he can put the phone down, it rings with an incoming voice call. It's his dad again. He can barely face talking to him again after last night's long and emotional chat. Despite living in Northern Ireland with his new wife, his dad had a strong relationship with Sara, she was always his favourite, and he had been hers. The residual jealousy tempts him not to answer, but then just thinking of such pettiness changes his mind.

"Hi Dad, are you okay?"

"Hi Son, yes, I'm fine." He pauses, Alex senses his old man's reticence to go on.

"What's up, Dad?"

"I know you said not to come, but I've just landed at Stansted."

Alex's mind is in disarray again. With multiple teams on the ground and emails and phones to monitor, he hasn't got time to keep his dad out of the shit, but he cannot allow anything to happen to him. "Dad, you don't understand how serious this is. These people won't stop with Mum, Tom and Sara – they will do whatever it takes to deter us from tracking them down. That means taking any opportunity to get at me, Lucy, or anyone on our team."

"No, Son, you don't understand. I'm going to see my little girl one last time, nothing's going to stop that." His exposed, embittered passion strikes at Alex's heart, he is overcome as his dad's outpouring and the vision of his sister's body laying pale and torn on a mortuary slab saps him of his last shred of mental resolve. Alex breaks down into sobs.

"Argh, Dad. I'm so sorry." His cries are loud and coarse, he convulses on the sofa as his body writhes with the frustration of this feeling of emptiness, the strain and anguish rips in his throat making it hard to swallow. He does his best to focus on what needs to happen to ensure his dad's safety, again putting his mind to task acts as his salvation, bringing him back to purgatory. "Dad, just stay where you are. I'll have someone with you as soon as I can. They'll keep you out of harm's way."

"I've got a hire car to collect, I've got an appointment."

"Okay, Dad, collect your motor, then text me the make registration and where you are. I'll see if I can get someone to you inside an hour."

"Okay, Son."

"Take care, Dad." Alex ends the call and busies himself on his phone passing as much detail as he can on his Dad and his location to John – hopefully he'll have someone decent nearby.

*

Not 30 seconds after receiving another notification from her security shadow, Alex hears Lucy's key in the door. He hopes he can hold it together for at least some of the evening, he fears his continual shows of weakness will eventually turn her off him.

"Hi, how are you feeling?" she says as she drops her bag just inside the front door.

"A bit better." he lies. "My Dad's flown over; I've got him waiting in a car park at Stansted for one of John's men."

Lucy rolls her eyes lightly, knowing that this is the last thing that Alex needs. "How is he?" she asks.

"Distraught." Alex says, trying not to think of the feelings aligned to the word, trying to make it just words, like an ambivalent news reader, passing on the facts without sentiment or involvement. He takes away the need to explore the anguish of the situation and operationalises the conversation. "With John's guys tracking us two and Dad, we have an increased chance of finding someone connected to the Interest Group. I'm not sure how comfortable I am with using you and Dad as bait though."

"Maybe they're focused back on the candidates?" Lucy offers. "I'm looking at the chap that appears to have declined their offer to meet, he seems interesting."

Alex looks at Lucy with intrigue. "I thought he'd be a dead end?"

"Maybe, but he seems to be a little misunderstood. His record shows no hard evidence of him having any kind of hate agenda or religious involvement, other than attending mosque for prayers. He's got that 'wrong place, wrong time' thing going on; he seems to have fallen in with a bad crowd and been around when some of them had been up to no good, but when I've dug a little deeper, he has done some good things in the community, he's into lots of sports, and even has a live application profile on the Army recruitment database."

"What have you got in mind for him?"

Lucy smiles. "I'm shaping a case to put to Charlie. I think he's a possible asset. I'll have him followed for a few days, make sure he's what I think he might be, then make him an offer he can't refuse."

13

Tree house

The walk from the building site is silent. At three a.m. there is not a soul to be seen, not a car, no noise, not even the undertone hum of civilisation. The men navigate the short route easily. The local authority's policy is to keep the street lighting on overnight, as might be expected in an area of above average crime rates, though Spider and Jambo would rather the light were lower for this phase of their mission.

The density of the properties thickens noticeably as they head deeper into the residential estate, even from the little they have seen of the town, it is clear that this is one of its least affluent areas.

As they turn onto Candidate 23's street from the west end they have a line of sight to the house, despite the crowded parking of vehicles on both sides of the road. "I got lucky with the van," Spider says quietly, "opposite side of the road from the house, just a few yards from our tree." Spider had deployed a few hours earlier to conduct a brief recce of the location and to pre-position the unremarkable and untraceable old white Ford Fiesta van.

"Sweet." replies Jambo. He takes in the detail of the terrace as they proceed towards the target house. The slight uphill gradient of the street means that the footing of each of the buildings protrude above the pavement more at the distant end. The faces of these floating concrete bases are each painted in seemingly random colours, some not receiving a new coat in recent decades and the colour barely discernible, certainly not in this low, artificial light. Though relatively modern in design and brick selection, in a mix of browns, red and cream, the walls of most of the houses appear to have a film of algae growing on them. "Things don't seem to have worked out so well for our Hamza." Jambo says under his breath."

There is no pattern of consistency to the door and window fittings; some wooden framed, some PVA – all fairly grubby and untidy-looking. Many of the houses have gates or second doors to passages to the rears of the properties, again there seems to be no logical pattern, just some have been bricked up to make more space inside the tiny houses.

Walking on the left side of the road, Jambo eagerly looks down the street to see if he can start picking out the detail of the target house. He knows that it doesn't have its own rear access, but the house on its near side, number 40, does, behind a faded, wooden slatted gate – or at least it did when the street-mapping app's images were taken; that could have been five years ago. He knows the footing and window lintels of number 42 were painted white and that the front door is set back from the facia of the house by nearly a metre; another flagrant waste of space in the generic design of the terrace that many of the neighbours had corrected over time.

As well as the obvious, but far from precise visual marker of the clump of large trees opposite the house, he knows to look for the back of a road sign immediately outside the front door – he almost misses spotting it as its drab grey surfaces fade against the background of dappled walls. Eyes on target property.

*

The van is parked in the penultimate bay before a minor junction that turns in towards the block of flats opposite the target property. Spider slows as they approach the van. Jambo continues on past the nose of the last car, turns to face diagonally across the road at the target premises and edges back to rest against the corner of what is the last house in the row. Past the entry way to the flats is the tree and hedge lined green that forms the garden of the flat complex. He looks up into the branches of the thick beech tree as Spider opens the back

Joseph Mitcham

doors of the van in near silence; their attention to detail paying dividends, as the freshly greased hinges and lock mechanism function with minimal noise. Spider slings a coil of rope over his shoulder, walks past Jambo without acknowledgement, and carefully into the foliage.

Taking another deliberate look around his arcs of view, Jambo walks back to the rear of the van, leans in and edges his fingers under a roughly cut plank with a few items neatly stacked on top of it. He gently lifts it out, his primary focus on not dropping anything, while slowly closing the van doors with his backside.

Walking into the darkness beneath the trees, Jambo spots the dangling rope under the second and largest tree in the short row. He places his payload down beside the collection of loops. The ends of the darkly stained plank have vees cut into them with a bevelled angle, there are also multiple holes drilled through them at a range of angles and directions. At one end there is a larger hole bored out - Jambo sets about threading everything onto the end of the rope, starting with the plank. He secures the items with an exaggerated slip knot, gives a sharp tug on the length that ascends into the shadows, and makes his way into the greenery at the base of the trunk of the first beech tree.

*

As he steps across from where the great frames of the two trees merge, on the ladder-like branches of the beech tree onto a thick bow of the horse chestnut, Jambo is struck by the accuracy of Spider's description of the way the branches of their host tree form layered plains, between which are clear arcs of view across to the house. Jambo climbs inwards and up a further layer to where Spider has nestled himself into a comfortable working position, straddling a saddle formed by a fork in the tree's trunk, facing away from the house towards the flats.

Spider has already wedged the plank horizontally between the trunk just beneath where he is sat and another thick branch that points away from the house. Yet to untie the rope the other items remain on its upper surface. He gestures with his head for Jambo to move over to the plank and uses his downward facing hand to suggest that he put some weight onto the plank.

As Jambo manoeuvres into place, Spider takes a screwdriver from his map pocket and a long, green, anodised decking screw, selects one of the pre-drilled holes and begins to screw the plank down into the soft, moist wood of the chestnut.

Jambo surveys the view from just above the plank and is content that they have good enough line of sight, balanced with cover from view. He has to move his head around significantly to find good views of the front door and ground floor window, but he is happy. His job of providing ballast for Spider over, Jambo pulls open the small draw-string bag looped onto the rope and takes out the jumbled balls of rope and string. He hooks one of two thick metal rings onto his middle finger and lets the rest of it drop down through the canopy. Attached to the ring is a single green plastic rope and an almost black mesh of string net. He climbs up with his arms, standing on the plank, deep into the next layer of foliage and checks the cover from view that this space has in all directions. Satisfied, he ties the rope with multiple knots onto the trunk. Being careful to have three points of contact at all times, and trying not to step on Spider, who has now got his own bodyweight on the plank and is working on securing the distant end to the tree, Jambo walks off the plank and along the limb that it is being firmly secured to. The limb splits laterally; Jambo follows the right branch, which is still robust enough not to flex noticeably under his weight. Extending the dark mesh out until he gets to a second ring. He identifies a suitably stable branch just beyond the range of the ring at the same height that he has tied the other end off at. Pulling the second rope, attached to the second ring, tight around his selected branch, Jambo ties off the hammock. As he walks back towards Spider, he hangs his weight off the middle of the hammock to check that he has made it taught enough.

Spider opens another, larger, draw-string bag and takes out a hand drill. He bores 8mm holes into both sides of the trunk, pointing

Joseph Mitcham

downwards slightly. Once happy with the depth and angle of the holes, he takes two dowls, each with an end whittled down, stained dark brown and each threaded through half a curtain of leafy camouflage scrim and plugs each into one of the holes, creating an added layer of protection from view to hide behind. He then screws in a bracket on the left rear of the trunk, low down to the plank onto which Jambo attaches a digital SLR camera. Lastly, he screws two phone holders into the trunk, next to each other, central to the plank and as low down as he can get them. Jambo clips in the two phone handsets, onto which he has taped improvised black-out covers over the screens.

Spider takes a small plastic box from the now almost empty bag of goodies; the three lit white LEDs on the front of it indicate that the charge is full. He pops the lid, removes and fits the tiny black earbuds and stows the box away – first watch begins.

14

Candidate 35 - Tariq

After spending the night confirming functional communications with the men on the ground, Alex had slept in. He wakes to the smell of bacon wafting through the open bedroom doorway. His need to feel Lucy's presence as strong as his desire for breakfast, he walks through to the kitchen in the designer pyjama bottoms that she'd bought him, wearing them between getting up and getting dressed was one of the few conditions that she'd attached to his staying here.

He rubs her shoulders and slides his hands down her upper arms and sneaks his fingers under them and around her waist. "Don't get any splashes on this lovely dressing gown." he says as she flips an egg over. He kisses her on the side of the neck.

Lucy turns her head and kisses him impatiently. "Make yourself useful, butter the rolls."

*

"I do love an egg and bacon banjo." Lucy bites into her roll, being careful to spill the yolk onto her plate and not down her chest, which would have forced her to perform the strumming as billed by the sandwich's name.

"How are the spook team getting on with their 20?" Alex asks between mouthfuls.

"There seems to be a bit more of a sense of urgency now the candidates have been allocated to the agents. So far, we think we've lost two of them to IG recruitment. I'm not sure we've got your level of detail on their digital activity, but probably got bigger teams on the ground, so tracking movements will be more effective should any of them get the call.

"How was last night?" she asks.

"Good. We've got all 29 teams out and in place. I've got alerts set up for incoming emails. I've got some work to do this morning to refine the recording of calls, if you've got any time; you could give me a hand with listening to some of them?"

"Maybe. I've got a call to make about Candidate 35."

"35?" Alex says, unable to recall the individual.

"The one who declined IG's kind offer."

"What did Charlie reckon to your plan?"

"She thinks it's got potential; she's got someone with a bit more agent-handling experience identified to help me – he's ex-Forces too."

"Oh?" Something about Lucy's tone worries Alex. His natural insecurities maybe accentuated by the recent trauma in his life, he feels a weakness inside himself at hearing Lucy talk about working, he assumes closely, with another man – another military man; he knows what devious, snaking sods they can be.

"Yes, Matt, he's bringing extra resources from his department, he's already got a team out tracking Lima Three-five. Assuming we find the target approachable, we're going to set up an interception."

Alex's concern is elevated, not just at the potential competition from another man, but that he knows that Lucy will want to be at the forefront of any engagement on the ground.

*

Hitting Home

"Sapphire One, this is Sapphire Three, target entering gaming café on Croydon High Street, over."

"Sapphire One, roger. I have audio, rotate with Sapphire Two, fall back to cover position." The Security Service team leader sits in the blacked out back seats of a 2011 BMW 535 Touring, the big old estate car has all the room she and her technician need to operate from their laptops and communications devices. The vehicle fits in perfectly with the area and is more agile and less conspicuous on the move than the vans that they would have employed on operations up until recently. The Two callsign opens the front passenger door and departs to take on overwatch from his Three around the corner at the top of Mint Walk.

The team leader listens intently to the sound transmitting across the mobile network from the target's phone microphone as two coffees are ordered. "Are you getting this?" she asks the tech, receiving a firm nod and thumbs up from him.

"Hey, Tariq, bro, how yer doin'?" The voice sounds more distant and has a much more casual, lucid tone than the one that ordered the drinks.

"Salam, my friend, how are you?" The second louder and clearer voice has the humble and familiar tone of the target that she has come to know over the earlier morning.

Sapphire One finds herself enjoying the friendly small talk between the target and his friend, they are both in good humour. Their discussion incorporates a number of names and places that will be recorded and checked out in the background, all details being passed back to the office by the tech. The conversation moves on to something of immediate interest.

"Are you still thinking about joining the infidels?" the distant voice asks.

Joseph Mitcham

The target laughs lightly, "The Army? I don't know. I don't think they want me; I had to put in an appeal cos of that thing with Jamal and his brother."

"That was ages ago!"

"I know. It would seem that 'having dickheads for friends' is a barrier to getting in. Ironically, it'd probably be easier to join the Police."

15

A step forward

Trying to keep pace with the notifications that have mounted up on his phone, Alex sifts through the email inboxes of the 29 remaining candidates. He has set his filters to be too sensitive and almost every email has triggered a warning for him to check. He opens the Notmail account belonging to Candidate Lima Two-three, to his shock, there is a recent email thread with an address made up of seemingly random letters and numbers. Alex feels an all-consuming hot sweat coming as he opens the message window.

"You are a good man, we need you. Become a servant to the cause. Can you meet me today?"

"That sounds interesting. Who are you?"

"The force behind the current movement. Meet me this afternoon, 1pm at Stockwood Park."

"Where exactly?"

"Walk up Farley Hill until you see a red and white gate into the park, from there walk into the centre of the green. Do not bring your phone."

Alex checks the time on his phone, 1225 hours. He flicks through the open app windows on the screen and calls the Lima Two-three team.

"Hi, Alex. We know." Jambo says, having anticipated a call from him over half an hour ago.

Joseph Mitcham

"Sorry guys, I missed the emails coming in."

"We're on it, not a lot else to do up that tree other than look at the ghost. I've deployed forward to the park; my bravo remains in the OP at least until the target sets off. John's mobilised from London to come and assist, he's 20 minutes away; I'm looking for a stop-short for him to park up at."

"Anything else happened at the property?"

"Neggers, Cheggers." Alex assumes that means 'no', recognising 'neggers' as negative, though he's not old enough to have enjoyed the entertainment of Keith Chegwin. "Since that last email his phone's been off, unless your software's packed in?"

"The software's fine. He's having the same reaction to initial contact as most of the other recruited candidates; dropping comms, going offline."

"Roger. I'll keep you updated on what goes down on the ground."

*

The houses of Farley Hill sit back from the main road, behind a long parallel service road which is shielded from view from the park by interspersed trees and sections of hedge on both sides of the main road. Surveying the location that he has selected for John to arrive at, Jambo stands on the broad strip of grass between the roads, which is hatched into with small banks of parking spaces. He is provided with cover from view from the park by the low hanging branches of one of the small, individual trees.

The parallel roads are orientated on a south-west to north-east diagonal, and he has chosen a spot near the south-west entrance to the service road. He walks along the grass back towards the other entrance, which is directly opposite the red and white gate referenced in the recruiter's email. Swinging the folded lead belonging to his imaginary dog, Jambo thinks about where he will position himself and what he will do to remain inconspicuous should he find himself in line of sight to his targets for any significant duration – I need to think of a decent dog name.

As he walks, he notices a blue Ford Mondeo creeping slowly down the road towards him. He opts not to look directly at the vehicle occupants, knowing that eye contact would risk blowing his further usefulness in the surveillance operation. Instead, he catches just enough of them in his peripheral vision to determine that there are at least two people in the car. He keeps moving past the next source of cover, a thick clump of hedge, and pushes in behind it. The Mondeo slows further before pulling across the road and halting alongside the curb. Jambo photographs the vehicle on his phone and checks the quality to ensure the registration can be made out, then forwards the image via the encrypted app to Alex, John and Spider with the caption 'possible target vehicle, minimum of two suspects. John - will find you a new location'.

*

Spider has made his way silently to ground level outside Lima Two-three's house and stands innocuously behind the thin hedge, looking at the detail of the Mondeo on his phone as he waits for the candidate to emerge. He checks the time, knowing that it is a good 20-minute walk to the suggested rendezvous point. At almost exactly 1240 hours, the front door opens, and the young, smooth-looking Hamza Mohammadin steps out onto the raised step. Spider has a good enough view to confirm that his target is of average height and build, tanned skin, black hair, tightly shaved at the sides, with a longer tufty-styled crop on top. A good-looking young lad, he has a shifty demeanour to his body language; that youthful swagger that might otherwise be an indicator that he's up to no good. He steps down onto the pavement and turns to his left to head west.

Spider pauses in place to allow Mohammadin time to get out of useful visible range, then heads off in the opposite direction, emerging from the bushes at the junction onto Tennyson Road where he crosses the road and heads south, making a beeline for the far corner of the large triangular park from where Jambo had been conducting his recce. The plan has been devised for him, Jambo and John to cover sections of the park based on the points of the triangle, however if Jambo has correctly identified the recruiting party, this may yet be refined. Spider tabs on at speed to maximise his time on location.

*

John gently pulls to a halt into the last parking bay on Whipperley Way, just 20 metres from the junction with Farley Hill; he is just over the road from the red and white gate, perfectly placed to watch Mohammadin land on his initial RV marker.

John relaxes back in the seat of his white Audi A6, which is hot and emanating fumes of smouldering rubber and carbon dust from its hard run up the M1. He fits a pair of wireless earbuds, then transfers the Bluetooth connection to them from the in-car system. "In position." he says, his eyes fixed on the road that cuts in front of him.

"Acknowledged. Stay in your car and watch for Lima Two-three. How's Mike doing?" Jambo asks, passively fighting all urges to move his hands to his mouth or ears as he speaks.

"Will do. Mike's mustering the cavalry and standing up the ops room. We have a number of callsigns en route to points along the main transport corridors around the town. What are your locstats?" John asks, needing to know Jambo and Spider's location statuses for his own situational awareness.

"I'm tucked round the corner, behind a hedge to the west of the expected RV." says Jambo. The large, expensive properties to the south-west of the gates, line the road, creating a border between it and the park. The perimeter hedge of the back gardens of the first two houses juts out much further than the others, creating a prominent corner; the recess it forms gives Jambo a good fallback position.

The hedge is actually a tightly planted row of dark, soft conifers, which offers Jambo perfect protection from view from head to toe

Hitting Home

and enables him to get a clear view through the well-defined leaves. This part of the park is also off the beaten track, with no one much else around to wonder what he is up to.

"I'm in position - mobile on the path bisecting the park, running north-south past expected RV." Spider says as he strolls casually along the strip of multi-coloured tarmac that provides pedestrian and light vehicle access to the Stockwood Park Pavilion. The path is lined with huge oak trees, his vision only impaired infrequently and momentarily by their massive trunks. He nods kindly to a dog-walker, attempting to appear relaxed and unoccupied. His plan is to hide in plain sight, ambling up and down the path, maybe altering his appearance by removing or donning an item of clothing, putting on or taking off his small backpack, each time he completes another repetition of the 300 metres or so of the stretch of path.

"Remember gents, any possibility of being compromised; we walk away – we cannot risk being blown." John's words mean more, purely because they are from John. "Our main effort is to keep the chances alive for the other teams, even if we lose this opportunity."

His overtly aggressive nature and usual 'take no prisoners' attitude, are the context that give his words gravitas. They are all aware that the prize; their unifying purpose, is a route into the Interest Group's organisational structure; any hint of one of their candidates or recruiters having been tracked will ensure that they will all disappear a further layer into the unknown.

*

As he approaches the north end of the path for the second time, Spider looks directly ahead to where it emerges from the park and joins Farley Road's footpath. He instantly recognises Mohammadin's gait and the colouring of his clothing in the middle distance, further up the road. "This is Lima Two-three Bravo. Eyes on Lima Two-three, eyes on Lima Two-three." he repeats the key information to ensure that Jambo and John are both alert to it. "He's heading west on Farley Road, approximately 250 metres from John's location, wearing light blue jeans, brown hoody, clean fatigue." A military parachute jump without an equipment bundle or weapon is referred to as 'clean fatigue'; John and Jambo understand this means that Mohammadin isn't carrying anything.

John's view is screened by the houses to his left and sits tight. Jambo strains his eyes to look across the open green and along the perimeter to its northern-most corner. At this range, over 300 metres, his view is inhibited by the tree trunks and saplings which, whilst fairly sparse, seem to blend as his angle of view foreshortens them together.

Knowing where Lima Two-three is, that Spider has him tracked, and that he is exposing himself to the open ground to his right, Jambo turns his attention back to watching for the recruiting party - had he not seen the blue Mondeo; this is where his focus would have been – switch on, Jambo – he tells himself off for letting such an assumption cloud his tactical considerations.

Jambo visually sweeps his arcs of view, from south of his position, around in an anticlockwise direction, back to Farley Road. He doesn't see anyone who would meet the description of a prospective recruiter for a terror organisation - just one elderly dog-walker who is heading into the trees away from him to the east. He decides he will be less conspicuous by taking a laying down position on the grass. He moves a few metres to a nice flat spot and sprawls out on the ground. He lays face down, head pointing towards Farley Road, but turned with his left cheek down, giving him clear, if sideways, view of the hub of the recreation area.

"He's stayed on Farley Road; he's crossed over and is on the north side footpath. Now 100 metres from John's location." says Spider. "I'm walking almost parallel, a little behind. Now looking for suspects in the central park area."

"Roger." Jambo acknowledges. He identifies what must be Lima Two-three on the path and keeps track of him as he pops in and out of view between the patches of greenery, flitting his eyes further to his right during the brief periods when the primary target is out of sight.

Hitting Home

"Eyes on Lima Two-three." John's voice has an air of excitement about it as he gets his first sighting of a live target since kicking his last into the path of a high-speed train.

John watches Mohammadin step out to cross Farley Road from the corner of its junction with Whipperley Way with increasingly stilted swagger as he nears his destination. Hamza's natural confidence and arrogance seem to dry up as the reality of meeting someone from the 'real deal' organisation gradually dawns on him.

"Any sign of a greeting party?" Jambo asks over the open two-way voice channel.

"Wait one." Spider whispers. Jambo looks to his three o'clock to try and see what has Spider so preoccupied. At 200 metres the trees seem denser than they can possibly be, he can't see anything.

"An IC6 male in his fifties just walked past me, he seemed interested in something to the north – might be our guy."

"IC6?" John asks, having done more kinetics than he has surveillance ops.

"Arabic or North African." Jambo enlightens him. "I think I see him, there's someone amongst the trees heading that way."

"Lima Two-three is stood at the gate looking like a lost puppy." says John, "He's stepping over it, now moving slowly south-east towards the lone tree at the centre of the green."

Jambo waits patiently with his head resting in the grass, even closing his eyes to ensure that any first impression he is to make with either party is that of a sleepy layabout. He adjusts his position on the ground so that his eyes naturally centre on the lone tree. All three of the team are well over 100 metres away from what now looks to be nailed on as the RV for this meet. "We need to start thinking about how we are going to get a decent photo of the recruiter if this is the best range we're going to get."

"I've got the SLR, but not the long lens." Spider says. "If the recruiter comes back the same way; I can get a shot."

"Roger, let's plan on that for now." says Jambo. "I've got eyes on both parties, looking like they will come together at the lone tree. Standby."

As the distance closes between Lima Two-three and his recruiter, John sits and watches from his car wondering what needs to be fed up and back about the progress they've made. This might be the only candidate found in the act of recruitment from both the parallel lists - can he trust his darling Charlie to let him get on with it, or would she insist on having Security Service agents take over the tracking of the recruiter? What about Alex? John trusts Alex implicitly, but knows that he's shit with secrets, especially trying to keep them from the likes of Lucy and Charlie. Maybe I can use Lucy's ambition to keep this right?

16

Unexpected interview

Tariq approaches the ominous-looking cream brick building with a sense of trepidation. Its early Victorian design gives it the appearance of a dungeon. Many of its windows have been bricked up and the few remaining on the ground floor being covered with a dusty, mysterious mesh. The huge, heavy, double wooden door is painted black, but for the white lettering and union flag of the British Army's branding – 'Be The Best'.

He pulls the knot of his tie tight and straight and brushes a few bobbles of fluff off his suit jacket, then presses the intercom buzzer.

"Good afternoon. Do you have an appointment?" comes the instant and gruff reply.

"Yes, my name's Tariq Nasruddin."

"Okay, someone'll let you in."

"Thank y…" The speaker crackles and the lights on the intercom panel go out.

After a few seconds of patient waiting, the door clicks and opens inwards. Tariq's expectations of a mildly rude middle-aged man bulging over the beltline of a set of sweaty combat fatigues are blown away by what he sees. He tries not to stare at the beautiful, young, tanned woman in highly tailored cream shirt and green skirt. "Tariq?" she asks. He nods, his mouth gaping open slightly. "I'm Corporal Lucy Butler." Dropping back to the rank she had been just a few months ago seemed like it might make things a little less intimidating for Tariq, convenient as she has also failed to purchase rank slides for either of her subsequent ranks.

"I didn't think you opened on Saturdays?" Tariq asks as he steps inside.

"We don't." says the grumpy Sergeant standing in the hallway. He fits Tariq's expected description of staff perfectly.

"No, we've had this huge backlog of applicants what with the new recruiting software, so we're getting as many of you through as we can. Would you like a cup of tea?"

"Yes please."

"No problem. Sergeant Evans, be a love, would you?"

*

Lucy has Tariq to herself, having made excuses for the office's cranky resident senior. Tariq seems relaxed having talked through his difficulties negotiating the convoluted recruitment process. Lucy has been her charming self, expressing her concerns and empathy for his prolonged ordeal with the system. She feels that now is the time to broach the meat of the afternoon's business.

"You're doing everything right, I'm sure that you're well within the tolerances for all of the generic criteria. What have you got down as your choices of Arms and Services?"

"My mum says that I need to get a trade, so I was thinking about Royal Engineers or Royal Electrical and Mechanical Engineers." His smile and tone are a thinly disguised plea for advice. He pulls his fingers through the long quiff of jet-black hair of his school-boy side parting as his emerald-green eyes look down at the desk. Lucy is surprised at his level of vulnerability. At 24 years old, he barely looks 18.

"Getting a trade is a good idea, but with the high intelligence scores that you have, that might be a bit of a waste of your potential." Lucy leafs through the pages of his file, touching the tips of her front teeth with the end of her tongue seductively as she thinks.

"You could be a Royal Signals Communicator, or even join my cap-badge; the Intelligence Corps?" She is encouraged by his inquisitive expression. "An Army Intelligence Operative has some easily transferrable, and very lucrative skills if you're worried about having a future after the Army?"

"That sounds good." He smiles enthusiastically.

"You know they brought me in specially to speak to you today; they think you've got what we're looking for."

"Really?" Tariq says, gleefully surprised.

"Yes." She looks him in the eyes and smiles, enjoying his moment of elation with him, squeezing every second out of the positive direction of conversation.

"The only possible stumbling block we have where my cap badge is concerned is that your criminal record would need to be looked at in fine detail." Tariq's face drops.

"You must have seen what's in there?" he says, sadly looking down at the buff cardboard folder on the desk between Lucy's hands. She stares back at him without expression, without judgement. "I'm appealing it. It was nothing to do with me." Still Lucy says nothing, silently offering him the opportunity to appeal to her.

"I got in with a bad crowd." Tariq tries his best to line up the counts against him and knock them down in order of priority. "The Patel brothers, Jamal and Kalif – I had no idea what they were up to. They never showed me what they had in their shed."

"They never showed you what was on their phones?" she asks, doing her best to keep her voice low and neutral. "Never shared any files or images with you on messaging apps?"

"Well, yes, but…" he pauses, thinking about how things so awful could ever be justified. "… I never took any of that seriously, not as a supporter of that sort of thing. It was just shocking content, it was horrific, it got a reaction, you know, it just made you want to watch it more – like a train wreck." Tariq immediately regrets his choice of words, with the Belton Tunnel attack still making the daily news headlines. Lucy ignores his poor selection of simile.

"I mean, I was never interested in the ideology or would ever want anything like that to happen." The image of a flashing blade and a decapitated head rolling across the floor plays in his mind's eye. "It was violence like that that my family came here to escape."

Lucy knows that Tariq had arrived in the UK from Iraq in 2002, aged nine. His Uncle had been tortured and killed by Saddam's regime, and his father had been threatened with a similar fate for his active role in the Kurdistan Democratic Party. The family had been smuggled out of the country by sympathisers of the party and had funded their long journey across Europe.

"How did your father react when you were arrested?"

"I've still got the bruises." Tariq says, allowing the smile to return to his face briefly.

"I never asked them to send me those videos. I never sent them on to anyone else – you can check."

"We did." Lucy smiles confidently allowing a hint of arrogance and authority to slip into the persona that she presents.

"My dad brought me and my sisters up to be thankful to this country. We have as much trouble understanding why these people do the terrible things they do, as you do."

Tariq is saying everything that Lucy wants to hear, but far from being sold, she feels the tug of her natural control measure pulling at her. She will not fall into the trap of collecting evidence that supports her argument - a challenge is required.

"It's a shame that we had to destroy the whole country to get rid of Saddam. It's like the entire Muslim world has started to crumble since he fell."

Tariq returns a look to Lucy that shows his awareness of this being something of a test. "Whatever Iraq was before Saddam fell, it was not any kind of place that I wanted to live in, not without freedom, without choice. I would rather it be bombed to the ground and have a choice of which crater to live in than live under a dictator like him." Tariq seems pleased with his answer.

"As for religion, you might loosely call me a Muslim, but it is not a significant part of my life. I consider myself British and want to live my British life with the freedom that comes with it."

"How far would you go to protect that freedom?" Lucy asks. She gives him a stern look. "You'd join the Army? To get a trade and make something of yourself?" She shoves his folder into the middle of the table. "What about getting your hands dirty? Putting yourself on the line to protect our freedom?"

Tariq is riled by her attack on his valour. "Of course, I'd go wherever you'd send me, I'd do my duty."

Lucy shuffles herself in her seat, readying herself to take the plunge. "What about here?"

Tariq is confused by the vagueness of the question. He tilts his head, beckoning more information.

"What if you could help us fight the fight here and now?" He still doesn't understand. "If you could help us get to the people behind these recent attacks – would you?"

Joseph Mitcham

Tariq's look of confusion turns to one of concern. He stammers, struggling to find the words he wants. "I told you, I'm not into anything like that. I don't know anyone who is – it's not my thing."

Lucy picks up her mug and turns it in her hands, trying to find the cleanest section of the rim before taking a small, slow mouthful of Sergeant Evans' finest brew. "Do you remember getting an email a few days ago?" She pauses further, taking another sip whilst analysing his reaction. "An invitation to 'become a servant to the cause'?"

Again, Tariq's eyes flick up and to his left, they have done consistently throughout the conversation, giving Lucy confidence that he is actively recalling memories. The notes that she has made have been more about anticipated levels of truthfulness than about anything specific that he has said. "I had an email like that." he says, unsure about exactly what it is that he is admitting to.

"We think that whoever sent you that email wants you to be one of the next perpetrators of a serious atrocity."

Tariq looks shocked. "Are you reading my emails?"

"You're on the Watch List, Tariq." Lucy knows that this is no justification, but she glosses over it for now. "What did you make of the message?"

His eyes linger top left again. "I don't know. I didn't know whether to take it seriously or not at first, then I figured, 'serious or not - it's going in the bin'. I didn't think any more of it after that."

"So, thinking about it now; would you rather help stop them, or let them get away with another Pavilion Gardens or Belton Tunnel?"

Tariq loosens his tie and undoes the collar button beneath it. "What would you want me to do? Email them back?"

"That would depend on you, on what you're willing to do." She tilts her head down and looks up at him. "We wouldn't ask you to put yourself in any direct danger, not against your will, but ideally we'd want you to go along with whatever they want until we are able to identify and gather enough evidence to restore security."

"Would I be working for the Army?" he asks, a hint of excitement apparent in his voice.

"Actually, no. Though I am Intelligence Corps, I'm currently working for the Security Service, and you would be helping the team I've been seconded to."

"Seriously? The Security Service? MI-5?"

Lucy nods.

"That's cool."

17

Lead out

"I wish the bastard still had his mobile with him." Jambo says, his eyes half open, as aware as he needs to be that the targets are still where they had met.

"That'd be too easy." John replies.

"We have movement." Spider says quietly, trying not to let the woman, sitting a metre along the bench from him, hear him. She has made a good imaginary wife for the sake of appearances whilst Mohammadin and his recruiter have talked for the past four minutes. "They're coming my way, picking up the path that intersects with mine and leads towards the Equestrian Centre."

"There's only there or the complex entrance that they'll be going for." Jambo reasons. "Can you head for the Centre's car park and I'll run round to the South Entrance."

"Moving now." Spider replies.

"Do you want me out on foot?" John asks.

"Stay in the car John, you're hardly inconspicuous, mate. Get yourself down to the housing estate east of London Road, but park facing back west. Assuming the target gets mobile, you'll be on the spot as first car." Jambo is having to think several moves ahead as the situation begins to develop; he needs to keep his assets optimally placed if he is going to be able to keep watch over the recruiter without being compromised.

"Roger." says John.

Jambo remains in place, keeping watch as the targets walk beside each other; an unlikely looking pairing. His eyes struggle to adjust as they enter the shadows of the trees of the main concourse; their path cutting across it. He sees them wait politely for a loose group of people to clear the junction before crossing and continuing towards the Equestrian Centre. Now confident he knows where they are going and that his movements are well out of their field of view, he gets to his feet and begins to run at a fast jog with a 'sporting gait', trying to appear as if it's for fitness.

*

Spider enters the Equestrian Centre car park totally focused on finding somewhere suitable to get a good shot at most of the possible angles of the location. He momentarily forgets himself, striding around looking from left to right. The ticking of the engine draws his attention to the blue Mondeo idling over to his left at the northern-most corner. Fuck. He dares to look at the windscreen. To his relief, the driver is hunched over, likely looking at his phone.

Darting into the cover of the last of four rows of cars that dominate the small, freshly tarmacked parking area, Spider is at a loss as to how he is going to get a decent shot of the targets without reasonable cover or a long lens. The Mondeo is diagonally to the front-right of the last car in this row. Stooped over, Spider retreats into the gap between the fourth and third rows and moves along towards the Mondeo to check out his limited options.

Resting on his knees, his arms folded on the bonnet of the penultimate car in the strip, Spider considers getting under one of the cars or retreating out of the car park towards the complex exit. As he looks over that way, he realises that the car that he is resting against is old and is unlikely to have an alarm. He looks down the side of the tatty Vauxhall and along the line of the passenger door window to see a red button raised above the trim – unlocked.

18

0035

At the top of the stairs, Lucy holds open a door immediately on the left, she smiles invitingly. The situation is made to feel all the more ominous by the dark, shadowy cold of the building; it is as daunting on the inside as it is on the outside. Tariq reaches the top of the steps, still unsure of what he is getting himself into.

"Tariq, this is Matt." Lucy says as she shepherds him into the large, stony-grey room. There is an unoccupied desk, but Matt stands from one of the three chairs placed casually around a low coffee table.

"Good afternoon, Tariq." Matt thrusts his hand out to him. Tariq finds himself further intimidated by Matt's refined appearance; everything about him oozes quality. His slightly receding, tightly cropped brown hair, piercing blue eyes, and the finely chiselled features of his remarkably handsome face have Tariq in awe. He admires the tailoring of his crisp, modern, navy-blue suit which gives clues to the perfectly toned body beneath. Tariq shakes his hand doing his best to conceal his nervous admiration. "Take a seat."

Matt is as smooth-talking as he is attractive. His self-belief, based on his abilities, knowledge and a fair helping of arrogance, inspire confidence and a willing to please. After going over much of the same ground he had watched Lucy cover with Tariq, he feels that he has earned enough trust to begin describing what he has in mind for him. Tariq has been lulled into a state of willing by the combination of Matt's positive, supportive attitude and his confidence-inspiring polished Cambridge accent.

"The first thing you need to remember is that what we're trying to achieve relies on maintaining secrecy. We cannot allow the people that we're trying to track know that we are on to them. Do you understand that?"

Tariq nods.

"That's good for you, because if anything should ever look like coming out or you think you may have been compromised; the safest thing to do is to simply walk away, just disappear." Matt smiles. His intent is to instil the principle that Tariq's safety is paramount to the operation, aiming to provide him with the sense of security that will be vital to their success.

"You will need to reply to the email invitation with a simple message agreeing to meet up. The meet is likely to be arranged somewhere public and not more than 20-minutes' walk from your house. You will be told not to take your phone, but we will have you wired for sound and have a covert team on the ground; you'll be as safe as can be."

Tariq's mind is buzzing, trying to compute what this all means for him, what he will need to do, how much he will need to think. He's never been a good liar; it doesn't come naturally to him. "Might they search me for bugs and wires?" His reference materials for the realities of this proposition come from the television shows he's watched and the novels he's read – he has no real idea of what to expect and fears ending up in a dangerous situation that he will have no control over.

"We have the best devices available, Tariq." Lucy leans in to reassure him. "We're world leaders at this." Her smile puts him at ease for a moment.

Matt goes on, "They may provide you with a new phone; if that's the case, we should be able to isolate it on the network and exploit whatever opportunities that it presents. Even a basic analogue handset offers us the chance for microphone access."

Tariq sits looking a little overcome and perplexed. "Are you okay?" Lucy asks. He looks to his hands, resting in his lap as he tries to pick out the most important of the plethora of outstanding questions.

"So, what do I have to do? Once I've met with whoever it is?"

"Just go with the flow." Matt says with an injection of energy into the conversation. "Forget about us and what your true motivations are. Play the role, put yourself into a frame of mind as though you are genuinely there to help them to do whatever it is that they are trying to do – and do it. You need to demonstrate willing, be useful. Try and remember details of people, places and what is going on around you, but don't take notes – if you forget things; don't worry."

"What if they want me to do things that are illegal?"

"We will be watching, if we need to step in, we will. You might have to break a few eggs to make this omelette – we've got your back, okay?" Matt's gesturing eyebrows and gleaming smile are like a comfort blanket; Tariq is already beginning to feel like one of the team.

"Okay."

Matt smiles at Lucy, then looks at the small black Peli case on the desk.

Lucy stands up, walks over to it and snaps open the two clips on either side of the case's handle. The industrially rugged matte plastic box looks like a professional piece of kit. Lucy lifts the lid and takes a cheap-looking smart phone from it. "You can use this to stay in touch until you leave for the meet. Use the encrypted application for voice, text and multi-media messaging." She hands it to him.

"As we said, we don't use anything with wires these days." Lucy takes a bulky digital watch from the Peli case. "I know this looks a bit cheap and nasty, maybe that'll stop anyone from wanting to take it from you. Nevertheless, almost the whole of the space inside the body is

Hitting Home

battery storage, incorporating a highly sensitive, voice-activated sound recorder. The watch mechanism itself takes up a tiny fraction of the space."

Far from being dismayed at the watch's lack of style and elegance, Tariq is in wonder at the technical capability it possesses. "This is cool. I don't usually wear a watch." He says as he straps it on."

"Do you wear a belt?" Lucy asks as she picks up a heavily woven grey canvas belt. "I'm guessing you won't be wearing that suit for the meet?"

Tariq laughs coyly.

"This should go with whatever casual trousers or jeans you'd usually wear." She points at where the material folds back on itself from the buckle loop – there are two lines of double stitching two centimetres apart. "There's a GPS micro-transmitter stitched in here, we can track you wherever you go, but we should never end up far enough away to have to worry about that."

"Wow, this is proper James Bond stuff." Tariq says inspecting the belt at close quarters.

"We'll call you Double O 35." Lucy laughs. Matt gives her a stern look.

"Why 35?" Tariq asks.

"No reason." Lucy says.

"I'm sure you'll have lots more questions, and that's absolutely fine. Matt says. "Note them down in your new phone and we can talk more before we launch into anything."

"Did anyone know you were coming here today, Tariq?" Matt asks.

"Yeah, my friend, Zeb."

Joseph Mitcham

"Good." says Matt. "Can you send him a message, by which ever means you usually would. Tell him you were rejected by the Army and that you're pretty upset about it."

"Make it clear that you're pissed off." Lucy adds.

19

On the move

"I'm in a good position, less than 25 metres from the suspected target car." Spider scooches down behind the steering wheel of the Vectra with his camera held ready to move into position to get a shot of the targets inbound.

Having taken a significant short-cut across the green, Jambo breaks into a slow walk to catch his breath. "I'm 100 metres south of the car park. I can see them coming your way – they're crossing the grass and will enter the car park on the west side. One of them is on the phone."

Spider looks half left to the prominent gap in the hedge. As he sees the two figures heading his way, the Mondeo moves off towards the gap. "Shit." He fears he'll miss the photo opportunity if the car collects them at the gap.

The Vectra's driver door is wrenched open. "WHAT THE FUCK DO YOU THINK YOU'RE DOING?" The hulking owner of the car looks fresh from the weights room.

"Oh fuck." Jambo and John say almost together.

"SHUT THE FUCK UP AND GET DOWN." Spider snaps with maximum aggression. The man is stunned, he thinks for a second, looks at Spider's camera and drops to a squatting position inside the door.

Joseph Mitcham

Spider drops his voice to a low whisper, "Half left, blue Mondeo, potential terror suspects. Give me one minute, and please - shut the door."

"Good save." says John.

"Confirm we're not compromised." Jambo says, not convinced that the shouting would not have been heard by the targets at such close range.

Spider says nothing, he lets the camera's shutter click do the talking.

*

"Both suspects are in the car. That's three in the vehicle including the driver. They're moving off now." Jambo says as he walks through the gap in the hedge to see the Mondeo follow the access road around past the paddocks.

"Roger. Standing by. I'll dial in our other mobile callsigns." says John.

Jambo scopes the car park, trying to locate Spider, and sees a burly man stand up amongst the cars and open a door.

Spider pivots towards the car owner from the driver's seat. "I'm sorry, mate. I needed somewhere to watch those guys from, and your car door was open." Spider says, still wary of the big man, whose aggression does not seem to have completely quelled.

"Are you Police?" the man asks, stepping back defensively as he sees Jambo approaching from between the two cars in front of him.

"No, mate, we're not Police. We're working with another Government agency on an anti-terror case." Spider says, standing up out of the car.

"Where's the van?" Jambo asks impatiently, "We need to get on the road."

Hitting Home

"Still up at the target location." Spider says, his face showing signs of embarrassment at his lack of foresight. "I didn't want to risk the target recognising it." he bluffs.

"Vehicle turning south onto London Road. I'm pursuing." John says into both their ears.

"This is Mike Two-three Bravo, I'm heading down London Road now, I'll be right behind you. John." One of the mobile volunteers says from his burgundy Ford Focus.

"This is Mike Two-three Alpha, I'm joining the M1 southbound at junction 11, I should make it down in front of the target vehicle." The Mobile Alpha callsign accelerates in his ageing black Nissan Qashqai to ensure that he does get out in front of the Mondeo.

"Roger." Jambo acknowledges the location statuses of the mobile team members. "Don't suppose we could borrow your car, mate?"

*

"I can't believe you've brought the fuckin' civvy along." John says as Spider turns off the roundabout onto the southbound M1 slip road.

"We're all 'fuckin' civvies' now, John." Jambo says back to him.

Once Jambo had explained that he and Spider were ex-forces and that the men in the Mondeo represented a real danger to the public, big Trevor had been more than willing to lend them his car, for what they had convinced him will be a low-key tail.

Poor Trev still hasn't cottoned onto the fact that Jambo and Spider are wired into a digital conversation. His confusion at their seemingly spontaneous outbursts doing nothing to help right his disorientation at the situation that he finds himself in.

Trailing John by over two minutes, Spider quickly moves into the right-hand lane and stays there, firmly, but politely progressing through the weekend traffic, ensuring that his lane etiquette is faultless, even at speeds approaching one hundred miles per hour, he does not wish to attract unnecessary attention as a potentially reckless driver.

"Come on, Jambo, where are you?" John asks as he passes another junction entrance.

"We're half a mile from the Hemel Hempstead junction." Spider says.

"You must be close; I'm just going past it." The target vehicle is just in sight, blurring into the horizon with the train of vehicles. The mobile Bravo callsign has slowed and allowed the target vehicle to overtake it and is sitting three cars behind.

"Mike Two-three Bravo, target still on M1, passing A414 exit now."

Rotating the duty of lead car every five miles or so, the four-car surveillance team are never nearer than 100 metres to the target vehicle, allowing greater distances to open up between junctions, but on this stretch on the M1; there is minimal opportunity to allow line of sight to be broken, slip roads breaking off from the motorway every other mile or so.

"This is Alpha, he's indicating off at junction four, that's the A41."

"Roger, drop back, let Bravo slot in. We'll hold back in reserve with John." says Jambo. The built-up area that they are heading into makes remaining covert much more difficult. Jambo cannot risk being noticed, certainly not before the destination is even reached. The two mobile callsigns are expendable assets, if they end up getting too close; they may simply drive off never to be seen again. It is vital that Jambo and Spider remain out of the picture for as long as their vehicle is not essential to maintain contact. "Stay behind John." he says to Spider.

As the vehicles snake off the motorway the traffic becomes unnecessarily heavy; the more nervous drivers slowing to negotiate the curves of the flyover as the A41 crosses to the south side of the

M1. "I'm going to need to jump forward a bit or risk losing him at the roundabout." says the Bravo driver. He lurches out into a barely big enough gap in the right-hand lane and passes four cars before returning to the left lane just in time for the dual carriageway to end. His darting manoeuvre being 'par for the course' in this part of the world, he is now only two cars behind the Mondeo.

Jambo opens the maps app on his phone to try and anticipate where their journey might be heading. Breaking from the M1 at this juncture indicates that they will be heading into the suburbs of Harrow or Edgeware. The long gap between the Bravo and Alpha cars is concerning, as this could result in the lead car becoming isolated and therefore needing to take greater risks to maintain contact with the target.

"Mike Two-three Bravo, left at the roundabout."

Fortunately, the weight of traffic is from their direction and the cars heading into London dominate the junction; the surveillance team all make it onto Edgeware Way unbroken. Jambo watches his icon move along the road on his phone screen, wondering where they can be going as they head back towards the M1 – maybe crossing back over the motorway into Barnet?

The Bravo driver interrogates the huge green road sign, trying to anticipate which way the Mondeo will go at the roundabout; will it be straight over towards Mill Hill? Will it be left to Totteridge? Or right to central Edgeware? He is so focused on the sign; he almost misses the Mondeo deviating off the road ahead. "Target has turned left onto Mountain Grove. It's access only, so it's either his destination, or they're doing some counter-surveillance. I'm too close to follow – driving by."

*

Jambo follows the road on the mapping, the Grove is 300 metres long, with a left turn at its end where it becomes 'Rosedene', which loops back in a semi-circular arc and re-joins the grove near to its entrance. "Alpha, proceed onto Mountain Grove with caution. Let us know if it's safe to follow on." says Jambo.

"Roger. Turning onto Mountain Grove now."

Jambo and Spider smile at each other in anticipation as they await an update.

"Target not seen."

There is a confused pause.

"Just saw his back end – he's turned onto Rosedene. I'm continuing on Mountain Grove."

"Roger. Follow the grove to the end and turn left, that'll bring you back round head on to him." Jambo says. "Unless you're worried that he's made you? John, can follow you in?"

"Negative, I barely saw him, there's no way he spotted me. Standby for my update."

Spider parks on the grove with John in front and the Bravo behind. They wait patiently.

"The gardens are thick with foliage, I might have missed him." the Alpha says, sounding worried.

"Target vehicle sighted at house number eight. No suspects apparent."

20

Up to the challenge

Tariq has walked the 20 minutes from Croydon East train station in a daydream. He opens the front door to his scruffy block of flats with a new perspective; no longer feeling like he belongs in the humdrum of the mundane life that he has allowed himself to get comfortable in.

After little more than an hour with the beautiful people of the Security Service, he feels elevated, special, as though the true meaning of his being were about to be realised. He feels better, cleverer, switched on. His suit, though nowhere near as nice as Matt's, gives him an added sense of superiority within the context of his family's crappy flat. Being given a specific mission has brought him the direction and purpose that he has been missing and he truly feels as though he can accomplish anything.

He wastes no time in getting down to business; he lifts the lid of his tired old laptop and turns his attention to his phone whilst giving the almost obsolete computer the minute or so that it needs to fire up; he opens a social media app to message Zeb.

"Time wasting fucks - said I'm too much of a risk to be in the British Army. They threw out my appeal and told me not to bother reapplying. Well fuck them – I'll show them a risk."

He laughs to himself as he hits the send icon, trying to imagine his friend's reaction when he receives it. He turns back to the laptop, opens the internet browser and clicks onto his email shortcut. His deleted items folder is teeming with spam and junk mail, but it doesn't take him long to find what he is looking for. He hits the reply button.

"Salam my Brother, this sounds interesting. When might we meet?"

Tariq spends the next hour exchanging messages with Zeb, embellishing on his story of rejection by the Army, whilst concurrently imagining what scenarios he might find himself in on his new adventure and what questions he might ask Matt and Lucy. He has difficulty in coming up with anything and is conscious that his window of time to think about it is finitely framed. This pressure is compounded as an email notification pings in the corner of his laptop screen.

"Come to Wandle Park at 10am tomorrow morning, I'll be at the Bandstand. Leave your phone at home."

Tariq tries to smile as he hits reply once more but finds himself shuddering inside. He thinks about Matt and Lucy, drawing down confidence from theirs, he feels his inner strength returning.

"I will be there and ready."

*

"How's it going in Edgeware?" Charlie asks, speaking into Lucy's mobile, which lays in the middle of the desk on speaker mode.

"We've been lucky;" John says cockily from the comfort of his car, "the house next door seems to be occupied, but let's just say that they've not paid much attention to the garden. The bordering hedge to our target house is like a jungle and we've managed to get Spider in there with his surveillance kit. We're hoping to catch one of the neighbours from across the street and buy our way in for a frontal view of the property sometime this evening."

"What about the rear?" Alex asks, dialled in from the flat.

"Negative. There's a large shed, without windows, plus we're not sure if they're using it, apart from that; there's no decent cover."

"Have you managed to collect any intelligence yet?" Charlie asks.

"No." John says bluntly. "We can't even confirm that the three people in the car went into the property, that's just an assumption based on where the car is. There's no room for taking risks, we have to stay back and be patient." Something Alex never thought he'd hear John say. "What's going on 'spook-side'?"

"Of the 20 candidates, four appear to have been recruited and gone off grid." Charlie says with an unimpressed frown. "A further three have been approached by email, one of those yielding a potential meeting planned for tomorrow in Liverpool."

"Similar proportion to how ours are shaping up." Alex says. "What's happening with our potential mole?"

Charlie gives Lucy a look of a thousand daggers across the table. "Wait one." she says and places the phone on mute.

"How much have you told Alex about your plan?" She doesn't let her answer, "Recruitment and handling of covert assets has to be at the highest level of classification, you should know that. It's not for open discussion, even with Alex."

Lucy knows that she has made a fundamental error discussing her idea with Alex, knowing what it might develop into. "I'm sorry." she says. "Alex is aware that there is a lead, he knows his name and codename, and clearly he's familiar with the case file."

Charlie frowns intensely baring her teeth a little and shaking her head. "Well, it looks like Alex is in the circle, but you must brief him that it goes no further, especially not to John or Mike."

Lucy nods meekly, "What shall I brief now?"

"Nothing, blow it off as a dead lead. You can fill Alex in after."

Again, Lucy nods. After a pause to gather her thoughts, she unmutes her phone. "Apologies, I was just checking my messages from Matt. It looks like that's a dead lead."

Charlie seizes the initiative to change the subject, "Alex, how are the 29 looking?"

"Just Lima Two-three picked up that we're aware of."

"What the fuck do you mean 'that we're aware of', Alex?" John snaps across him angrily. "My blokes are fully aware of what's going on with the targets they've been assigned. They're more than capable of tracking these dickheads."

Charlie and Lucy are as stunned as Alex at his outburst.

"Sorry, mate. I didn't mean anything by it; I know you've got it covered." Alex is getting to know John well; he knows that something is bothering him. "Are you okay, John?"

John puffs out heavily over the line, "Mate, I'm just a bit threaders. Since those Watch List targets dropped off the radar on our watch, I can't help feeling that we're being seen as second rate, and we're fucking not."

"Listen, Hun, that's absolutely not the case." Charlie leans in, "If I've given you that impression, then I'm sorry, Darlin', but you guys are a part in a bigger game."

"Roger." says John despondently. "If you haven't got anything else for me; I've got to boost." Without much of a pause, he rings off.

There is an awkward pause on the line as Charlie and Lucy look at one another with disconcerted looks.

"As I was saying," Alex begins where he left off, "Just Lima Two-three picked up, but three more candidates' accounts have received invitations. I'm working with John and Mike to ensure their blokes have what they need.

"Thanks for the update, Alex." says Lucy.

"Yes, thanks, Alex." Charlie breaks in, "What Lucy briefed earlier about Candidate Lima Three-five – that was for John's benefit. Lucy and Matt have actually made some good progress, but it needs to remain classified. You haven't mentioned his name or Lima Three-five to anyone else on the team, have you? Even John?"

"No," he says, unimpressed by the lack of trust that they are willing to show in the wider team, "to be honest, I can't even remember his name."

Charlie picks up on his disappointment. "Alex, any situation where we have an asset working for us, it is imperative that we keep those in the know to an absolute minimum. I don't even know his name, it is just the three of you, and that's how it's going to stay. Got it?"

"No problem." Alex says sulkily. He turns to Lucy, "So how did it really go?"

"I met with him earlier today. He's a nice young man, very keen, possibly a bit excitable, but I think once he's had a chance to get used to the seriousness of the situation; he'll be fine. We have a meet with the recruiter planned for tomorrow morning."

"Tomorrow?" Alex exclaims, "That's not long for him to 'get used to the idea'. Is he going to be in the right place to be able to manage it? He could ruin the whole operation if he blows this."

"Our team will be close by at all times." Lucy says, her own doubts and fears obvious in her voice.

"There's nothing they can do to salvage the operation once the mistake is made." Alex reinforces his concerns.

Lucy looks up to Charlie; the responsibility lies with her. "The juice is worth the squeeze." she says, being the woman that she is, she backs Lucy's plan to the hilt. Having given it the go ahead; she must give her full confidence and commitment.

"This individual represents a unique opportunity for this mission. Having an asset inside their organisation gives us a chance to get some real information. Chasing the genuine candidates might lead us to the recruiters, possibly connect a few more dots, but without their cooperation; I can't see us getting much further while we have to watch from a distance – we'll get interventions and prevent some terrible acts, but this lad can do some digging, see things we'll never be able to otherwise - maybe even help us nip this whole group in the bud.

21

Recasting the line

"You are an absolute star, Lesley, thank you Darlin'." Jambo says taking the tray of bacon sandwiches from the lady owner of the house. He had managed to get talking to her as she had walked to the shops the evening before. Having shown her his old Army ID card, a spare that he'd never handed in, he had talked her into letting him and the boys use her spare room to keep an eye on the potentially dangerous people going in and out of number eight across the road.

"You're very welcome, Jambo." His nickname doesn't sound quite right from the lips of a white-haired lady in her late sixties, "I've taken a pack-up and flask to John and the boys around the corner; they're happy enough. You just give me a shout if you need those mugs topping up." He smiles at her from the 'off-shift' nest he's made for himself on the floor as she turns and walks back towards the stairs.

Activity at the target property has been minimal since arriving on location yesterday afternoon. A delivery of takeaway food had arrived in the early evening, the door having been answered by the driver of the Mondeo. The same person, identity unknown, had left the house at 0746 hours on foot. John and one of the mobile callsign drivers had pursued him to a petrol station where he had bought a range of supplies, mostly cooking ingredients, and come straight back. The team have still not had visual confirmation that Lima Two-three and his recruiter are present, though the amount of food going into the house certainly suggests that there is more than one individual in there.

Spider has taken the majority of the watch shifts overnight and has the position set up on Lesley's old computer desk behind a small gap in the curtains. He twitches in the seat; "Looks like we've got some movement."

The driver steps out of the front door of number eight, presses the button on the key fob and opens the driver's door of the old Ford.

"Mobile callsigns, standby." Jambo says into his mic.

The driver is followed out of the building a few seconds later by the recruiter. The older man presents a calm demeanour, pausing on the doorstep, allowing Spider the opportunity to get some clearer shots of him, he walks slowly over to the car and climbs into the passenger seat.

"What's going on?" John asks over the open call, sounding like he's still got half a mouthful of bacon sandwich.

"The recruiter and his driver are in the Mondeo. Have you still got both your mobile maties with you?"

"Roger, we're all sat here in my motor enjoying Lesley's lovely breakfast." Jambo hears John chivvying the men, reverting to his 'in barracks troop sergeant' tone, "Come on fellas, get back to your cars. Take your scoff with you."

"I'll leave Spider here watching the house. Can you get him some back-up?"

"No problem. Are you coming with me?" John asks.

"No, I'll catch you up." Jambo says before hanging up the call. "Fancy coming for a drive, Trev?" Jambo says, giving the bed a shove with his foot.

*

Joseph Mitcham

Tailing the blue Mondeo south through the heart of the capital and across the Thames had been a nightmare for the team. The alternating lead trailing cars had to fight with the aggressive traffic to stay within the optimal distance; it had been wearing on the drivers, particularly Trevor, who has had no training for such a challenge – Jambo ensured that his stints at the front were short, which also suited his requirement to maintain the lowest profile of all the vehicle occupants.

Without Spider, his right-hand man, on the ground; Jambo will be on his own unless he makes the call to take the 'visual landmark' that is John, or one of the mobile callsigns, neither of whom he knows. From what he understands about his target he doesn't anticipate the recruiter to have any great level of security awareness, and he certainly doesn't have the ability to out-pace him or otherwise give him the slip – easy enough decision.

"Did you not want to go home then, Trev?" Jambo asks his volunteer driver.

"And miss out on this little adventure? You're joking, aren't you?"

Jambo lets the small talk die before it begins and consults his phone's mapping app for parking locations that the target pair might be heading for. This part of South London is peppered with green spaces, any of which would be suitable for the recruiter to meet another candidate, but equally there are business centres and community hubs that might host any kind of meeting, transaction or collection.

Filing off the slip road from the A236 behind the Bravo car, everything feels fraught again as they navigate into the quieter side streets.

"He's gone into the car park at the end of Westfield, I'm peeling off."

As Trev proceeds carefully down Westfield Road, Jambo spots the bright brick pillars either side of the car park entrance. He interrogates the overhead view of the area on his phone but cannot see any other ways in nearby. The access road into the car park is nearly 50 metres long and doglegs round to the left. It is well shaded by the thick deciduous trees; Jambo assesses that he will be able to slip in unnoticed on foot, as there seems to be plenty of other people walking around inside the grounds to lose himself amongst.

"Just pull up here, Trev. Cheers." Trevor parks the car tight to the curb 75 metres short of the park gates. "Wait here, this should only take ten minutes."

*

Jambo jumps out of the Vectra and jogs slowly up to the pillar on the left side of the entrance. He stands back from it, so as not to appear as though he's peeking around a corner, but takes the same angle of view, keeping most of his body out of sight. He further conceals his focus by holding out his phone and concurrently starts to organise the mobile units' cover of the area.

"John, anticipate going back the way we came, get the lads positioned." Jambo steels another look around the corner of the brickwork, "Target vehicle has parked up - both subjects remain in the car."

The Mondeo faces into the centre of the park, looking out, under the high canopy of trees. Jambo senses that he has stood still for long enough and ventures into the grounds, stepping over the low, single bar fence on the right side of the road and heads off around the north side of the green where a large group of young men are playing football.

The lads are unruly, and the game is energetic. As Jambo walks in a wide arc behind the makeshift goal of piled up items of clothing, the ball comes bouncing out of play, rolling to a stop by Jambo's feet. He drags the ball back under his toes, then flicks it into the air towards the shirtless goalie, receiving a "cheers, mate". Looking down the field

Joseph Mitcham

of play and beyond, he identifies his target vehicle - occupants still yet to move.

22

Into the abyss

Wanting to look the part for his role, Tariq had conducted some internet research on how a 'man of action' should dress and had visited a local outdoor shop. Wearing his new, snug, black and grey walking trousers with his special new belt, and light brown, round-neck base-layer shirt, he feels set to take on the world. He checks the time on his new watch, 0942 hours, almost time to set off. He wonders if the watch is recording now and how much noise is needed to set it recording. He steps outside and shuts the front door of his flat, not knowing when he might return.

*

Walking down the steps of the footbridge over one track, he continues under the viaduct of a second, the convoluted footpath seeming to be squeezed into the limited space between them, weaving its way through the entwined rails. He stares up at the ageing brickwork of the viaduct as he passes under the archway; the individual bricks have a purple sheen to them but appear to have retained their strength and integrity over what must have been a century in place.

Emerging from the darkness of the tunnel into the brighter, but still shaded walkway at the south-west edge of the park grounds; Tariq already has his bearings from years of visiting the park on a near daily basis as a younger teenager. He focuses on readying himself mentally for what lies ahead.

Joining the path to his left that runs through the trees around the edge of the park, he has a partial view of the bandstand through the alleyway between the trees that the path carves. He closes his eyes and imagines himself as a carefree and careless individual who is at liberty to do whatever he likes; he feels the freedom to do whatever is asked of him and has no one to answer to – how much more straightforward could this be?

The path splits and opens out around both sides of the bandstand, there are clumps of trees behind the structure to the left and right. The area is busy with families and groups of children playing, running around and climbing on the railings of the empty, ornate platform.

Tariq pauses on the cusp of the scene to look around – no one stands out as being a likely terror organisation recruiter. He checks his watch, 0959 hours, he looks around the peripheries of the area, down the possible approach routes, though the path behind him and beyond, to where it continues around the park to his left, but neither view extends far into the trees, owing to the curve of the circular path.

As he begins to slowly walk around the bandstand in an anticlockwise direction, he sees a figure step out from the trees behind it to the right. The man looks old, he is dressed in baggy, dark-green shirt and cream slacks that fit snuggly around his bloated waist, but hang like sails over the rest of his lower half. After sharing a split second of eye contact, the man beckons his recruit with the wave of a single finger.

23

FUBAR

Jambo had maintained strict discipline and barely looked at the car whilst acting as a ball-boy for the footballers. He had left them to it to track parallel to the recruiter, following the circular path from the car park, in a southerly direction, into the trees. Pre-empting the likely rendezvous point, Jambo had been patient and waited more than long enough for the Mondeo driver's attention to wander from his colleague's security before taking a direct route across the green.

Sitting on the North bank of the stream that sections off the southern quarter of the park, Jambo leans back on the palms of his hands on the soft grass, takes in a deep breath and basks with the sun on his dusty dry, dark brown skin. Absorbing the heat through his clothes, the warmth, greenery, and the sights and sounds of families enjoying the park, make him feel like he has stepped into the normal life of an untroubled civilian, something that he has not experienced since he was a teenager.

Keeping his target in peripheral vision and feigning busyness with his phone, Jambo barely flicks his eyes up as the young man begins to head north from the east of the bandstand. What is attracting Jambo's attention is the runner with his foot up on the park bench immediately to his front, who is quietly talking to himself as he rests his hands on the top of his trainer, apparently not doing up his shoelaces.

"John, possible spook tailing at the RV." Jambo immediately becomes self-conscious – if I've spotted him; has he spotted me? He lies back on the grass and closes his eyes.

"Ignore him. He'll ignore you." says John.

Jambo had anticipated the possibility of encountering 'blue forces', but thought that they would be more difficult to spot – who knows, maybe there are others I haven't seen? The target and the approaching candidate are now third on his list of priories after minimising his profile on the scene and spotting other Security Service team members. Have they been told I'm on the ground? Jambo makes this into a game of professional standards; there are reputations at stake – who can conceal themselves the best? So far, he judges that he is in front.

He sweeps the tree line with his eyes for other malingerers – no one being that obvious. He visually interrogates everyone in the area around the bandstand once more, then he checks that all of the dog walkers on the green have dogs – testing against his own favourite ploy. He fits all of the minimal, but necessary movements of his head and body into plausible actions centring around getting into a comfortable dosing position.

30 metres west of his position, to his right as he lays, there is a couple sitting talking quietly, her flowery blouse makes her look older than her face appears from this range. There is something familiar about the man, but Jambo does not allow himself to look at him for long enough to get a proper look. His attire is casual, a light linen shirt and blue jeans, but there is something not quite right about their body language. Neither of them is looking directly at the target pair, but then neither are looking away from them either. There is certainly no eye contact between them as they chat.

Jambo turns his attention back to the spoof jogger, who is now resting his backside against the back of the bench and stretching his hamstrings. He looks directly at the couple as he says something else to himself. Jambo smiles but foresees potential difficulties with their combined exit strategies. He risks becoming reliant on the Security Service operatives' abilities and spatial awareness not to compromise them all at the point when the targets move off from their RV.

Hitting Home

Making the assumption that the recruiter will head back to his car with the new candidate in tow, Jambo looks at the mapping of the park on his phone to try and find a way back to Trevor without adding to the crowd of people that might all move in that direction.

*

1012 hours, the recruiter gives the new candidate a friendly tap on the arm and they both turn towards the bandstand and begin walking. They pass the structure on the left side as Jambo sees it, heading into the trees to pick up the shaded path, back towards the car park. "Target and candidate moving onto northbound path, heading back to wheels." he says quietly.

The jogger raises his knees to his chest alternately, hugging them each to stretch his glutes and then begins to move towards the green archway made by the trees. He pushes an elbow high over his head with his other hand, maintaining his facade to those around him, despite his targets being unable to see him.

As the jogger disappears from view, the couple get to their feet and begin to walk at speed, north across the green. Jambo holds tight, trying to estimate how much distance the target pair have covered. He looks to his left, following the line of the stream to where it emerges from a culvert that goes under the circular path. As he looks above it; he sees the recruiter and his new recruit pass across a gap between the trees.

"Moving now, heading straight back to Trevor." Jambo stands up and walks at best speed along the brow of the bank, making a beeline for the gap in the trees to the path. He sees the jogger pass by at a pertinent distance from the target pair some 20 metres in front of him. Jambo breaks half left to cut the corner and walks between the trees to hit the path just a few metres behind the Security Service agent. Continuing on his vector, he crosses the path into a disused carting track. He marches to the back of the track and pushes into a sparse hedge and climbs the chest-high wall behind it.

Shuffling over the industrial sized waste bin on the other side of the wall, Jambo hits the ground running, following Cuthbert Road he sprints around the outside perimeter back to Westfield Road and sees the faded silver Vectra half way down, exactly as he'd left it. Nearer to him on the other side of the road, he sees John's white Audi, repositioned to face away from the park. Jambo smiles and tips him a faint nod as he passes by.

*

"You all right, Trev?"

"ARGH Jesus, Jambo, you scared the shit out of me." Jambo laughs as he settles into the passenger seat and resets his focus back on the gap between the salmon pink pillars of brick at the top of the road.

"They'll be heading back up this road in figures few, we need to get round the triangle so we're facing the right way to follow." A perplexed Trev looks back at Jambo. "Drive down there, turn left, then left again." Jambo says trying to keep hold of his patience.

As they are about to round the first corner, Trev spots the Mondeo moving along the track out of the park. "There they are." he says.

"Best move a bit quicker then." says Jambo. "Target vehicle exiting onto Westfield."

"Roger, I'll go lead." says the Alpha call sign from the black Nissan which is parked up half way along the road that Jambo had just run down – Jambo raises his hand to him as Trev accelerates past.

"Target vehicle now on Westfield." John says, his eyes fixed on his driver-side wing mirror.

"Moving now." says the Alpha.

"I'll follow on." says the Bravo.

Hitting Home

As Trev turns left, for the second time, Jambo spots the maroon Ford Focus half way up the road. "Slow down, Trev. Let him out in front of us." Jambo points to the Bravo car. "We've got John to slot in before us, too."

Trevor pulls in to the gap left by the Focus amongst the line of parked cars; his instincts for covert driving slowly developing. "That's it, give it a few seconds."

"Target car has turned north onto Factory Lane." John says, pausing with concern. "Mike Two-three Alpha, you have a BMW up your arse; gun it so I can get out in front of him."

The Qashqai lurches forward with a sudden gear change – John is ready and noses the powerful Audi out, sticking to its bumper, then slows to further irritate and frustrate the driver of the navy blue 5 Series.

The alpha callsign makes it out onto Factory Road just about in visual contact with the target car. John watches the Bravo vehicle go past as it emerges from Cuthbert Road, which joins Factory Lane just metres before Westfield on the apex of the bend under the fly-over. John waits until he can see Trev and Jambo reach the corner and pulls out. "Follow on quick Jambo, don't fuck about."

"Roger." says Jambo. "Go, Trev, GO, GO." The big man takes the hint, launching the big old Vectra out of the junction. The impatient and angry driver of the navy BMW isn't in the mood to wait and jumps out of Westfield immediately to their left, trying to beat him out but pulls straight into Trev's path.

The shock of the explosive burst from the airbags is more violent than the impact itself, but Jambo's over-riding thought is that his part in the mission is over for now.

"We're out of the game. Fucking prick in the BM pulled out on us."

"I'll come back for you." says John, "We know where they're going."

Joseph Mitcham

*

"Are you okay, Trev?"

"Yeah." he smiles, rubbing the chalk dust from his eyes and poking his ear with his little finger. "I'm fine; the car's a bit fucked, like."

"We'll sort you out, don't worry, mate."

Jambo gets out of the smashed Vauxhall, burying his anger at the driver of the other car, knowing that there's nothing that can be done about it now.

"Are you all right, fella?" Jambo says as he tries in vain to open the driver's door, but the Vectra has done a good job of mangling both offside doors well into the safety cage of the car's body. Both door windows have shattered. As Jambo reaches in to grab the side impact airbag, he recognises the linen shirt. He pulls back the deflating curtain - "Nice shirt… Boss."

24

Combined efforts

Matt's extremely high intellect and physical capability had made him a dangerous quantity as a Special Forces officer. He had barely touched the ground at Royal Marine Condor as a Second Lieutenant before breezing through SBS Selection – he had relished the opportunity to show what he could do and devoured the challenges presented by the course.

He had jumped the queue on early promotion to sub-unit command, coming out of the SF environment to represent the Royal Marine cap badge as an exchange Company Commander with 1 Para. Jambo had met Matt several times around the SF bazaars but knew him best from serving time together at the first battalion. He had been one of his Platoon Sergeants while on a break from the SAS, back with the battalion for some 'down-time', but Matt's unique style of leadership, combined with his insatiable ambition and broad streak of arrogance, had made it far from a period of relaxation for anyone.

"I take it you were following the candidate?" Jambo asks as Matt climbs through the window of the buckled BMW, which he has reversed back against the curb.

"Were." Matt says angrily, frustrated at losing the tail on his target. "Hopefully my other callsigns are with him."

Jambo says nothing.

"What about you? I take it you're working with Charlie's unofficial team?" Matt read's Jambo's raising of his eyebrows as an affirmative.

Joseph Mitcham

"What brought you here? Were you on the recruiter?" Matt answers his own questions as he goes. Have you got anyone else following him? Do you know where they are going?" Matt's questions keep coming as he expresses his thought pattern aloud, but Jambo is coy and looks on as Trevor scrapes the remaining fragments of the front of his car towards the curb with his instep.

Jambo has a nicely settling operation going on and the situation at the safe house is likely to build into a rich hive of activity and information – the last thing he needs is the confusion that Security Service involvement would inevitably bring. As he drags out his silence on the matter, John's white Audi screeches around the sharp bend under the flyover, past the scene of the crash, and halting across the road from the three men.

*

"Roger, I'll pick it up from his place in Wembley. Cheers." John ends the call, jumps out of the car and walks over to join Jambo. "Don't worry about your car, Trev. How do you like that one?" John asks, pointing back to the A6.

"Very nice." says Trevor, looking at it with coveting desire.

"Well, drop us off in Brent and it's yours."

"Mega, cheers!" Trevor says, the smile immediately returning to his face.

Jambo introduces John to the former Royal Marine and Special Forces officer. "Matt's working with Charlie – in some capacity."

"I've been brought in to try and get some traction with this emerging group. I'm working with Charlie and Lucy."

"So, you're on the payroll with the spooks now?" Jambo asks.

"Yes." Matt is curt and has no intention of taking them through his career history. He checks his mobile screen. "Look I really need to get after that target. If you guys know where they're heading; I'd appreciate it if I could ride with you."

Jambo bites the bullet; "Okay, we tracked the recruiter and a candidate to a house in North London yesterday. We believe he's heading back there with your target now."

"Great. What's the address? I'll get a team up there." Matt says keenly.

"No. I've seen you and your operators in action, and you can stay well out of it." Jambo says with authoritative contempt.

Matt is taken aback, but again finds himself without much of a defence. "You don't understand, I have to be on the ground." He hesitates - Jambo and John look at him without sympathy. "Okay, just me then?"

Jambo stares at Matt, eye-to-eye, trying to judge how he will behave, whether the through-and-through officer can let go of the idea of command. "This is my operation – what I say goes."

"That's fine. I just need to be nearby."

*

Trevor proudly drives his new acquisition out of the customer car park, waving a fond farewell to Jambo as he goes. Jambo gets into the front passenger seat of John's new vehicle, a grey Mercedes E-Class. They set off north-east on the North Circular.

"Spider's confirmed the Mondeo has returned to the Edgeware property and all three occupants have gone into the house." Jambo says, looking at his phone screen. "Our candidate from yesterday hasn't left the building, and no one else has been seen going in or out of the house either.

Matt sits in the back seat keeping an intermittent check on his phone. "What sort of coverage do we have on the target property?" he asks.

"Not much, just line-of-sight from a house across the road. We've tried a laser microphone but there's not much talking going on at the front of the house, other than idle chit-chat. We could do with getting inside and getting it bugged, but that's too high risk."

"Roger." Matt acknowledges. "So, do I have this straight? You guys are working indirectly for Charlie Thew?"

Jambo knows nothing of Charlie Thew; all he knows is that he is helping out John to track down the organisation that had killed his long-time friend and mentor, Craig Medhurst. He says nothing.

"Charlie's asked us to keep an eye on what's going on with a few potential bad lads, we're hoping to find links from them into the bigger picture." says John.

"As I understand it; there are two lists of potential candidates for recruitment into this 'Interest Group' and you're tracking over 30 of them?"

"Something like that." John replies, "How many of your 20 have you got?" he counters.

Matt pauses. "I'm not sure on the numbers, my colleague is keeping tabs on the detail."

"Lucy?" John asks.

"Yes."

"She'll take your mind off things." John laughs.

"Yes, she's quite a woman." Matt says with a thoughtful, respectful tone.

25

Coming into focus

Alex clings on to Lucy, nestling his head tight into her bosom as they sit together on the sofa. "I'm so sorry, Sweetie. I wish there was something more I could do." she says, rubbing the top of his shoulder. He has done his best to fight through the waves of intense grief but has been unable to get images of his joyous, happy mum and doe-eyed little sister from his mind; the pain that harps through him is unrelenting.

Alex cannot reconcile the loss - neither the loss of them as central characters in the story of his life, nor the loss of them as points of reference of his place in the world – he now finds himself without an anchor point, no grounding, no one and nowhere to call home, except Lucy. Though here, in her flat, he still feels like a temporary lodger, a bit-part player in her story; an unnerving sense of precarious insecurity runs through him, and it will not let his mind rest.

"Things will get easier; it's just going to take time." She says mournfully.

"There's no way you could possibly know how I'm feeling." he snaps.

Lucy looks mortified. "No," she pauses, "I was too young to remember my dad being killed." Her face saddens sharply.

Alex's heart sinks. "I'm sorry. I'm such a dick."

His self-involved quagmire is jeopardising the one good thing he has left.

"I don't know where I'd be without you." Alex instantly regrets his choice of words that make him sound needy and weak. "I mean, you've been great." He's still not happy; he tries to convey what he is truly feeling in a more manly way. "There's nothing I can do to bring them back, but together we can get some payback."

Making a conscious decision to show some positivity, Alex kisses Lucy on the cheek, firmly squeezes her shoulders, and gets to his feet. "Right, a brew and into action."

*

"How's the tea?" Alex asks.

"Marvellous." Lucy smirks, glad to see Alex in better spirits. They put their mugs on the coffee table, bounce back onto the sofa and slide their respective computers back onto their laps.

"How are we getting on then?" Alex asks, sounding as upbeat as he can.

"You mean apart from the colliding teams in Croydon? Not too bad."

Lucy lists through the Security Service targets that have been contacted and gives updates on four candidates who have been picked up and taken to other safe houses in Liverpool, Birmingham and Manchester, and three prospective recruitments that look to be going ahead over the next 48 hours; two of them to be met the following morning.

The intelligence gathered by both elements of the operation has given the pair some significant insights; each of the candidates has received an approach from a unique email address, but these addresses do not each represent an individual recruiter. Indications from the Edgeware safe house and a similar pair of candidates tracked to a single address in Birmingham; it would seem that the recruiters may be operating within regional areas of responsibility and are cohorting their new soldiers.

"It may be that we end up with a network of safe houses up and down the country." Lucy says, making light of the big jump in the intelligence picture.

"What do we do with that?" Alex asks, knowing how delicate things are going to get.

"We can't move on them without risk of scaring the whole organisation further underground." she replies.

"We need to keep a close eye on them - they could launch these new recruits any day." Alex says, "It's not like their recent attacks have required much planning or logistics."

"Agreed; the parallel teams have that taken care of. We need to work with Matt and focus on Tariq to get what he can from him." Lucy picks up her mobile phone and dials Matt on encrypted video call. "Hi, Matt. How are you getting on?"

Alex is dismayed to see that Matt is every bit as good looking as he had imagined, one of those smarmy sods that know they're attractive - he hates him even more.

"Hi Lucy. Good; I'm in place across the road from the Edgeware safe house. Our man is in the target property with another of the recruits, a chap from Luton, Lima Two-three - Hamza DeSousa."

"You managed not to lose him then?" Alex snipes from over Lucy's shoulder with uncharacteristic spite.

"Yes. Unexpected situations like that are what the tracking device is for." Matt says calmly. "It was just a shame that I had to be the only one on my team that knew about it."

"No harm done, and it doesn't sound like there's room for a whole other team up there?" Lucy buffers the conversation between the two men.

"Quite, though space isn't my main concern at the moment. What is bothering me is that we have this brand-new asset working in complete isolation. If he were older and a bit more worldly-wise; I wouldn't have an issue leaving him to it, but I think we need to know more about what's going on in that house."

"John says there's no way of getting in to install anything; what are you suggesting?" Lucy asks back to Matt, but Alex jumps in.

"I could take a look at the local network? See if there are any hooks into anything useful?"

"Great." says Matt, "I'll send you an image with the route into the stakeout; there are a couple of fences to negotiate to get into the rear. How soon can you get here?"

Alex looks at the time on his laptop screen and visualises the tube journey. As much as he might like to spend the rest of the evening consoling himself in Lucy's warmth, he knows that he may hold the key to tracking down his family's killers. "I can be there in about an hour. Is John there?"

"He's a street or two away, heading up the mobile call signs. I'll see you at about 2100 hours.

26

Getting inside

Alex almost never sits down on the tube, no matter how quiet it is, but tonight, on this most quiet of nights, he sits huddled in the most secluded seat he can find in the unnervingly open a brightly lit carriage. On a mid-late Sunday evening, there are few other travellers heading North on the Thameslink. No one is taking any notice of him, but he feels vulnerable and exposed.

Consumed by his sadness, the faint glow of positivity that he had absorbed from Lucy had drained from him the instant he'd left the flat. Alex can feel the gloom manifested on his face as a sulking frown which feels like a weight pressing down on his cheeks, physically pushing out a pet lip – he has the feeling of a simmering five-year-old. He should be using the time to run through the plays he will need to make on his laptop, but he cannot get past the negative thoughts plaguing his mind. Not thoughts of his parents or sister, but the new man in Lucy's life, even thinking this way casts another couple of layers of guilt over him.

*

The overhead, day time image on his phone bears little resemblance to the area he finds himself in -waist deep in nettles and catchweed in a thick border of trees and bushes in the southern boundary of the Rosedene properties. He looks back over the heavy, broad-panelled fence and gets a lock on the house that is hosting the stakeout - diagonally across to his left, a couple of gardens away.

Joseph Mitcham

The thickening greenery makes accessing Lesley's garden, or that of her immediate neighbour's, impossible. His footing on the steep bank is aided by the small patch of foliage that has been flattened by those who have trodden the route before him.

As he tries to find a grip on top of the fence, he feels a personified version of the same nervousness he felt as a kid when jumping over the neighbours' fence, feeling the terror as he would run to retrieve his football.

The immediacy of the challenge to complete this final leg of his journey undetected takes the edge off his primary concern - coming face to face with the man that Lucy seems so taken with. Can he possibly be as smooth as he had appeared on the video call?

Alex fears for the strength of his relationship with Lucy. Things have moved so fast with so much energy; might the fizz be getting lost as realities are realised, as his underlying depressive nature comes to light? He puts these thoughts out of his mind as he launches himself over the fence.

*

Alex taps gently on the large, double-glazed window pane of the back door. He looks with trepidation through the square of glass, scanning the back of the curtain for clues to movement. He flinches as the material is snatched back. He is greeted by the friendly face of an elderly lady. She smiles at him and opens the door. "You must be Alex?"

"Yes. Lesley?" he replies in a hushed voice. "Very nice to meet you." Alex surprises himself as he feels his natural charm begin to flow from nowhere. "I love what you've done with your garden, it must be lovely out here in the sun?"

"My back garden's never had so much attention; so many young men through it in a day. Come in, love, let's get you a cup of tea."

Alex maintains his composure as she leads him through the door, straight into her homely dining room. He looks through to the conjoined kitchen to see a svelte figure presiding over the kettle. "Get another cup out, Matt; Alex is here." Lesley says, as though talking to a member of the family.

Matt bends to take a mug from the cupboard by his knees, places it on the side and turns to make his way over to them. Alex's heart sinks as he locks eyes with him. His glinting smile might rival Brad Pitt's, emanating positivity and friendliness, Alex can feel his hatred being unlocked by Matt's personable look. "Hi, Matt. Nice shirt." he says grumpily surveying the muscular bumps in it as he shakes his hand.

"Yes," Matt says, looking down at his sleeve with a wry grin, "I've been out on a little undercover jaunt in the park this afternoon and my kit's not caught up with me yet."

"Are they still trying to pry it out of your BMW?"

Matt laughs, again on the back foot of the conversation. If he is annoyed or riled; he shows no sign of it, seemingly taking Alex's barracking in good humour. Alex feels his desire to provoke him into confrontation waning, he is finding Matt as charming and likeable as Lucy has, and evidently Lesley is too. Charmed by his apparently submissive good nature and manners, Alex feels a barrage of frustration building within him.

"Tea?" Matt asks.

"Yes please." Alex says politely, sensing his own resignation to give Matt a fair chance at a working relationship. He slides his small backpack off his shoulder. "Is it okay for me to set up here?" he asks.

"Of course, love. Do you want the wi-fi details?" Lesley smiles.

"Yes please, I just need the ID, thanks."

Alex slides his laptop out of his bag and flips it open on the table. Lesley places a business card-sized slip next to it. "It's a BT one."

"Thanks, Lesley. I won't be logging into it, it's just an easy one to discount from my search."

Alex logs into his computer and immediately launches a software window. Matt places a mug of tea down and looks over his shoulder at the columns of white text on the plain black rectangle in the middle of the screen. "That looks complicated."

"That's all the wi-fi networks in detectable range." Alex points out the column of network names "The 'Service Set ID' is a good place to start. We can see Lesley's here, with the greatest signal strength – we can discount that one." Alex right clicks and removes it from the list.

"The power looked low on that one." says Matt.

"It's measured in decibel milliwatts, confusingly, that's always shown as a negative, so the smaller the number; the stronger the signal."

"Seen." Matt says, showing real interest.

"It's all well over my head." Lesley says, "I'm going to take my cup of tea up to bed. Goodnight boys."

Alex spends the next ten minutes showing Matt how to narrow down the field of possible networks that might be the one in use at their subject property. This includes moving the laptop around in the room and even out into the back garden to observe the effect on signal strengths. He checks the potential ages of the routers, filtering out any old models based on their assumption that it would have been bought new when they set up the safe house. Not all of the assumptions that they have made have been bulletproof, merely a best guess at this stage to give them some options to try. Alex settles on a VirgilMedia profile.

"Now what? You don't have the encryption code to access it." says Matt.

"I know, a minor hurdle." Alex opens another software window on his screen with 'Wi-Fi-battler' emblazoned across the top of it. "This is a fairly crude programme that can breach WPA2 encryption in a matter of minutes." Alex sets the software to work.

"Who the fuck is this?" Jambo bawls at Matt as he bursts angrily into the room.

"Calm down, Jambo." Matt says coolly, barely turning his head. "This is Alex." Matt realises a weird irony as he introduces Alex. "I take it you've not met?"

"Alex, Alex?" Jambo asks.

"Yeah. I take it you're with the Lima Two-three group?"

He nods; "Call me Jambo."

"Sorry, I should have let you know I was coming; I didn't think."

The fiery Afro-Caribbean is still simmering. "Don't just be inviting people in here without telling me, Matt, regardless of who they are." Jambo's dusky brown eyes seem to darken further with his glare.

Matt stares back at Jambo, half acknowledging him, but half not. The arrogant smirk that breaks on his face is the first clue to Alex of the hidden menace that he may yet prove to be.

*

Before Alex has finished his brew, the software has done its job. He now has access to the router, sight of any connected devices, and an easy route into them.

"How is it looking?" Jambo asks.

"I think we might be on the right track. There are no wi-fi devices connected to the router, and only one hard wired system." He taps a few more buttons. "A new model Mac laptop wired directly into the router - who does that? And not even using it for a TV connection."

Joseph Mitcham

"You think we're on the money?" Matt asks.

Alex nods, but he is already working his way into the settings of the MacBook Pro. He has access to the camera and the microphone and adds shortcuts to them to his desktop. He leaves the camera for now, knowing that turning it on risks compromising the asset. Jambo and Matt lean in as he opens the microphone. The anti-climax is palpable, as only background static can be heard. Three sets of ears lean in further as breaths are heard and a heavy laboured sigh. The men look at each other, each unable to rate the significance of what they are hearing.

"I'll set it up for voice activated recording." Alex moves on the next priority; email and messaging sites associated with the asset. He then has other recently accessed internet pages to trawl and will be concurrently sucking across the content of the laptop's non-system memory drives and anything else that might be plugged into the device.

27

Liverpool crew

"All stations, this is Zero, we've got movement, over."

The safe house in Liverpool, for all intents and purposes, was the same as the one in Edgeware. A large, secluded house in a quiet, unassuming neighbourhood. The surveillance team has a broader street with no approachable friendly neighbours who might host them in the way that Lesley has done for Jambo.

The individual teams have accumulated in the vicinity of the house, four so far, including one of the Security Service crews. John had tried to steer negotiations through Charlie to install Mike as the local lead, but with them owning the truck that overwatch is being performed from; he was on a hiding to nothing, and he'd had to bow to them bossing the location. The reality of the situation is that this allows Mike to let someone else do the leg work, coordinate shift patterns and all the other niff-naff and trivia. He is free to focus on the tactical detail and has joined one of the mobile call signs.

Sitting in the passenger seat of Jeff's Grey Mercedes C-Class, parked over 100 metres down the street from the safe house, Mike raises an eyebrow to his old mate. "Lima One-four Bravo, acknowledged. What's happening over."

"Uniform Five-three has left the house. He's heading towards the white Toyota."

The Liverpool safe house would seem to have been up and running for longer than the Edgeware property – three occupants, including a recruiter and driver, have been noted on top of the two Lima designated candidates that have been tracked to the house and one Sierra candidate from the Security Service's list. The unknown occupants have been designated 'uniform' numbers. The first identifying the safe house – Liverpool being 'five' Uniform Five-one had been confirmed as the recruiter, Uniform Five-two as the driver - Uniform Five-three is a close match for one of the seven candidates who had been recruited before Lucy's plan had rolled out.

The house has been quiet; the only activity of note was that Uniform Five-three had left the house yesterday - was followed to a supermarket west across the Mersey on the Wirral. He had sat in his car watching the store from 1100 to 1700 hours, from opening until closing.

Mike looks at his watch, "Almost opening time at the Superstore. What do you reckon? Fancy getting out of this street for a bit?" Jeff smiles and nods.

"Hello Zero, this is Lima One-four Bravo, we'll take the Toyota."

"Zero, roger, out to you. Red Ten, you go too, acknowledge."

"Red Ten, roger, out."

To keep things simple, the Security Service team members have moved onto the same mobile phone communications app that the unofficial team are using, keeping a single group call active for 'all-informed' communications; the two men can talk to and hear the whole team through Jeff's handset. All call signs have maintained their handles; Red Ten is a lone Security Service Operator in a Black BMW 3 Series, parked a few cars in front of them.

*

With a good idea of where he is heading, Jeff has tracked the Toyota at a good distance to the car park of the huge store. Whatever sort of reconnaissance Uniform Five-three might be on, he is taking no such care; parking front and centre to the store, facing through the empty disabled bays, pointing nose-on at the store entrance. Perfectly timed, Jeff arcs round in front of the Toyota, as Uniform Five-three looks down to his lap. Mike steals a glance beyond his friend as Jeff follows the one-way route, turning right towards the back of the car park.

There is not much cover in terms of other cars at this time in the morning, so they are unable to park anywhere near the target car. Jeff loops around two columns behind the target car into a space that offers a good balance of visibility and concealment. He edges forward into the space gradually as the white Toyota almost disappears from view behind the car diagonally in front. "Perfect." says Mike, craning his neck back to bring the Corolla back into view.

"Hello Zero, this is Lima One-four, in position with good arcs on Uniform Five-three. He's in similar position as described yesterday, remaining in the vehicle. We are to his 6 o'clock, Red Ten; his four."

"Zero, acknowledged. Remember main effort is remaining covert."

"Lima One-four, Roger out."

28

Back to Belmarsh

"You ladies must like this place?" says the ever-smooth Governor Davidson, stepping into his staff conference room. His impeccable grey suit as pristine as though he'd just walked out of the tailor's shop. "The refreshments are on their way." The two women stand to greet him. Between them they are able to weaken the knees of most men, but their presence only seems to invigorate his character.

"As nice as you keep this place, and as lovely as your company is, I can think of other places I'd rather be." Charlie says with a cheeky grin.

"Thanks, Rod." Lucy smiles back at him. "It's lovely to see you again."

Charlie has been back to supervise further interviews, both with Zafir Abdulaziz, the Pavilion Gardens and Millbank bomber, and Majid Jaleel the Pavilion Gardens attacker. Nothing much had come of those interviews, both maintaining their silence – maybe a lesson learned from Charlie's expert manipulation and exploitation of Zafir at their first encounter. Lucy has not returned since then.

"Prisoner Alfredi should be ready for you any minute. I know you're on a short timeline, so if there's anything I need to know about him or any of his possible associates; now might be a good time to bring them up." An astute man, Rod fully understands the complexities associated with such a prisoner. Access to agents with the knowledge that Charlie and Lucy possess is a rare opportunity to be taken advantage of.

Lucy resists the urge to speak up and looks down the edge of the table to Charlie. "Eee," Charlie sighs out in her loveable Mak'em way. "I know you've been very supportive of our requests."

"Yes, we have invested great resources in keeping Prisoner Alfredi isolated from the rest of the remand population." he interrupts.

"Quite, and I'm afraid I can't go too deep into the reasons for that, but you can imagine the kind of people Alfredi is connected to, and what messages getting to him might do for our investigation?"

"Yes. I understand. There's no need to explain any further, but I must manage your expectations." He pauses. "My officers are the best in the Service, that's how they get to be here, but that does not guarantee that they can't be got at. It happens from time to time. Whether it's blackmail or greed, it can never be mitigated against completely."

"So, you think they might have been able to communicate with him?" Lucy asks, her voice full of innocence.

"Of course, they can communicate with him, and him back to them, no doubt." Charlie says dismissively, almost laughing. She levels her tone; "Thank you for your efforts, Rod. Alfredi's isolation over the past nine days will have certainly slowed down the passage of information, and may even have let a little useful information seep through to him that Lucy will be able to extract."

"Me?" Lucy shrieks, her mouth hangs open, gawping at Charlie.

Charlie ignores her for now. "You have some core members of what we think might be an emerging network inside your prison, and from what we are finding in the course of our investigations; it may well grow further as those who survive their planned atrocities are detained."

The Governor breathes out a sigh as one of his junior administrators opens the door and pushes in a rattling metal tea trolley. "Thanks,

Martine. Leave it there, that's fine, my love." Martine gives Charlie and Lucy a smile and almost undetectable flick of the eyebrows that says, 'what's he like?' The two agents both give her the same thankful, but sympathetic look as she closes the door.

Rod stands and sets the cups onto saucers. He talks as he begins to pour the milk, "I don't need to ask about who you mean." He looks at Charlie sternly. "Prisoners Jaleel and Abdulaziz have been as thick as thieves since the latter arrived. No coincidence, I take it, that they and Prisoner Alfredi committed atrocities that are yet to be plausibly claimed by any named organisation?"

Charlie's expressive eyebrows need no words to substantiate an answer.

"Together Jaleel and Abdulaziz have built quite a posse around them, and I don't just mean in terms of numbers." Rod goes on.

"What do you mean by that?" Lucy asks.

"They have been very selective; it's not the 'tough guys' or the 'big-timers'. They have kept people like that on side, but at a distance. They have surrounded themselves with the clever and the focussed." He hands the women their drinks in turn. "I don't need to tell you; this is a rich recruiting ground for people like them."

"Rod, you don't know the half of it." Charlie says, feeling a want to confide in him about how the Interest Group are recruiting with the UK Terror Watch List as their tailored candidate reel. Normally tight-lipped and never usually one to even consider giving away information, she feels at ease with the suave, meticulous older man – he has that 'father figure' vibe going for him, he'd make a great interrogator.

"As you can understand, Rod, a lot of what we're dancing around is heavily classified. You've been good to us - we always enjoy coming to see you, and I cannot go into detail, but as you have observed;

there are and will be perpetrators, seemingly unconnected to anyone, who would be best kept away from each other."

Rod holds his hands up from the tabletop, "I get it, I'm on the page, but if you could get me an order on paper; that would ensure I got the funding to go with the special measures that I'm expending on goodwill at the moment on Alfredi, and I could get placed on the other two." His expression is pained.

"Eee, we're working on it, Rod, we're working on it."

*

"When were you going to tell me that you wanted me to lead on this?" Lucy asks feigning, but not really feigning anger.

Charlie doesn't quite manage to conceal her mischievous smirk. "Well, you did all the work prepping the baseline questions, it felt like I was going to be robbing you of an opportunity."

Lucy shakes her head, unsure of how she feels about it. As a trained military tactical questioner and interrogator with operational experience of personnel exploitation in Afghanistan, she is no stranger to being front and centre in the interview room, but she has a lot of personal connection to this case. "This animal killed practically all of my nan's neighbours, some of them were her good friends. I'd met some of them." She scowls angrily down at the table.

Charlie stares hard at her until she lifts her head and makes eye contact again. "I know." She pauses to let that sink in. "I thought that would be a keen motivator for you. You'll have the resources of passion and emotion, just make sure that you use them as weapons in the armoury, and don't succumb to them."

Lucy holds her gaze, unsure whether to feel inspired or appalled.

Lucy had spent many happy summer weeks at her nan's, back before her grandad had died. Her dad having died in Service with the RAF, her mum would drive her down to Folkestone on a Friday night and they would spend the weekend together as a family, before leaving her there, returning to High Wycombe for work, for a week or two at a time. Lucy had spent as much time there since joining the Army, visiting her nan over the majority of her leave periods; she was there so much, she'd even listed her nan's house as her primary leave address.

"Okay." she says, summoning her strength, "Let's find out what he knows."

*

Despite several brews in the conference room, all moisture in Lucy's mouth seems to disappear as she follows Governor Davidson along the curved corridor, passing pine door after pine door, she just wants them to go on endlessly, but soon enough Rod stops. "Are you ready?" he asks quietly. Lucy nods with resignation, like a junior soldier accepting a weekend guard duty from the Regimental Sergeant-Major. He opens the door.

Far from the haze of intimidation that she was expecting, there is no atmosphere in the room at all. Alfredi sits, looking withdrawn and submissive in his chair next to his solicitor, a disinterested-looking, balding middle-aged man in a scruffy suit.

"Good morning. I'm Agent Butler of the Security Service, this is Agent Thew. May I ask who you are?" Lucy asks pointedly to the woman sat in the corner. She doesn't look particularly threatening, more like a badly dressed teacher.

"That's Mrs Waring." says the solicitor, "Mrs Waring is our independently appointed 'appropriate person'."

"Appropriate person?" Charlie spits back at him. Lucy gives her a cutting look, displeased at her getting involved.

Lucy remains standing, positioning herself to dominate the room. "Are you trying to tell me he's been classified as some sort of vulnerable adult?"

Alfredi's lawyer pulls a sheet of paper from the inside of the card folder in front of him as though he is pulling an ace from his hand. "He was clinically evaluated last Thursday; this is the report. Mr Alfredi has a mental age of 12." He reads from the report; "Alfredi has deficits in intellectual functioning and has limited capacity for: judgment, reasoning, problem solving, planning, abstract thinking, learning from experience and academic learning – all previous Police interviews are rendered inadmissible."

Lucy's initial angry reaction quickly subdues as she realises that whatever punishment that this diagnosis may help Alfredi to avoid may be a small price to pay if it is genuine. A subject of limited mental capacity will make for much easier interrogation. We might actually learn something.

29

Supermarket swipe

Alex's head snaps up from his laptop screen at the soft knock at the back door.

"They keep coming." Lesley says jovially, looking up from the frying pan. The novelty of having her house alive with colourful and relatively young characters has still not worn off.

The door opens and John's shaven, badly scarred head pops in. "Oye-oye." he says, a lot more quietly than he usually would. "Good morning, my lovely." he smiles. "Lesley, not you." he laughs at Alex.

"Dick." Alex says, quietly enough for Lesley not to hear and with a smile on his face that, despite his best efforts, he cannot suppress.

"What would you like, John? Sausage and egg again?" Lesley says, her hand on the fridge door handle ready to respond.

"Yes please, Lesley. Shall I make the brews?" he offers.

*

John sits down with his brew. "Have you got anything from inside the house yet?"

"Jambo said there'd been some conversation late last night, mostly friendly 'getting to know you' stuff, but this morning we heard what we think was the recruiter and driver discussing a potential move tomorrow."

Hitting Home

"The fuckers aren't hanging about, are they?" John says, baring his teeth and twitching his head with anger.

"It wasn't news, really. It was in line with emails received by one of our other Lima candidates; they are being tapped up at a steady rate. The picture of safe houses and recruiters is shaping up quite nicely. The real work is going to be linking the recruiters to the hierarchy of the group."

"Ah, thanks, Lesley, you're a star." John says, beholding the over-sized soft bap that she places down in front of him. Four ends of halved sausage droop from both sides, skirted with lightly browned egg white. "Can't beat a sausage banjo."

As he struggles to find the optimal angle to pick up the sandwich, his phone buzzes in his pocket. "Perfect timing." he says, taking the handset from his inside pocket of his soft, comfortable looking black leather jacket. "Hi Mike, can't a bloke eat his breakfast in peace?"

"John, we might have a situation in Liverpool. How far are we willing to let things go before we can break cover?"

"What's going down?" John asks, his persona snapping into sharp focus. Alex recognises the change instantly and looks in with concern.

"Uniform Five-three started to look a bit agitated."

"Alex has identified him as Shiranga Khann." John interrupts.

"Yeah, well he's out of his car and taken something from his boot, something long, maybe a weapon. He's concealing whatever it is under his coat and he's making his way over towards the supermarket."

John thinks through the realities of the policy that they're following and what breaking cover might do to their mission. "Mate, you're going to have to hold back, at least until he goes noisy, then by all means step in and end it – then get the fuck out of there, no trace."

*

Uniform Five-three walks across the busying road and between the bollards of the customer drop-off lay-by. He is almost hobbling as he tries to hide whatever he has under his knee-length coat against his leg. Mike and Jeff are out of the car, pulling baseball caps down over their brows with their gloved hands. They thread their way across the car park which is now peppered with cars. "I would've thought he'd have waited for it to be a bit busier than this?" Mike mutters. His fast walk breaks into an 'Airborne shuffle' as Uniform Five-three disappears from view into the store.

Mike politely, but firmly skirts past a doddering elderly couple, inciting 'tuts' as they show their displeasure at his impatience to wait. "Sorry." he says over his shoulder, but his focus is on re-establishing visual contact with his target. He doesn't need to look far; his eye is caught by the sweeping brown cloth of the assailant's long coat as it is flung back to reveal the long wooden handle of an axe. "Shit," Mike says, as he breaks into a sprint. There are waist-high troughs of fruit between him and his target, his route is not straight forward. In that instant, Mike forgets that he is meant to be remaining covert until something happens, but he cannot hold back his need to stop what is about to happen.

Uniform Five-three raises the huge felling axe high above his head as he steps forward towards his first intended victim. Gasps and screams emit from those who have taken notice, and the shock ripples out through the few shoppers spread thinly across the open fruit and veg area.

Mike weaves between the stands of apples, trolleys and shoppers. Still quick and nimble for his age and size, but he is too far away to save the old man, who is barely aware that anything is going on. He begins to turn, reacting to the shrieks of terror, but before he is even half way around, the axe falls, smashing into his skull, swatting him down, forward against his trolley, which rolls free, crashing into the soft fruit display chiller as he crumples to the floor.

Hitting Home

As Uniform Five-three plucks the heavy blade from his victim's head, Mike arrives, just a second too late. He connects at full tilt, with all his weight, into the ribs of the killer, scuttling him to the grimy floor. They skid to a halt in a mass of flailing limbs at the feet of a petrified young mother who flinches forward in a reflex action to shield her baby.

As a Tri-Service Judo champion, with more than a passing interest in mixed martial arts, Mike is quickly in control, positioning himself to prevent incoming blows and to facilitate his own attacks, but he has the wherewithal to sense Jeff calling him, "BACK UP, BIG FELLA."

Landing one last hammer-blow to the nose, Mike pushes himself down the torso of the almost unconscious Khan as Jeff lets swing the axe. In a pitiful attempt at being merciful, Jeff has reversed the axe - the back of its head thumps into the skull of his victim. It hits with such force that Khan's head completely caves in, leaving the few remaining spectators in no doubt that he is dead and that their ordeal is over. The young woman snaps her head away from the gruesome sight of the concave pit of blood and deformed features, and narrowly avoids splashing vomit into the face of her screaming son.

*

Getting to his feet, Mike wipes his face, conscious that he has blood on him from the scarlet incursion into his peripheral vision. He only succeeds in smearing it down his cheek. Jeff lets the handle of the axe slip through his gloved hand until the top corner of the cutting edge hits the floor, a few droplets of blood splash down onto the tiles from the impact. He drops it from his grip and the shaft lands gently on the limp body of his victim. "Now what?" he says.

Mike thinks about their situation. The plan was to get straight out of there, but presentationally that poses a problem – two 'have a go heroes' that successfully intervene and then mysteriously disappear might stimulate unwanted interest from the press and they, or more likely their car, wouldn't be too difficult to track down, if it has been caught on CCTV – Jeff's false plates would raise even more questions.

Equally if they stick around and their identifies are made public; it won't take a lot for the Interest Group to realise that they weren't there by coincidence.

Mike distracts himself by checking on the victim. He steps across Khan's legs and walks across the aisle to where the old man's body lies. As respectfully and forensically aware as he can be, he rolls the body over. He is immediately struck with a sense of recognition, he knows the face, then he sees the Royal Marines' lapel badge on the old boy's jacket. "Oh, fuck, no."

30

Lighting the touch paper

Alex's laptop bleeps with a notification from his hacking software application. "Oh, brilliant." he says with enthusiasm.

"What's that?" John asks from the kitchen as he washes up the breakfast things.

"A mobile phone's just connected to the target router. I can get straight into it and embed my spyware. I'll have microphone, speaker, camera and access to all files in a few seconds."

"Gleaming." John says, his hawkish features bending into a demonic grin. "What are your plans for the next few days?"

Alex conceals his mild irritation at the demand on his attention whilst he is trying to forge on with his technical work. He taps in the final line of code and hits the send button. "I was thinking about getting back to town and speaking to Charlie's tech team to make sure what I've done here is being replicated at the other stakeouts."

"Me too, I need to start pushing with what the next move is once we've got what we can out of these locations. We can't just sit around waiting for these characters to start wreaking havoc. We might need to get a bit more intrusive if we're going to find out where the orders are coming from." The snarl that has been stretching his macabre features suddenly relaxes. "Plus, it'll be nice to see the girls."

Alex's laptop alerts again. "They're talking." Alex turns up his laptop volume.

Joseph Mitcham

"Marhabaan 'akhi hal kulu shay' ealaa ma yaram?"

"Shit." John says, but Alex doesn't seem too concerned, he lurches for his phone. He taps on the search engine icon and opens the translator, selecting Arabic to English, then presses the microphone symbol and holds the phone close to the laptop. "Hopefully, we'll have just missed the pleasantries." he whispers. As the voices continue, the app churns out the dialogue on the small screen:

"I will plan to meet our next soldier on Wednesday, he is keen, I think."

"Very good. We have enough room for another?"

"Yes, and we will soon be moving two of our current guests on." The voices on the call speak quickly, but clearly, the translator seems to be working well. John's phone rings in his pocket, he looks at it, silences it, then puts it away. "It's Mike, I'll call him back."

"I must select the two best recruits for a special mission."

"That sounds interesting, my brother. Do these soldiers need to have any special skills or talents?"

"No, they simply need to be able to follow instructions and not be noticed. It goes without saying that they need to be of the strongest conviction and of powerful being." John pulls a frown as he reads the text from the screen.

"I'm recording it, I'll get Charlie to get us a proper translation."

"This will be our strongest message, yet. We shall hit their bitch up where it will hurt most." Alex and John look at each other, further confused by the strange form of words.

"When will it happen?" the second voice asks.

"A call will come at 10 a.m. on Thursday, I will know everything then."

As the discussion dries up, John's pocket buzzes. "Mike again." He presses the handset to his ear. "Oye-oye, nob 'ead. What's up?" John smiles at Alex, loving his own banter, but Mike is silent at the end of the line. John remembers that the situation in Liverpool was turning potentially serious. "Everything okay, Mike?"

"John." He pauses, trying to find the words. "Khan, he went into the store. He had an axe."

"What happened?" John's mind races with what might have gone wrong, what might be causing Mike to be so reticent. "Did you step in? Have you blown it?"

"No, John. We left it as long as we could. Maybe too long. He only swung the axe once, only took out one person."

"We always knew there would be collateral damage, Mike, we have to accept that. You did the right thing. Did you take him out of the game though?"

"Yeah, yeah we did, John." Mike's voice is low and quiet, "But the one we couldn't save, it was your Uncle Bobby."

*

John's childhood is a place of dark memories for him. His Father was never in his life, having left soon after his conception, and his mother had dragged him along as she suffered in a downward spiral of unemployment, bad men and drink, leading to drugs and a muted, painless death while John lay sleeping upstairs as a miserable twelve-year-old boy on a dirty, threadbare mattress - the future had looked bleak for him. His fate in the hands of social services and with no willing foster families available to take him on, he had looked to be consigned to a children's care home.

It was only by chance that Robert Gallagher had heard about the death of his sister whilst on shore leave. The Royal Marine took the adolescent John under his wing. Having never been married or having kids of his own, it was a new challenge for him as he retired from Service as a Warrant Officer following a career of highs and lows. Robert had been the embodiment of 'old school', and that, in the eighties, was hardcore.

John's teenage years were a learning curve; Uncle Bobby literally knocking him into shape. Never malicious or vindictive, Bob was training him up, as much as he was bringing him up. It was a love-hate relationship which was a dichotomy typified by John's decision to join the Paras and not the Marines - Bob couldn't be prouder or more pissed off.

It wasn't until they were out from under each other's feet that their relationship really blossomed. Bob had softened, had even taken up with a lady-friend. John had never called him 'dad', but in his heart, that was how he saw him.

*

"I'm so sorry, Lesley. Don't be upset." Alex says, doing his best to try and salvage the situation. "John's just had some awful news – the worst kind of news."

Sitting sideways into the corner of her sofa, her head buried deep into an over-sized gold velvet cushion, Lesley trembles with fear. Alex perches on the arm of the chair next to her and places a hand on the shoulder – she flinches violently, a reflex action, he assesses, so persists. He rubs the top of her arm gently. "John's just lost his uncle in another one of these terrible attacks."

Lesley raises her head slowly, "Oh, poor John." she says, raising a hand over her mouth. "You're not having much luck, you fellas, are you?"

As soon as he heard about Bob, the same thought had gone through his mind, but now he takes time to think through the observation. It was immediately clear that his family had been targeted. He had considered Lucy's nan's lucky escape to have been incredible incompetence if it wasn't a coincidence, but Uncle Bob's demise leaves no doubt in his mind. "Come on, Lesley, let's go and order you a new kitchen table."

31

What's the damage?

John has been silent in the car all the way down through North London, Matt and Alex's attempts to cajole him provoking no response. Not a word is said as they walk through the underground car park, nor in the lift up to the reception area of Thames House.

Matt does the talking as they verify their credentials at the security kiosk. As they cross the lobby, heading toward the café, they see Charlie and Lucy standing waiting for them.

Charlie throws her arms out as John nears, "Eee, come 'ere Chuck." She hugs him tightly.

Alex almost forgets his own grief for a moment, so intense is the atmosphere around John as the stubborn block on his emotions seems fit to burst – he has never seen the big man in this state. Anger is a natural part of mourning, but whatever the other stages of it are, rage will be John's primary setting until it can be released through suitable vengeance. He pulls back from her embrace, kisses her on the forehead and looks her in the eyes for salvation.

Charlie looks back at him. Her sympathetic expression turns to one of concern mixed with fear. The furious grimace etched on his face and dead black of his eyes making even her afraid of what he might be capable of in this frame of mind. She pulls him back into her arms to try and calm him.

The group turns collectively and walks past the café seating area and head towards the meeting rooms. Alex dawdles, hanging back. Lucy looks to him as she slows to match his speed. "I know we have our banter and take the piss," Alex says, subdued with sorrow, "but when I see him like this it puts everything into perspective. To see him distraught like this, a gladiator of a man, a special forces warrior, it breaks me. My own loss has been hard, but I'm a mortal, I kind of expect to be hurt and weakened, but to see John this way makes me feel like there is no hope; like they can get at anyone."

*

The atmosphere in the meeting room is sombre and painfully awkward. Cliff has returned from operations in South London, but even he, as one of John's closest friends, struggles to know how best to approach him. He stands with his hands out to his front, not quite relaxed, but not outstretched. John meanders past Charlie, who holds the door open, and walks straight into Cliff, giving him a firm pat on the back. "Mate, I'm so sorry about Bobby."

Alex, Lucy and Matt follow in behind Charlie and everyone takes their seats. Dev tips a sympathetic nod to John who forces an all too temporary smile back at him.

"Thanks for coming in, everyone." Charlie says, doing her best to inject a modicum of positivity into the room. "As you're all aware, things are moving at quite a pace. So far, between our combined lists of 50 candidates, we have seventeen actively recruited and accommodated in at least seven safe houses around the country, ten of these individuals we have tracked to these safe houses, the other seven we have to assume accepted the offer and were recruited to those safe houses, and possibly others, before we got on the trail. We are also tracking a further four who have agreed to meet with their respective recruiters. This is all over and above whatever manning they had to start with, which we believe to be in the region of 40, which may or may not include the seven pairs of recruiters and drivers.

"Observations of the safe houses by our combined teams would indicate that there are at least a further five suspects already in those safe houses, not including the 14 in the driver – recruiter pairings, which would seem about right if we've caught sight of most of those early recruited candidates."

The room is silent; everyone outwardly uncomfortable with such a force being only partially known and with limited monitoring. The Interest Group's lack of boundaries with regard to the damage it is willing to do, mean that it is a truly terrifying prospect while the team's hands are tied when it comes to being able to intervene.

"We were all shocked at the attack on Alex's family," Lucy says, placing her hand on his thigh, "but now with what's happened to John's uncle, it is clear that the Interest Group is actively targeting members of our team's families." Solemn nods of agreement circulate around the table. "Charlie and I interviewed Samir Alfredi, the 'Folkestone Slicer', yesterday. He let slip that his primary target was my grandmother." There are looks of surprise and shock from her peers. This news seems to break John's trance of self-isolation; he looks in at Lucy with an expression of compassion. "By chance, she had taken an unscheduled trip to the shops and was away from the house for the period of the attacks."

"This raises a raft of questions." Charlie says, pre-empting the anticipated barrage. "How far does their knowledge go on our team? Where are they getting their information about our families? Do we all need to alert those closest to us? Do we need to provide them with protection?"

"How are we going to stop them and remain covert?" Cliff asks.

"That's not necessarily an issue." says Matt. Cliff tilts his head at him with interest. "Think about what they know about what we know. At the very least we know that three separate attacks have been made on family members of the team that took down the top tier of the UK Terror Watch List."

"What do you know about that?" Alex asks defensively.

"Worst kept secret in the Security Service, Alex." He cuts him off. "It would be natural for anyone involved with that team to take measures to protect their family members – it wouldn't surprise me if they stopped these targeted attacks now that it's clear what they were doing. And that's why I'm not overly concerned at Mike and Jeff's rapid appearance at the attack today – it's no jump in deductions that we might have made from Folkestone to Peterborough for you to have been protecting your own since then."

"So, you think that they'll move on to other targets now that our attention will be on protecting our families?" John asks. Matt nods.

Alex thinks through what he heard at the stakeout, about others that might be in play. He interjects; "What if they know more than we think? What if they know about people outside of the Watch List team? What if they know we're on to them? Maybe not to the extent that we are, but they have got to know that the investigation hasn't ceased."

Alex looks around the table, as though asking why no one else can see the elephant in the room. "They must know that there are other agencies working to find them, even if they don't know that we're collaborating. What if they know about you?" he says, fingering Matt, Dev and Charlie, "Our Police and Security Service colleagues?"

John comes to life, "Alex did some sterling work up at Edgeware. Using what we assume is the recruiter's phone as a bug we were able to listen in to a conversation - it sounded like they're shaping up for a bigger action, against our 'bitch'."

"What?" Lucy shrieks, "They want to have another go at me?"

"Or they know of me," Charlie says calmly, "which would mean that we have a real security issue."

"I sent the recording of their chat to your tech guys, they said they would get it to a translator, but the straightforward online translation said, 'We'll hit their bitch up where it will hurt most'." Alex keeps his focus on Charlie, knowing that what he has said would strike at his beloved Lucy, but his instincts tell him that it is someone relative to Charlie that they are targeting.

The group take time to think through what they've heard. Each assessing the risks to their family members, to the investigation, and the opportunities that the new information brings.

"Where are their instructions coming from, Alex?" Charlie's first thought is not for her family, or anyone else's, but to progressing the investigation into the Interest Group's higher echelons.

"We don't know, but they are expecting more detail on the task from a scheduled call - they're using good communications drills, so I'd imagine that whoever it was would have been on a burner phone that will only appear on the network for the calls that they need to make. I'll work with your boys to see if we can get any more detail from it - any other connections.

"Let's look at it logically." John says, his motivation stoked. "As far as we know, they stumbled onto the Watch List plan when Tony Blunt turned up to our orders group." The radicalised former Paratrooper had been quickly rooted out but then disappeared with knowledge of some of those involved before he could be permanently silenced. This breach is thought to have led to Alex and Lucy being intercepted on multiple occasions as the Interest Group sought to secure a copy of the Watch List.

John goes on, "As well as me, he might have seen Cliff, Mike and any number of other blokes that turned up for it. From there it would have been easy for them to follow us to meetings with Alex, Lucy..." he pauses thinking over some of the names of those no longer with the team, those who have met their end along the way. "Let's just say, we're all in scope, as is anyone that any of us have met with outside of secured locations."

"That assumes that they are using visual surveillance alone." says Lucy. "Their awareness of their digital footprint is indicative of a strong technical competence – they may have gained access to our unencrypted emails and phones."

"I'd like to think I'd have spotted any spyware going onto my phone," says Alex confidently, "but I'll run a scan. I rarely use unencrypted means, so there wouldn't be too much of a compromise by me if it's clear."

"What about getting inside our organisations' networks?" Lucy asks.

"What? Hacking into the Police or Security Service systems?" Dev reacts.

"The infrastructure isn't that secure." Alex says, knowing them like the back of his hand, "but they'd need a decent operator for that."

"We should consider the strong possibility that they have a HUMINT source." says Matt, knowing that the relatively low complexity of human intelligence is well within their capability. This idea draws an uncomfortable look from Charlie. "If they're well-funded; they are more likely to be buying the intelligence than they are to be finding it for themselves."

"Bribing someone within one of your outfits." John says, just to make it plain.

"You'll be able to check that quite easily." says Alex. "There will be a clear digital footprint in the personnel records. I can check Lucy's personnel file, and my and John's Regular Reserve record to see if they've been accessed and by who, yours too Cliff. I can work with the Police and Security Service HR teams to see about yours." he says to the others.

"What are we going to do about alerting families?" Lucy asks. "My nan is still in that house all on her own, and my mum is alone at home too."

"Well, we know the locations of the safe houses now, and we have eyes on all of them, with teams ready to deploy and protect anyone that they go after." says Cliff.

"There are a few holes in that plan, Cliff." Lucy says with irritation. "For a start, we only know about safe houses that have had new recruits since we began tracking 'some' of the entries from the list. With the numbers they reportedly have, there might be several more ripe activists out there who could be in or on their way to safe houses that we don't know about."

Cliff cups his hand over his mouth, thinking through the permutations of the situation.

"What about putting security watches on the families?" John asks.

"Who, though?" Alex asks. "I've got grandparents, aunts, uncles, cousins, there could be any number of relatives, and who's families are we looking at? We have no idea how far into our structure they've seen or what methods they're using to learn the details of the families." Alex's stark assessment of how little they know is unnerving, bringing a sense of collective vulnerability to the group.

"From what Alex has heard, priority has to be with Lucy and Charlie." says Matt.

"Right." agrees John. "Ladies, get me a list of names and addresses, and I'll have the lads deployed. It can be overt or covert, whatever you want, but best let them know they are coming."

*

The team break for some much-needed air while John and Cliff make the calls to activate their men. Within 30 minutes, there are 12 operators on the road, each heading to an exposed potential target. The distributed network of committed former colleagues means that none has far to travel – within the hour, all minds will be at rest and the team will be able to refocus on the task at hand.

Back around the table and with a much more positive buzz in the room, the posture switches from the defensive to the offensive.

"Did you get anything else of use from Alfredi?" Matt asks Lucy.

"He'd been at the South London safe house. He said that there were five other men there; that marries up with what Cliff's team has observed."

"They've had another one in since." The big man adds.

"He knew nothing about where the orders were coming from." Lucy continues, "He said that they were not allowed to have phones, there was no computer access. All his instructions came through the man who recruited him, and he didn't even know his name."

"Or he wasn't going to tell you?" says Matt, unconvinced.

Lucy smiles emptily at his comment, a sign of irritation from which Alex takes gratification. "No. He was fairly tight-lipped to begin with, but I think we won him over, he got quite friendly and talkative by the time we'd finished with him."

Charlie nods, "I'd agree with Lucy; he isn't quite 'all the ticket' is our Sami. He doesn't have the mental capacity to withstand questioning for very long."

"Who does, from you two?" Dev smiles. His comment brings further welcome relief to the room.

"That set-up is consistent with Edgeware." says Alex. "No other devices on the wi-fi, just a single smart phone that pops up for scheduled calls over an encrypted app."

"Where do we go from there?" John asks, "We need to focus on whoever it was the recruiter is getting instructions from."

Alex nods. "Yes, I'm standing by for that call to come in on Thursday, then I'll attack the number and see where we go from there."

"Two days is a long time, Alex." Charlie says dourly. "How about you and Lucy take a little trip to see Jon Banbury and see if you can't accelerate things?"

Alex nods, already smiling at the thought of seeing the quirky professor again."

"That's great, thank you, Alex." says Matt. "I have a team standing by to begin the chase as information starts to come in."

John's reaction is instant and aggressive. "From what Jambo tells me about your lot's efforts at covert surveillance, you best be leaving that to us." He glares across at Charlie but takes no solace from the uncomfortable look on her face.

"I'm taking the opportunity to reorganise resources." she says with limited enthusiasm. "Matt's people will withdraw from the safe houses outside of London and take over Edgeware and Dulwich in their entirety. They'll also take on any leads to the Interest Group hierarchy."

"For fuck's sake, that makes no sense." John rages. "We've got blokes from Hereford, SRR; the best in the business, and there's you and your idiots, standing out like a bulldogs' bollocks – I can't believe you've let this get political."

"Oh, fuck off John." she unleashes on him, "Of course it's bloody 'political'. This is the UK's number one priority for national security – the Prime Minister is involved, giving clear direction through her COBR briefings – I have to have our own people on this at the centre of activity."

John settles, still clearly not happy, but even in his emotive state, he can see the difficult position that his other half is in. His frustration at having badged SAS blokes and men and women of the Special Reconnaissance Regiment on hand to do exactly this kind of task continues to eat away at him.

"There's plenty of opportunity for us to be involved, still." says Alex. "All these recruits need keeping track of, and there are still another 22,000 names of the Watch List that we haven't even looked at yet."

"It's a backwards step, Alex." Cliff cuts in, chopping the air with a straight hand - the 'Brecon chop'. "We've got the skills to bring this to a swift conclusion."

"Well, Cliff, that's part of the problem." Matt says with his arrogant lilt, "We need a legal and accountable conclusion, so please; leave it to us."

Cliff says nothing in reply, just stares back with a quiet fury burning in his eyes. John looks at each in turn, then to Charlie and just catches the slightest of winks from her.

*

The door handle puts a sizeable dent in the plasterboard of the conference room wall as John flings it open and storms out into the corridor. Cliff and Alex follow, skipping steps to catch up, neither wasting their time trying to calm him down, allowing him to simmer in his own juices for now. As they step out into the main lobby area, Lucy runs to catch up with them. "Guys, wait." Cliff and Alex stop and look back.

John turns, but continues walking backwards, "What's the point, Lucy? Working with this lot's a waste of our time. You can crack on with them if you like, but I'm done."

Lucy smirks, holding her grin at him; his mood breaks instantly. "Ignore Matt. You know this is Charlie's gig. You know what she wants." She walks between Cliff and Alex and pushes John playfully on the shoulder and breezes past him. "Come on, I'll get the brews in."

*

The four sit in a lone booth in the corner of the labyrinth-like seating area – the location designed to accommodate anonymous, clandestine meetings; they have all the privacy they need.

"I feel a whole lot better now I know that mum and nan are being looked over." Lucy says, cupping her drink in her hands.

"I've got Mike checking the names of anyone that Blunt might have known from the Hodgehill orders session, then anyone that could have been seen and associated with our project from then on." says John. "We have to assume they've followed our core team everywhere and that they've heard our conversations.

"Charlie's asked for her parents and her sister to be watched – I'm going to redeploy Jambo and Spider to Sunderland now they're surplus to requirement in Edgeware."

"We're putting people on Dev's folks and his sister too." Cliff adds.

"There are still questions to be asked about how they got the details of our family members." Alex says angrily. "I could understand them following me as a one off." Alex knew that he was putting himself and those close to him at risk as the man with the plan – the man with the list, but he had not anticipated the Interest Group coming after the other members of the team, let alone members of their families.

"They've either got some serious detective skills, or they've got someone with access to our systems." says Lucy. There is a quiet pause as the group collectively think about the channels of information that might lead to their nearest and dearest.

John plants his cup down firmly on the table. "There wasn't anything else on that pen drive they took off you, was there, Alex?"

Until that moment, Alex had only felt stronger resolve within the team after the blows inflicted and victories won by the Interest Group, but John's insinuation physically knocks the wind out of him. The trusted bond that Alex had felt that he had built up with the naturally suspicious, hard-nosed Hereford operator, feels like it has been washed away with those few words. He slams his drink down, causing it to splash out onto the table, but wrestles to contain a verbal, or worse; emotional, outburst. He looks John in the eye, bites down on his frown and shakes his head slowly, showing the depth of his disgust with a raw saddened scowl. Still holding eye contact with John, Alex sees the instant change in his bearing; he looks to be genuinely disappointed with himself.

"Guys, we've got to keep it together." Lucy says, desperately. "There's a reason why they're going after us – they know that we are a threat to them. They know that if they break our spirit, if they can break our cohesion, then that threat goes away."

"I'm sorry." John throws his hands out in submission. "I'm out of order." Alex feels consoled a little but still weakened by the latest reminder of the delicacy of their relationship.

"If we can identify their source; that might offer us another route to their organisation – I'll work on that." says Lucy.

"There might be another way too." says John, rubbing his chin, the cogs of thought clearly grinding. "Whatever they've got planned for 'our bitch', whether that's you," he nods at Lucy, "or Charlie, it's a bigger job with two or more of their better recruits being placed on it – that'll require some level of planning, and potentially some higher-level involvement."

"We can track the two they send from Edgeware and see who they hook up with." says Alex.

"That might take some negotiation to keep Matt's team off it." says Lucy.

"Roger," says John, "but that's our new main effort."

32

Inside the den

It has been an unnerving two days in the Edgware safe house for Tariq. Living in the general darkness of the house. Shielded from all natural light, to prevent any prying eyes, has been wearing - the cheap 40-watt bulbs give a nauseatingly dim glow, he finds himself constantly checking his new watch to see what time of day it is.

His movements within the house have been limited. Spending almost all of his time in the lounge at the front right of the house; the large room doubles as sleeps for him and the two other recruits that he shares the space with. They have the freedom to move between there and the bathroom for use of the shower and toilet, but are under strict instructions from their recruiter to stay out of all the other parts of the house.

As something of a runt amongst the three, Tariq has the sofa for a bed, which is not quite long enough for him to sleep on comfortably, not that his runaway thoughts would let him sleep that much anyway. The other two have inflatable single mattresses which stand in the corner of the room through the day, with their new, clean, but very plain blankets and sheets folded and piled in front of them – not quite the perfect military bed-blocks that Tariq had envisioned himself folding, nor the soft and comfortable duvets that, in reality, he would have been issued, either.

Whilst down the pecking order, Tariq is on friendly terms with both the other two, though he has developed a healthy fear of the elder; Hamza, who seems crazed and determined to do harm to someone, be it for a cause or for fun.

Hamza had only been resident at the safe house a day longer than Tariq, but he has seemed settled and at home, like an established soldier relaxed in his environment and bossing his peers without sign of fear of the people with real authority.

Kashif, on the other hand is physically bigger, only of just above average height, but with a broad frame and muscular build. By no means a bodybuilder, he appears of soft constitution with a bit of a belly on him. Despite being resident in the house four days longer than Hamza, and his size advantage, he seems to have quickly capitulated his position as the senior recruit in the room.

Kashif has his own strong beliefs and is clearly ready to serve his chosen cause but does not have the drive or wherewithal to compete with Hamza's levels of intensity and conviction. Tariq assesses that Kashif is of quite low intellect, having observed him agreeing continually with Hamza's endless rantings, ambivalent or unaware of the countless contradictions and obvious embellishments and untruths that lace the boisterous young man's rhetoric.

The young men have seen very little of the driver, who they know resides in one of the upstairs rooms. Their recruiter has had a fleeting presence in the room, joining them for some meals, interacting with them as their oracle; their sole point of information on the outside world. He has told them tit-bits about the 'great organisation' that they have joined, and how it is growing, but nothing of tangible value or use. He had brought them news of the success in the Wirral supermarket, embellishing the tale, glorifying it beyond the quickly thwarted attack that it was.

The old man has withheld his name, preferring to be called 'Alab', Arabic for 'father'. From his physical appearance, dialect and dress, Tariq discerns that his new Alab originates from the middle east, maybe Jordan or Syria. Having changed out of the ill-fitting shirt and trousers that he had worn whilst recruiting Tariq, the old man dodders around the house wearing a light, baggy cream coloured, ankle length dish-dash, haphazardly banging his stick against doors and walls, and the occasional recruit.

Though physically infirm, the old man still seems to have retained all of his marbles and has been sharp in his dealings with his young charges. His general angry authoritarian nature is tempered with quieter moments of kind nurturing when he is sat in the room with them.

Tariq has done his best to build himself into the fabric of whatever organisation it is that he has let himself become a part of; he has acquiesced to the rhetoric, going along with everything his Alab and his peers have said, even adding to their ramblings when he has had the confidence and felt the gumption to project convincingly.

Being the youngest of the three, of slightly lighter build than Hamza, and with his newly established links to the security services constantly on his mind, Tariq feels nakedly vulnerable. Having to think carefully about every sentence that he utters has been exhausting. In an effort to overcome the draining nature of his current existence, he has begun to try and trick himself into believing that he is a true member of the team, to forget where he has come from, who has sent him. He plays a dangerous game in his mind, already confusing himself as to what is right and wrong. His tiredness and the constant talk in the room of what gloriously terrible things they might do, have Tariq in a delusional state.

*

"Vehicles are good for killing a lot of kafir, but it's not pure - it's not real killing." Hamza says with a sadistic smile.

"What do you mean?" Kashif asks, "Our brother, Majid Jaleel has become a hero for what he did at Pavilion Gardens."

"Yes, but it is not the act of running down so many that struck fear into their hearts, it was for what he did after that – putting cold steel into the flesh of his victims – that is what brought true terror to the park that day. Taking it to them, up close and personal is where it's at."

Joseph Mitcham

A grin grows on Kashif's face as his head nods with growing enthusiasm. He looks over to Tariq, who is staring into space again. "What would you do to bring down the kaffur, Tariq?"

Hamza shuffles in the plump armchair, agitated at Tariq's lack of engagement. He holds back from issuing a rebuke as Tariq's head slowly lifts from the pillow that it rests on.

"I had an idea." he says quietly, his tone invokes interest from the other two who lean forward intrigued. "I play the slow game, sign up to join their infidel army." Tariq speaking at the wall before him as though entranced, "Play the good little ethnic soldier, learn how to use their weapons, maybe even carry it on until I've built up some experience with firing them. Then on a day when there is plenty of ammunition, I load up with as much as I can, pretending to help the other soldiers, then boom – I strike, shooting all of the other recruits with loaded weapons first, then the instructors."

"Wow." Kashif says, surprised by the usually placid Tariq.

"Then, with my pockets full of ammunition, I steal a vehicle and head into the nearest town and find the biggest groups of kafir that I can and spray them with bullets."

Hamza and Kashif fall silent as they appreciate Tariq's idea. Tariq's expression remains blank, still staring at the wall.

"I'd keep firing until armed Police take me down. If I should run out of ammunition before that; I'll just get back into whatever vehicle it is I have and go hunting pedestrians until they come for me. No surrender, no escape."

A feeling of lucid relaxation melts over Tariq as he lays, feeling detached from himself - his state of exhaustion has peaked to the point where he finds it impossible to maintain his conscious pretences. He finds himself immersed in his new persona, feeling reborn as a new person.

The door crashes open as the old man clumsily stumbles in his usual manner; he has a broad smile on his face as he steadies himself with both hands clasped over the top of his stick. Gesturing in turn with his head, "You two have been chosen."

33

Exploring

Lucy focuses on the middle lane traffic that might move into her way as she motors along the right-hand lane of the M40 as she stretches the legs of her sporty little Mercedes convertible. Alex is unsure if she is taking notice of anything that he has been saying.

"Go on, I'm listening." she says, dropping a gear to lunge forward, deterring a slower car from cutting in front of her.

"Are you getting your driving tips from John?" he asks. She shoots him a sneer.

"As I was saying," Alex goes on, "My old Chief Clerk from York, he's a bit of a ninja on JPA, so I asked him to check out our records to see if anybody had been looking at them."

The Joint Personnel and Administration system is a clunky but largely functional piece of software, that manages a vast amount of personnel data including pay, pensions, personal appraisals and postings – every detail of every Service Person, serving and recently retired.

"And?" Lucy asks eagerly, desperate for news that might lead them towards the Interest Group's core and help shut down any vulnerabilities in the team's security.

"Well, our records were both looked at, at about the same time, nearly three weeks ago, along with John, Mike and Cliff's Regular Reserve records."

"Shit." says Lucy, taking her eyes off the road fractionally too long for Alex's liking.

"It gets worse." He pauses to give her time to get her mind back on the motorway. "The account that was used to look at our records belonged to a senior clerk at Army Headquarters."

Lucy gasps, holding her mouth open to express her shock.

"But when they've dug deeper, it's turned out that this clerk doesn't exist."

"Spoof soldier?"

"Yip." Alex says knowingly.

Many soldiers have heard the urban legends of entire platoons of soldiers being created by some devious clerk who had coined in the salaries amounting to hundreds of thousands over the years. The tale ends with the clerk being found out when they had come to the end of their career and needed to hand off their imaginary body of men to someone else or risk the eradication of the soldiers' raising red flags.

"I've heard of it done for cash, but never for the exploitation of the data access that they would give."

"I know, it's a new one on the SIB too, but it's in their hands now."

Alex's former colleague had quickly passed the case to the Royal Military Police's Serious Investigation Branch.

"Make sure Charlie knows about this, she'll be able to intercept and assist their investigation."

*

The motorway traffic had been merciful, and having cut through what there was, Lucy takes her foot off the accelerator to make the countryside drive up the A40 a bit more relaxed.

"How are you feeling?" She asks him as she settles down to 45mph at a considerate gap behind a couple of pensioners in a little green Japanese microcar.

"I'm fine." he says, far from convincingly. "You know how I get when I'm busy; it takes my mind off things." The corner of his mouth jerks with the emotion as his mind wanders to his mum being burned alive in her car, but he holds himself together.

"I know." she says, but her tone indicates that she is better attuned to his feelings than he has given her credit for. "Is there something else though? No issues with John or anyone else on the team? Something with me, maybe?"

Alex pauses, sensing that she knows exactly what is bothering him, but he's not sure he wants to open this particular can of worms, knowing that it is likely to result in his standing within her reckoning being further weakened. Lucy holds her silence in a way that only a trained interrogator can, making the silence feel like a void that must be filled. He cannot help but open up to her.

"It's definitely not you. You're perfect." He feels himself squirming as he struggles to find the words he needs. Getting this wrong could make things worse, or even bring things to an end entirely. "John and the blokes are all fine, they're toeing the line for a change."

"What about the other team? Charlie, Dev," she looks across at him with searching eyes, "Matt?"

"Argh, the beautiful Matt." He responds with a complete change of tone, as though his mention is an unexpected and new strand of conversation. "You seem to be getting on well with him?" With Lucy bringing his name up, he sees the opportunity to find out more about what she thinks of him.

"He's an incredible guy, professional and driven, quite cute too," she says, the look on her face doesn't say enough to tell Alex whether she is winding him up or not, her eyes are fixed on the road, her smirk shows no sign of breaking into a grin. He waits for the 'but' that he hopes is coming. Lucy tortures him, pausing as she bursts on the accelerator to glide past the old couple in their tiny Nissan. "He's out for himself though - nice when it suits him, but I don't trust him."

Alex knows how important trust and a nice personality is to Lucy. His own breach of her trust, when he took the Watch List from her office, might have been the end to any chance that he had with her, but his confession and openness about it had been a clear demonstration of his true nature. His concerns are calmed for now.

Alex twists the dial on the centre console, zooming the satnav view out. "Where are we going anyway? I thought we should have been on the M3, not the M4, and now we're heading North?"

"The Prof's investigations have gone outside his usual realms of materiel exploitation – he's had to get some outside help."

"Where are we going then?"

"The Doughnut."

34

Doughnut

Government Communications Headquarters, GCHQ, an organisation steeped in as much myth and legend as the old biochemical labs of Porton Down. It may be argued that the codebreaking and cypher operations performed by GC&CS, as it was during the Second World War, was the difference between victory and defeat.

Moving to Cheltenham in the fifties, it only took up residence in the perfectly circular 'doughnut' in 2003 relocating the main body of the workforce from the old buildings in Oakley from the east of the town to the west.

Not quite a 'GCHQ groupie', but Alex has always been intrigued by what goes on inside the doughnut; what new technologies and methods they are developing and what level of capabilities they are able to achieve. He had been privy to briefings from GCHQ Liaison officers whilst serving on the communications detachments in some of the more sensitive and high-level military decision-making centres that he had served with, and had never failed to be impressed by the content and accuracy of what he had heard.

The security protocols are almost identical to those of Porton Down, where they had met the professor just two months ago. Had it not been for the signage, Alex might have thought that's where they were – the same visitors' car park, similar guard hut-come-waiting room; the same polite, but not cheerful, Ministry of Defence guard.

"Lucy, Alex, how have you been?" The bouncing character of Jon Banbury brings life and colour to the room, but for the dark corner of it that Alex inhabits.

"Hi Jon." Lucy says in a subdued tone, "It's been a tough week."

The naturally clumsy professor's exaggerated blink and grimace express his anger at himself for letting Alex's turmoil slip his mind. "Argh, er, yes." Flustered and embarrassed, he is temporarily lost for words. Alex knows the professor well enough to know that he only ever means well and feels for him, with his clear social awkwardness. "I'm so sorry, Alex. How are you doing?"

"Don't worry, Jon. I'm fine." he says, forcing a smile. "It's cheered me up a bit coming on this magical mystery tour. I've always wanted to have a nosey at this place."

Jon takes Alex's cue to change the subject and to indulge his desire to explore the grounds of the Government's largest Privately Financed Initiative project to date. Handing them their temporary security passes, the professor escorts Alex and Lucy through security.

Even at just 100 metres away, Alex almost doesn't recognise the main building as they emerge from the guard room; the scale of it is so vast that its curvature is barely noticeable. As they make their way along the concourse, the clouds' reflections contort and move over the three-story tall walls of glass, giving away its shape.

They cross the road to follow the footpath around the VIP visitor car park and then over the building's orbital ring road. One of the three huge, largely decorative, aluminium roof sections swathes down, giving them cover from the sun. "I bet it's going to be warm in there." Alex says, looking up above the ground floor's Cotswold sandstone, past the entranceway's aluminium cladding, to the expanse of dark, heavy-looking glass walls.

"You'd be surprised." says Jon as he holds his pass up to a sensor set into the wall by the main door, "This is one of the most energy efficient buildings in the country – it somehow manages to stay cool in the summer and warm in the winter."

As they walk into reception, Alex is surprised at how open and bright everything is and that the temperature is comfortably cool. Jon smiles at the guard, as he scans his pass on yet another sensor, and invites Lucy and Alex to do the same with theirs. Alex looks across to the inside of the building and sees a chunk of the raw, exposed sandstone with the organisation's emblem carved into it.

The building is actually more like two buildings, the inner circle is connected to the outer by only the glass ceiling, the gangways between the open office areas of the upper tiers, and the floor of 'the street', the unbroken space along which the entire building may be circumnavigated. As surprised at how far off his expectations were, Alex is every bit as amazed as he thought he would be.

"They say you can get between any two places in the building within five minutes." Jon says, "A deliberate design feature to aid collaborative working, so I understand."

As they turn left onto the long open walkway, Alex feels as though he is in a shopping mall, rather than at the heart of a world-leading intelligence, cyber and security agency. "How much time are you spending down here, Jon?" Alex asks.

"More than my wife would like." he says grimly. "Since you introduced me to this little problem, I've been rather sucked into this new project, and it's keeping me down here for weeks at a time."

"Sorry, professor." Lucy says kindly.

"It's not so bad. The hotel's nice and it's a break from the kids if I'm honest. Oh, here we are."

Jon veers off the centre of the street and leads them into a magnificent stone column that encases a stairwell and lift, each beautifully crafted from the same sheets and tubes of brushed steel as they have seen functionally decorating the building throughout. "Are you okay with the stairs?" Jon asks. "Of course you are." he says.

Expecting to go up to the massive open spaces of the first or second floors, Alex is surprised to be heading down. They descend the two short flights, to reach the basement level. The corridor seems to follow the same curve of the street, though much narrower, just a normal corridor's width, but is still as impressive in its design. They turn left, heading back towards the front of the building past several heavy, but smoothly polished oak doors. Jon slows as he reaches the third. He slides his pass through the reader, grasps the handle firmly and leans in in anticipation of the weight of it. "Welcome to Project Dowding."

*

Alex is struck dumb by the beauty of the huge golden object that dominates the room. It has the look of a metallic chandelier. Hanging from the high ceiling, it nearly reaches the floor and is over a metre at its widest. Looking far from like something on the cutting edge of technology, it looks like an antique – like something from a Jules Verne novel. The rich colour, gives it away as 24 carat gold of most of its component parts, tells Alex that the machine demands the highest possible level of conductivity. At its core is a broad tubular column from which sprout narrow metallic tubes that disperse around the rest of the structure like nerve stems emanating from a spinal cord. "It's bigger than I thought it would be." Alex says failing to mask how impressed he is.

"What is it?" Lucy asks.

"A quantum computer." Alex replies. He has seen pictures of such machines online, but the secretive nature of their development and use means that he has little idea of how it works or what this particular example is capable of.

"This is 'Dowdy', currently, the world's most powerful quantum computer." Jon says, smiling over to one of the technicians who glares back at him. "Alex, Lucy, this is Marco Silva, the mastermind behind Project Dowding." The young man, who looks to be in his mid-twenties with a Spanish-Italian, western European glow to him, puts on a smile, waves, but then turns straight back to his monitors.

"You're quite correct Alex, she is quite a big old beast, almost 50 percent bigger than any others that we know about, more importantly it is the most powerful by a number of orders of magnitude."

Alex walks up close to the computer to eye the detail of its internal workings. The machine is separated into four layers by circular gold plates, held rigid by six horizontal pillars perforating the plates at their edges. The top 'floor' looks simple from the high angle of view that Alex has, appearing to be a series of hundreds of coiled tubes spanning from the top to the bottom of the tier. The other layers are filled with what look like solid gold panels each covered top-to-bottom with columns of what look like fuses. Each 'fuse' connects to one of the fine, metallic tubes that emanate from the central column, the fitting connecting each of these individual units is a bulky gold hexagonal bush – hardly the micro science that Alex would have expected, but in line with the images that he has seen.

"What applications does it have?"

Jon has an excited look on his face as he rolls into a well-rehearsed brief on his new toy.

Quantum computers have long been the eagerly anticipated future of the security industry. Since they were first conceived; there had been talk of them cracking multi-layered crypto enciphered passwords in fractions of seconds that might take a conventional super-computer decades to breach. The Security Service had quickly identified the need to be ahead of the game and had employed Marco and his team of like-minded developers to ensure that Britain kept in front of its adversaries, with the express aim of developing the ability to defend itself from such devices.

"The original intent was to build the thing so that we could figure out how to defeat it, and that remains the main aim, but what Marco has been able to do with her as an asset has blown our minds – she opens up an entirely new level of intellectual analysis.

"I take it that's going to be of some use to us in locating the higher-level members of the IG?" Lucy asks, cutting to the chase in that way that she does.

The professor grins. "As something of an initial operating experiment, we fed in five years of UK telephone network data – as you can imagine, a vast amount of information. We set some basic rules and defined relevant terms. From this, Dowdy was able to identify strings of relationships – who was talking to who, in what groups, as interwoven clusters of caller groups.

Alex and Lucy look at one another and then back to the professor, still unable to see how this wealth of information might translate into useful intelligence on people using handsets with no attached identities.

Aware of their building scepticism, Jon goes on, "We began to filter the information, aiming towards people using the telephone network for nefarious activity. We focused on the 'burner phone', telling Dowdy to look at contract free numbers that appeared on the network for limited time to limited contacts. We were able to build a picture of a hierarchy of discreet networks, ranging from low to high grade - the lower having more contacts, which in turn might be less discreet, maybe registered numbers, they would be connected to the network for more time. The highest-grade groups only appeared on the network for short periods, only had limited contacts, which were similarly low-profile, the call and messaging traffic would be low to non-existent, pointing towards the use of encrypted applications. We also looked at the lifespan of use of the numbers, which indicated an effort to affect counter-surveillance, or that those phones had been employed for the use of a particular criminal act or job."

Alex and Lucy smile as they realise how high up this hierarchy the Interest Group's caller communities would sit, and how Dowdy might have been able to piece together far more of the puzzle than they could have by interrogating individual accounts from one or two phones.

"Of course, this intelligence is of national significance." Jon says with pride. "We have set up a Security Service led task force and are already started working with every UK Police force to exploit it."

"But you've got something for us?"

The professor laughs lightly. "Lucy, my dear, when you asked me to help locate Tony Blunt you spawned my idea to explore the opportunities of data mining. Without the Interest Group conundrum that you brought me, GCHQ might not have got around to pushing this project with operational data for a year or so yet. Rest assured, you have been at the forefront of my thoughts and a real driver for us.

"So, what have you got, Jon?" Alex asks, becoming impatient with the professor's uncharacteristically magnanimous build-up.

"Well, it hasn't been straight forward. We knew that we were looking for a high-grade network, but of the ones that we had logged; none of them matched the geographical profile that we were looking for. We were at a bit of a loss until the locations of the safe houses started to come in." The professor walks over to one of the large computer monitors on the wall-mounted desk top that circles the perimeter of the room. He nudges the mouse and brings the screen to life, showing a map of the UK with the footprint of safe houses marked.

"We were unable to link the handlers' numbers that you have been able to get us to any significant branches of any common network, just one or two contacts each, but none of them common to each other. We ran deeper searches focusing on these general locations and the timing patterns of the periods of activation of the handsets." The professor presses an arrow on the keyboard. "We were able to identify a shadow network consisting only of eight numbers – one from each of the conurbations hosting a safe house, the eighth has been in Manchester, but on its last transmission had moved to Sunderland of all places."

"Charlie's home town." says Alex musingly.

"Really?" the professor replies.

"Our bitch." Alex says, bringing a confused look to Jon's face.

35

Balance of probabilities

As they approach Swindon signal strength returns to a decent level. Alex dials in Charlie.

"Hi Alex." Charlie's voice sounds weary.

"Hi Charlie. I'm in the car with Lucy on our way back to London, you're on speaker."

"Oye-oye nob 'ead." Alex hears in the background.

"You can guess who's here."

"Hi John." Alex and Lucy say together.

Alex explains the professor's findings. After taking in the news, Charlie remains silent, but John is eager. "So, there's another set of phones being used away from the safe houses speaking to someone up in Sunderland?" he asks rhetorically. "Are we sure they're our guys? We've not tracked anyone leaving the safe houses to make calls."

"There haven't been any calls since we started watching them. From what we heard in Edgeware; I'd say there'll be one tomorrow at 1000 hours."

"I'll get back up to Edgeware tonight." John says keenly.

"I wouldn't bother." says Alex dismissively. "I've got the phone number and will try to get my spyware onto it next time it gets switched on – we'll be able to hear the conversation and not have to risk being spotted conducting surveillance on the ground. Plus, you'll just piss Matt off going up there."

"Fuck Matt." John pauses. "Sorry ladies."

Alex ignores him. "I'll inform all the stakeouts of the likely activity and ask them to keep out of the way."

Still Charlie says nothing. John is already constructing what intervention will look like. "I want my top team up there and ahead of them. I'll take Mike. Jambo and Spider are there already. Are you coming?"

"Let's not get ahead of ourselves, John. It's a bit of a jump to assume that they're mobilising a force up to Sunderland." Charlie says.

"What the fuck else are we going to do? This is a strong lead; we can't ignore it – worst case - we just redeploy back down." The silence on the call from both ends tells John that there aren't any showstoppers. "So, are you in or what?"

Alex looks across to Lucy, who smiles back at him. "Yeah, why not."

John laughs. "I'll get Mike up there today; he can sort us a house and start scoping the place."

*

It has been a quiet drive along the motorway as Alex and Lucy both reflect on the developments and how the emerging plan might play out. Alex breaks the silence; "What are the chances of your boy being selected for the Sunderland job?" Alex asks.

"That's a jump, isn't it?" Lucy smirks as she throws his words back at him. Alex laughs back at her. "It would certainly put the cat amongst the pigeons."

Both know that John will never let go of anything that threatens Charlie or her family, and that Matt's main effort is keeping track of Tariq. Having both of these driven characters with misaligned objectives in one place is a recipe for disaster.

Let's chat with Matt. Lucy says, pressing a button on the slick black plastic centre console. She turns a dial, flicking through the encrypted app contacts displayed on the small screen in the dash.

"Well let's think this through." Alex says in a minor fluster, "Do we need to tell him? Can't we keep Sunderland to ourselves?"

"No. Matt will track Tariq to wherever they deploy him, and he'll bring a whole team with him. If we manage him properly, we might get him to buy into working with us."

Alex can see the logic, but still holds reservations about Matt for a number of reasons. The group dynamics don't bear thinking about, with both John and Jambo despising Matt, and Mike being there to throw fuel on the fire in the way that only he does. Despite his aversion to the idea, Alex concedes.

Lucy flicks the tiny dial switch on the steering wheel.

"Hi Lucy."

"Hi Matt. I'm with Alex. Can you talk?"

"Yes. It's calming down a bit now; we had another arrival, one of the Sierra designated recruits."

"Great," Lucy continues, "we've got some new information."

"Send, over."

Alex is pleased to see Lucy roll her eyes at Matt's use of radio voice procedure on a two-way voice call. She fills Matt in on the detail of the shadow network and how they expect the two selected recruits to be moved sometime after 1000 hours tomorrow.

Hitting Home

"Charlie's given primacy to John and his team for whatever is happening in Sunderland. It might be nothing yet, but we need your guys to keep clear."

"That's a lot of 'ifs', Lucy - If Tariq is selected - if they take him to Sunderland."

Alex is pleased that Matt has remained calm and not reacted to the potential side-lining by Charlie.

"Listen, if it comes to pass that two of the suspects from here mobilise to Sunderland, then I'll leave them to John, but at the end of the day, I'll be following Tariq and will be making direct contact with him as soon as I can isolate him."

36

Down the rabbit hole

Alex had busied himself sending his malicious software to all eight of the phones on the shadow network, but none of them had yet been switched on. John had left London 'early doors' to get up to Sunderland before the calls were likely to begin. Conversations overheard in the other safe houses supported the anticipation of further instructions from Sunderland and the surveillance teams at each location were standing by to track individuals emerging from the target buildings over the course of the morning, knowing to give a wider berth than usual.

John accelerates across the Wearmouth Bridge, unsure which of the three lanes he needs to be in. The historic arched structure is beautiful, painted in duck-egg green, and takes him high over the water of the River Wear to its North bank. The river itself is steeped with maritime industrial history; the shipyards of the city made it the global centre for ship building, turning out millions of tonnes of cargo ships that kept world trade afloat for a century.

The river serves to split the 'city by the sea' into two very different segments; the South being predominantly commercial, and the North, with its Marina and seafronts, a magnet for tourists, but both somehow equally plagued by poverty and deprivation.

John takes a right turn into St Peter's Ward, then left into the neat lattice block of terraced houses, heading deep into the thick residential area just inland from the Roker seafront. He pulls up outside of the address on Ripton Street that Mike had given him. The street is typical of the area; one of the poorest neighbourhoods in the country and it is easy to see how a population of 300,000 have been squeezed into a relatively small corner of the North-east. With high unemployment and evictions all too common, it had taken Mike minutes to find a property that was immediately available.

Mike opens the door and steps out onto the street as John gets out of the car. "I'm surprised you didn't melt the tyres." he says looking at his watch and then down at the wheels of the Mercedes. It had taken John less than four hours to cover over 270 miles.

John smiles. "Nice spot." he says, raising his eyebrows sarcastically as he surveys the house and wider, lateral neighbourhood.

"I did a quick estimate – most of the potential targets are this side of the river, the marina, seafront, Nissan plant, the football stadium."

John nods. "Where are Jambo and Spider?"

"They've got a flat on the South side; lovely little place called Hendon, right near Charlie's sister's gaff."

John nods some more.

*

Alex sits at one of the hot desks in the team office at Thames House, not wanting to be alone again on Lucy's sofa. Almost dead on 0930 hours things start to move. He monitors reports of target personnel leaving the safe houses in ones and twos. By 0945 the surveillance teams are tracking movement from four locations, only Bristol, Birmingham and South London seemingly not playing.

As well as having an open voice call to all boots on the ground, including John and Mike, Alex has patched in one of GCHQ's listening operators. Close monitoring for any activity on the eight phone lines is being observed by the nameless operator. Until Alex's spyware is accepted; this, and the physical observation on the ground, is the only way to determine what is going on.

"Primary focus needs to be on the potential control station." Alex says, reminding the operator of the importance of the number last seen on the network in Sunderland.

One-by-one, the surveillance teams report their targets arriving at parks or other well-populated open spaces, and one-by-one the operator reports the phones appearing on the network.

At 0955 hours, the report that Alex has been waiting for comes in; "Target number ending 798 has appeared on the network. Location is Sunderland – South, somewhere near Mowbray Park."

"Did you get that John?" Alex asks.

After a quick search on his phone's mapping app, John replies, "Roger, we'll be there in five minutes. Jambo and Spider are nearer, I'll give them a shout."

As John and Mike race around the infuriating one-way systems of the city, caller 798 makes his first call. Whilst a phone tap is legally in place on all numbers, the call is made over encrypted VOIP, Voice over Internet Protocol, so with neither the caller nor the call recipient taking Alex's baited spyware trap; they are unable to listen in.

"Hello, Zero, this is Lima One-four Alpha. Uniform Six-two has received the call. He's not saying much – he's defo on receive."

Alex checks his file; Lima One-four was a recruit picked up by the Manchester safe house. He wishes that he could hear what is being said. As he focusses his mind on how he might get around the challenge, a notification pings on his laptop – the spyware programme alerts him that his malicious link has been clicked by a user of one of the other active handsets. He grins - grins so hard that he trembles, his teeth feel like they might crush themselves. He feels that this success, this small success, is somehow significant. He looks over to Lucy – she is listening to the group call intently, oblivious to the work he is doing concurrently, oblivious to how he is feeling. He holds back the intense desire to tell her what he has achieved, he savours it as he watches her – she is fixated on her screen, her busy, beautiful eyes seeking out solutions. For the first time since the detonation at Millbank, just a few hundred yards down the road, he feels like they might win.

*

"We're here," John says, stopping as firmly as he dare; avoiding any screeching of tyres, "We're at the North-east corner of the park – where are we heading?" They abandon the car with two wheels up on the curb, cross the road and enter Mowbray Park near to the duck pond, almost stepping into slow-motion, relaxed, happy gaits in the idyllic, lively green scene they find themselves a part of.

The place is alive with the sound of trickling water and laughing children. Mike and John look at one another as though both questioning themselves – their common vision of 'Sunderland' had not included such a utopia. The pond before them forces them to turn left or be channelled along in front of the museum and its huge glass-encased winter gardens.

The path immediately splits; the right fork following the flower bed around the pond, the left follows the east side perimeter of the park to the south. The men take the right branch, but in just a few metres the path splits again, forming something of a web of routes through the grassed area, with a small, concreted area around a beautiful white statue. John heads straight for it, getting away from the trees and bedding which has thickened into a small cluster of trees to their right, shielding the pond from view.

"He's mobile, in the north-west quarter, heading round towards you by the looks of it." the spook operator says over the 'all-informed net'.

The Interest Group caller has remained active and has been tracked, by triangulation, moving steadily up the western edge of the park. He is yet to call the only phone that Alex has access to, but the Manchester eyes reports their man ending his call, and a second surveillance team report calls in that their target, Uniform One-two, establishing contact – North London – Edgeware – Matt, himself, is on the ground.

*

"I'm dialling Jambo in." Mike says. "He's coming in from the south-east entrance."

John glances at the emotive memorial of a woman holding a dead child as he strides towards his selected area of grass and sprawls himself down on his back, feet towards the pond, doing his best to blend in amongst the mums, grandmas and their toddlers. He props himself up on his left elbow twisting his shoulders away from the direction of likely enemy approach.

Mike stops next to the statue and scopes the area. Apart from the pond and its thick green border; the north half of the park is sparse of features, just well-kept open green areas surrounded by neat, bordered pathways and peppered with immaculate flower beds. He sees little option for a decent observation point, other than trying to clumsily hide in one of the tree lines that flank the park, but there are too many people watching for him to execute this effectively. He evaluates the area to the south, but quickly rules it out; a high retaining wall partitions the park, with a single path over an ornamental bridge presenting the only obvious route through. "Jambo, there's a choke point between the north and south sections of the park. You stay in reserve within sight of the break – John and I'll cover the north."

"Roger."

Mike doesn't much fancy emulating what John is doing – one thorn amongst the roses is probably enough. "Any update on the target?"

"He's still in the north-west corner of the park."

"I'm gonna head round the water the other way." Mike says, looking down to John.

He strides back the way he had come, slowing to an amble as he turns onto the flat north edge of the pond. He strolls gently, taking in the sculptures that are placed around the concrete and ceramic space, which acts as a huge sun trap, the heat reflecting in off the walls and glass of the Museum and Winter Gardens.

He looks everywhere but over to where he expects to see the target. As he surveys the area, he notes that most of the few men that he has seen in the park appear somewhat dishevelled and possibly drunk. He untucks his Polo shirt in an attempt to look a bit rougher and bends down to pick up a discarded Special Brew can from the floor. As he continues along past the impressive cylinder of glass full of tropical greenery, he adjusts his movements and mannerisms accordingly.

He takes his first look across the water – his field of view is limited by two small islands of trees to his left and right. Between them, he has a clear view of the path that is shielded from John's view by the small copse.

"I think I've got him." Mike says, feeling free to fix his gaze on the man, who's head is buried in conversation, pressed against his mobile phone, bimbling along the path less than 40 metres across the water to Mike's front. "A young guy, maybe late twenties. IC6, possibly of Arabic descent. Black hair, short on the sides, but long on top, flopping down over his ears, something of a miss-match to the neatly trimmed, inch long beard that he sports. He's wearing dark blue jeans and a grey jacket."

"Any chance of capturing an image?" Alex asks.

"Not from here." Mike replies.

"I've got a camera." Jambo says.

Joseph Mitcham

"Roger, Jambo, standby in place. Out to you. John, he's heading your way now."

*

John rolls over onto his stomach to face south, away from the target and begins to play with his phone, not even risking a glance as the target emerges from behind the trees. The slick-looking Interest Group lieutenant hangs up his call, briefly raising his head to check his surroundings as he passes parallel with John, picking up the perimeter path south.

John watches him dial another number from a scrap of paper pulled from his pocket.

"I've got dial tone." says Alex calmly.

"Lima Three-three Alpha, our target, Uniform Six-two, looks to be answering a call." The driver from the Liverpool safe house would seem to be the weak link that took Alex's bait. All call signs on the group call fall silent as Alex broadcasts the spyware enabled audio over the line.

"Hello, brother." says the call recipient.

"Salam. Hal tatakalam lughat Allah?"

Oh shit, Alex flicks open a window on his phone and scrabbles for the interpreter app.

"Errr, only a little, not enough, I'm sorry."

The caller grunts in disgust. "Very well. You have two new soldiers for me?"

"Yes, they are ready, the best of the four we have left."

John snarls at the grass, his blood boiling at the thought of the person on the call being involved with plotting the death of his uncle.

"Good."

As caller 798 reaches the retaining wall he follows the path to the right and gets on with his instructions. John stands up and walks towards the path that bisects the main green, heading south to follow the caller towards the bridge. He maintains his listening watch as he walks.

"You must bring them to me in Sunderland between Dhuhr and Al-'asr on Saturday. Call me when you are 20 minutes away. I will have a new number then. You must also have a fresh phone and number specifically for this job – do you understand?"

"Yes, brother, but how will I know your new number?"

"The same way you got this one – it will come."

"Where in Sunderland shall we meet you?"

"I'll tell you that when you call."

"He's heading your way, Jambo." John says as the caller embarks on the sharp incline onto the antiquated steel bridge up to the higher ground of the southern section of the park.

*

The south of the park undulates significantly offering Jambo plenty of opportunity to find cover, but equally limiting his ability to maintain 'eyes on' - the ground makes the maze of paths between the hills more of a labyrinth. Jambo has assessed that with still at least a call and a half to make, the caller will be spending a while here, so guesses that he will follow the central path that leads to the greatest selection of routes. He takes cover in a thick bush beyond the caller's first option to deviate left, into a dead end that is the play park, or right leading directly to an exit gate onto Burdon Road but hopes that the caller will take a course straight ahead, which should offer the perfect view for a decent shot of him.

Joseph Mitcham

The close and less populated nature of this part of the park means that Jambo has been able to slip into the bush unnoticed by anyone. He manages to find a line of sight to the bridge and holds his position.

"Your recruits must arrive with nothing, only wearing plain tracksuits. No personal possessions – I will provide them with everything that they need."

Jambo can hear the words from his ear-buds echoing from the direction of the bridge; he begins to apply pressure to the shutter release. The caller emerges from the mouth of the bridge, head down, his fingers busy terminating the call. A touch more weight on the shutter release brings his target into sharp focus, but Jambo is worried that he won't get his shot. Faced with a choice of three routes; the caller pauses and looks up. His eyes shoot left, past Jambo, towards the park, and then back to the right.

"Got him." Jambo whispers as the target steps off without altering course. "He's heading south on the central path."

Jambo checks the preview of the image on the LCD screen. Happy with what he sees, he stows the camera in the baggy pocket of his jacket.

The coast clear, Jambo pushes out of the bush and walks over to the entranceway to the bridge and nods to John, who is making his way over the grass towards him. Whilst not needed, Mike has hung back, looking over the memorial wall and pathway for names of soldiers he knew.

"Gents, we need to start thinking about the onward chase." Jambo says, knowing that he can cover the park's southern half alone. "John – you head back to your car and standby. Mike – take one of the exits on the west of the park and start making your way down Burdon Road towards the south-west corner of the park. I've got him covered while he's in the grounds."

*

Jambo turns around to see caller 798 disappearing behind the green slope to the right of the path. He sets off at a steady run up the bank of the hill, slowing as he reaches the summit and lowering himself into the prone position.

"Lima Two-nine Alpha, our target, Uniform Three-two, is receiving a call."

"Roger, confirmed, Caller 798 is on a new call. He's walking up a hill feature on the west side of the park."

"Lima Two-three Alpha, this is Alex." He keeps his name in clear over the unofficial net whilst talking to Jambo; his ego not strong enough to designate himself as the controlling 'zero' callsign. "By my count, this is his last call."

"Roger. Thanks Alex, out to you. Mike, John; standby for target to exit the park on the west side. John, there's a lay-by just up from the Civic Centre car park."

"Moving now." John says, the revs of the engine clearly audible over the call – Jambo's head shoots over his right shoulder; from his position on the high ground, he can see and hear the fast-moving Merc rocket south along Toward Road. Looking back to the target, Jambo is happy that the caller has no line of sight to any of John's route until he gets onto Burdon Road, and even then – aggressively driven cars are the norm and are no cause for heads to be turned.

"Where are you, Mike?"

"I'm almost at the south-west corner of the park."

"Good." Jambo says, craning his neck to get eyes on the crossroads – the drop down to Burdon Road from the park's perimeter wall reduces towards the south and he can see Mike through the railings. "Once you're there, cross Burdon Road and start making your way back north, I'll let you know when he moves."

Jambo watches the caller walking laps of the monument to Jack Crawford, the local hero of the Battle of Camperdown, the man who had famously 'nail the colours to the mast'. Completing the recount of his script for the final time, Caller 798 switches off the phone and begins to walk swiftly down the path.

"Guys, he's moving south."

"Shall I stay here?" Mike asks, knowing that there are no other exits along the western perimeter south of the monument.

Jambo scours the potential routes. "Fuck; there's a bridge over to the Civic – best get back up the road sharpish." The path that the caller is following bends to the right onto a footbridge that spans from the high ground of the park across to a raised area at the back of the Civic Centre. From Jambo's oblique angle, he cannot see an onward route, other than doors into the building or the steps that double back down to the road below.

"Fuckin' one-way system." John snaps, "I'll be two minutes."

"He's over the bridge and walking towards the building." Jambo says, getting to his feet, he jogs steadily down the hill and joins the path leading to the footbridge. The Civic building is based on two hexagonal loops which are conjoined by their upper floors. As Jambo's angle of view changes, he sees the gap in the lower floor that cuts straight through the building. "He's heading through the complex."

Jambo scrolls over the mapping images on his phone. "He's heading for the Park Lane Interchange. There's a Metro station, bus stop, taxis or a route through into the city centre.

"Fuckin' hell." John sneers angrily, having just made it around to the bottom of Burdon Road. "I'll do another lap."

Hitting Home

"Mike, come up the steps on the left." Jambo says looking over the railing of the bridge at his friend as he shuffles down the hill towards him.

Jambo picks up his pace as he hits the brown tiles from which the floor and steps are made, and which the Civic Centre's brickwork matches exactly. A ground-breaking step forward in architecture in the 70's, the Council building is now, largely unanimously, condemned as an embarrassing eyesore. The pointing is failing, with weeds sprouting from the crumbling grout, and leaks plaguing the internal electrics and soft-tiled ceilings within.

The weight of visitor traffic on the walk way offers Jambo good cover, and he is comfortable to be within 20 metres of the target. The path is slightly down hill and everyone walking towards the town seems to be in a hurry – the lunchtime rush of council officers maybe.

Jambo settles behind two young women, the flowing dyed red hair of the one on the right offering him cover. This colouration is common in many ladies, young and old, in the city, as an unsubtle nod of support to their beloved Black Cats - Sunderland Association Football Club. The women talk work as they walk, discussing the merits of a manufacturing park.

Slouching his gait, Jambo keeps a wandering eye on the target as they leave the shade of the building and feel the warm breeze coming off the green space behind the Civic Centre.

Looking beyond the target, Jambo sees that the path leads to a roundabout; the Park Lane Interchange is directly across the junction. The road to the right of it leads to the extensive retail centre of the City. The road to the left provides access in to the interchange from Stockton Road, and to the right is the entrance of the Civic's underground car park – Where's he going?

Caller 798 turns left, following the path around the roundabout, past a couple of cars dropping off passengers for the bus or metro station, but then he stops at a third vehicle, a silver Volkswagen. Jambo just manages to avert his gaze as the caller looks back as he pulls the door open.

Reaching the curb, Jambo doesn't break stride, stepping out to cross the road that leads into the car park. He walks on, the opposite way around the roundabout, only turning his head for long enough to read and remember the vehicle registration as it pulls off erratically.

*

"John, where are you?" Jambo asks.

"I'm on Stockton Road, about 100 metres from the interchange turn."

"Target is in a Silver Golf about to exit onto your road."

John sees the red lights of the junction ahead. Already feeling like he's on a hiding to nothing, trying to conduct a surveillance operation as a single mobile unit, he can sense that this is going to be difficult to say the least. He moves into the left of the two lanes and leaves a decent gap to the car in front as he anticipates the target vehicle emerging from the road joining the junction from his right – will they go left, or right?

The first car through the lights, out of the interchange turns right, heading off in front of John, but the Golf comes out behind it and turns left, shooting past and quickly shrinking in John's rear-view mirror.

By the time the lights turn green the Golf is almost out of sight. John waits patiently for the three cars in the near-side lane to move through the junction. The driver behind him less patiently honks her horn as John remains static, as she hesitates to drive around him, John pulls further to the left briefly, then spins the wheel down, full right-hand lock and squeezes the throttle, arcing the car across the full four lanes, just making it around without scraping his rims on the curb. A clear road ahead he must judge his pace – fast enough to catch up to the Golf, but not so fast that the occupants become aware of him. The

Golf is out of sight along Stockton Road, so John makes the most of the opportunity to get his foot to the floor.

As he rounds the tight left bend onto the short edge of what is becoming his favourite one-way triangle, he approaches the lights for the third time, the Golf is just getting up to cruising speed beyond them on green. John carries his speed as they switch to amber, and then red, but goes on.

The Golf continues past the end of Mowbray Park and through another set of green lights, which change with John well short of the line. As he flirts with the idea of running them, a Police patrol car pulls out from his left. "SHIT – lost them."

37

Nose-bleed territory

A heavy feeling has weighed on Alex since getting off the train for their incidental connection at Peterborough, and it isn't Lucy's suitcase. As he steps onto their next train at Newark Northgate he manages to force a bitter-sweet smile. Lucy senses the culmination of his lapse into grief, places a hand on his back and gives him a warm, sympathetic smile. He had not said a word during their short hop on the bus-replacement service. The alternative transport having been in place since Belton Tunnel was completely destroyed along with two trains and most of their passengers; this trip has been a miserable tour of recent tragedies.

Their luggage stowed; the pair sit opposite each other across a table in the almost empty carriage. Emerging from his funk, Alex tries to focus on the task ahead; "So we're expecting anything from five to 11 new recruits to arrive in Sunderland tomorrow afternoon."

"Yes, joining Caller 798, plus however many other chaps he might already have assembled up here." Lucy says, completing the verbal picture of enemy strength.

"What are the chances of Tariq being one of them?"

Lucy shrugs. "What have they got at Edgeware? Three potentials?"

"Four with the one they picked up on Wednesday."

"He's a switched-on young lad and physically average – he might be just what they're looking for."

"It would be a bonus having tabs on one of them, even if we can't talk to him." Lucy says thoughtfully.

Alex frowns, "Matt has tabs on him – we don't."

*

John stands at the end of the platform; his eyes are everywhere – he looks stressed and remains uncharacteristically silent as the pair approach. "Oye-oye." he says, more quietly than Alex has ever heard him utter his expected greeting before. They quickly clench hands and John gives Lucy a hurried kiss on the cheek. "I've swept the station. Jambo's right outside in the motor with good arcs on all approaches."

"I take it you've had no luck locating our friends, then?" says Lucy.

The big man twitches his head with frustration.

*

The three are silent as the jittery ride on the escalator nears its end, bringing them up from the underground platforms to the gloomy, grotty ground-level entrance floor. A few steps and they are out onto the street.

Alex immediately spots John's car as they step out the doors of the scruffy city centre train station and walks half left towards it. Jambo in the driver's seat is doing a better job than John had at maintaining environmental awareness without attracting attention; he gives Alex and Lucy a smiling nod as he sees them. The pleasantries are warm, but brief - clearing the high footfall area is priority.

Jambo turns left and left again at the end of the street. "We'll take you on a bit of an orientation drive, so you know what's what."

The road broadens as they approach a major junction, Jambo indicates right and turns onto Burdon Road. "That's the Museum and Winter Gardens," he says pointing to the building now on their left, he keeps his finger pointing left as they pass it, "and this is Mowbray Park where we intercepted Caller 798."

"South of the Wear is the city centre, most of the residential area, and the port. On the north is more housing, the Stadium of Light, which is just over the bridge on the left, and the seafront and touristy bits." John gives the broadest of 'ground in general' briefs.

As they drive south between the park and the Civic Centre everyone in the car follows the line of the footbridge with their eyes, looking to see the path taken by the mystery target.

"What lovely architecture." Alex says sarcastically as he takes in the angular brickwork of the Civic.

Jambo pulls up to the red light at the end of the park. "This is where I lost him," John recounts. The lights turn green and Jambo turns left following the south edge of the park. "They came down here and I got stuck on a red."

Jambo waves his arm towards the built-up area beyond the park to his left, "We've scoured all of Hendon; that's the estate around the docks to the east of the park. Once they were out of view, they had routes north through there and on towards the bridge, or south to other estates or out of the city altogether on the A1018 – they could have gone anywhere, to be fair."

At the bottom of the hill Jambo takes the first acute exit off the roundabout following the A1018 north. The terraces of houses briefly give way to more industrial properties, small outlets, units and the odd shop. "This area has one of the highest crime rates in the country." Jambo says as they reach a mini roundabout and turn right into more tightly packed houses.

Some open grassland comes into view as they approach the end of the road. "This is the Town Moor, it backs onto the old railroad tracks that serviced the port, but it's been out of use for decades." Jambo says pointing at the horizon of trees and overgrown shrubs beyond the heavy wall.

They turn left and follow the perimeter of the green. Jambo pulls up to the curb at the entryway to a court of nicer looking houses. "That's Sheryl's house." He points down the back-left of the broken horseshoe of houses.

"Sheryl?" Lucy asks.

"Charlie's sister. She lives there with Allan, her husband, kids, Sophie and Arron, both primary school age. Charlie's mum lives with them too, but she's pretty much housebound."

"How's the close protection working?" Alex asks.

"As I said, we're not expecting anything to happen before tomorrow when their main body arrives, even then I'd anticipate at least a few more days of planning before they try anything. Still, Spider's leading the effort on the ground, following Sheryl on her walks to and from work."

"What does she do?" Lucy asks.

"Some sort of project worker at the Council, working out of the Civic Centre." Jambo points beyond Sheryl's house. "We're holed up over there." he points at the gable end of the terrace just visible past Sheryl's house. "We keep out of the way – Sheryl's not best pleased that we're here and thinks it's all a bit unnecessary."

*

Jambo continues to 'hand-rail' the green, north past the Port of Sunderland security gates where the road bends to the left to track the course of the Wear back inland.

"We'll head over to the north and meet up with Mike. He's been looking at some locations with your brief in mind." John says.

The consensus emerging from Thames House is that the most likely course of enemy action would be to attack members of Charlie's family as part of a 'bigger picture' attack, in a comparable manner to what had happened to Alex's parents, and what might have happened to Lucy's nan.

They join back onto the A1018 as it sweeps round the final stretch towards the Wearmouth Bridge. "I've got Cliff coming up in a spare car first thing tomorrow." John says as Alex and Lucy admire the construction of the iconic bridge and its views across the university campus and out to sea.

"Have you got enough assets to track the recruits coming into the city?" Alex asks.

"We'll have three vehicles including Spider's van, plus however many cars come up from the stakeouts. We'll end up with at least seven by the time the last package arrives."

As the car snakes along the one-way system of St Peters Ward, Alex envisages the difficulties of trying to follow a vehicle covertly through the complex web of routes, hampered by frequent sets of lights, crossings and difficult junctions. Not quite to London standards of an aggressive driving environment, but there certainly seems to be some offensive posturing and lane changing going on.

The road bends round once more, taking them back on themselves towards the river. As they approach the north side of the university campus, the road splits – Jambo turns left towards the Roker seafront.

*

Emerging onto Whitburn Road the sea view is obscured by the wall that separates the path from the steep embankment down to Marine Walk. Jambo parks the car nose on to the path. Alex feels a slight unease as he sees Mike walking towards them. He is smiling, but the smile does not mask the man's incredibly aggressive and domineering persona – Alex's sentiment is not helped by knowing that Mike played a part in the killing of the Interest Group assailant at The Wirral just four days ago.

"Alex, Lucy, welcome to Sunderland." Mike says jovially, like some kind of odd holiday rep. "This is Roker seafront," he says, encouraging them to step forward to the wall, "popular tourist spot for all the usual seaside reasons, nice beach, water sports, amusements and restaurants."

Alex and Lucy take a moment to digest what they can see – the thick arcing stone concourse of the North Pier spikes out nearly a mile through the narrow, milky yellow strip of sand to dominate the view, with the red and white striped Roker Lighthouse at its tip. The sand turns to shale as it curves round to the north towards the rocky outcrops of Cliffe Park.

Directly beneath at the bottom of the green slope on the other side of their wall is a modern-looking water sports centre with people of all ages clad in wetsuits scurrying around inside its grounds with sail boards, looking like ants carrying sections of leaves. Further north along the promenade is what looks to be a brand-new row of shops and restaurants.

"It looks like there's been a lot of investment?" Lucy says.

"Yeah, but still not a great target though – too spread out," Mike says, almost sounding disappointed, "unless you're a marauding gunman." He looks to the clouds thoughtfully imagining what carnage might be inflicted by such a course of action. "You could walk down the pier though, picking people off – nowhere to go." he says menacingly, almost entranced. "Let's walk." he says, snapping out of it, back into his 'cheerful tour guide' role.

"I'm going to head back to relieve Spider." Jambo says, getting back into the car.

"Lucky boy. Save some for me." John says, laughing at his own joke in his typical way.

Joseph Mitcham

*

Passing the mini roundabout that they came in on, the group follow the Pier View slip road down to the front. Having seen all there is to see of the promenade from above, they continue to head south along the coastal path, rounding the fenced compound of the yacht club past the nub of the inner north pier and onto what becomes the north bank of the Wear. Alex keeps having to remind himself that he is 'at work' and forces himself to stop trying to hold hands with Lucy. Even with the two angels of death flanking them, her allure has him wanting her. She catches him telling himself off and gives him one of her priceless smiles.

The path cuts in behind the club's grounds, the river's wall angling in to form the basin of the densely packed marina. Hundreds of small vessels rise and fall with the movement of the water against pontoon walkways within the awkwardly shaped expanse of water enclosed. The high concrete walls make the little boats look quite inaccessible.

"This looks fab." Lucy says, again surprised that such a nice location exists so close to such rundown areas.

"Nice, but not a target; we've discounted it already." Mike says, hastening his stride.

The pathway continues along the river, cutting away at a stony old slipway for a way before coming back to the water's edge at the end of the university campus grounds. "This is the National Glass Centre; it belongs to the uni." Mike says as they turn right, off the path that continues in front of it, to walk around to the back of the building. The roof line slopes down to meet them as they reach the car park. Alex is amazed to see that the roof is effectively a ramp made, in part, of glass tiles.

"Don't look down." John says as they begin to ascend the subtly impressive structure.

*

Alex steadies himself on the railings at the front-centre of the roof's edge. The breeze has stiffened somewhat with the 12 metres of elevation. He looks across the water to see an enormous crane extracting a huge cast plate of steel from the bowels of an immense cargo ship.

"That's the docks' deep-water berth." Mike says, sharing more of the knowledge that he's collected over the past couple of days. "All the smaller freight goes in through the lock." He points to the left of the quay. "It opens just before high tide to let traffic through and closes at peak tide to maintain the water level." He points to the other end of the perfectly straight stretch of concrete, "Most of the buildings between the docks and the bridge are university digs, but there are some private flats and a couple of businesses. On this side," he waves his arm at the area adjacent to the glass centre to the west, "is the main campus of Sunderland University."

"Is this any better a target than the seafront? Or even the shopping centres?" Alex asks.

Mike returns him a stern frown. "I've been looking at the local forecast of events and there is going to be a maritime festival hosted here next weekend, it should attract a decent crowd."

"That's interesting." Lucy says, raising her eyebrows at Alex – he acknowledges her with a nodding head. "Is there anything else happening in the next month?" she asks.

"The stadium has home fixtures on the 12th and 23rd. They get a pretty good attendance as well, by all accounts."

"Jesus." Lucy gasps. "Imagine the damage they could do there?"

"It's a worry." Mike says calmly. "It's certainly what I'm looking at as their primary option."

"And the twelfth is this Tuesday – would three days up here be too quick for them to get organised?"

Joseph Mitcham

"I'd say so." John says.

"The target doesn't even have to be something so obvious." Alex says, "They've shown that - hitting a conference centre, train tunnel, supermarket… petrol station."

"I reckon you're bang on, Alex, but the manpower they're putting into Sunderland stinks of them gunning for something big and high profile." says John. "Peterborough and The Wirral were big deals to us, but they were in and out of the headlines."

"A stadium attack would fit the bill." Lucy says.

"I'll go through my list with you, Lucy." Mike says. "There's more in Sunderland than you'd realise; there's the Empire theatre," he points over a couple of fingers left of the bridge, "the university itself, the Nissan plant just on the outskirts" he thumbs over his shoulder, "I could do with your green slime input to do a full analysis."

Lucy smirks and rubs two fingers on her cheek in Mike's direction. "No problem."

*

"This is nice." Lucy says, thinly veiling her displeasure at the standard of their temporary quarters.

"Sorry, Ma'am, not up to your standards?" John quips, mockingly placing a downturned hand on his hip and wiggling his bum.

"Come on, we've got a call with your good lady in 'figures few'." says Alex, struggling in with the luggage from the street.

The four sit around the table as Alex dials Charlie.

"Good afternoon, I've got Dev here with me in the office. How are you enjoying Sunderland?"

"It's a bit of a dump to be fair." Mike says reactively.

"How very rude!" Charlie shrieks, bringing a giggle from everyone but Mike who almost breaks a blush.

"It's not half as bad as you make out, Charlie." says Lucy.

"Anyway, how are you getting on?"

"We've just got in from a whistle-stop tour around the key landmarks." Lucy says, "Mike and I have a bit of research to complete, looking at potential targets."

"Jambo and Spider are keeping tabs on your sister, but nothing to report." John adds.

"But still no luck pin-pointing our caller?"

"No." John says bluntly.

"Well hopefully that'll become academic tomorrow and the recruits will lead us to him." There is a pause. "Well, if that's all you've got; Dev has some updates."

"Hi everyone. Lots of news, some of it good. Interviewing continues with Samir Alfredi; it would seem that he was conducting reconnaissance of Birdbrook Fields for over a week. He'd been screening out properties with more than one occupant," as Dev pauses, Alex looks to Lucy to see if she is okay, but her frown shows more anger than upset. "but he's remaining tight lipped about who was calling the shots.

"I've been speaking to the lead investigator of the Wirral attack - the axe used by the terrorist was the same make and model as the one that Tony Blunt used at Belton Tunnel." Dev says, giving the news a few seconds to sink in.

John stares hard at the phone in the middle of the table. Mike can see that his friend is disturbed by what he is hearing. "Do you think that's just a common procurement thing? Or is it supposed to be a message?" He asks.

"I'm not sure, but either way, there are connections to be made and leads to be followed. We've not hit on anything yet, but there can't be that many outlets for that sort of axe – we might get lucky and be able to trace the buyer or buyers.

"I took a call from Professor Banbury's office at DSTL. They have worked back, linking historical numbers likely used by the recruiters, several of them network in to phone numbers used by the Sadeeqis."

The father and youngest son of the Sadeeqi family, were silenced permanently before there was a chance to properly question them, but they had been shaping up as the best potential lead the team had had towards the senior leadership of the Interest Group.

"Unfortunately, that's looking like another dead end… as it were, but some useful background. I've asked the prof to keep looking for more links to other potential suspect numbers."

"I've got nothing from the histories of the safe house properties, and nothing worth mentioning from the likenesses of any of the unlisted suspects."

"The recruiters and drivers?" Lucy asks.

"Yeah," Dev replies, "and the car registration from the Park Lane Interchange was a fake – it belongs to a Mazda in Guildford." The mood at both ends of the call dips as Dev knocks away each of their most promising leads one after the other. "Is there anything else you've got for me to chew into?"

"I could do with you coming up north with me if there's nothing pressing there." says Lucy, hoping that she'll get support from Charlie. "Having an experienced Police head up here would be useful for local liaison."

Lucy looks to Alex as the sound of Charlie's nails tapping on the desk emanate from the speaker of his phone. "I think I'll come too. Ain't sin me ol' mam for a while."

38

Full presence

Alex sits on the floor of the grotty bedroom, the power socket too far away for him to sit on the bed while his laptop charges. He wonders whether the dark patches in the carpet are a deliberate pattern, or simply mildew.

"You bring me to all the best places." Lucy says sleepily, rousing from her slumber. She turns herself over and scooches back against the pillows.

"What time did you and Mike finish last night?" Alex asks.

"About one, I think. You were out like a light."

"Did you come up with anything?"

"Not really. I still fancy the stadium." She swings her perfect, tanned legs off the side of the bed and bends down over her knees to get closer to him. "What are you up to?"

"Checking in on the safe houses. My software hasn't picked up anything significant from the phones or laptops in any of them."

"All quiet before a 'major muscle move'." she suggests. Alex bobs his head. "How soon before Prof Jon can isolate the new phone numbers?"

"Theoretically as soon as they've all been used to call Caller 798's new number, he could get a new data cut from the phone companies, run a new search and have it today, but I'm not sure if he can make that happen. Even if he can; our caller might never use the handset again and it'd be a wasted effort."

"Charlie can make it happen – it's got to be worth a shot."

"Yeah," he says, still tinkering with his computer, "I'm still a bit worried about the physical tracking of them into the city; the roads are a bloody nightmare."

Lucy stands and picks up a towel from the top of the chest of drawers. "Mike's done well with the provisions – he must have been an SQ in a previous life." Although the shell of the house is in a poor state, Mike had spared no expense in furnishing it with everything that the team would need to live comfortably for a period of weeks, his attention to detail that of someone with experience as a company or squadron quartermaster sergeant.

She wraps the towel around herself and heads for the bathroom.

*

Alex and Lucy emerge into the kitchen to more faces than Alex expects to see, Lucy having forgotten to tell him that they had new arrivals in the early hours.

"Good afternoon." Dev says sarcastically.

Charlie stands from the chair across from him. "Eeee, good to see you." she says, air-hugging Alex.

"Oh, yeah, they drove up late last night." says Lucy.

"Morning." Cliff says from the open-plan kitchen, where he stands assisting Mike.

John takes the brew orders, and Mike confirms that everyone is getting egg and bacon banjos regardless of what they might want. Small talk and catch-ups out of the way; they eventually all settle around the table for a working breakfast.

Hitting Home

Charlie begins - "We've got Interest Group recruits being brought into Sunderland this afternoon. We know there are two coming from Liverpool, but unconfirmed numbers from Birmingham, Manchester and North London. All we know about the reception party is that there's one planner, we're currently calling 'Caller 798', and one other, assuming his driver is a player."

John takes over, explaining the expected scheme of manoeuvre, "The aim is for one car from each stakeout to track the recruits from each safe house. Three of those will be my blokes, only the one coming from Edgeware will be from Matt's lot – they all know to inform me as soon as they set off. We'll operate the same method of comms as we've been using; an open voice call using the encrypted app – Alex will ensure that everyone needed is added.

"We have three cars here. We'll be pre-positioned a junction down from the first Sunderland turn off from the A19. There's a service station just off the junction down from the A1018. We'll have plenty of notice, but I set 1130 hours as our 'no move before' time. I'll ride with Mike in my car, Cliff and Jambo will be solo. Our main effort is to identify the location of IG accommodation in Sunderland."

"We are sure they're definitely coming by road?" Alex asks. "Are we ruling out a train move? Thinking back to the instructions Caller 798 gave to his Liverpool contact; I'm not sure that we can."

John looks perplexed momentarily as he thinks through the potential curveball. "There's only one station, with one exit – it wouldn't be an issue with a bit of jiggling, but good thinking, Alex."

"So, hopefully by the end of today we'll know the location of a house full of extremists." Charlie says, pressing a hand down lightly on her man's forearm. "What's the plan with local force engagement?" she asks.

"I've got an appointment with one of Northumbria Police's Counter-terror Security Advisors on Monday morning, we'll see where that takes us." Dev says, reaching for the vibrating phone in his pocket.

"I'll need to speak to the Chief Constable to make sure we're not stepping on any toes." Charlie says, but Dev isn't paying attention.

"Breaking news;" he says as his eyes remain fixed on his phone as he reads the message to the end, "We've got a result from facial recognition – Caller 798 is Sharif Jhiani."

"I know that name." Lucy whispers, "from the target packs."

"One of the disappeared?" says Alex.

39

Prepare to move

Tariq has taken every opportunity to find out more about what his mission might entail from his Alab, but the old man has remained tight lipped, only telling them that Saturday, today, would be the day, and that they need do nothing to prepare, but pray.

The routine in the house has become ever more numbing for all of the recruits, but Tariq has struggled to keep his mind on track, forcing him to immerse himself yet further into his assumed persona.

Hamza has been speculating non-stop about what they will be called to do, goading himself into unbearable fits of explosive excitement at his thoughts of carnage and destruction. Tariq has begun to interact more with his roommates, exploring barbaric fantasies, conjuring more of his own vile stories of murder and mayhem.

The arrival of Rashid, Tariq's third roommate, had provided him with some respite from Hamza's incessant talk of bloodletting, but the novelty has soon worn off on them collectively. Rashid has about as much to say for himself as Kashif. Traveling from Morocco, leaving a destitute family eight years ago, he should have had fantastic stories of his complex route to UK shores, but he lacked the personality and verve to bring them to life, coming over as something of a dullard. What set him apart was that he had some real form; having recently spent three years in prison for a deeply violent assault, his resultant deportation still pending, thanks to an immigrants' rights support charity stepping in to defend him.

What Rashid lacks in voice and imagination, he makes up for with the frighteningly calm, but evil look ever-present in his eyes. The eldest of the four, he is of similar height to Tariq, but has the rugged muscular maturity that a tough life has developed. His thick mop of untidy, curly black hair is flecked with grey, his beard is trimmed to mid length, but otherwise unkempt. Tariq has given the tramp-like man a wide berth, fearing that he is the most dangerous of his companions.

"Hamza, Tariq, you leave in five minutes." Alab says through the half open doorway from the hall.

"Brother," Rashid says, standing from his place on the sofa from which he has displaced Tariq, "Why are you taking this pathetic juban if this is such an important mission?"

Tariq looks up to Rashid from his nest of cushions on the floor, as the ruffian stands over him, but says nothing.

"Brother Rashid," Alab says to him calmly, "it is good that you are so keen, but there will be a mission for you, that will be just as important to our cause."

Rashid snarls, not satisfied with their local leader's answer. "Then use him for that mission, I will not stay here rotting in this room another day." His anger boiling, Rashid lashes out with a foot, kicking Tariq in the face – the blood flow is instant, he clasps his nose fearing that it is broken.

Rashid pauses to gage reaction, his Alab is hesitant, unsure of what to do. Rashid seizes upon the weakness and lets fly with his foot again. Tariq's senses are awash with adrenalin, but his path to flight is blocked - he is forced to fight. As he lurches back out of the bony bare foot's trajectory, he grabs at it and pulls it into his chest. Rashid waves his arms, trying to keep his balance, as Tariq kicks out at Rashid's other ankle. The older man topples back, his head crashing down onto the hearth of the fireplace. Tariq feels his opponent go limp the instant that his head impacts, but does not relent, keeping a firm grasp of the leg, he repositions himself and kicks out with his heel at Rashid's face.

Tariq continues his lateral stamps until he becomes aware of the other three men watching him, not with concern for one of their number, but with the avid interest of spectators at a football match. He throws off Rashid's foot, which slumps lifelessly against his other leg. Tariq gets to his feet and faces up to his Alab to await whatever discipline is coming.

"You have proved that you are the man for this mission. Go and clean yourself up. There are new clothes for both of you in the bathroom. Put them on and leave everything else you have."

*

Bending down to dab his feet dry, Tariq stares at the two piles of clothes on top of the white-painted, wicker linen bin. New white sports socks turned into each other sit on neatly folded black brandless boxer shorts. The outer items appear to be sportswear. He puts on the boxers and unfolds the red and white striped top; a Sunderland Football shirt. As he dons the top, he realises that his special belt will be surplus to requirements. His mind then runs to his watch — how literal was my Alab when he said 'take nothing'? He picks up his watch from the shelf above the sink and puts it on. The short sleeves of the football shirt offer no cover; it stands proud and conspicuous on his skinny wrist.

"Are you done?" Hamza calls from the landing.

"Just a second." Tariq finishes dressing and opens the door. Hamza stands waiting, a placid expression on his face. "How is Rashid?" Tariq asks.

Hamza's face remains solemn, "He's dead."

Tariq's mind races, his throat dries as he considers how much trouble he is in, how sorry he is. His eyes well, thinking about the bloody mess that he had left laying on the floor downstairs – why did he have to kick me? Why did I have to kick him so hard, so many times? What the hell possessed me? What if I could have saved him by rolling him over? He places a palm to his forehead; a tear rolls from his eye as he closes them.

"Don't be soft, I'm only kidding, he's fine. Kashif has made him some chai, he's nursing a sore head in the kitchen, broken jaw too by the looks of it."

The blood seems to fill back into his veins as the elation of relief surges through him. "Oh, you bastard." Tariq says, incensed and exasperated.

"Sorry." Hamza laughs, patting Tariq on the shoulder as he brushes past. "How's the nose?"

Tariq's numbing level of bewilderment does not prevent him from recognising the change in Hamza's treatment of him. Throughout the six days of his almost constant company, he has not heard Hamza say sorry to anyone, even their Alab - Hamza's posture and attitude has definitely altered towards him. Tariq turns to see Hamza leafing through his pile of clothes.

"We're a team now, Tariq. No one's going to mess with us when we get to wherever we're going."

Tariq smiles, feeling like another weight has been lifted off his shoulders. "Sunderland by the looks of these shirts."

Hamza's top is a more subtle grey polo shirt branded with the Black Cats' emblem on the chest, the tracksuit bottoms are the same. "Where's that?"

"Up north, I think. Isn't it in Newcastle?"

"COME ON YOU TWO, IT'S TIME TO LEAVE." their Alab shouts from the hallway.

40

Sunderland bound

"Hello, all stations, this is Red Four, Uniform One-two returning to safe house in the blue Mondeo with a full tank of fuel."

Matt makes a rare trip up to the stag position in Lesley's spare bedroom. He stands looking over the shoulder of his operator who watches over the eyepiece of the long-lens camera mounted on a tripod at the end of the repositioned bed. Within a minute, he sees the Ford drive past, then reverse into the drive of the house opposite. Already knowing that the travel window is open, Matt checks the time - 1126 hours.

The driver gets out of the car and walks the few steps up the rest of the drive. As he raises his arm to bring the key to the lock, the door opens. He turns about, and heads back to the car.

"Looks like they're going out for a spot of football, Boss." the operator says as he catches sight of the two young recruits.

"Can you ID them?" Matt asks, unable to see for himself through the cover of the net curtains.

"Yes, Lima Two-three and Lima Three-five."

"Are you sure it's Three-five?"

The operator tries to conceal his contempt at being questioned by his boss, but confirms, "Yes, Sir, Tariq Nasruddin, the young skinny one – I'm positive."

"Red Four, this is Red One, we're looking good for a long trip north. I'll jump in at the junction with Edgeware Way." Matt mutes his phone and puts it in his trouser pocket. "Tell Terry she's 'got the con'." Without a goodbye or thanks, Matt runs down the stairs, grabs his crash-bag from the hall and bounds out the back door.

*

"Dev, be a luv and put the kettle on would yer?" Charlie asks with her pussycat pout. He folds the lid of his laptop down and gets up from the dining room table, which is looking like a full hot desk straight out of Thames House. He collects up the mugs and steps into the kitchen.

"Lima Three-five?" Lucy pre-empts the topic of the chat that Charlie wants without Dev present.

"We're going to have to handle this carefully to give Matt the space he needs to work Tariq effectively."

"Surely we can bring the guys in on it?" Alex asks.

Charlie pauses, practicality battles against her years of training and experience. "No. We keep Matt a close and welcome member of the team, we need to ensure he feels free to keep us in the loop."

"What about splitting out the accommodation plan a bit? It's getting pretty full in here, what about if Matt, Alex and I move over to stay with Jambo and Spider?"

"And leave me here with the three stooges? I love 'em, but eee gods. There are three bedrooms at Jambo's place; I'll send them there for now. We might need to consider a third property if our tracking drivers stick around."

"Have you had any updates from Matt on Tariq? Has he confirmed the tracker is working?" Lucy asks.

Charlie pinches her lips together, "Nada, but let's not worry about that for now. We just need to remember – the boys and Dev don't know and don't need to know."

*

The front door clatters open. John, Mike and Cliff bundle in, returning from a long morning of searching for the elusive Silver Volkswagen. Although the plan is to follow the recruits to Caller 798, Sharif Jhiani, the team would be able to minimise the risk to the operation by knowing where they were going and reduce the need for potentially obtrusive surveillance.

"Re-fill the kettle." Charlie calls to Dev.

"Find anything?" Alex asks, already knowing the answer.

"No." Cliff grunts.

"Have you been listening on the group call?"

"Yeah." Mike says, a mischievous grin breaking across his face.

"Red One's on his way." Alex says, stoking John's fire. Mike smirks.

"Fucking bellend." John bites. "He best keep in line or he'll be getting a dig."

The big men take seats around the dining room.

"The Manchester car is less than an hour away." Lucy says. "They'll be the first to arrive at approximately 1300 hours, quickly followed by Liverpool, then there should be a bit of time before Edgeware gets here. East Birmingham will be later this afternoon. We've got seven recruits in transit, five Lima designated, six Uniforms. We're not sure about the drivers; they've all been on driving duties with their recruiters and running people about, so I'd assess that they're vocationally employed and likely to return to their respective safe houses once they've made their drop offs."

"We have to be ready for anything once they get into the city." John says, his mind focused only on the task immediately in hand. "They might have more than one location, they might conduct a handover that sees a quick change in direction or mode of transport – we have to stay calm and deal with whatever comes up."

Dev brings through a tray of hot drinks.

"We'll have this and get out to the start line." John says, swiping one of the mugs.

41

Cat and mouse

The afternoon is something of a learning experience with the first two attempts to track the arriving recruits failing miserably. Taking the second major road into the city, the A690, the tracking convoy had lost the target vehicle at a set of lights as they approached the city centre.

Resetting for the arrival of the Liverpool party was fraught, as timelines were tight, John and the operative from Manchester had remained pre-positioned in the city at points along the A690, but the others were still heading the wrong way down the A19 as the target car came up and exited on the A1018, leaving the single vehicle to follow it, again losing contact behind a slow car that was impossible to pass on the long straight along the seafront.

The stifled web of roads around the city with channelled routes, one-way systems and limited places where cars are able to stop, make having cars forward difficult, but equally they are wasted behind in convoy, as rotation is proving difficult. The team opt to have one car on each route as far along as they have managed to track the first two cars, and all others to follow behind.

*

"All stations, this is Red One, we are one mile from the Seaham, Murton junction."

"Lima Two-three Alpha, acknowledged, reception party moving off." Jambo pulls out of the service station car park in Spider's little white van, followed by John in his big Mercedes and Cliff in his recently acquired Audi A4 Avant.

"The traffic on the A19 is steady, we'll aim to get Jambo out in front of him and the rest of us will hang back." says John.

"Target passing the exit to the junction now." Matt says, from the X6, 300 metres behind.

Jambo hits the gas but is confident that he will make it out ahead of the Mondeo. He speeds down the slip road, nestling in behind a pensioner-piloted Honda Jazz and in front of an articulated truck. As he joins the carriageway, he can just see up the slip road in his near side wing mirror – John is off the roundabout and teetering slowly down. He knows that he has about a mile and a half to let the target pass him. The blue Mondeo appears as if by magic from behind the artic and cruises by, pulling in front of Jambo in plenty of time to make the next exit, but it passes the A1018 exit. Matt's car has maintained its distance from the Mondeo, but John is up on his rear bumper.

"Hold your position, Jambo. I'll move up. Make way, Red One."

The big black BMW teeters in the right-hand lane, though well clear of the little Honda, seeming to hesitate before moving in. John angrily hits a burst of speed to get past, narrowly missing the BMW as he cuts in on him and moves up to within 200 metres of the target, keeping one other car between them.

*

Having John on point is a blessing as the section of dual carriageway of the A690 ends and the route begins to wind its way into the city as a single carriage road. He manoeuvres aggressively through junctions and roundabouts to keep his distance from the target car within tolerances.

Having pushed his luck in the mirrors of the Mondeo, John allows Jambo to pass him as he turns left, north, onto the A183 where the roads are forced around the outside of the commercial centre. The operator from Manchester has joined the party and is a car in front of the target, but is a bit of a spare part, and is forced to let the Mondeo by and join the convoy.

"He's in the right lane, but not indicating." Jambo says, now two cars back. The Mondeo drives up the hill and takes the second and last exit onto St Mary's Boulevard. Following the line of the river east towards the Wearmouth Bridge. Jambo stays in the left lane, anticipating a move across the Wear to the north of the city.

The Mondeo holds its position in the right lane and stays there as the road splits out to three lanes beyond the building site. The traffic is fairly light and Jambo is able to drift over as the lanes split further, two to the left over the bridge and two on the right – straight over onto the A1018 towards Hendon, towards Jambo's base location, or right onto Bridge Street and into the largely pedestrianised city centre.

"Red One, you take the lead from me after this roundabout, I'll let you undertake me."

The big BMW four-by-four switches lanes instantly and pulls up just behind level with Jambo as the short queue at the lights begins to form with the Mondeo at the front right. Jambo pulls off slowly, watching the Mondeo turn right. The spooks' car pulls across in front of him, but slows, obscuring Jambo's view of the target car.

"This is Red One, target car has stopped just off the roundabout, the first parking bay along Bridge Street."

Get moving Matt - Jambo edges forward trying to pressure the black SUV in front to move on knowing that Uniform One-two will be nervous and on the lookout for unwanted attention.

"Cliff and I'll go straight on and dump the cars. Let us know where we're heading."

Joseph Mitcham

The X6 continues along the street looking for the first available turn – left into Bedford Street, Jambo follows, his eyes are on his rear-view mirror as he approaches the left turn, he moves as slowly as he can get away with to see what they are up to – "Both passengers are on the pavement." he says as he rounds the corner.

"We're in a bus stop just over the roundabout, less than a minute away." John says.

Jambo pulls up behind Matt on the double-yellowed curb. There is a large barriered private car park, but no legal spaces on the road. His instincts tell him not to leave the vehicle where it could generate unwanted attention, but Matt's demeaning frown at his hesitation reorders his priorities.

*

The blue Mondeo, light of its cargo, whizzes past. It just makes the lights at the end of the road as Jambo and Matt walk around the corner back onto Bridge Street. They have a clear view of the pavement all the way down to the roundabout but cannot see the target individuals. They do see the stark figures of John and Cliff coming round the corner; John shrugs his arms out as he spots Jambo.

Jambo surveys the potential escape options as he walks. The building on his right is the back side of the offices associated with the gated car park – no entrances onto the road. Over the street is a variety of grotty looking fast-food restaurants, hairdressers, a Catholic Centre and a church. The targets didn't have time or the cover from view to get out of either end of the street on foot without one of the tracking pairs seeing them.

"What do you think?" Matt asks as the four converge at the drop off point, "One of those shops?" tipping a nod across the road.

"Underpass on the corner." John says, turning to walk back the way he had come.

The other three hurry to catch him up. "We're sticking out like the dog's proverbial here, fellas." Jambo says. "If they're doing any kind of counter-surveillance at all; we're blown."

"Jambo's right, chaps." Matt says stopping in his tracks. "We've got one more bite of the cherry – let's get back to the start line and wait for the last car.

42

Last chance

Alex, Lucy and Spider are deployed to the possible exits from the underpass system as the car transporting the final pair of recruits, from Birmingham West, enters the city on the A690. Cliff has been shuffled to the front – he has John immediately behind him followed by the MI-5 BMW.

The group call is quiet, with all drivers close enough to see the target car, and nothing worth relaying to the pedestrian members of the team. The Red Skoda Octavia follows the same route as the Mondeo had done. Cliff stays in the centre lane as St Mary's widens and allows John to slip by to his right and onto the tail of the target car. All of the other friendly forces' cars move across too. "We're 100 metres from the Bridge Street roundabout – John's behind the target. I'll continue onto the A1018 and cover the main east exits of the city. Ground call-signs; standby."

The lights are red at the roundabout, Cliff has no traffic in front of him and has no option but to pull up alongside the Octavia. He stops half a car's length back, able to see the backs of the heads of the three occupants, but they all remain facing forward.

As the lights turn green Cliff's left toes maintain most of their pressure on the clutch and he feathers the accelerator. The red Skoda is even slower off the mark, so Cliff decides to leave the others to it and accelerates off to find somewhere on the other side of the city centre to wait.

Cliff drives onto the roundabout, passes the Bridge exit and onto the A1018. The Octavia follows the curve of the roundabout initially to the left, but stays on the tangent, cutting across to the outside lane. Matt and his driver are far enough back to be able to drift across into the empty lane, but John is forced to remain on his course, right onto Bridge Street, else risk compromising himself with a conspicuous manoeuvre. "For fuck's sake," John blasts, "he's gone straight over."

Alex jumps up from the low wall at the south end of the bridge and starts running towards the roundabout.

John rephrases his last; "Target car heading east on the A1018. We have one car in front of it, Red One now lead chaser, followed by our three other mobile callsigns."

The Octavia settles after its rash movement and cruises along the high-walled, single laned side of the carriageway as it curves to the right between the outskirts of the city centre to the south and the drop-off of land to the river valley to the north.

The team have barely had a chance to think about the possible routes that the target car might be taking, when, without indication, it swings off the road to the left.

"Red One, target has pulled off into a small car park; it's surrounded by a low wall overlooking the river."

The car park is merely a narrow strip of tarmac with rows of spaces on the near and far side, the far row curls in at the ends to make use of the space outside of the entrance, and exit which is at the east end.

"We're turning right just past the car park entrance, towards the city – we'll try to establish eyes on." Matt sounds relaxed, almost blasé, having almost lost the target. "The target looks to have stopped near the middle of the car park." he says looking back through the rear window. "Cliff, come back around the next roundabout and park up in the west side – there are plenty of spaces. All other mobile units:

Joseph Mitcham

turn right at the roundabout, park up and start looking at likely routes."

*

Alex slows through the gears from sprint, to jog, to walk as he nears the car park and begins to lose the cover from view provided by the over-grown trees and bushes that bulge from behind the wall. The wall and path bend round to the left, around the perimeter of the long narrow car park. He sees the back of Cliff's black estate reversing towards him into a parking space. "I'm here on foot, west end of the car park." he says, trying not to make his breathlessness too obvious over the call – he quickly mutes his mic.

Alex spots the Skoda about half way down the row of cars nearest to the river. He scopes the immediate area around it and spots a gap in the wall – an overwhelming urge to have a closer look at the Skoda takes hold of him. "Have we had eyes on the car the whole time?" He asks, pulling his baseball cap down and stepping off, he taps Cliff's window as he walks between the cars and heads out onto the tarmac along past the ends of the long row of vehicles.

The silence on the call further worries Alex, no one able to confirm that visual contact was maintained between Matt turning off towards the city and Cliff making it back from his excursion to the roundabout. Alex's view of the side windows of the Octavia is obscured by the adjacent car but as he nears, his view improves. Just as he begins to gain sight of the rear window, the Skoda starts up, coughing a light grey haze over the black ground. Alex is caught in no-man's-land – he'll be spotted if he continues his line behind the car should it reverse out and he'll be seen if he changes course to go in front of the cars. He slows his pace, knowing that he is still out of view of the driver. He moves in close to the bumper of the next car – he is still three cars away from the target.

The Skoda revs, the clutch bites and the car begins to reverse. The tail shows signs of arcing towards Alex, but as soon as he sees enough of the rear passenger compartment; he bolts in between the nearest two cars.

"Target vehicle has no passengers on board – the recruits are gone. Possible escape route is a set of steps down towards the river." He checks that the Skoda is on its way before jumping out from cover and hesitantly looking over the wall. "Confirmed – steps from the car park down to a low road that follows the line of the river east-west."

"Roger - Panns Bank." says John, "Lucy, Spider, you move onto the bridge and keep watch – that's the only way off the bank to the west."

"There in one minute." Spider acknowledges.

"Alex, you stay where you are. All mobile units – follow me round to the east, we'll park up and start sweeping the bank on foot."

43

Not seen

John and Mike stand at the edge of Fish Quay, looking down over the railings at the tenuously moored little fishing boats, as they wait for the others to finish the sweep of the south bank. They are as far east as the secure perimeter of the Port will allow them to be – outside the locked and infrequently used gates onto Corporation Quay. The high retaining wall beneath the properties along the road above and the steep grassy bank offer them good cover from view from all directions but for the west – as good as it gets for their rendezvous with the team.

"It seems wider from this side." Mike says, looking back across the water to the Glass Centre.

John is too angry to engage in small talk. "Where the fuck did they go?" he snarls.

"They'll turn up." Mike tries to humour him.

The team members begin to appear, each shaking their head as they come into range. They have searched the strip of land clearly defined by the river to the north and the A1018, turning onto the road that leads through north Hendon and along to the main Port entrance – High Street East. Lucy and Spider are the last to arrive from their distant standing observation point.

"What do you think?" Cliff asks no-one in particular, "Did they know they were being followed?"

"Hard to say." Lucy offers.

"We knew it was going to be a tough terrain to conduct mobile surveillance in." Matt says, "We've not seen them employ such good counter-surveillance techniques before – but this Jhiani character seems to be a bit more switched on than their other operators."

"Whether they knew they were being watched or not; they've got to be along here somewhere?" Alex says looking back past the grassy bank and beyond along Low Street between the small block of flats to its left and the fish market and Quay restaurant compound that sits on Fish Quay on the river side.

"We shut the area down quickly enough and would have seen them if they crossed any of the routes out?" Everyone nods their agreement with Lucy. "So, we just need to keep watching for them on the main exit routes – they've got to be in one of the buildings in this strip."

"That might not be so easy." says Mike, "Hendon isn't the sort of place where strangers can just stand on street corners or sit around in parked cars without attracting unwanted attention."

"We can use our imagination." John replies, "Rent a couple more properties in strategic positions, fast rotating roving patrols. Are you blokes alright to stay up for a few days?" he asks looking at the three men who have driven up from Manchester, Liverpool and Birmingham – they each nod they're willing.

"We'll stay up too." Matt says unprompted, nodding at his politely smiling colleague.

"Nah, you're alright, mate – this is our operation." John says dismissively.

"We've got other things to be getting on with; I'll leave the ground work to you." He doesn't wait for a response; "Come on Nick." He walks curtly through the group. His grinning driver gives an apologetic expression under his shades and sets off after him.

*

The mixture of businesses and restaurants along the south bank make disparate groups of people a common sight in this patch, so the core group of the team are relaxed about walking back to the cars together up on High Street East where few windows of residential properties look out.

"That cock ain't moving in to our digs." John says, still fuming at his exchange with Matt.

Alex sees an opportunity to help Charlie along with the accommodation plan. "Won't you want to be over here now, John? It'd be easier for you, Mike and Cliff to move in with Spider and Jambo, wouldn't it?"

"Maybe."

"Matt's a bit of a tube sometimes," Lucy says disparagingly, "but he'll be a big help to Charlie and me getting plugged into the local Government and Police.

"If you guys are going to move this side of the river; we'll keep him out of your way on the north." she sneaks a wink to Alex.

*

Arriving back at the house, Charlie is keen to consolidate what they know. "Seven recruits dropped off - all likely in the area of the south bank. We know all their identities, and that of their new handler, Sharif Jhiani, who we believe is a skilled operator and who was apparently saved by the Interest Group from the Watch List killings."

They have all read Jhiani's file – he had moved across from Pakistan with his family when he was five years old, been relatively well educated and worked in his father's flourishing printing business. He had become increasingly troublesome through his teenage years with a record of offences that had grown in frequency and seriousness. It would appear that his high level of intelligence and ability to plan were what made him worth saving from the Watch List target plan. "What are our next steps?" Charlie asks looking around the table.

"Find their base location." John answers up.

"Identify their target." says Mike.

"Start shaping discussions with the local Police counter-terror and FIB reps." says Dev.

"FIB?" Alex asks.

"Force Intelligence Bureau." says Lucy. "We should find out which local councillor has the portfolio responsibility for events – maybe get an introductory chat with them?" she adds.

"I like that. Just be careful not to set any hares running." says Charlie. "John, Mike, Cliff – you fellas get yourselves sorted in your new place and set up your routine monitoring the south bank. We'll get on with the other parts of the operation from here – our business is in the city centre but it's worth keeping this footprint on the north; it's where most of the potential targets are.

44

A little more rope

After the excitement of the final few minutes of his trip, Tariq's heart rate slowly returns to a normal rate as he sits on the sofa in the living room of his new home. He is nervous amongst the presence of the other new soldiers and finds himself missing Hamza momentarily.

The man who met them at the mouth of the underpass enters the room carrying a huge Moroccan-style chai teapot. He is followed by Hamza who walks around him and places a tray laden with ornate cups and saucers, a bowl of sugar and a large plate of Khudri dates.

The young soldiers all slip down from the comfort of the sofas and sit cross-legged around the tray, making room for Hamza and the charismatic man with the teapot. Hamza 'plays mother' and holds the cups up in turn for their new leader to pour the tea into.

"My young brothers, welcome to Sunderland." he raises his cup in toast. They follow his lead and drink a gulp of the bitter brew that they have each sweetened to sickly levels.

"My name is Sharif. Our leaders have given me the honour to lead our mission here. I am sure that you are all eager to learn of what we will be doing, but please be patient, as there are many pieces of the plan to be formed yet."

Tariq feels a sense of elation as Sharif addresses them. To be treated like grown-ups feels alien after days of being told the bare minimum. Although Sharif has told them nothing, he is engaging with them as an equal.

"We are well-funded, and you shall want for nothing. We have food delivered from the supermarket, and you may each add to the order using the computer. I have bought for you lots of new clothes, mostly from the local soccer team's shop. The sport is extremely popular in this city and most people of your age wear the team's clothes like it is some sort of uniform. If you wear these clothes and obscure your faces with caps or hoods; in the next day or so, you will be free to go where you please."

There is a buzz amongst the young men; all excited at the prospect of getting out with the freedom to explore.

Sharif explains the layout of the large apartment and how their routine will work, with each responsible for allocated chores. Having no cooking skills and a hatred of cleaning; Tariq volunteers to look after emptying the bins and washing up.

With everyone happy with their domestic roles, Sharif shows them around the apartment. There are three bedrooms, two larger ones facing to the north with great views of the river and the bridge, the third room is smaller and to the front of the building looking down onto the busy road. "Any preferences on which room you would like to be in?" The young men seem confused, not having been given many choices about anything over the past few days.

"What about you, Sharif?" Tariq asks politely.

"I have the sofa; I hardly need any sleep."

"Tariq and I will take this room if that is fine with you, Alab?" he gestures towards the slightly smaller of the two north-facing rooms, quickly working out that three men will have to go in the biggest room and two in the other. The two from Liverpool take the biggest room with the singleton from Manchester and the two from Birmingham are left with the box room. The bigger of the two from Birmingham does not look too impressed with his lot. He glares at Hamza, but more-so at Tariq.

Joseph Mitcham

*

Hamza walks around the first bed, past the window and around to the second. Almost in tandem, they jump on their beds like children. "This is nice." Hamza says, stroking the plain, but soft sky-blue bedding.

Tariq rolls over and looks at the furniture, which is all on his side of the room. He gets up and investigates the chest of drawers that nestles between the door and a tall cupboard. On top of it are two sets of items piled neatly next to one another. "Look at this." he says, selecting the left pile as his, he inspects the large leather pouch that sits on top of the other things. He unzips the toiletry bag to find everything that he would need for personal grooming, all top brand stuff – he tests the aftershave on the back of his hand, "hmmm."

He places the bag on his bed and looks to see what else he has – a wallet. He unfolds it and opens it out to find £200 in twenties – he turns and flashes it towards Hamza. "This is more like it he says."

Hamza rolls off the bed and walks over to join him.

"These are nice." Tariq says, rubbing his face into one of the four towels he has in a variety of sizes.

Hamza ignores his pile and pulls out the top drawer; there is a pile of socks at each end, all still with the glossy paper band packaging around them. He pulls out the other drawers, but they are all empty. "What's in the cupboard?" he asks.

Tariq opens it, "Nothing."

"Argh, my London boys. Are you pleased with your room?" Sharif says, peering in around the door.

"Yes, Sharif, it's fantastic, thank you." Tariq says gratefully.

"Here are your clothes." He says, holding out two bulging carrier bags. "The sizes should be about right, but you will be able to buy your own things if they are not suitable."

Tariq empties his bag onto his bed and begins sorting through the garments. "Wow look at all this, Hamza." The clothes are mostly sportswear, but they are all fashionable brands and the underwear is a top marque designer label.

"More Sunderland stuff?" Hamza says dismissively.

"Some of it is but look at these trainers – I've never had trainers like this before."

Hamza pockets his wallet, closes the door and returns to his bed. He lays back and stares at the ceiling as Tariq folds his clothes away into the drawers. "Keep an eye on that guy from Birmingham." Hamza says with a concerned tone. "If he gives you any trouble; do what you did to Rashid. I've got your back, brother."

45

Where's Tariq?

The north-side house is a whole lot quieter without the boys around; without their banter the place is beginning to feel like a grown-up environment. Lucy and Charlie sit down in the living room, both with laptops perched on their knees tapping away. "When are we expecting Dev back?" Alex asks placing a tray of teas on the battered wooden coffee table.

"At least an hour. I've told him to do a bit of research in the community – see if he can find some likely meeting places with groups who might be sympathetic to the IG cause."

The sound of the key in the lock reverberates through the wooden door frame and echoes about the house. "Hi Matt. Want a brew? The kettle's just boiled. Is Nick with you?"

"Yes please, Alex, coffee white, none - just me though; Nick's on a task." There is a quiet moment as all around the table ponder what task Matt's cheerful team member might be on. Charlie isn't in the mood to waste time and cuts to the chase with Matt, "What happened to your track of Tariq?"

Matt looks to be squirming a little, a mixture of anger, frustration with an overtone of aversion. "The signal did not move from Edgeware." he says, looking Charlie in the eye. "Both the recruits had complete changes of clothes on from what they wore into the house. I would assess that he would have been prevented from retaining the belt."

"What about his watch?" Alex asks as he places Matt's tea on the dining table.

"I don't know – I didn't get good enough eyes on myself."

"So how are we going to find him and re-establish contact with him?" Charlie asks. "Poor little sod will be scared shitless."

"I'm sure your boys will turn them up soon enough." Matt's mocking tone irritates Alex. As much as he wants to accept Matt into the team, he cannot help but feel that he is a problem waiting to happen.

"Well, until they do; you can make yourself useful and go with Dev and Lucy tomorrow to meet the local plod."

Matt doesn't look pleased, but he stays silent. In the pause, Charlie notices Lucy's thoughtful expression, "What's up, Chick?"

"I'm just a bit worried about Tariq's mental state. Like you said, he's probably terrified, not having had any contact with us for nearly a week – that'll have felt like an eternity in the company he's been in. Then being moved half way up the country with no tracker."

"It's not ideal, but he's a strong lad." says Matt.

"You'd normally have wanted weeks to prepare someone for a challenge like this though." Charlie says, backing Lucy's concerns.

"What if he's cracked?" Lucy asks. "What if he's felt so abandoned, that he's lost his will to help us? If they're looking after him and making him feel welcome; he might have turned."

"It's a microcosm of the main factors that cause radicalisation in day-to-day life." Charlie says.

"This puts us in a seriously difficult position if we don't know that he's with us." Alex says. "Without knowing if he's on our side or not; how can we even approach him without knowing if we're compromising ourselves?" Alex looks at everyone around the table, hoping for some pearls of wisdom from Charlie or Matt with their years of experience – he wishes that Jambo or Spider were here. "Whether he's told them about our investigation or not, if he thinks we haven't been able to follow him up here, because he ditched his tracker, he'll think he's got a clean slate to become a part of whatever it is he's joined."

"Let's not get carried away. He went into this knowing it would be tough. I think of myself as a fairly good judge of character, so leave it with me." Matt says coolly. "Once we find him; I'll handle it."

46

TLAs

The fresh air is a delightful change from the stale old house; Lucy breathes it in deep as she walks with Dev and Matt out from the maze of terraces and onto Newcastle Road, as the A1018 is branded north of the river.

They cross the wide junction where the one-way loop returns from the University, the bridge looms large in front of them. Lucy cannot help but search the faces of everyone they see, hoping that she might spot one of the IG recruits; that she might spot Tariq.

The faces are mostly young, but not necessarily fresh-faced. There is a stream of students moving across the river from their accommodation, down to the campus that dominates the bulging knuckle of low ground where the river bends round to the north-east.

"Quiet day yesterday." Matt says.

"Yes." Lucy replies, "Alex and I went for a walk along the beach and up to Cliffe Park as far as Seaburn – it's beautiful up there.

"I think Charlie went to see her mum and sister. The boys stayed on task; roving patrols around the south bank but didn't find anything." She looks across the river as they approach the bridge, wondering which of the buildings might be hosting the cell of would-be terrorists. "What did you and Nick get up to?"

"Nothing much, just trying to come up with ideas of how to find them.

"Who is it we're meeting today anyway?"

"Sergeant Dan Mason from the CTU, and PC Sam Brendell from the FIB." Dev says.

"You Police like your TLAs more than the Army." Lucy laughs.

"TLAs?" Dev asks.

"Three letter acronyms."

*

Charlie had spoken to the Chief Constable, then his deputy, and then his assistant, before finally losing her rag and demanding that a desk-level meeting be set up for her team members to speak to officers that could bring relevance to her investigation. Lucy is unsure of how receptive or helpful the officers are likely to be.

The Sunderland City Centre Police Station doesn't do much to inspire their confidence. Set into the floor space of a small shop, the paint of its blue and white fascia long-since losing its shine, the colourful, but out-dated decals that decorate the glass panes are peeling off at the corners. Dev pushes on the rickety aluminium-framed door.

"No one home?" he says as the others file into the tiny reception area. He presses a button next to the service hatch. The three look at one another with expressionless faces, an air of anticipation that they might be about to be kept waiting.

"Good morning." They are pleasantly surprised to see a female officer appear at the kiosk.

"Hi, we're here to see Sergeant Mason and…"

"PC Brendell?" she interrupts. "That's me." she says cheerfully.

*

Whatever negativity that Charlie has created with the upper echelons of the Northumbria force, it has apparently not filtered down to either of the two officers. PC Brendell, in her heavy black combat pants and Force polo shirt, walks them through to be squeezed into interview room one – the only interview room or potential meeting space in the station big enough to accommodate the five of them.

The trim, blonde PC, edging towards the back end of her forties, seems to shrink as she sits down next to Sergeant Mason, who is on the scale of build of a rugby forward; he is rugged and robustly set - his dented face tells a tale of a rough-and-tumble life. With introductions and brews made, they get down to business.

"Have you had a chance to look through the pack I sent you?" Dev asks.

"Yes, some interesting individuals. I'm guessing you're going to tell me what they've got to do with Sunderland?"

"We believe that they have formed a terror cell under the leadership of Sharif Jhiani." Dev says.

"Our team observed Jhiani passing instructions by phone from Mowbray Park on Thursday." Lucy blurts. Dev and Matt's subtle clinching reactions, and Sergeant Mason's raised eyebrows tell Lucy that she has over-stepped the mark, her brow boils at the stupid mistake.

"You've been out and about on our patch already? That would have been nice to know about." he says with a smile. Too long in the tooth to bicker and with a healthy interest in what the Security Service delegation have to say, he teases her, rather than make an issue of it.

"Apologies for that; it was all rather 'quick and dirty'." Matt steps in. "We believe there could be a threat developing somewhere south of the river, near the port."

"Hendon?" PC Brendell remarks, "Lovely spot." she says with a flick of her eyebrows.

"Any idea what they might be planning?" Sergeant Mason asks.

All three draw back from the table with subtle, unconscious shrugs. "We believe they are affiliated with the emerging terror group responsible for Belton Tunnel and the other recent high-profile attacks." Lucy says. "It could be something on that scale, considering the size of the cell. We've done some research on what the possible targets might be, but we wanted to get your thoughts."

"They've missed most of the summer programme." Sam says, "The half marathon and 10K is our biggest risk event. The Black Cats are the obvious target."

"Black Cats?" Dev asks.

"The second-best team in the north-east." Dan says smirking sideways at Sam. "No longer Premier League unfortunately, after getting beaten more than Phil Collins' drums last season."

"Six wins in a row against the Magpies, I think you'll find – are you still giddy about getting back out of the Championship?" she bites back. Dan is silenced; the banter, though delivered with a friendly smile, strikes a nerve. "Yes, Sunderland Association Football Club. They have one of the most loyal fan-bases in the… football league." she says, clearly narked at having to drop the 'Premier'. "Attendance is still consistently over 25,000 at the Stadium of Light."

"We've done a bit of analysis and that's come up as the most likely target." says Lucy.

"We hold Security Advisory Group meetings with the stadium security team a few days before each match." Dan says, "We did the one for tomorrow's match against Nottingham Forest on Friday. We'll be meeting again on Thursday the 21st for the Cardiff game."

"Cardiff on the 23rd would give them enough time to get organised; I think we should focus on that until we get any more intelligence." Dev says, sounding happy to have something to work to.

"The stadium's head of security is one of our former colleagues; a reet good lad." says Dan, "He has a background in counter-terror and event security assurance. If you want to come to the next SAG, we can introduce you?" Dev and Lucy nod as they write the date into their notebooks.

Dan finishes his drink in a long gulp. "Honestly, man, you must have an asbestos throat." Sam says, putting her own mug back down on the table. "The SAG is usually a formality; the plan is pretty much unchanging. We give the risk assessment a skate over, confirm security guard and cop numbers – they are adjusted based mainly on the opposition's proximity and the track-record of their fans. Forest has a core of nasty bastards that tend to follow them around, but we consider other compounding factors," Sam pauses, "drawn from whatever intelligence we have to hand."

"We'll need to put something out to our officers and try to find these guys." Dan says, sensing that there is some good Police work to get his teeth into. "We have the eyes and ears of the city – if they're here; we'll find them."

The response from the Security Service side of the table is stilted; the three confer silently with looks at each other.

"That's where this is going to get a little complicated." Matt says, "As we've said, this cell is part of a group that appears to be very well organised, and we've got few leads on the identities or locations of any of their key people. If any members of this cell get an inkling that we're onto them; then we push the whole network further underground."

"We want to work with you, but we don't want cops out scouring the city for these men." says Dev. Sergeant Mason looks perplexed and frustrated. "All we need for the moment is your local knowledge, and for you to bolster your assets around public events until we can find them."

"We need to at least register the threat." Dan says, anger starting to creep into his voice. "I can't demand more resources based on nothing."

"The national level is heightened; that justifies increased security across the board." Matt says calmly, "We will square enhanced central funding through your Chief Constable – just ask for what you need, and you'll get it."

Sam's eyes wander to the ceiling, "So, let's say you find this group and track them to whatever nastiness they are planning – how are you going to stop them without it becoming clear that you've been onto them?" Her question is met with an uncomfortable silence.

47

Shopping

Leaving the meeting having not been able to satisfy the officers' concerns, Matt seems in a hurry. Alex is nearly knocked sideways as he jumps to stop the station's front door from slamming closed. "Matt, wait." he says running to catch up. Matt barely acknowledges him, but Alex pushes on; "I've been meaning to ask – do you and Nick want any help? Anything technical… or anything really?"

Matt eyes him with an authoritative caution. "Thanks, Alex, but we're fine."

Alex looks up and down the empty side-street and goes on in a quieter voice, "Are you onto anything?"

The station door opens again, and the others emerge.

"I'll see you back at the house." Matt says staring hard at Alex. He turns and walks off towards the heart of the city.

*

"And then there were three." Lucy says light-heartedly. "I'll dial Charlie for a back-brief." Alex and Dev fit their earbuds as Lucy initiates a group call. They keep walking, following Matt's lead, but don't make an attempt to catch him up.

"How are you getting on?"

"Hi, Charlie, we've just met with the local Police – they're not best pleased that we won't share the intelligence."

"Hmm, standard. Their Chief Constable wasn't too pleased about it either, but they all know the score. We're going to need to box clever, as they might play the legal game and try to force the issue on public safety grounds, so it would be really useful to find this cell quickly and figure out how we're going to get them off the ground efficiently. I'll speak to John about that." Dev glares at Lucy, understanding Charlie's meaning. Alex just smiles, his sympathies all but evaporated for the unconvicted, potential criminals.

"Anyway, update on Jhiani – not much, I'm afraid; Manchester CTU haven't seen anything of him since he disappeared on the night of the Watch List killings, so he's in breach of probation rules if nothing else."

Walking through the peripheries of the east side of the city centre from the bridge to the Police station they had seen a multitude of restaurants and takeaways from a broad variety of cultures, it seems like there is nothing else in Sunderland other than eateries. As they deviate through the Market Square, there are more shops, but no real attractive brands – Poundworld is the most recognisable. "I hear that most of the decent shops are in the shopping centre." Lucy says, steering them to the left towards the entrance of the mall.

Inside, the centre lives up to its reputation and there is every name that you would want to see. "Superfly?" Alex suggests going into the ultra-trendy clothing store.

"A bit young for me." Dev says. Lucy turns her nose up too and they continue to window shop.

*

Hamza rifles through the piles of skinny jeans trying to find his size in the right shade of stone-wash. The young men are enjoying their liberty, and their spending money - both have a pile of bags across the floor next to the changing room. "This is nice." Tariq says, pulling back the curtain and stroking the fine, soft cotton shirt flat over his chest.

"You look good, man. You look how an off-duty soldier should – very smart, and very cool." Hamza says, pouting back at him.

"Not as smart as Sharif; he's way cool." Tariq says, awe inspired by their new leader.

"He is a very cool individual, brother, and very smart too." Hamza checks over his shoulder that there is no one in earshot, "I think his idea is a good one – it will make heroes of us."

"Do you think we can pull it off? It seems to be a daring plan."

"We can do it, that is why we were selected; what could possibly stop us?"

*

Ger, or Gerard, which nobody ever calls him, even his mum, walks pigeon-toed in his funky green suede Adidas daps, past Debenhams and into the Bridges shopping centre through the south-west entrance. He holds the door for a well-dressed, pretty young lady and her two companions. He smiles at her, then frowns at them as they take a fraction longer than he would have liked them to take. He mumbles angrily under his breath.

As a middle-aged bloke in jeans and a Sunderland t-shirt, Ger melds into the fabric of life in the city. Still with a full head of medium length hazel-blonde trusses and a few days of growth, he moves erratically; giving the appearance that he might be drunk, but he is not – not this week.

His Service has left him with demons that have taken him on a journey of drink, drugs and raucous football thuggery – but his love for his daughter is giving him the strength he needs to drag himself out of despair. The past week has been torturous as he has fought to clean himself up.

Though he feels intensely uncomfortable walking the streets, he cannot face the confines of his bedsit, where the walls seem to close in on him inch by inch. A walk along the river has the ever-present temptation of the final jump to freedom, so he puts up with the pressures of society and tries to make the best of it, absorbing the positivity where it exists and trying not to attract any unwanted attention.

With a good few years of experience in the Light Infantry, latterly becoming the Rifles, Ger has developed high standards of personal fitness and self-administration, but has failed to achieve them recently, slipping further and further over the past four years since being forced to leave under the 2013 redundancy programme. Without meaningful qualifications, he has been unable to find work, making life miserable for him. This had rolled on to affect his family life until things gave way nearly a year ago.

His self-pity runs away with itself, as it tends to do, as two young Asian lads in Sunderland shirts, larking about, cross his path, nearly hitting him with their swinging clusters of shopping bags. He growls at them, but they don't even notice him.

"Ha'way," he says aloud, angry at himself for being on another downer, "lighten up man."

48

Belter

"The Black Cats nil, Nottingham Forest…" Dev pauses to let the tension build, but neither Matt nor Alex look up from their cereals. "One."

"At least their stadium didn't get blown up." Lucy says walking over from the toaster.

The last two days have been tense, with no sign of the cell members. John's boys on the south of the river have decided to expand their search patterns to take in a broader area, and from this morning will have men roaming on the north bank and in the city centre.

"Where's Charlie this morning?" Alex asks.

"She's got an early meeting with one of the city councillors." Lucy says as Matt reaches for the phone buzzing in his pocket.

"Hi… Really?" Matt says without emotion, staring at the table. "I'll be there in ten minutes." He nonchalantly slides his phone back into his pocket and takes another sip of coffee.

"Anything interesting happening?" Dev asks. Everyone looks at Matt with hope.

"No, just Nick chasing shadows again, I should think. What have you all got planned?"

"I'm digging into Jhiani's background; see if I can't find some clues to what sort of thing he might be thinking about doing." says Dev.

"I'm due a catch up with the professor to see if he's identified the phone that Jhiani used to guide his new soldiers into Sunderland." Alex says, already reaching for his laptop from the sideboard.

"Sam Brendell's sent me some more ideas for potential targets, so I'm planning on bringing that together with Mike's notes to see what else might be under threat." says Lucy, but Matt isn't really listening.

He stands up from the table and downs the rest of his almost cold coffee. "I'm going to head south of the river to check something out. I'll be back in an hour or so." He walks into the hall and grabs his jacket on his way out.

*

Matt walks at a brisk pace, keeping an eye on the specialist app on his phone. He cuts south, through the St Peter's estate, to join the road that runs behind the university campus. As the bridge comes into view, he checks the app again and slows to a dawdle. Making it half way across the bridge; he still isn't seeing what he needs to see, so stops and leans on the thick steel railings.

His eyes scan the river and the paths either side, but then are drawn to the steel-clad block of flats – a wall of balconies on the north side, but the shiny curves of its other faces give it a modern appearance. He looks at the hundreds of windows, each with different coloured curtains, blinds or patterns of nets – very few are left free of obstruction to view inside.

A few minutes pass, and just as Matt considers relocating, he sees what he is looking for on his phone screen. He sends Nick a text 'moving now' and continues along the bridge.

As he comes parallel with the wall of balconies, Matt strains his eyes to try and see over the major junction to the path approaching from the opposite side – exactly where the two Edgeware recruits had eluded the team four days ago. It is too far to see without knowing the detail of what he is looking for. Taking a final look at his phone, he decides to trust the tech and makes his way into the underpass.

*

"Matt's up to something, you don't need to be telepathic to know that." Alex says. Lucy raises her eyebrows to concur.

"And who's his weird little sidekick?" Dev says from the sink as he washes up the breakfast things.

"The lads are calling him 'too nice Nick'. Alex smirks.

All three of their phones ring simultaneously; Dev fumbles with his wet hands briefly, before giving up and settling with sharing Lucy's handset on speaker. It is John making a group call.

"Morning all. Jambo thinks he's identified one of the targets, we're scrambling now to get out in support. Wait-out." He hangs up without hesitation.

*

Matt composes himself as the natural light is gradually replaced by the dull glow of the underpass strip lights. Pedestrian traffic is light, but he anticipates that there will be a handful of people in the tunnel at the point of interception. He rehearses his approach in his head, knowing that he will have a matter of seconds to get the key points across. He steps sideways as he senses his target nearing. He leans up against the wall and feigns concentration on his phone screen.

As new faces come into view under the downwardly curved ceiling further down the passage, Matt scans for Tariq, but he is caught unawares as he spots Hamza DeSousa walking behind a small group of students. As DeSousa nears, Matt's eyes flick to his waistband; he spots the colours of the belt that he had given Tariq.

Matt forces his focus to push away from the mis-intended target, looking back to his phone. As DeSousa goes by, Matt looks through the following faces to see who else might be out with him; he is faced with a second shock - Jambo staring back at him with an initially confused expression, quickly turning to one of riled suspicion.

49

Fishy

The weather is still nice enough for Alex and Lucy to take a table on the first-floor restaurant's extensive balcony that overlooks the river. Set on Fish Quay on the south bank, they have great views of the bridge to the left, the campus across the water, and the towering industrial cranes of the port to their right. Despite the huge jump in progress made in the last hours, neither of them is particularly looking forward to the back brief that they are about to be part of.

Still not 1130 hours, the restaurant is barely open and still otherwise empty. "Oye-oye." John says, almost curtly, as he and Jambo storm over to them like charging bulls and sit down with a sense of urgency.

"Lima Two-three, Hamza DeSousa confirmed entering the underground car park under the Echo Building." Jambo says, making sure that the basics of what he has seen are understood.

"Great stuff." says Lucy trying to stoke some positivity. "Dev is already working on getting us a list of residents. I doubt they'll be named, but we should be able to narrow down which flat they are in with that and a bit of close observation."

"I also saw Matt in the underpass; he was acting strange – any idea what he's up to?" Jambo adds.

"No." Lucy says simply. "He's been working a few angles with Nick, I think, but they don't seem to have come up with anything."

"Something wasn't right with him; he seemed to be waiting for something in the underpass but seeing DeSousa caught him by surprise. He's up to something."

"I've tried reaching out to him; offered some tech support, but he didn't want to know." Alex doesn't want to add any fuel to the fire; the team is dysfunctional enough where Matt and Nick are concerned, but he has a feeling that whatever Matt is up to is not anything that will benefit the combined team or its mission. "He left after a call from Nick this morning – he must have gone straight to the underpass." he muses.

"So was Nick tracking him through the city?" Jambo asks rhetorically. "They've upped their game if he was."

"Whatever he's up to, it would be nice to know – we're supposed to be working together." says John. "We agreed to let him come up onto what was agreed to be 'our patch', the least he could do is pay us the courtesy of telling us what he's up to."

"I'll see if Charlie will have a word with him." says Lucy, keen to get back onto a more constructive discussion. "How's the surveillance plan developing?"

"It's looking good." says John. "Mike's found somewhere with arcs onto the Echo Building - remember where we lost them; the building by the underpass entrance? It's a horseshoe of units, and there happens to be one empty with a window that faces directly onto the pedestrian entrance. He's currently negotiating a short-term lease with a few extra parking spaces so that we can set a base there – access and egress is from the rear, so it's ideal for launching mobile callsigns."

"We'll continue foot patrols in the vicinity of the building and the routes from there to the city." says Jambo. "I'm sending Spider in for a recce this afternoon. If Dev can get us that list of residents; it'd be a massive head start."

50

Maintaining eyes on

The step forward of locating the embryonic terror cell seems to be energising the team and bringing back morale. As he parks his van in a loading bay between the multiple underground car park and service entrances to the back of the Echo Building, Spider has a melodic hum going on that isn't a planned part of his act. Wearing black overalls emblazoned with the orange branding of the local housing association, he jumps out of the vehicle and drags a compact set of steps and a black Peli case to the edge of the van's floor pan.

He waits patiently, feigning industriousness by tapping out crude messages to Jambo on his phone. Early in the afternoon, there are few people around to take any notice of him, but then few residents are likely to emerge from the car park. As he begins to consider traipsing around to the front entrance, he hears the gratifying mechanical clunk of one of the steel roller-doors setting into action.

With still a third of the door left to clear, a bright red Nissan Leaf lurches up the ramp, the radio antenna pinging off the heavy footstrip of the door. The Chinese student in a hurry is long gone before the door is fully open, giving Spider ample opportunity to enter unchallenged.

*

Wasting no time, Spider locates the central column of the building, the single point of entry into the upper floors from the car park via the stairs and lift beyond the heavy fire door. Spider sets his steps to the left of the door and opens the Peli case. He extracts one of the camera pods from the sponge lining of the case and climbs the steps.

The pod is a sleek, black conical shape, with the business end at the point. Spider flicks the small switch that is set deep into the centre of the flat base. He pulls out his phone and checks the associated application to see that the camera has registered via the mobile network – he sees his own face moving back and forth across the screen as he waves the pod in front of him.

Satisfied with the function check, Spider peels the shiny, donut-shaped paper seal from the surface of the base, revealing a thick ring of green, jelly adhesive. He holds the pod aloft as high and as far right as he can reach and presses it hard against the white painted breeze block wall.

*

"Ha'way, man. Wha's gunnan on?" Spider says to himself out loud as he pushes through the fire door. Supremely confident in his 'cover package', he is immersed in his character so much so that he feels like a genuine maintenance technician doing a genuine job – he cracks on as though he is.

Taking the stairs up to the ground floor, he places a second camera over the door of the lift, sited to catch the faces of residents returning through the front entrance. The list of residents, procured by Dev, shows that floors two up to five are fully occupied by permanent long-term social housing tenants, so discounted as likely.

Floors six through eight are higher-end student digs, sub-let through the university, and the top two floors are privately owned or rented – Spider assesses that the cell could be anywhere on floor six or above.

Taking the lift up to the tenth, Spider works his way down through the floors, using the stairs between landings. He places cameras above the set of lift doors on each level, offset to the left to capture footage of anyone taking the stairs from the west end of the building.

By the time he descends to the seventh floor, he has perfected the art of shoving the fire door open with the ball of his foot with the correct weight to open it far enough without causing a clatter. He steps through sideways, left foot first, to get the steps, beginning to weigh heavy on his right arm, through behind him.

He turns to his left to walk the few metres to the lift doors and becomes immediately aware of a group of people coming out of one of the flats at the far end of the corridor beyond him.

*

Spider looks, smiling, straight at the cluster of men as they make their way towards him. He recognises DeSousa, who leads the group. Other faces are familiar from the pictures of the cell members that he has seen many times over the past few days.

"Morning, fellas." he says, pressing the button on the lift control panel, "Going down?"

"Yes, thank you." Hamza says without expression.

"Is there a problem with the lift?" another of their number asks from the rear of the pack.

As Spider gains a glimpse of the inquisitive, bearded man; another flicker of recognition sweeps over him - Sharif Jhiani – the boss man. "Nah, man." he says in his best enthusiastic Mak'em accent, "I've just fixed a knacked button down on three and I'm checking all the others."

The lift arrives to rescue Spider. The young men begin to file in. "After you?" Jhiani says, gesturing for Spider to get into the lift.

"Ha'way, man, I'll take the stairs." Spider says with as much finality as he can inject whilst concurrently counting the men into the lift. He bends down to pick up his kit, standing upright in time to see Jhiani staring at him intently as he slowly passes him.

As the doors close, Spider stands frozen, trying to work out what his next move will be. After rousing Jhiani's interest, he is loathed to place a camera immediately at the site of the compromise. He considers that having identified the cell's dwelling, the need for cameras on each floor is redundant.

Spider takes his phone from his pocket and navigates through the app menus to the ground floor camera, just in time to see the eight men walk across the cramped lobby and out of the front door. He sends a message to the 'all station' group – 'Cell's base location identified - Echo Building seventh floor. All cell members exiting the building now, heading west."

Spider walks down the corridor, eyeing the door that the cell members emerged from with the intention of gaining entry. 'Flat 78' he adds to the message stream. His approach becomes more cautious as it dawns on him that his first message wasn't quite accurate – he had identified several of the known members, but he could not be sure that all eight were the eight that they knew of – and there may be additional unknown members within the cell. Might there still be others inside? He pauses, facing the door, weighing up the risks; his mind cuts back to the team's main effort – remain undetected. He looks up to his left and the end wall of the corridor and clicks open the Peli case.

51

Outing

Cliff and Jambo get a dab on from the office unit around to Bridge Street and down into the underpass.

"The cell over the bridge, following the path round towards the campus." Nick says from the cover of the St Peter's Metro platform, housed in a small glass structure which seems to hover on the left side of the road, north of Wearmouth bridge – the Monkwearmouth Railway Bridge running parallel to the road bridge, just metres up river. The group meander along the path across the road from him.

"Roger," Matt acknowledges. He waits patiently keeping check in his wing mirror. "Seen, coming onto Bonner's Field." Parked amongst the slightly less shiny motors awaiting service and repair from the back-street mechanics; he hopes that he won't attract their attention. The industrial units are just down from him, on the north side of Palmer's Hill Road; squeezed in along the slope down towards the north bank. The road cuts diagonally behind one of the peripheral blocks of university buildings and ends at a gate with pedestrian entry onto the lower green area of the river bank belonging to the campus.

The eight factional brothers spread out across the tarmac as it becomes clear that there is no traffic. Matt sits back in his seat, going unnoticed behind the lightly smoked glass of the X6. As the group funnel through the gap to the side of the gate, Matt nods to Nick, who follows them on foot. "I'll move round to the Glass Centre car park." Matt says, starting the engine of the big black BMW.

*

"We're over the bridge and will head down the steps onto the river bank." Jambo says over the group call.

"Negative." says Matt, "Keep your powder dry and stay out of view, Nick and I have this covered. Fall back in reserve to the north of the campus."

"Fucking arsehole." Jambo fumes off the net.

Cliff grins at him, finding his frustration amusing. "You know he's right, mate." Four pairs of eyes are a lot to keep in cover, particularly if those they're trying to observe are on a recce, actively looking around and taking note of things. Two massive black blokes, twenty years older than the average student, strolling around an open area trying to make themselves inconspicuous – that would be a stretch, even for men with their skills. "Chill out, mate. Let him be the Charlie."

Jambo laughs and shakes his head wearily. "I just hope those pricks don't fuck it up."

*

Having driven around three-quarters of the Rokcr one-way circuit, Matt breaks off towards the sea front, then turns right down into the river valley to the National Glass Centre car park. He drives down the first channel between the cars, which runs parallel to the back of the sloped roof, and parks at the back, putting three rows of vehicles between him and the oddly shaped building. The height of the 4x4 and the slope of the building ensure a clear view of the entirety of the Glass Centre's roof. He gets out and makes for the viewing platform.

"They're proceeding slowly east. Jhiani is doing a lot of pointing and gesturing." Nick says over the group call.

The platform is popular with tourists visiting the city by the sea. The top edge is smattered with people in small groups taking photos and taking in the views. Matt assumes a position on the front edge of the roof a few metres along from the right corner with good views south and west. Looking across to the dock hinterland, he sees teams of people setting up galvanised temporary barriers along the 200-metre length of the deep-water berth. His gaze falls back across the water and he becomes aware of another team of men in hi-vis vests placing pallets of materials on the rough ground in the gap between the Glass Centre and the other campus buildings – setting up for the maritime festival. He looks up-river and scans the near bank where the broad path sweeps around the central, prominent campus building as the Wear arcs round to the right to head directly west towards the bridges.

At a range of 250 metres, the individual figures emerging from behind the media centre are indistinguishable, but Matt recognises the target group before half of them are into his field of view. "Eyes on." he says without movement.

He watches with interest. From just their movements and gestures, Matt places the members into a hierarchy of dominance. As they get nearer, he is able to identify them and is not surprised to note that Tariq has maintained a submissive posture within the group. Hamza DeSousa is clearly establishing himself as a leader, but all cues point to Jhiani as the individual with real dominance; they circle him and look to him for reassurance as they walk in fits and starts along the pathway.

The group stands together in a loose circle on the outskirts of the gravelled area, pot-marked with boulders where the skeleton of a stage framework is beginning to take form. Jhiani speaks to them calmly; he offers little movement, occasionally raising a single finger before him as he talks. What is he telling them?

Matt turns to his left, away from the group and looks straight down through the glass roof tile to the pavement below – it looks a lot further than nine metres. He watches on as the eight young men walk directly underneath him and in through the front entrance, making their way through the centre's open-plan shop, up the staircase and onto the upper floor where the lobby is flanked by halls filled with historical and artistic displays of glass theme. He loses sight of them as they approach the rear exit.

Holding his nerve, and position, Matt sees the men moving together ascending from the entranceway that tunnels into the centre of the sloped surface. They file round the end of the railings, back on themselves, to head up onto Matt's side of the rooftop.

The personalities within the group are displayed further as they climb the gradient of the roof; the bolder, more exuberant individuals thrusting on to get to the top, others, less excited or less fit, being left behind. Tariq is at the back of the straggling cluster – Matt smiles.

*

Talk of the mission, even in such scant detail, has Tariq's mind in a state of dichotomy. He is really beginning to enjoy the lifestyle as a member of a functioning team where he is respected and has the freedom to do pretty much as he wishes, but this is brought into horrific reality as Sharif describes the outline stages of what they are here to achieve.

He sees the first members of his team reach the top of the wave-like roof and feels the need to not keep Sharif waiting and puts a little more spring in his step to catch up. He becomes aware of someone walking towards him, he begins to deviate out of their way, but they move in the same direction. He looks up to gain eye contact and feels a debilitating shock spike down his back as he locks eyes with the MI-5 agent.

"I'm in the black BMW," Matt says, tipping a nod in the direction of his car, "come and see me."

Tariq's head goes into a flat spin; trying to compute the turn his situation is about to take. As he re-joins his new friends, Sharif talks on quietly, but Tariq is oblivious – his mind tumbling through a cycle of wondering what Matt knows, how he has tracked him down and what he might expect of him – and how that might impact the dynamics of his new life.

"Are you okay, Tariq?" Sharif asks.

*

Matt sits patiently watching Jhiani conduct the gaze of his followers. He relives the moment that he locked eyes with Tariq over in his mind. The look of shock might have been expected, but there was something else; was it fear?

He watches intently as Sharif keeps his men at the front edge of the roof for a good ten minutes, pausing his outpouring every now and then as sightseers get close.

Their interest now seems focused on the commercial area of the port. Matt wonders what they might be planning, relieving his own boredom by concocting his own ideas of what might constitute a 'flag-level' attack.

Soon enough, the group turn and walk down the roof. Matt spots Tariq approaching Sharif, whispering something in his ear – Sharif nods. As the group returns to pavement level, just over four car lengths away from him, they turn to head west, back off into the main campus, but Tariq peels away from the snaking group and heads back towards the entrance channel at the centre of the roof's base. Now where's he going?

*

Tariq staggers back into the Glass Centre bewildered. Feeling his heart throbbing in his chest, he rushes through the foyer and down the stairs hanging onto the banister, having no confidence in his legs' ability to support him as his senses are overloaded by stress and confusion. He wanders, seemingly without aim, into and through the ground floor restaurant and takes a seat near to the west-facing, tinted glass wall, his eyes locked onto his group of compatriots.

"Good afternoon, would you like to see a menu?" The waitress fails to notice his catatonic state. "Sir?"

"Er, no, thanks." he says, his eyes remaining fixed on the seven men walking away from him. He lurches to his feet and brushes past the young girl.

*

Matt tries to read Tariq further as he walks between the cars towards him. His gait is unsteady, his expression plain, hinting at nervousness. Still perplexed at what might be going on inside the young man's mind, Matt tries to stop himself fixing any predisposing thoughts about Tariq's loyalties and what he may or may not have been up to in the ten-day period of obscurity. Matt knows that he needs the freedom of movement within the coming conversation and must not stovepipe himself before it even begins – his training kicking in.

Tariq takes one final look around before opening the door and jumping up into the front passenger seat.

Matt looks sympathetically across at the lad. At closer quarters, he reads Tariq's face as one harrowed by recent experiences. He gives him a moment to adjust to his company. "How are you?" he asks eventually.

Tariq shrugs, lips pinched. "I thought you'd lost me."

"No," Matt laughs lightly, "we had no way of making contact whilst you were in the safe house. We followed you up from London, and I've been waiting for the right moment to reach out to you."

Tariq forces a smile. "I thought I was being left high and dry. I had to leave my belt in London, then I saw Hamza wearing it the other day – that was a surprise."

"Yes, gave me a bit of a shock too."

The icebreaking nicely, Matt moves the conversation on, "How are you getting on with the members of the cell?" He chooses his words carefully, making sure that he keeps Tariq separate from the others when referring to them, not describing him as, or inferring that he is, one of them.

"Fine. I had a bit of a run-in with one of the older recruits down in London and that seems to have brought me some kudos with the guy that I came here with – he's looked after me since and has been bigging me up to the other lads up here." Tariq looks into his hands solemnly, "I hurt the guy pretty bad, might have broken his jaw – I can't get into any trouble for that can I?"

Matt smiles and uses the steering wheel to pull himself round to face his young asset. He drops his smile, "Tariq, you don't need to worry about that."

Tariq's expression is telling – Matt knows he needs to give him full assurance so that the young lad can have one less thing on his mind and give him some respite.

"Tariq, you're bullet-proof." Matt reaches back and drags his laptop case through between the seats, slips a sheet of paper out from the side pocket and holds it up in front of Tariq. "This memorandum is signed by a judge of the Queen's Bench Division, describing an understanding that you, Tariq Nasruddin, are 'exempted from prosecution for any criminal acts committed in the course of your duties, as may be required in order to integrate with, and earn the trust of, target actors'."

Tariq takes the page from Matt and looks it over with intrigue. Matt's smile returns, he gently retrieves the letter and slides it back into his bag.

"You can do what you need to do and not have to worry about compromising yourself, whether that's illegal parking, breaking someone's jaw - even killing someone – got it?"

Tariq smiles back at him, "Yeah, got it." His head raises, tilting back to the headrest, some of the weight seeming to lift from him.

"Now, we don't want to be losing touch with you again." Matt says warmly. Tariq looks concerned. "Don't worry, no devices, we're going old school. When you want to talk to me, hang a plain coloured towel out of your window – someone will be watching at the top of every hour."

"You know which window?" Tariq asks, his eyes narrowing with suspicion.

Matt smiles and tips a nod. "Hang a towel out and I'll meet you in the coffee shop at the east entrance to the Bridges shopping mall on the next half hour. You got that?"

Tariq nods into his lap. "What if it's shut?"

"Not a problem, just go there and keep walking past it across the square, and I'll be around." Matt likes that Tariq is starting to show some interest and is thinking practically. "If it's an emergency; drape a Sunderland shirt, or anything red, at any time, and I'll get to the car park along from your building as quickly as I can."

Tariq nods again, "Got it".

"If I need to speak to you, which shouldn't be often – I'll wait until you need me if I can, you'll see a bright orange bike chained to the railings by the river right under your window."

Tariq nods and seems suitably relaxed. Matt decides to warm up into the meat of conversation with an easy line of questioning, still unsure if Tariq's state of mind is up to dealing with the gritty detail; "How are you getting on with Jhiani?" he asks.

"Good." Tariq says with a burst of enthusiasm that he quickly thwarts. "He's a cool guy, very laid back and is very switched on." Tariq's face sullens, almost apologetic for his feelings towards Sharif. Tariq describes the living conditions in the flat and his relationships with the other members of the cell and what their daily routine involves, helping Matt to build a picture to frame events within. As the chat becomes more relaxed, he decides it is time to move on to a more sensitive topic.

Matt looks out over the Glass Centre roof and through the gap between it and the back of the University's media centre to its right at the open campus area. "Has Sharif discussed the nature of the cell's mission?"

"No," Tariq replies almost too curtly, "not specifically." he adds coyly. Matt says nothing, just raises an eyebrow and waits. "This trip out today is to get a closer look at the river. There is some sort of shipping festival happening here at the weekend, Sharif showed us where they are starting to set up for it on the campus and over on the quayside in the port." Tariq beams a little as he looks at Matt for his reaction, but Matt is struggling to take in the fact that the focus of the cell's attention is looking to be an event in just three days' time.

Bringing himself back into sharp focus, Matt fights for eye contact with Tariq. "What does he have in mind for the event?" he asks boldly.

"I don't know." Tariq says innocently. Matt looks down his nose at him with narrowed eyes. "Honestly, I don't. We were just looking around; Sharif was telling us how the stage and entertainments were going to be on this side of the river and the ships would be over at the port." Tariq reaches round to his back pocket and pulls out a badly folded flyer. "He gave us all one of these. He was telling us about when he thought the busiest times would be."

"When did he think would be optimal?"

"Sunday, late-morning."

Matt nods his acknowledgement. "Is he worried about the security services? He's not told you to keep a look out for anyone?"

"No. He's said we have to be vigilant, but as far as he's concerned; we're well under the radar."

52

Sagging

After just a few minutes inside the purple-brown brick, fortress-like civic centre, Alex feels entombed. The building's state of disrepair is even more evident inside – as he walks along the long first floor corridor, flanked by Lucy and Charlie, he notes frequent patches of water damaged tiles on the ceiling. The walls and skirting boards are chipped and scuffed, the carpet looks clean, though worn thin. The atmosphere is surprisingly bright and friendly, buoyed by the workforce's collective personality.

As they follow the flow of uniforms and suits around another of the southern hexagon's 60-degree corners, Alex sees a growing mass of officials swarming a refreshments table. Those with their brews and biscuits secured make their way through the door opposite. A loud, familiar voice cajoles the hesitant and shepherds the malingerers, sending Alex in to a mild state of confusion. As the face of the shepherd comes into view, he is flummoxed. He double takes from her to Charlie.

"You're twins?" Lucy says.

Charlie snaps an angry grin that shows that forty-…ish years of receiving reactions of surprise and subsequent delight have worn thin.

"Eeee, yer ald cow." Sharon says loudly and warmly as she sees her sister. She strides towards them and gives Charlie an enthusiastic, but light hug – as keen as each other to keep hair and make-up pristine. "Three minutes older, she is." Sharon still seemingly not at Charlie's level of exasperation at the 'twins thing'. "Let me introduce you to some people."

"I'll get some drinks." Alex says, keen to sidestep the pleasantries.

He picks up on a positive buzz amongst the group as he queues. He finds himself talking to strangers; everyone seems very polite, keen to introduce themselves and find out where he is from.

He sits down next to Lucy at the back of the packed room, crammed full of Council officers from various departments and representatives from a multitude of security and maritime agencies. Only now does it dawn on him why everyone has been so engaging; eyes everywhere in the room flick to Charlie, like Christmas lights on a slow twinkle, not a second goes by without someone snatching a glimpse of her. He senses that it is not just the novelty of Sharon's twin in the room.

*

From the centre of the table out in front of the tightly banked rows of delegates, the ageing, overweight but apparently lively Councillor, Fred Crawford - portfolio holder for events, introduces the meeting, "Welcome to the final Security Advisory Group, for the Sunderland Maritime Festival." he begins.

A mobile phone rings in comically loud and embarrassing fashion, "Sorry." Charlie says, snatching it from her bag and looking at the screen before silencing it – fookin Matt.

Sitting to the Councillor's right, Sharon finishes taking her notes and gives him a smile as his opening remarks culminate, before inviting the festival project director, a mardy looking middle-aged woman, sitting the other side of Fred, to give her updates. She would seem to have the attitude that this is all a bit unnecessary.

Alex listens with interest as Shelly talks through the final detail on the layout and operational plan for the event. She describes how fifteen ships of varying sizes and mast configurations, will be in port, moored mostly inside the locked dock basin, but the three largest galleons will be out on the river alongside at Corporation Quay – the deep-water berth that Alex has viewed from the roof of the Glass Centre. There is to be some entertainment on the north side at the university campus, mainly to 'appease the councillors from St Peter's Ward', but the event organisers' primary focus would seem to be maximising footfall through the port.

Each of the emergency service reps provides their final updates in turn, Sergeant Mason giving his empty shell of a counter-terror update with embittered tone, his eyes continually scowling across at Charlie and Lucy. Other agencies are invited to contribute by exception, with nothing more than trivia and waffle ensuing. Sharon gladly moves the meeting on to the risk review.

The top page of the risk assessment has been reproduced as a handout - A3 sheets are passed between the rows of seats. "This being the first time that the port has ever been opened to the general public, we've come a long way from scratch thanks to all of your efforts." Sharon talks through the enhancements to risk mitigations made since the last meeting, detailing the protections and segregation of the more vulnerable industrial parts of the site to the south and east of the basin.

Alex is beginning to feel that he has heard enough about the types and gauges of temporary fencing when Shelly eventually moves on to the still-developing site entry policy. "As most of you know, we couldn't get the x-ray machines we talked about at the last meeting, but that was probably a rabbit hole we needn't have gone down. In consultation with the Police and Gate-guard, our security force provider, we have concluded that rigid entry points with, mandatory searches, is a bit of a waste of time. The porous nature of the north site being basically open – if anyone were determined to make an attack; they'd simply go for the zone on the campus, which, will have crowds just as large, if not more so in the evenings when the musical acts are in full swing. We will of course have the security team in place, but they will only be conducting a 25% bag search.

Joseph Mitcham

Alex sees the logic of the argument but is horrified at the thought of there being no real barrier between such a large public event and the cell that they have been tracking. He senses that he is not the only one in the room uneasy with the decision. Dan Mason glares over his shoulder at Charlie looking angrily frustrated. Out of nowhere, he pipes up, "I'm happy with that as long as there's been no change to the threat level."

"Well, Sergeant Mason, you tell us." the big Councillor laughs.

"Nothing from me, Sir. I don't know if any other agencies have any updates?" he says malevolently, looking side to side before turning to face Charlie and levelling a stare that puts her in an awkward position.

All eyes are on her, waiting for a response. Reminding herself of the operational imperative to maintain secrecy, she absolves the guilty feeling that grasps her. As it melts away, she stands up, "No updates from London," she says with heavy authority, "but we'll be working closely with Sergeant Mason and his team to ensure you have a safe event."

The room breaks into a noisy bustle as the meeting ends. The delegates make the most of the margins to get the real work done. Sharon pushes through to the back of the room, "Sis, Councillor Crawford would like a chat down in his office if you've got a minute."

*

Sharon shows Charlie in to the long, but narrow office, then backs out, smirking at her as she shuts the door, like she's a naughty school girl being walked into the headmaster's office. The room is sparse, but functional, none of the historical fineries that adorn the walls outside. Councillor Crawford turns on his swivel chair and stands from his wall-facing desk. "Come in, please. Ms Thew? or is it Agent Thew?"

"It's 'Charlie', please, Councillor." she replies, extending her hand to meet his. Only now does she fully appreciate his size – he must be at least 6' 5"… and 18 stone. His bulbous nose, feathery ginger hair, with school-boy parting and gentle voice gives a soft edge to his presence, but she doesn't allow herself to fall for his charm.

"Please, call me Fred." he says, gesturing for her to take a seat at the small glass-topped table. "Sharon tells me you're getting on great guns down in London. It's good to see a Mak'em doing well for themselves." he smiles.

"Thanks. I've been very lucky." she says. The temptation to prolong the small talk and delay the inevitable comes and goes, she decides to grasp the nettle. "What is it you wanted to talk to me about, Fred?" She stares hard into his eyes without expression. His bravado and smile seem to evaporate, leaving him at a loss for words momentarily, knocked from his well-exercised routine of softening up his opponent in whatever debate or negotiation that he's in.

"Charlie, listen, I've been around the block a few times," he begins, "I know how things work, and I know you're not in Sunderland for a family visit, dropping into my SAG to see your sister." He pauses, throwing his hands out flat on the table, his look willing her to share what she knows.

Her loyalty towards her city pulls hard on Charlie's conscience, but she knows she cannot give anything away. She takes time to select the right words for her response. "You don't have to worry, Fred. I'm not going to let anything happen in Sunderland."

"But there is a credible threat?" he asks, anger starting to build in his voice. "Don't you be messin' on, trying to be clever," his voice raises further, "you nip whatever, or whoever it is in the bud, and if you'd be good enough to make sure it's done before the weekend – that'd be just fine, thank you very much." The seasoned campaigner takes a deep breath to calm himself, as Charlie looks on unmoved.

"My business here cannot be disclosed, but we are working with the Northumbria force to minimise any threat. Our mission is of significance to national security, and I'll conclude it as soon as I can, but you have to know that I'm working on a much bigger picture than one event or group of people."

"So, there is a 'group' of people, and they are looking at an 'event'?" Fred sneers irritably, shaking his reddening head. "I'll tell you this, young lassie," he says, waggling a finger at her, "if anything happens in my city; it'll be your head on the block."

53

Teamsters

"His head's all over the place at the moment, he went a long time without us having a touch on him." Matt says to Nick as he slides the key into the lock. He steps into the hall of the St Peter's base house. "He's a good kid, I'm sure…"

John slams Matt against the dining room wall by his collars. Nick draws back a fist but freezes as he catches sight of Cliff and Jambo stood growling over each of John's shoulders with faces of granite.

"WHAT THE FUCK ARE YOU PLAYING AT FELLA!" John pushes Matt's jacket up, pressing into his neck. Matt tries to push him off, but John anticipates, pulls back slightly and swings his uninjured leg wildly, sweeping Matts legs from under him. John drops down over him on one knee and points a finger, millimetres from Matt's eye. "What was that about in the fucking car park?" his voice now menacingly quiet.

Matt's face boils with frustration, but he remains still. The pair dead-eye stare at each other as they each think through their next move.

"Okay." Matt says eventually.

John jumps to his feet, doing his best to mask the pain in his right leg.

*

Jambo slides Matt and Nick's teas down in front of them with contempt. He sits down at the dining room between Matt and John. Cliff plonks his and John's mugs down and sits the other side of him.

"Well? What's the sketch?" Jambo asks impatiently.

Matt's anger and frustration turns to arrogance as he decides what he wants to tell them. "We identified Lima Three-five as a potential CHIS from his record and early communications, or lack of them, with his recruiter."

"Lima Three-five? At Wandle Park – where you stacked into me?" Jambo says, joining the dots together, realising that he had been present when the Covert Human Intelligent Source had made first contact with the enemy.

The three cannot help but look impressed as Matt describes how he recruited and prepared Tariq, unaware of his elaborations and his omissions of anyone else's input or even knowledge of the project.

"Does Charlie know?" John asks.

Matt's smile twinkles as he sees an opportunity to create more mischief, "Of course she does." he smirks.

John's anger bubbles and Matt's glee glows in an aura around him as the five men drink their brews. They all look round as they hear the front door open. Charlie walks into John's tirade, "Why didn't you tell me about our little mole?"

Charlie frowns, non-plussed, but unsurprised.

"How do you know…" Alex blurts.

"Oh, so you're all in the picture over this side of the river, are you?"

Alex shrinks back into the hall - Lucy looks to the floor.

*

With Cliff and Jambo leaving to relieve Spider, the kettle can just about cope with the next round of brews. Alex and Lucy pass out the mugs. Alex gestures for her to take the empty seat between John and Nick, as he moves to perch on the edge of the sideboard behind her.

"As you should be all too well aware, covert sources are kept at an extreme 'need to know' classification." Charlie says, not directing herself at John specifically.

"Extreme?" John laughs, "Seems every Charlie and his dog knows about this one." He starts pointing sequential fingers at everyone else in the room.

"Don't feel left out, Hun." Charlie says patronisingly, immediately disarming John. "I don't know the asset's identity, Lucy and Alex know because they identified the individual. I brought Matt in to help Lucy with the recruitment, and as far as I know; Nick doesn't know the name or any other details other than what he looks like to track him." Nick shrugs innocently with raised eyebrows.

John's temporary calm threatens to erupt, "We've been running around like dick heads looking for these characters, but conker-bollocks, here, has known where they are the whole time. We're supposed to be a bloody team."

Charlie says nothing, just lets him air his gripe.

"I had no choice not to say anything." Matt says, trying to sound pragmatic. "But now the secret is out, we can work together." His grin is sardonic.

John stares back at him, the dichotomy battling in his mind of wanting to be fully involved, pitched against his distrust of the Security Service agent.

The friction, all too obvious, stirs Charlie, "We will be working as a functional team. The intelligence picture will be drawn by Matt and Nick, based on the source. Alex, I want you on the case getting whatever you can from the flat digitally. John, you will lead ground surveillance, while Lucy, Dev and I focus on liaison with the local players. Got it?"

Everyone nods.

54

ROC Drill

Lucy stands over the model of the event zones that she has constructed with pride. Covering most of the living room floor, it is neatly depicted, with shapes cut from brightly coloured card representing the spaces, buildings, routes and waterways of their mission's 'area in detail' from the university campus to Hendon, and the length of the river from the dock entry gate to the Wearmouth Bridge. Green plastic toy soldiers are placed to represent the event security guards, police and she holds a handful in reserve to represent their team members.

Charlie, John, Alex and Matt file in for the Rehearsal Of Concept drill, though this will be something of a reverse engineering of the process – their concept unable to be developed without the knowledge of what the cell has planned.

"We're going to look at what we've deemed as the three most likely courses of enemy action." Lucy begins. "We've ruled out a hostile vehicle attack, as the Council has acted on outputs from the Pavillion Gardens' lessons loop and have a robust anti-vehicular plan in place. What we're looking at it is what a group of eight men can achieve on foot with what they can carry, or what they can make use of within the event space.

"Our first scenario is a crowd surge attack with bladed weapons, where marauding knifemen attack a concentration of the gathering public, causing disproportionately high casualty rates through crush and stampede injury." she states matter-of-factly.

"Less for the bomb blast, that's how most of the other deaths were caused at Pavillion Gardens. Jaleel's rubbish truck and machete combined didn't kill as many as the thought of them did." says Alex wistfully.

"This type of attack might be initiated on either or both of the event spaces. On the Campus site the crowd would likely be shepherded towards the river, where they would be crushed against the robust steel railings. In the port, the crowd has much more open space to disperse into, but the terrorists would likely steer them towards the water's edge at this corner of Corporation Quay." She points with a broken child's snooker cue at the knuckle of hinterland at the east end of the deep-water berth where the water channels south towards the lock's entry gate. "The temporary barriers only go to the end of the last hull, leaving plenty of exposed quayside where they could potentially drive hundreds of people off into the water."

"Assuming they go for the port option, that's fairly simple to defend." says Matt, "We make sure that there is adequate sharp-shooter cover over the entrances, then make sure that they get their bags searched, at which point the Armed Police do what they do.

"Tomorrow is the first day of the event, it will be relatively quiet, I'm sure they'll be doing recces – we should make sure that the ground Police presence and bag searches are on the entrances and approaches to the grounds that we do not want them to use."

"Next up," she continues her delightful narrative of terror, "marauding firearms attack from one or more event entry points." Lucy pauses, but no one else seems to want to join in. "Unlikely to want to risk a clumsy start, should they get pulled at the bag search, I'd assess this type of attack would be initiated from outside the entrances with the biggest queues."

"Giving them a juicy target set to start with." John says thoughtfully.

"Similar to the first scenario," Matt says, "relatively simple and easy pickings for the snipers."

"Hmmm." Lucy isn't happy with the lack of initiative being shown at more efficient ways at preventing the potential loss of life.

Matt's phone buzzes in his pocket, he takes it out and sees the message preview: 'Nick – white towel'.

Lucy pretends not to notice his distraction and pushes on. "The last one is an incendiary attack on one or more of the vessels on show at the event. Now this one…"

"Listen, Lucy, I know you've put a lot of effort into this, but it's all a bit of a waste of time until we get some firm int. Speaking of which, I'm going to have to leave you guys to it. Hopefully I'll be back in an hour or so with more news. If you want to make yourself useful; speak to Dan Mason and sort a meeting out for late this afternoon with him and whoever's leading their armed unit."

55

Police support

Lucy and Dev stand waiting outside the Sunderland City Centre Police Station as a smug-faced Matt walks towards them fresh from his meeting with Tariq. "We're good." he says as he pushes the door open and holds it for them.

Sergeant Mason is waiting for them behind the counter and ushers them straight in to the interview room.

"Agent Matt Tailor, Sergeant Dev Jackson and Staff Sergeant Lucy Butler, this is my colleague from the armed police unit, Sergeant Jerry Richards."

Jerry has the look of a seasoned field officer, between him and Dan, Lucy feels that the Police side of the operation is in good hands. Jerry stands to shake their hands and say hello.

"We've got our plans in place and our officers briefed ready for the big weekend." Dan says seeming cynically eager to set his skittles out ready for Matt to smash down.

Matt chooses to listen, hoping that what they have in place will be suitable.

"We have four beat officers who will be on roaming patrol, two each side of the river, and a further four officers from Jerry's team, who will be stationed at the main access point on Low Street into the port, and the other pair will circulate in coordination with the unarmed pair on the campus."

"Is that it?" Lucy exclaims, "Eight officers?" with not so much disappointment but genuine fear in her voice.

"Without any solid intelligence of a credible threat, there's no justification to exceed the resources we've already applied, this is already double the number of officers that we'd have dedicated to a localised event like this." Dan says impassively.

"Unless you've got any updates for us?" Jerry adds.

"Okay, gents, let's not play games. You chaps can't do your jobs without decent intelligence, and up until now, we haven't had much to offer, but please cut the bullshit." Matt smiles. "I know you have more officers available than that. That is unless your Chief Constable's requested funding for a further 12 officers is a fraudulent one?"

The officers' expressions of disappointment are broken by cheeky smirks. "Can't blame us for trying." says Dan.

Matt resets his position at the desk in a more open posture. "We have new information that a cell of eight or more individuals are planning a potential attack at the festival." He lets this sink in for a few seconds. "The attack is most likely to happen on Sunday, late morning as the footfall peaks. We believe they will be armed with a mixture of heavy blades and blunt force weapons, coordinating initiation at the two entrances to the port event zone."

"Thanks, that's a bit more than helpful." says Jerry, "Deeply worrying, but helpful."

"As we mentioned in our previous meeting," Lucy says, "it is vital that we do not allow the members of this cell to know that we're onto them, so please, only tell your officers what they need to know. And where possible, minimise your profile at the event."

"We have to make the credible threat clear to our officers, there's no two ways about it." Jerry says, but we've decided that the most effective way to cover such a large space, even with the additional officers, will be to use a large proportion in a sniping capacity. The industrial cranes along the main berth of the port mean that we can cover most of the ground for instant effect."

"We'll have armed cops on the relevant entrances too, that's what they'd be expecting as a minimum." Dan adds. "Out of interest, what's your source?"

"Grade one, that's all you need to know." Matt replies.

56

Green recce

Alex and Lucy had done their best to enjoy the walk through the Campus event zone as best they could, wanting to present as a pair of carefree tourists, but their knowledge of what might be coming kept their faces grave.

The recce of the north side space told them nothing much they didn't already know. What had hit home was how porous and open the event zone is, with unchallenged pedestrian routes in from all directions.

Both of them try not to stare at the Echo Building as they cross the bridge. "We can't let them do it again." Lucy says emphatically.

"I know. We won't." Alex says, wanting to reassure her for a change. "We're on them, the place will be crawling with armed police and ex-special forces – they won't know what's hit them."

The couple hold hands as they round the corner and head down the steeply sloping road past the ominous block of flats. There are more pedestrians than usual on the path heading east along the river, the Maritime Festival has only been open for an hour on its first day, but it is already attracting a moderate level of attention. Any visit of a tall ship or naval vessel to the port is novel and draws people in their hundreds, sometimes thousands, but a cluster of galleons, and access to the port seems to be enticing people out of their homes.

The path turns away from the water's edge and behind the abruptly obstructive perimeter fence of the Fish Market complex, taking the flow of public onto Low Street. The tall blue pickets of the port gates wide-open, visitors are welcomed uninhibited. The view along the street and through along the length of Corporation Quay gives a foreshortened picture of the bustle of human traffic, but there can still only be five hundred to a thousand people within sight.

The security at the gates appears to be in line with what was briefed - loose. Two unarmed police officers stand forward and to the right of the gates and there are marshals in hi-vis vests just beyond the fresh hold of the port, ushering people through, not actively doing anything.

"THIS ONE LOOKS DODGY." Spider shouts to Cliff.

"Excuse me, Sir, would you mind stepping aside and opening your bag please?" Cliff says with a burgeoning grin. The 'one size fits all' fluorescent vest is tight over his shoulders and the Velcro is just hanging on under his pecs.

Alex and Lucy follow Cliff over to the table. "You fellas having fun?" she asks.

"Hardly." Spider says as he pretends to go through Alex's rucksack. "The targets have left their building; we're expecting them to arrive on site in the next ten to 20 minutes. We're operating a group call with Jambo and Mike, they're up on the main entrance, John's on the prowl. I can dial you in if you like?"

"Yeah, cheers." Alex takes a single earbud from his inside pocket and presses it into his ear, then accepts the call on his handset.

*

"They're amazing, aren't they?" Lucy says.

"What, Spider and Cliff? They're alright. I wouldn't go as far as amazing."

"The ships, you dick." She nudges him with her elbow, they both laugh.

"I'm more impressed by this." Alex says, looking up through the enormous structure of the industrial crane that they are walking under. Its steel wheel hubs are similar to those of a train and are supported in two linear trucks that run parallel under the superstructure of the hulking mesh of welded metal. The wheels rest in triple-width train tracks that run down the entire length of the quay and beyond, around the corner to the outer basin of the lock.

"Are you looking for the Lima Tango guys?" Lucy asks, as he continues to look up.

Alex doesn't reply, feeling a little frustrated at not being able to spot the police marksmen.

The pair walk the length of the quay, trying to maintain their operational focus, but the impressive spectacles and vibrancy of the festival make it difficult for them to remain objective. The row of vast warehouses, that run parallel to the quay, are barely visible behind the food vans, trade stalls and side-shows that compete for the attentions of the smattering of patrons.

"There's one." Alex says, taking pleasure from spotting the head and shoulders of a dark figure on the roof of the warehouse. "He'll have good arcs from there."

From over the apex of the roof at the eastern-most end of the structure, the fire arms officer has clear views of the main berths on the river and around the knuckle of the port hinterland to the lock basin.

The sparse crowd thins down to almost nothing as they pass the last of the three ships and turn right towards the port basin. The lock chamber is bigger than either of them had visualised from the schematics and maps that they had used in their planning. The rectangular reservoir has sheer concrete walls on all sides, but for the giant gates at the river end, and at the distant end; a dilapidated-looking swing bridge, that was probably yellow, but is now more orangey-brown with rust. As they move closer, they see that entry across the bridge is closed off with a barrier and security marshal keeping visitors away from the industry and business sites across the water. A few geeky-types are photographing the bridge, but otherwise pedestrian traffic ceases.

"That's the main port entrance usually for industrial traffic." Lucy says pointing to their right at the guardhouse at the top of the steep slip road that winds up from the end of the swing bridge. The road sweeps round to their right, cutting across the contours of the bank to the high ground of Hendon. The guardhouse stands only a few metres away from the back of the warehouses that face onto the river.

"Shall we go and see Mike and Jambo?" Lucy asks.

"Let's get down to the end of the port first, we'll see them on the way back."

They walk on past the bridge along the road that tracks the lock basin south. The perimeter fence is on the other side of the road, separating it from the bank of thick small trees and rough greenery.

The scale of the main basin soon becomes apparent; it is like a rectangular lake, its edges disrupted with irregular breaks and cuttings. They see a long line of smaller masts and furled sails at the water's edge and note a few people meandering between the quayside and the concessionary stands.

"They've got the shitty end of the stick in here." he says looking around the sparse, dusty area. The hardstanding of the quayside area is broken and gravelly, and the outer edges away from the water are littered with industrial refuse. There are lumps of concrete, bent and buckled formations of metal and piles of aggregate; solidified with grass growing over them. There are broken sheds, trailers, rusting lumps of iron – it's a real tip.

Scanning around, there is nothing much to the west, just the perimeter wire fence before the bank that dictates the shape of the port land. Turning counter clockwise, Alex's eyes follow the road behind the food stalls until it disappears behind a cluster of four huge towers. "What's in them?" he wonders out loud looking at the towering white cylinders.

"Some sort of storage silos." Lucy says without certainty.

Alex nods and continues his scan of areas beyond the event zone. There is a sharp narrowing of the water that sections off the final 200 metres of the dock; the square basin has several industrial-looking ships moored inside it. Beyond the water, behind a tall, galvanised picket fence, is a hazy mass of buildings and structures. The industrial landscape continues around to the east and thins back to warehouses and cabins up towards the other end of the swing bridge and beyond to the north-eastern peninsular of headland, where Port Control is situated.

"I don't know why they didn't just put all the boats in the river?" Lucy says, concurring with Alex's poor rating of the location.

"Silt." Alex says dismissively. "It'd cost them millions for them to dredge berths not already in use, plus the tidal range of the Wear is six metres – that's too much for these tiddlers to manage - their gangways would be up and down like yo-yos. Inside the lock the Harbourmaster controls the water level to within about a metre.

"This is the Class B ship." Alex says, pointing at the middle vessel of the five moored alongside the first stretch of unbroken quayside. With only two masts and much smaller than the Class A ships on the river, the vessel, flying a Dutch flag, still dwarfs the others. "Come on, let's go and see Mike and Jambo".

*

"Hi Mike." Lucy says as they reach the search tables adjacent to the guard hut, but he is busy going through the bags of a young mum with three small kids and a pushchair in tow.

"Hi guys." Jambo says, stepping out from the cover of the hut.

"Thank you, Madam. Sorry for any inconvenience" Mike says, as he sends the cranky young lady through. With no one else coming his way, Mike turns to greet them. "Culmination of my career, this – bag search in this dump."

"OYE-OYE nob 'ead."

"Hi, John." Alex says without even turning around. John hands Mike and Jambo brews in brown card disposable cups. "We must have missed you back there?"

"That bodes well for you finding anyone." John says sarcastically, looking down at his hi-vis vest.

"We're giving the punters a hard time at this gate today, hoping to promote the use of the Low Street entrance." says Jambo.

57

Red recce

Alex and Lucy leave the lads to it and follow the road from the main entrance north. Their route curves westwards to become the old High Street East road, circulating back towards the other entrance.

"I'm feeling a bit guilty for not offering to do a stag on the gate." Alex jokes. Lucy says nothing. He looks up to her from the concrete and is startled to see her focus fixed straight ahead. His eyes flash back to where she is looking – Hamza and three other cell members walking in pairs - Tariq is just visible between the shoulders of the leading two. The group are silent and have grim looks on their faces.

"Relax." Alex says under his breath. "Look, you can see the ships from here." he says loudly and with as much enthusiasm as he can muster.

"Four targets approaching Low Street entrance." Cliff says over the group call. "Lima Tangos advised."

"Wow, aren't they beautiful?" Lucy says, bouncing into life, shaking herself from her trance. The pair step onto the grass to let the four young men past. They stay off the path to let other pedestrians by. Lucy looks over her shoulder at the same instant as Tariq snatches a glimpse back at her – they lock eyes for a split second – is he smiling?

"Four targets heading towards west entrance." Alex gives his report. "Matt's in pursuit." he adds as he spots the MI-5 man casually strolling past on the opposite side of the road. "I'll add him to the group call."

Joseph Mitcham

"Roger, I'll brief my Lima Tango if they come this way." says Jambo.

*

Word seems to be spreading about the ease of access at the Low Street entrance. As Alex and Lucy carefully step down the steep crumbly path across the grass bank that separates the port road from the low ground of the quayside; the concentration of people is markedly busier. Despite the greater footfall, without a bottle neck of searches at this entrance; there is still no queue. The atmosphere is building as the crowds grow and excitement rises as some of the ships signal that they are about to open for tours.

*

Mike fights to conceal his contempt for the potential terror activists, biting down his snarl as they saunter towards the small disorderly queue of people waiting to be checked through at the main entrance.

Jambo hams up his interactions with the members of the public as the four get nearer to their table. "Good morning, ladies." he says to a group of teenagers, "Have you come to see the ships? Or just me?" They fail to find him funny.

"Smile girls, it might never happen." Mike says, forcing himself to get involved.

"Afternoon, gents." Mike says boldly moving with vigour towards the group of young Asian men. He places his hand on the first one's shoulder, gently, but carrying the momentum of his full weight through his palm to take Jhiani off balance. "No bags?" he says maintaining his friendly tone without a glimmer of acknowledgement of his heavy-handedness. Jhiani shakes his head mutedly. "You don't mind if we give you blokes a quick pat down, do you?" John asks but doesn't pause for them to surrender to the request.

Both the SAS men sense the anger coming from the group, Jhiani in particular, his eyes boiling.

*

With sniper eyes on all target individuals and no offensive action expected from the cell until Sunday, the tracking of the eight men is kept loose by the team. John and the boys keep their hi-vis vests on - hiding in plain sight.

Individually, they wander from marshal post to marshal post, maintaining tenuous visual contact with the target groups, but trying not to encroach nearer 100 metres to them. Coordinating the handover of responsibilities as the nodes of targets come together by the swing bridge, Jambo stands in overwatch, whilst making small talk with the guy managing the loan pool of wheelchairs at the bottom of the slip road.

"There seems to be a lot of interest in the perimeter along the line of the railway track." Jambo says, picking up on Jhiani's arm movements, waving at the embankment and fence in front of it.

"There's nothing much there." Alex says.

"Not near enough to the main crowds, certainly not a premium spot or choke-point." John adds.

58

Gold

The tension in the festival's Gold Command Centre, deep in the guts of the Civic Centre, is intense, even without everyone having full knowledge of what is happening on the ground.

Surrounded by stern senior blue force officers and irritable Council officials, Charlie feels the pressure building. She has managed to keep news of the cell's presence in the main event zone to her and Chief Constable Chanders, who's response has been considered. He beckons her towards the small brew room along the corridor with a playful waggle of his finger and mock discerning look over the rim of his heavy, dark framed glasses. His thick side-parted blonde hair belying the age inferred by the wrinkled, leathery skin of his face.

"Tea or coffee, Darling?" he asks, in a voice as camp as a row of pink tents. Charlie hasn't quite worked out if he is gay, wholesale eccentric, or both. Never having met his wife, she is not sure whether she is real, fictitious or maybe of convenience. Guy's every movement and word is pure theatre, with deliberate embellishment - his mannerisms and prose-filled monologues endear him to everyone, but there is no mistake that he is not one to be crossed.

"White coffee, please, Guy." she says perching herself at the end of the counter as he grabs two mugs from the tea trolley.

"You know you're playing a dangerous game. young lady." he says quietly in a tone as close to serious as she has heard him use.

Charlie tilts her head to check the corridor is clear. "Eeee." the weight of the situation evident in her sigh and all over her face. "I know." She pauses, uncertain that she wants to say any more. They both take sips of their drinks. "You know what the bigger picture is, as well as I do." The chief constable bites down on his lips and gives a sympathetic frown. "As soon as these characters make a move; they'll be nipped in the bud," she says solemnly, "but until then, all we can do is watch and wait."

"Well, my dear, you know I'm behind you, we're supporting you with everything you've asked for," his building magnanimous posture begins to deflate, "but as much of a positive spin as I can put on it; it's your decision, made against my sage advice." He looks up from his brew, "That is to say; if this does go tits up – you're on your own."

Charlie feels the balance of pressure squeezing her. Between scuppering a national level investigation and risk the lives of members of the Sunderland public as effectively bait in her trap - her position is precarious, if not impossible.

"I fear it's going to be another two sweaty days in here, then." he smiles, lightening the mood.

59

Cover of darkness

The team continued to observe the cell for a further hour, in its sub-groups and together as a unit – there were no further clues as to their intent. The cell had left through the Low Street gates and moved straight back to their flat on foot.

Alex and the majority of the team congregate around the picnic tables of one of the recently closed beer tents on Corporation Quay. The calm view down the river is spectacular; through the masts and the rigging lines of the largest of the tall ships, the sun sets behind the iconic pair of bridges. The Echo Building stands tall on the south bank, but tonight it seems more of a shadow than a silhouette.

The port has been closed to the public for over 45 minutes, there are now just a few stereotypical 'drunken sailors' wandering around trying to find their ships. Charlie's heels screech across the concrete, having stormed straight to the port the minute that the operations centre had shut down to its overnight skeleton crew. "What have we learned?" she asks before even sitting down. The torturous day has taken its toll; she looks and sounds browbeaten.

Cliff does his best to take a positive; "The way they all deployed out to this single space and tested both entrances would suggest that they will be focussing on a concentrated attack on the primary event zone."

"Maybe." says Matt, making no effort to sound enthused, "We'll have to see what they do tomorrow. They may just be taking the event spaces sequentially."

"Why were they so interested in the fence line?" Lucy asks. She receives only shrugs in return.

"Looking at the mapping," Alex says, turning his laptop around on the table, "there's nothing between that fence and the Hendon estate, but a dis-used railway line, apart from that it's mostly bushes, a few trees - just scrub land."

"I'll check it out in the morning," says John, "before the gates open."

"If you could get it cracked and report in before our morning briefing with the CTU, that'd be a big help." says Dev. Lucy nods in support.

"No worries." says John.

"We haven't got much…" Lucy pauses as she notices the expressions frozen on John and Cliff's faces. "What is it?" she asks.

John holds up a finger as he receives the end of the message. "Roger, acknowledged. Nice one, Spider. Out." he says, then silences the mic on his headset. Everyone but Cliff looks at him, waiting, holding their breath. "We've got a couple of Charlie's leaving the Echo – likely moving by car."

"Nick's nearby in wheels." Matt says eagerly.

"Spider's got Jambo up at the stakeout, they can cover it between them." he nods at Matt. "I'll dial you and Nick in."

*

Jambo sits behind the wheel of Spider's little white van in the parking bay adjacent to the stakeout on Bridge Street, exactly where Tariq and Hamza had been dropped off six days ago. The traffic coming from across the bridge, into which the target vehicle would merge, is still busy, and is an incoherent blur of headlights.

"Red One in place at the exit slip of the St Mary's Car Park." says Nick. Jambo is confident that Bridge Street is the least likely route that the target car will take but having Nick in an alternate start point hedges against it. Their main risk is that the target gets too far ahead while they wait for the lights to change.

"Red Toyota Yaris emerging from the car park with two on board." Spider says.

"Moving now." Jambo says, echoed by Nick. "Were you able to ID them?"

"Negative."

Jambo rolls up to the lights slowly, letting them turn to red. He looks across to the next entrance to see Nick teetering down St Mary's way with cars accelerating round him as his lights go green, their honking horns threatening to attract unwanted attention. Mercifully the lights change and the X6 takes prime place at the front of the queue in the centre lane.

"The Yaris is at the lights now, right hand lane, not indicating." Spider says calmly, watching from his window over the junction.

Jambo fears that he might be about to see the target car drive straight past. He checks around him – he could spin a J-turn back into his parking space easily enough, but the sharp movement would be obvious from across the junction, even from three cars back. He holds his nerve and trusts in the assailant's cavalier approach to indicating.

The headlights of the oncoming traffic arc across Jambo as they enter the roundabout and then back the other way as the majority of the vehicles snake round past him. "Target vehicle exiting onto St Mary's."

Jambo counts five cars past before the lights change for the A1018 traffic, most of which heads north of the river. Jambo knows he has some catching up to do. He spins the wheels of the little van and thrashes it, arcing onto and off the roundabout and down the outside lane of St Mary's.

Frustrated by the traffic, Jambo is only able to pass three cars before getting caught behind a slow mover. As the road contours down, he catches sight of the small red Toyota. As it passes Keel Square it is one of only a few vehicles not indicating left – it is still in the right-hand lane. Other vehicles intending to take the second exit stay in the middle lane, giving Jambo a clear run to the bumper of the Yaris.

"I'm back on St Mary's, where are you?" Nick asks.

"Turning onto Silksworth Row, heading west out of the city." Jambo takes a breath to reset his composure and eases off the accelerator. He negotiates the next roundabout with a respectable gap to the target car and follows it around the flowing curves of the trunk road that runs parallel to the river with a strip of industrial estate in-between - the remnants of the historical ship-building yards recycled and repurposed.

Expecting to take the second exit at the next big roundabout, he is caught off guard as the Yaris swerves off the almost unnoticeable first exit into what looks like a building site entrance. Jambo slows and continues round the junction. "He's exited at…" he struggles to check his phone mapping whilst holding the turn, "Carol Street. I'm doing a lap of the roundabout and going after him."

As he completes his lap, Jambo sees Nick has caught up and is waiting for him to pass. "I can see him turning left, 100 metres along Carol Street."

"Roger, that's a closed estate," Alex answers out of the blue, "no more than 200 metres square, it's just five strips of terraces – advise you dismount, it's going to be difficult to observe in there."

*

Jambo drives past the entrance to the estate following the newly built partitioning wall that separates the compact terraces from the still partially built houses on the north side of the road – unapologetic gentrification in process. The tall, modern, pale bricked wall appears, despite its picketed sections, as a shield to protect the view of the new residents from the ageing estate. Nick pulls up in front of the van and joins him on the pavement.

Jambo moves past Nick's car to observe through the next set of pickets. He has a clear view down between two of the rows of terraces, but this is an alleyway bisecting the back gardens, not a street. Jambo checks the mapping before forming his plan.

"There are three streets running to the south. The first is accessed back there," he points back towards the roundabout. "They'll either be down St Cuthbert's Street," he points over the wall at the centre street, "Cirencester Street," he swings his arm further to the right to the western-most row, "or one of the two short rows that run across the distant ends of these roads." Nick nods his understanding. "Most of the back alleys don't look like they take vehicles, so don't worry about them for now." Nick nods. "You take St Cuthbert's and the two rows at the end of it, I'll take Cirencester and the alley behind that, which doesn't back onto anything."

He eyeballs Nick who looks a little concerned. "Are you up for this?"

"Yeah." he answers unconvincingly. "I don't do a lot of field work." he says hesitantly. "We normally do things in bigger teams." A stout, sturdy figure, Nick's bent in nose and harden features give him an appearance that fits in with the rest of the field team, but his nature is submissive, polite and friendly.

"Well, it's time to put your big boy pants on, Nick." Jambo smiles playfully. "Come on, let's go to it."

*

Jambo sees Nick off down St Cuthbert's, where no red cars can be seen in the near distance. His gut tells him that the target is on Cirencester and that he doesn't need to worry about the nervous MI-5 man.

Reaching the corner of the terrace Jambo steals a peek down Cirencester. The street is crowded with parked cars. He can see figures moving on the pavement more than half way down on the near side, but at this distance he cannot confirm the presence of the small red car. He gorilla runs across the end of the road, mostly in the cover of the parked cars, onto the far pavement and begins to make his way down the road maintaining his crouched posture.

Snatching glimpses over the cars, Jambo sees the back of the Yaris nestled in behind a battered old Land Rover defender. Just beyond it he sees two dark figures standing outside an open door. The men are fully focussed on the door; Jambo decides to risk getting closer. Facing the targets, he creeps diagonally forwards, taking some of his weight off his feet and stabilising his movements by pressing down on the window seals and bonnets of the cars as he goes.

Two cars away from coming level with the targets, Jambo has a perfect line to observe through the driver's window and windscreen of an old blue Citroen AX. Whoever it is the two targets are visiting is back at the door and is handing them a large package. As he passes it over; its weight is evident.

"Nick, targets are on Cirencester. They have collected a large package. Get back to your car, get to the opposite side of the roundabout and turn around ready to pursue."

"Roger. Moving now."

"Get a sprint on, they'll be on the move soon."

Jambo notes the door number of the house, tracks back in silence, breaking into a run as he senses that he is beyond the limit of noise. He makes it back to the cars before Nick and three-point-turns as

Nick emerges onto the road. Jambo drops his window, "Other side of the roundabout." Jambo says curtly. Spider's nippy little van lurches off.

*

"Target vehicle is heading back towards city centre." Jambo reports as he pauses to allow the Toyota to crest the hill and almost get out of sight before giving chase. Nick, having only just arrived in position behind him, follows closely.

Eastbound traffic being lighter along St Mary's, and with a strong assumption about where the target vehicle is heading, Jambo is comfortable to leave a decent gap. To return to the Echo Building underground car park, the Yaris must either cross the river and follow the Dundas Street one way system, to return on the bridge's other carriageway, or head past the building towards the Port and drop down onto Panns Bank and double back. The Yaris crosses the roundabout seeming to favour the latter option.

Following the curve of the A1018 past the narrow car park, Jambo sees the Yaris take the first exit towards the Port.

"We know where he's going, I might as well head back to base."

"Roger." says Nick.

"Acknowledged." says Alex.

Jambo watches the small red car head down the road as he enters the roundabout to turn back to the stakeout. "Wait." he snaps back onto the line. "He's not taken the turn down to Panns Bank." Jambo arcs wide around the junction completing a full circuit and follows the target car onto High Street East.

"There's a second left that takes you down to Fish Quay." Alex offers.

"No, he's past that already."

*

"It sounds like they're heading our way with some sort of 'parcel'." John says.

"All of the armed call signs are stood down over night." Charlie says sternly.

"Don't worry about that." Cliff replies, "They're not going to attack tonight." A few hundred sailors, sitting ducks on board their ships, would be a juicy target any other time, but the weekend crowds are surely too good an opportunity to be missed.

"They've pulled up by the Town Moor, round near Sharon's house." John says to Charlie. She visibly quivers at the thought of her sister being vulnerable. "They're out of the car and moving across the green towards the Port's perimeter wall." he relays.

"This will be linked to them checking out the fence line inside the event space." Matt says reflectively.

"Shall we go for a walk?" Cliff asks looking at John. John pulls up the mapping on his phone.

"If they enter the scrubland from the Town Moor, they'll have to move through some pretty rough ground diagonally, north-east if they head to the spot they were looking at." he rubs the stubble on his angular chin. "Yeah, we can get round there and into cover in plenty of time. Come on."

*

"I think it's the two from Liverpool." Jambo says pulling the infrared monocular he'd found in Spider's glovebox away from his eye. Crouching behind a bin at the north corner of the oddly shaped Town Moor green, there is no nearer cover available without taking a significant trip literally around the houses; a journey he'd sent Nick on.

"One of them's gone over the wall." Jambo reports. He watches as the second cell member walks casually back to the Yaris and leans up against it.

"I'm parked up by your digs and walking through the Trinity Churchyard, I should be able to get within ten metres of the car." says Nick.

"Good work, but we're not going to be able to get much more from this side – we can't follow them into the scrub. How are you fixed, John?"

"Almost there."

Another minute passes and Jambo hears a call from over the wall. The second assailant responds by moving to the back of the little Toyota and opening the boot. He wrestles a weighty package free of the boot, tucks it under one arm and slams the boot lid down. Taking a firm two-handed grip of the burden, he hurries as best he can back to the wall.

Having to readjust his grip, he hoists the parcel up to chest height and presses it up on to the top of the wall. A pair of hands reach up from the other side and the bundle is snatched from view. Another call from the scrubland stimulates the second cell member into life, and he scrambles up, over and out of sight.

"In position under one of the burger wagons. If they breach anywhere along the west side of the hinterland; we'll have eyes on." says John.

*

John and Cliff, lay silent and still, their banter broken by the anticipation of the targets, their eyes scanning over-lapping arcs of the area of interest.

John touches Cliff's right elbow, drawing his eyes over to his right of axis. Movement in the vegetation up the slope of the embankment, visible over the top of the eight-foot wire fence.

"There's nothing like being tactical." John says sarcastically.

"And that's nothing like being tactical." Cliff laughs, knowing they don't really need to whisper with the amount of noise that this pair of characters are making as they descend the bank.

Nearing the bottom of the slope and becoming conscious of the open space of the Port grounds on the other side of the fence, the two now seem concerned about their signatures and step the last few metres quietly aided by the thinner vegetation and levelling ground. The leading taller figure places his payload on the grass and takes something from his jacket pocket. He turns towards the fence and takes a knee.

"He's cutting the fence." John says over the group call as the man makes the second snip.

As the first target works on the fence, the second unpacks the bundle, unrolling the rubberised sheet which loosens around its contents, scattering them onto the weeds with a slick heavy metallic clatter which immediately has Cliff and John's attention – the unmistakeable sound of badly handled firearms.

60

What to do?

"What's the sketch?" Alex asks as John and Cliff perch themselves back on the benches of the adjacent picnic tables.

"Not great." John says. "The hardware signifies some serious intent."

"Two AK-74s, very nice Bulgarian variants," says Cliff gravely, "and two chest rigs of non-standard mags; they're double the width of the standard issue."

60-round by the looks of them;" John adds. "I've never seen them before."

"And they've just left it all out on the ground?" asks Lucy.

"They've laid them out on a sheet and folded it back over the top – loaded, made ready, safeties off." Cliff explains.

"In reaching distance from the cut they've made in the fence." John adds. "They've covered the hole with a sheet of scrap metal."

"What are we going to do?" Dev asks. "We can't just leave them there."

"We can." Matt says dispassionately. "If we move those weapons, we blow the operation, we might as well all go home."

An uncomfortable silence chokes the discussion as they each consider the options.

"If we can't move them, can't we disable them?" Alex offers. "Take out the firing pins, or file them down?" he suggests, recalling something he'd seen in a movie.

"It's a good option." says Cliff.

"It depends on how far we're going to let them play into an action before we intervene." John says looking sideways at Charlie. "If we want them to go noisy before we nip them in the bud, that gives us an issue. If we're not willing to risk going that far; then we might as well, it'd be a safety net worth having."

"As poor as their skills might be, they're typically a paranoid bunch, I'd assume they'll have left things so that they'll know whether the weapons have been tampered with." says Matt.

"With the look we've just had, that ship's sailed, as it were." says John, seeming not to mind too much."

"What about scuttling them?" suggests Cliff.

"You mean block the barrel, cause a breach explosion?" John replies.

"Why not?" Cliff answers. "It would stop them from doing anyone any damage and might take one or more of them out of the game without our boys firing a shot. It might even cause some friction we can use between their group and the weapons suppliers.

"Just throwing it out there," Lucy says brightly, "but couldn't we seize the weapons, repair the fence, and arrest them when they attempt to retrieve them? No risk, a plausible explanation that the Port security discovered the breach and the local Police stepped in?"

Charlie smiles and shakes her head subtly. "That's not enough, Hun. It might put two of them away for a while, we can't incriminate the others without compromising our investigation."

Lucy is visibly annoyed at herself for her naïve suggestion, but her concern, and desire for a lower risk solution is clear.

"We need to keep things in perspective." says John. "They might have some Gucci kit, but they've shown that they are not good operators – classic 'all the gear and no idea'. The cell members have been recruited straight off the streets, brought up here and into that flat with no experience of these sorts of weapons. They take delivery, unwrap them, and expect to be able to carry out an effective attack with them?"

"What training are these guys going to have had? Watched a few YouTube videos?" Cliff says dismissively.

"How many hours of skill-at-arms training did you have in basic?" Cliff asks, looking at Lucy, Alex and even Matt. "Remember your first time on the range?"

They all smile, each reminiscing back to nervous, butterfingered experiences under the close supervision of overbearing instructors.

"At the end of the day, we know where they'll be picking up the weapons, and we've got another day to shuffle the sniper cover." says John.

"Where do you suggest we reposition them to? Under your burger van?" Matt asks with a thorny tone. "There are a lot of assumptions that need bottoming out before we can define the plan."

"We could do with getting into that flat and seeing if they have any other hardware." Cliff concedes.

"Is that a possibility if they all head out for another recce tomorrow?" Lucy ventures.

"I'll put Jambo in the stakeout and task Spider – that's his forte."

"Okay, Matt, you liaise with the Police and make sure the sharpshooters' arcs cover the new area of interest." Charlie says, grabbing her bag. "John, you lead on target and plan development."

"Wait." Lucy says, as something that Cliff had said strikes a chord in her mind. "What if we engineered a story of a parallel investigation? One that tracked the weapons, that said the cell had been compromised by the local CTU who stumbled onto their cell whilst monitoring arms dealers? Then we'd have them all."

The resignation to the failure of finding a solution evaporates from over the group. "Okay, that might work." Charlie says, relaxing the grasp on her bag. "Work up a concept, chat it through with Dan Mason in the morning, see if they have anything on the address where the weapons came from. We've got at least until the event sites open tomorrow to do what we need to with the weapons, 'til Sunday morning really.

"John, if we can get a cover story fixed, you can decide on how best to interfere with the guns."

*

At nearly midnight, most of the group follow Charlie to the Low Street gate against the flow of unsteady sailors and sail trainees. Just Alex and Lucy remain on a picnic bench together looking through the beautifully lit rigging of the centre-piece galleon with the glistening facia of the Glass Centre as its backdrop.

"I don't know what's going on here, am I missing something." Lucy says once the others are out of earshot. "They seemed to be more concerned about lining these guys up in the cross hairs than they do about trying to lift them."

"It's a tricky one." Alex replies. "No one wants to risk letting them get away with anything." His face cannot contain his feelings, his contempt and anger at the members of the Interest Group cell bubble on his brow.

Lucy cranes her neck to try and get in his eye line, her eyes asking more of him. "It's hard to stay objective though," he says, holding out as long as he can. "Knowing what these animals have planned, and the complete lack of mercy they'd have if we let them go through with it;" he shakes his head with disgust, "we should be putting them down like dogs."

Lucy puts her arm around her man's shoulder. "That's not like you." She kisses him on the cheek. "You're right with what you say, though; we've got to stay objective. I'd have thought about that arms dealer angle a lot sooner if I'd been thinking logically and rationally; we've all been affected by what's happened over the past few months."

Alex forces a grin. "Come on, let's go and get some sleep."

61

Revised plan

The Southwick Police Station could be mistaken for a modern church, it's modest neo-classical clocktower emerging from the dark brown tiles of the elongated rectangular roof, the dark brick body of the building presenting as one solid mass. Situated outside of the city on the north side of the river, a kilometre west of the Stadium of Light, it is a perfectly placed, tactical bound from most of the action – the ideal forming up point for major operations. Lucy strolls into reception. She flashes her warrant card at the window and asks for Sergeant Mason. An hour ahead of the morning briefing, she hopes to have an influence on what will be delivered.

Lucy quickly brings the head of the CTU team up to speed with last night's developments he takes a note to look into the arms supplier and it doesn't take much to steer him towards the required modifications to yesterday's plan.

"The guys on the warehouse might be able to get a sight picture on that fence line from where they are," Dan pulls a sheet of satellite imagery from a large buff folder on his desk, "but the angle will be low, it will depend on where they come out as to whether they'll be screened by the embankment."

Lucy puts the nib of her pen on to the paper at the point of the fence confirmed to her by John.

"Even if they can get a shot, if it's crowded, as I guess it will be, they are going to be hard pushed to avoid civilian collateral." Dan holds the edge of a long, clear ruler down on the image of the port. He moves the near end between the firing points along Corporation Quay, pivoting on the newly realised killing area, to illustrate that the lines of fire run to the southern event space where the smaller ships are moored.

"We can move one of the marksmen across from the cranes, but I'm not sure where we'd position them." he frowns. "There's nothing with elevation at the right angle." he scans his finger over the east side of the dock, slowing at any sign of a shadow.

"What about from on board a ship?" Lucy suggests.

"No, those vessels are tiny, even the biggest one isn't high enough and doesn't have enough bulk on its structure to provide the cover required."

"I meant the commercial ship, the one that's moored here." She points to the berth just south of where the festival ships are moored. "The thing is huge, its bridge must be at least fifteen metres above ground level, it's got a helipad on the front end, I'm sure you could lose a couple of officers on it."

"If the intelligence is good," Dan says cupping his chin, eyes fixed on the image. "I'm inclined to drop a gun team and put a couple more on the ground undercover, we can have them on the spot and more likely affect arrests."

"I like that." Lucy says, smiling.

"If I get a pair on the ship, leave one pair on the crane. leaving the other pair on the warehouse roof, we can have an extra pair to be focused on their potential entry point."

"How does that leave us for cover on the North side?"

"In terms of firearms cover? Just two patrolling officers and the marksmen on the crane and warehouse who can switch arcs at a moment's notice."

"Great."

*

Dan had delivered the amended brief to his team with a heavy heart, it being based on the fact that the weapons are to be left in place and untampered with. His hands tied by the MI-5 interlopers and that would not be changing unless the investigatory section of his unit is able to find a plausible link to the address on Cirencester Street.

As she gets back into her car, Lucy thinks about how the officers of the firearms unit had received the update pertaining to increased risk; like excited children - no signs of nervousness, just calm banter and bravado about the opportunities that might be presented. The reaction was similar to that of soldiers being warned off for deployment, a feeling that she had experienced herself, and as she reflects, she realises that she is feeling it now – her hands fumble the seatbelt buckle.

The mixture of excitement and trepidation felt has a different effect on everyone. The variable of the danger that one's role places them in multiplies against the level of appetite one has for getting amongst it. This manifests through each soldier's own unique personality, giving an infinite number of reactions, outlooks and behaviours.

It had not gone unnoticed that the marksmen had been particularly quiet. Extremely unlikely to come into the firing line themselves, their danger would be to take the shot, the responsibility of taking the life of the target, or worse, hitting an innocent bystander.

Lucy's own danger is that borne by the planner; taking her share of responsibility for shaping the situation that will unfold on the ground – has she done all that she can to mitigate against any of the stakeholders coming to harm? Not yet. She dials Charlie.

"Hi Hun, any luck with your Cirencester Street idea?"

"No. They've nothing on record. I was thinking, if you don't need me today, I could stay here and help out?"

"Eeee," Charlie covers her pause for thought, "Shouldn't think much else is going to happen today. See what you can find, it'll make things a lot simpler tomorrow if we can take those weapons out of the equation. I've got sign off from town to go ahead either way."

62

Just another day

Taking the scenic route, Ger scuffs his way down to the riverside. Dragging the soles of his immaculate Gazelles on the worn concrete steps of the path that cuts back into the bank beneath the Echo Building. He looks up at the untidy balconies, abused and unappreciated by the residents - students mostly, from what he's heard. He shakes his head, confounded at the lack of respect for what was a beautifully pristine building.

The festival had made the local news last night and again this morning. 15 minutes before the event site opens, there are already a few people down on the river walk where there would usually be near to none - they are all heading east towards the ships.

Reaching the bottom of the steps, Ger looks up to admire the complex structure of the underside of the Wearmouth Bridge before turning into the sun and heading towards the port.

His time in the Army was the only period of his life that he had ever spent away from Sunderland, other than odd weeks of holiday. Nowhere does he feel the conflict of pride and disappointment in the city more than along this river. Sunderland was a world leader in ship building - in the mid-1800s Sunderland produced over a third of the ships built in the UK.

As Ger follows the disturbed and broken block paving along the south side walkway he imagines the path peeling back, exposing the raw rocky orange soil banks, the sheet steel river walls disappear, the thousands of tons of silt that chokes the Wear dissolve away and the old yards rematerialize in all their glory. He sees the scene in a sepia filter; the wet and dry docks full of hulking great hulls in various states of build, the place is alive and busy, he hears the bustle and shouts in a gramophone quality.

All of his recollections of the yards are from documentaries and museum displays. The only ship building that had gone on in his lifetime was done behind the gates of the port, where the only remaining dry dock remains. Not really that interested in the maritime festival, Ger relishes the opportunity to get into the port to see what's left of that part of the history of his city - the only bit yet to be demolished.

*

As Ger passes the Fish Market on Low Street he sees the gates of the port being opened and the sizeable gathering of early visitors being let in – perfect timing.

The last of the crowd pass security as he reaches the entrance. "Excuse me, Sir, may I just give you a quick pat down?"

Ger feels his anger rising as he lifts his head to eye the enormous black security man. Something intrinsically tells him he's a military guy, so he restrains any expressions of aversion to the request. "Yeah, no problem, mate." he says compliantly. "Ex-squaddie?"

"Nah." the big man shakes his head with a smile.

*

The concourse of Corporation Quay is far wider and appears much longer than it looked from the other side of the river, he had spent many hours looking at it from the roof of the Glass Centre.

Everything about the port is huge on an industrial scale. The expanse of concrete is enormous, the vast, featureless warehouses that back-stop the hinterland to his right seem to go on forever. The towering cranes are beyond comparison with normal machines. Despite the enormity of their surroundings and the low tide dropping their decks nearly five metres below the dock, nothing can detract from the impact of the tall ships, they are still breathtakingly impressive.

The gangways down to the ships are still roped off. The event visitors stand peering down into the ships' miniature cosmoses, watching the crew members going about their morning routine and inducting the newly boarded sail trainees that have been lucky enough to secure a place for the onward voyages out across the North Sea to who knows where.

Ger walks by, paying little attention to the ships or the people, he takes in the detail of the two colossal cranes resting on their rails alongside each other at the near end of the quay. They appear modern, with an unblemished orange coat of paint and uninterrupted curves around the body of their mass that seems to float above the dark blue running gear.

Passing the two other ships and a third, smaller, older blue crane, Ger approaches the knuckle of Corporation Quay, where the river turns in to the entryway to the lock. The hardstanding to his right is cluttered with trade and craft stands, fast food wagons and seating areas creating a small village of attractions, but there is still a wide expanse of space that ends on two sides without warning with a sheer drop to the water.

He walks right to the edge of the corner, unnerved for a moment as he takes time to adjust to this odd perspective. He settles into the peaceful calm, the lightly rippling water that widens out significantly, past the marina on the far side, towards the two sets of piers that protect the waterway from the turbulent rigours of the North Sea. Forgetting everything else, he cannot recall such a feeling of pure tranquillity – is this the perfect place to do it.

Standing perfectly still, Ger closes his eyes and takes a deep breath. An avalanche of emotion hits him as he thinks about the course of his life, the people in it, out of it, the hardships he's battled, the barriers he still faces. Tears well in his eyes, he squeezes his eyebrows down against his cheeks to release the drops. His negative thoughts swirl but piercing through them all comes the vision of his little girl – his Katie. Her beautiful face jolts him out of his stupor. He purges the tears from his eyes with the palms of his hands and takes a step back.

63

Weighting

The tours onboard the ships are the main attraction of the event, and the combination of steep gangways, slippery surfaces, steps and elderly tourists make getting people through a slow process. By midday the slaloms of galvanised barriers outboard of each vessel are full of chatting adults and increasingly impatient children.

"A few more people than yesterday." John says, his mic open. He surveys the crowds massing around the ships in the dock from his uncomfortable vantage point, sat on top of a stack of steel ingots situated at the north end of the 'small ships' line up at the west end of the swing bridge. Each of the 6-metre-long ingots is nearly a foot thick, and are kept separated by wooden spacers. The commodity is one of the port's main sources of business and the place is littered with the neat, but unattractive piles.

"Crazy compared to yesterday;" says Mike from the main port entrance, "the queue's out of sight – typical of Jambo to jack on me when there's actually work to be done."

"Same down at Low Street." Cliff adds, "Do Mike and I really need to stay stagging on?"

"Mate, I told you, Spider's checking out the flat, Jambo's standing by for the north side, and I've got overwatch of the weapons stash. We can rotate after lunch."

"Be nice of Matt and Nick to take a turn on the ground." Mike says gruffly.

"Yeah, well, I'd rather keep that pair of clusters out of it."

"Fair one." Mike responds.

"Event control have just radioed; the port is almost at capacity, they're halting entry – moving to one out, one in down here." says Cliff. "Main entrance will change to be exit only. Executing in figures two-zero."

"It's busy, but not exactly packed?" John says taking another look around.

"50,000 people." Alex says, grabbing the ends of the top spacer and using the gaps between the ingots to climb up next to John. "Doesn't look that many when they're this spread out."

"We've got movement at the flats." Jambo bursts onto the group call. "Two targets leaving, clean fatigue, both in black hoodies."

64

All go

Matt rests his elbows on the wall at the top of the steps of the narrow car park, looking down and to the west to the base of the Echo Building. "Targets are following Panns Bank east, no scenic route today." he reports, now dialled in to the team's group call. He watches intently as the pair follow the route towards the port beneath his vantage point. "Plenty of human traffic for cover. Moving now."

*

"Acknowledged." Spider responds, but he is distracted by the developments on his laptop screen. "All six remaining targets are leaving the flat, nothing carried, all in various brands and shades of black hoodies."

Jambo rolls his chair closer to his mate's and leans in to watch. Neither say a word as they wait for the lift to descend. Spider flicks the ground floor camera to primary on his montaged view. The first pair walk out onto the ground floor foyer. Their movement is nervously stilted as they open the front door with edgy caution.

"Where are the others?" Spider asks. The first two disappear out of the front door.

Jambo looks up, over the screen and through the window across the A1018. "No idea, but those two are heading east."

Spider's eyes are fixed on his screen "The others are in the car park." he says, spotting them emerge into the smaller window.

Joseph Mitcham

"Nick, standby, potential vehicle move." Jambo says. He covers his mic; "Shall I go with him?"

Spider's expression mirror's Jambo's lack of confidence in Nick's ability. "There won't be anyone left here to watch." Spider says simplistically.

The pair watch on as the remaining group of four move to the Yaris, the back end of which is parked just in shot, though at the distant end of the small car park floor. The boot springs open, and the men crowd around as one of them bends down into it and busies himself with whatever is in it.

"What are they up to?" Jambo asks.

The man with his head in the boot passes something to one of the others, but there is no clear view.

"Are you sure there was only one parcel picked up last night?" Spider asks matter-of-factly.

Jambo freezes as he recalls the few brief moments that he had clear line of sight at the handover. Spider looks to him, concerned by the pause. Jambo shakes his head. Spider is worried further by the lack of narrative that accompanies the movement of his mucker's head.

Further items are passed to the man with his back to the camera. His baggy clothes look to stretch down with weight; the taught material of the dark hoody now giving clearer detail of the shape of his shoulders and the creases of the material are pulled tight towards his front.

"What was that?" Jambo says, catching a glimpse of something dark and angular being given to the man on the far side of the group.

"Rifle butt?" Spider offers.

The boot of the Toyota is closed, and the four men form a circle. They give each other pats on the backs and grasp at each other's hands. Finally, they tip nods to one another and the two that appear to be weighted down turn and walk towards the steel doors of the car park exit. The other two get into the car and reverse around to face the others.

"Nick, Red Toyota Yaris about to emerge out of the Echo car park, over."

"Acknowledged. I'm on my way round."

"All stations we have three pairs of targets moving out from the Echo. One pair on foot following Matt's heading. Another pair on foot and the third vehicle-borne; standby for their bearings."

The roller doors open enough for the two on foot to pass underneath it. They stumble out into the brightness of the midday sun and turn left up the hill, out of view of the camera. The Yaris is close behind and follows them out of sight.

65

Keeping tabs

The estimate takes place almost instantly in Jambo's head, based on the potential threat, and largely driven by the dispositions of friendly and enemy forces.

"Nick, watch at the roundabout and keep on that Yaris.

"I'm on it, he's heading east towards the port." Nick reports. Jambo watches Nick's unmissable BMW zip across the roundabout soon after the Toyota.

"Matt, keep on your pair, assuming they're heading to the port, once you get within sight of them entering, track back and see if you can find the other two.

"Cliff, Mike, you guys continue to man the entry points, but standby to rip out and get mobile." Jambo hopes that the 'Relief in place' from the security contractors is standing by as was agreed. "Spider and I will cover off the other two on foot, they're either heading into the city or across the water."

"Who's watching the flat?" Alex asks.

"Two of the lads are coming over from the house."

"Any more of them about?" John asks.

"Negative, all the other blokes have thinned out."

*

Hitting Home

Jambo keeps his eyes locked on the footpath to the left of the Echo Building as Spider sprints back through their complex car park. His view from the unit window doesn't allow him to see the pedestrian route from the Echo car park onto the bridge, but the only other route the pair could take would be south towards the front of the building or to the underpass.

"I'm at the underpass entrance on Church Street." Spider says, gasping for breath.

"Still no sign of them coming this way, keep moving." Jambo says, standing over the laptop, not sure if he wants to see them heading towards the city or not. It seems to take forever for Spider to negotiate the underground passage.

"I'm through." he says eventually.

Jambo sees his pal looking back to him, Spider is leaning against the path's railings, over the tarmac of the road to make sure that he is visible around the foliage that shrouds the aperture of the underground walkway. "I'm following on, you get after them." Jambo bolts from the unit, leaving the door flung open. He passes his two colleagues who have rushed over from their digs in Hendon. "Stay here, keep an eye on the flat – you're our reserve, got it?" but he doesn't slow down to hear their response. He runs at full tilt past the row of small businesses and around onto Church Street.

"You can take your time, Jambo, they've stopped for a bit of sightseeing on the bridge."

Jambo slows his run but is keen to get through the under pass and re-establish a visual.

"Hello, Jambo, this is Nick..." the hesitancy in his voice betrays him.

"Let me guess - you've lost them?" Jambo's mild Caribbean twang becomes more apparent when he's angry, but he keeps his cool. He slows as he approaches the underpass needing to get Nick sorted before entering the potential communications dead spot.

"Yeah, sorry, they went straight on at the High Street East roundabout - I had to give way to a slow car, now I'm stuck behind it heading south on the A1018."

Jambo tries to visualise the route – he knows that the A road curves around the outskirts of Hendon, then straightens southwardly to follow the coast. "We've got to assume they're up to something at the port site; take the first exit at the second roundabout, it'll take you down to the Town Moor – let me know if they turn up. Out."

*

Jambo emerges from the north side of the busy underpass a different person, putting the other elements of the tactical situation to the back of his mind. He is focussed on his own target pair. "I'm passing the Echo onto the bridge now."

"Roger. I don't think they've moved, they were not quite half way over. I'm sat on the grass waiting just over the north side."

Walking against the vast majority of the pedestrian traffic, Jambo stays close to the curb to keep out of the way, but also using the bodies as cover from view. The pavements are free of any other physical obstructions, less the broad sections of the bridge's archway, which curve down through the inner portion of the pavement. His selected route leads him up behind the dark, duck egg green hunk of the ancient engineering masterpiece. As he nears it, a gap in the crowds appears and he sees the targets, still leant on the thick railing, looking out over the river and across to the university campus. He about-turns, lays back onto the arch, pulling his phone from his pocket and holding it to his ear.

"First pair on the south bank have joined the queue at the Low Street entrance." Matt reports, bending slightly to casually lean on the riverside railings on Fish Quay. He jolts back to upright as he assesses the amount of rust at the ends of the flaky cylindrical beam that appears to have done well to take his weight.

"They'll be five minutes getting in, even without bags, unless control pulls the trigger on the site capacity early." says Cliff, who Matt can see at the top of the slight slope over the heads of the normal-sized people waiting in line.

Sure that his targets have not noticed him, Matt sets off back along the path to find his second pair. He doesn't have to wait long. Not even getting as far as the Fish Market compound, he sees the two suspect figures through the smattering of people late to the event. They have a look of paranoia about them, their movements are tense, not the confident swagger of the other two.

Not wanting to change direction in open view, Matt pushes on. Gaining as much information as he can from his peripheral vision, he slows as he passes them. He allows himself to steal a look over his shoulder. The pair gradually drift from the middle of the road, closer to the path to the right.

Comfortable that the targets are now far enough away through the steady stream of people and not taking any notice of who is behind them, Matt watches overtly as they cross over the path and gingerly begin to diagonally ascend the grassy bank to their right.

"Second pair of targets on Low Street are cutting across up to High Street East." Matt considers which route will add least to his profile. As he is about to turn and run around the small block of flats opposite the fish market, the pair falter half way up the unkempt green slope. "Check that. They've stopped – they're sitting down."

*

"There seems to be a decent crowd forming." Jambo says watching the small proportion of the campus gathering that he can see spilling from around the corner of the central buildings. Jambo takes another sly glance over his left shoulder. "Looks like we've got movement on the bridge – heading north.

"Acknowledged." Spider responds.

"Spider, you get ahead, we know roughly where they're going. We'll assume they're heading down for a river walk. I'll track behind, you push out on the far side of the campus and get ready to observe from the other side of the site."

"On it."

Wanting to keep his clean slate in terms of having not been seen by the pair of black hoods, Jambo delays his pursuit - he makes use of the time. "Nick, how are you doing with that Yaris?"

"I'm not having much luck. I've driven all the way through the back of Hendon, back to the port, now I'm combing the residential blocks."

Jambo can't help feeling a little sympathy for him, his options were limited as a lone driver trying to conduct mobile vehicle surveillance in a built-up area of single carriageways. "Don't beat yourself up about it. If they don't turn up, start looking around in the industrial area to the south, but chances are they've headed out of town."

Rolling his back off the steel slope of the arch, Jambo immediately begins cutting into the head start he has given his pair.

His target set is almost off the bridge before he gets to the distant end of the bridge's superstructure. He ups his speed as they round the corner into the mouth of the backstreet that cuts down to the riverside. The slightly concave slope enables him to see past the few people between him and them, they are still 100 metres ahead.

The bend in the street, as Bonner's Field turns into Palmer's Hill Road, is more pronounced than he remembers. He lets his weight carry him down the hill at a good shuffle as they go out of sight.

Sustaining the pace until he is around the bend, Jambo anticipates having eroded the gap to 60 or 70 metres, he focusses out to that range, to the partially gated path out onto the grass of the shallow, open bank, but they are nowhere to be seen. A bucket of shock and embarrassment hits Jambo in the face.

*

The incredulity that he, and no doubt everyone else on the call, had felt towards Nick will fall upon Jambo unless he finds the targets, and quick. He gives himself a moment before reporting in.

More of the bank comes into view as he nears the gates, but still no black hoods in sight.

Jambo applies logic, taking things back to basics; they cannot simply disappear. Forgetting his assumptions, he discounts where he thinks they should be and looks left and right at where they could be.

As the slope begins to level off, Jambo spots a narrow lane, off to the left, cloaked on both sides with brambles and vines. Its path bounces back up the valley wall; there is movement at the top of it – targets reacquired.

"Spider, they're cutting through the campus, watch for them coming through into the staff car park."

66

Walkabout

Buoyed by his pleasant morning at the festival, Ger feels happier than he has done in months. He has seen things that he has only ever been told about or has seen satellite images of on the internet.

The ancient swing bridge, the lock basin and its immense gates, all somehow still enduring and functional, despite their dilapidated exteriors, their mechanisms still work - their hearts still beat. He reflects on this and how it says so much about his city, maybe even about him - his esteem has raised a notch.

Even bearing the queues for half an hour, he has enjoyed being on board and chatting to some of the crew members of one of the smaller ships. He had taken delight in observing the bonds that they shared between them - that intimate camaraderie that only people with such close shared experiences enjoy. He envied them for having what he once loved about being a soldier, for what he sees glimpses of any time he meets another with military experience, serving or veteran. He looks down at the leaflet that he has taken, that details how to become a volunteer crew member, and smiles.

Tucking the folded piece of paper into the back pocket of his faded jeans, Ger walks past the last of the tiny Class D vessels, which is in stark contrast with the towering industrial ship moored behind it; it's shining black hull rising sharply up and out from the quayside, the mesh of its heli-deck protruding out far above his head. Ger looks the huge ship over with interest as he walks by, but then turns his attention to the group of four white, dome-topped cylindrical towers that dominate the ground further along the dock. He steps from the hardstanding of the event space onto the port's service road. Looking left and right to check for marshals; he squeezes through a gap in the barriers and follows the road south to explore a bit more of the unfamiliar hinterland.

Due to the pedestrianisation of the port entrance and the inaccessibility of the majority of the operational quays, almost all of the port's industrial lodger businesses have closed for the duration of the festival. Once a few metres down away from the crowds, the dusty service road becomes eerily quiet.

Passing the grain silos, and the empty old QE2 berth that services them, Ger wanders on feeling a little surprised that he's been allowed to go so far unchallenged. Reaching the bottom corner of the docks, he chooses to follow the road around towards the east side, ignoring the track that branches off straight ahead to the south, as the smell of sewerage that seems to be coming from that direction is non-too inviting.

67

Anticipation

As the two young men in black hoodies approach him, Cliff smiles, he imagines the taller one on the left fumbling around with the pliers while his shorter friend ineptly drops the weapons on the floor. He finds it difficult to imagine these two doing anyone any damage, even with access to such particularly nasty hardware.

"Good afternoon, gents. You don't mind if I give you a quick search?" His big hands encapsulate the entire shoulder joints of the taller assailant as he begins his cursory pat down.

"Thank you, fellas." he says standing aside and watching them through. Cliff immediately hands over his work station to one of the civilian security team.

"That's the first pair, through." He steps out of the checking area and into the small recess of space behind the open gate. "If they close the gates now, the queue will cause a concentration of people on Low Street – ideal target for those two on the bank."

"Roger." Alex acknowledges. "The Lima-Tango on the first crane has them in his cross-hairs, they wouldn't get a shot off."

*

Spider leans on the north corner of the first of the big, brand new university buildings. He watches along a south-easterly bearing down the wall of the oddly shaped and strangely orientated structure. Their selected route has taken them through the building's designated car park and out onto one of the main campus car parks that fills the gap between this and the main grouping of campus buildings. He watches patiently.

"I'm outside the front of the main campus area on the river, just round from the crowd." says Jambo.

"Roger." Spider replies. "Targets are crossing the main central car park into the hub of the campus." He steps off, crossing the car park entry road, picking up the path that border's the northern edge of the open space. The bays are all full, the university having exploited the opportunity to make some money from the festival by opening its available capacity to the public.

The long double banks of parking bays that flow west-to-east, and are perforated by beds of short, well-kept shrubs. The hoods walk through the bottom channel towards the main campus development. Spider speeds parallel across the top of the car park to get ahead of them, only slowing to check that they do enter the campus hub at the bottom corner of the car park at the other end of the huge building from him. Again, he steps up the pace to make it to an alternate entrance to the campus quadrangle.

As he reaches the latticed red brick square, Spider feels exposed as the broad pathway between the buildings faces almost directly onto the target pair – he hugs onto the wall to his left. The two cut a tangent across the distant side of the enclosed space, facing away from him, not once looking about them before disappearing inside the next pair of double doors.

"Jambo, they've gone into the university's media centre, the back of it faces out onto the stage area."

Joseph Mitcham

68

What's gunnan on?

Revelling in his illicit stroll, Ger has made it past the stench of the water treatment plant that borders the southern edge of the dock. He explores the east side, walking along the heavy-duty dock, between the triple berthed oil and gas vessels to his left and the warehouses to his right. This quay is perfectly straight and has a series of parallel rail grooves extending up and down it, seemingly leading to nowhere.

At the end of the basin, the warehouse ends and the concrete merges back out onto the road. Ger veers to the left to save his precious pumps from the thick dust and grime that has accumulated in the shade of the building, but as he does, he hears a car.

*

Dashing to the back corner of the warehouse, ignoring the mess, Ger peers round to see a small red car pull up to the front gate of what looks like some sort of processing plant. While he waits for the car to go, he takes a moment to admire the complex infrastructure and towering reservoirs of the plant, and wonders what all of the pipes and containers do – who in Sunderland knows how any of that works, let alone operates it?

As his mind occupies itself, one of the people in the car gets out and approaches the security kiosk. A tardily dressed guard steps out to meet him, his creased blue shirt half untucked. The pair exchange a few words, but then there is a sharp jolting movement, a jet of blood, and the guard drops to the floor.

Ger is struck dumb, his eyes are a flicker of blinks; he steadies himself against the rough block wall.

*

Tariq feels his breathing deepen and quicken, watching from the driver's seat of the little Toyota as Sharif drags the guard into his hut by his ankles. His head bobs as he swallows repeatedly to try and stop vomiting. He takes control of his breathing and takes a few consciously long, steady breaths as Sharif heads back to the car.

"Are you alright, Brother?" he says, as he climbs back into the passenger seat.

Tariq nods, trying to appear strong and brash. "Where are we going?"

"Straight ahead."

Tariq drives onto the main drag of the plant; all of the heavy works are to their right, with just a few office cabins and a small car park to their left. The plant narrows the further they progress, from being an opaque mass of metal, it thins and light begins to permeate through, until they come to a storage vat that stands over 15 metres tall and is as wide as a house.

"Turn in here and park as close as you can to that." Sharif says, pointing to the tower. "Don't worry about leaving room to get out, you can climb over."

Tariq turns in so that the wing of the car is almost in line with the over-sized safety rails designed to keep anything from encroaching too close to the structure. As he draws up at walking speed to be side on to the tower - Sharif puts his hand on the steering wheel and pushes it around a touch; the little Yaris crunches into the barrier and comes to a halt.

"Perfect." Sharif says. He looks at his watch - 12:51. "Perfect."

*

Joseph Mitcham

Ger looks into the guard hut, the poor man is clearly dead, his throat sliced, his gaping carotid artery a black, empty tube in the red-raw wound. His anger at the outrageous brutality, fights his fear and apprehension.

He crosses over the entryway and follows the edge of the plant works deeper into the grounds, trying to find something offensive along the way. He has not gone far before he sees a section of scaffold tubing that is being used to provide leverage on one of the heavy duty taps at the base of one of the smaller stainless-steel silos. He slides it off the long flat handle and feels its weight in his hands.

Setting his mind to the realities of the situation, the savagery of what he has seen, the nature of the environment, he tries to mentally grasp the seriousness of what might lay ahead. He marches courageously in the direction that the red car had gone.

Running out of real estate and any more serious infrastructure beyond it, Ger figures that the car must be behind the next and final tower. He holds his bar in the 'high port' position and edges around the curve of the giant cylinder. The back of the man who killed the guard comes into view first; he is talking. As Ger steps a little further, he sees the young man beyond him – their eyes lock. The killer stops talking and turns around. Ger steps into the open.

"What's going on here, like?" Ger says, gesturing at the car with his pipe.

Sharif says nothing, just looks at his watch – 12:53 hours. He puts his hand into his hoody pocket and slowly draws out a hand gun. He points it at Ger's chest.

69

Stepping up

"Hello Jambo, it's Nick. I'm at the south west perimeter of the port industrial estate."

"Any sign of the car?"

"Negative. The gates are closed, but the security chain has been cut. What should I do?"

"Keep looking but keep your head down. Out."

Alex thinks about Nick's findings and cannot help but think it of vital relevance.

"Here they come." John says, catching sight of the two dark figures over the heads of the crowd as they round the corner of Corporation Quay some 200 metres away.

Alex slips his laptop out of his pack and opens it up.

"What's up?" John asks.

"Just something I saw in the event risk summary." He taps away.

*

Having skirted clockwise around the quadrangle, Spider finds himself up against the side of the media centre entrance, the air reverberates with the humming music coming from behind the building.

Although the doors are glass, they are shaded; he can see nothing on the other side. Wary of triggering the automatic sensor, he cannot get anywhere near close enough to get a shielded view. "I'm going in."

"Roger, be careful."

Spider takes a few seconds to plan his strategy. With complete unknowns on the other side of the glass, he has risks to balance. The overriding driver is to not compromise the mission, that means not being caught snooping – he must behave as a member of the public, or in this case a student or lecturer. He takes a breath, a few steps back, then walks at the door as casually as he can.

The doors trundle back on their rails. Spider's eyes are all over the foyer; quick readout - clear.

As his eyes take a longer methodical look at the deep atrium that extends the length of the building as his route drifts to the right towards the only obvious cover available; the reception area, where the kiosk entry flap is raised.

The right side of the building seems to be a wall of rooms and offices with a narrow walkway on each of the two upper floors, the walkways are linked to the other side of the building by gantries that cross the atrium to the right side where there is a bank of lifts and a stairwell.

Spider takes a knee at the gap in the reception counter to consider his next move but spots a foot protruding from under the desk.

He shuffles in further to see the body of a young man laid in the foetal position facing away from him, in the dusty shade of the footwell. The branding on his pink bib says, 'Sunderland University Security'. There is a pool of blood slowly growing, filling the gap between his arms and legs.

Spider moves to check for a pulse but finds nothing. He takes the man's security pass from around his neck and puts it on. He stands up and checks that he is still alone. "All call signs, one times fatality in the

University Media Centre. Security guard with suspected stab wound to the gut. No sign of the assailants as yet."

*

"This wasn't in the play book." John says, jumping down from the pile of steel. He takes off his hi-vis vest and discards it onto the end of the wooden spacers. "Tomorrow was supposed to be the day." He turns to face Alex, putting his back to the pair of black hoodies as they saunter past.

"I've checked all other routes, none of the internal gates have been touched, the only route they could have come is onto the port itself." Nick says. "I'm just down from the south-west corner of the dock, what shall I do?"

"I don't like this." Alex says gravely. "Look." He spins his laptop round to face John.

"What's that?" he says, without the patience to look for himself.

"This is the Government's COMAH website."

"Coma? You'll put me in a coma, you boring bastard."

"Control of Major Accident Hazards, dickhead." He silences John. "I remember them talking about a 'COMAH site' on the security meeting last week, I meant to look it up. You can search this site by postcode, and it will tell you what dangerous installations there are within a range."

"And that's open source?" John says with surprise, "Fuck me, that's like a target catalogue for jihadis." Alex's expression reflects John's dismay. John reads the first few lines in the risk summary.

"We best get on to Char.."

"Did you hear that?" John interrupts. Alex nods. The unmistakable, if faint, double tap of a 9mm, "Over there." John points diagonally across the rectangle of water.

John clicks his mic open, "Nick, get yourself up to the event site."

"Dev, tell those sharp-shooters to wake up and let Charlie know we're heading to the COMAH site." Alex says as he shoves his laptop back into his bag, jumps down and begins to sprint after John.

70

Molten gold

Charlie strides over to the Deputy Fire Chief at the Blue Light end of the incident control room. "Chief Lawry, what can you tell me about the COMAH site on the port?"

The sportingly muscular chief spins around on her office chair, flicking her long red ponytail over her shoulder. She smiles up at Charlie. "The Tatersby Chemical Processing plant?" her face pulls a grimace. "It's the biggest risk on the Tyne and Wear register." She stands up, she is taller than Charlie, even in her flat soled boots - her heavyweight black trousers and Force polo shirt probably make her look shorter. "Luckily it's low likelihood, as it's so well regulated and gets inspected by us monthly." She smiles, hoping to have put the MI-5 boss's mind at rest, but Charlie has no look of relief.

Charlie looks around coyly and says quietly, "What if it were to come under terrorist attack?"

The question knocks the wind out of Chief Lawry's sails. "If it goes up it could level the port, and with an easterly wind; could put a toxic cloud over two thirds of the city."

"Smoke?" Charlie says hoping to be able to dismiss the risk.

Chief Lawry shakes her head. "That plant processes and stores methyl isocyanate, it's one of the nastiest compounds there is. It's used in pesticides, rubbers and adhesives. A flammable, volatile liquid, that reacts violently with water." She sounds well-versed in the consequences enough to tell Charlie that it is something she's thought about a lot. "Under accelerated combustion, which I guess is what you're talking about, there would be a runaway autopolymerisation reaction," she sees that she's losing Charlie with the chemistry, "basically there would be a massive release of a highly toxic gas."

"How vulnerable is the tower?"

"Security-wise, there's one guy on the gate, but in terms of the physical infrastructure, the main storage tower is a double-skinned, intercooled steel tower – more designed for keeping the contents at four degrees than for protecting against attack. A well-placed grenade would be enough to set it off."

"What if the worst happened, what would that mean for the city?"

The chief looks back at her in disbelief that this even needs to be considered. "The entire port would be wiped out instantly by the blast." She looks at the weather summary on one of the over-sized LCD screens on the wall. "With an easterly wind? The cloud would cover most of the city inside 30 minutes."

"So, we tell people to close their windows?" Charlie asks.

Chief Lawry takes a breath. "In India in 1984, in a place called Bhopal, there was a leak of methyl isocyanate, over 2,000 people were killed within days. Over the years, the company responsible has paid out for nearly 4,000 deaths. In reality, they think the incident was responsible for 20,000 deaths. That was a leak in an area with a widespread population. This would be an explosive release in a city with 300,000 people; mostly living down-wind."

"Charlie, my dear." Chief Inspector Guy puts a hand on her shoulder. She turns away from the fire chief with her jaw hanging a little.

"Darling, I know your operational necessities, but things are getting a bit 'twitchy bum'. We have to consider lifting these chaps before things get out of hand."

Charlie pauses for thought. She has known Guy for decades; they have crossed paths many times and she has been blessed with his advice and guidance throughout her career. She respects him as a shrewd and astute senior officer, so his intervention speaks volumes and makes her question her judgement of how far she has let things go, how much control she has allowed herself to release - she feels a bead of sweat building in her hairline.

Joseph Mitcham

71

It begins

The media centre being so open, with clear views into the rooms along the left wall, Spider's search quickly arrives at the emergency exit on the other end of the building. The door is propped open with a fire extinguisher and the pounding of the music almost drowns out the pulsating of his heartbeat. He looks through the window to see that the exit leads out and down one flight onto the grass bank that rolls gently down to the back of the crowd that fills the improvised arena.

The music is pulsing, and the crowd is animated. He scours the scene; he sees a black hoody. "Jambo, one times Charlie heading clockwise around the crowd towards the stage. No sign of the other one, yet."

"Roger, I'll get onto him, and I'll keep my eyes peeled for his mate."

Spider steps out onto the meshed platform, leaving the extinguisher where it is. His view is much improved, but he now feels exposed on the framework gantry. As he begins his more in-depth scan, he senses movement above him; he freezes – how loud did I just say that? How much cover is that fucking 'music' giving me?

He looks up slowly, he sees the soles of trainers, the shadowy mass of the figure, and held close against it, an assault rifle – there is no mistake, the muzzle is pointing straight at him; he dives backwards, falling back into the doorway. He gasps a breath and steadies himself as he realises that he has not been seen, or heard. "Second target seen – second tier of the media centre fire escape, at the rear of the arena crowd."

Hitting Home

Spider looks at the position of the man above him and where his buddy looks to be heading - "These guys are both in dead ground to the sharp-shooters. Jambo, you best get hold of the ground-based patrol."

"I'm on it." says Dev. "Lima Tangos are reporting activity at the arms cache – they're weapons free."

The Armed Police's 'weapons free' status means they now have a pre-authorised mandate to fire at will – a rare occurrence that only ever happens in the most complex, fast-moving and dangerous situations; this scenario qualifies without hesitation.

*

Mike throws his hi-vis vest to the verge as he runs down the slip road. He weaves through the sparse crowd, the people oblivious to what is about to happen. He bears right as he reaches the bottom of the slope, arriving on the event space as the second cell member stands and turns from the gap in the fence.

"GUN, GET DOWN." he shouts as the weapons are brought to bear.

Two high velocity rifle rounds thunder across the quayside in quick succession. The targets fall when hit, both with large chunks of their torsos missing, their black hoodies shredded from their bodies. The rifles clatter on the ground next to their twisted bodies.

"Thank fuck for that." Mike utters.

*

Seeing the pair of black hoodies getting to their feet on the grass bank, Cliff pushes through the queue. "Targets active at Low Street." he says. The noise of the rifle fire has unnerved the crowd, even as far round as Low Street and vigilance is heightened. There are screams as some bystanders catch sight of the weapons emerging out from under the clothes of the terrorists. Cliff runs to back up the pair of armed coppers who are already in standing alert positions, weapons trained on the two.

"ARMED POLICE STOP OR I'LL SHOOT." one of them screams, but their colleague isn't waiting. Another two 7.62mm rounds are delivered from a second Police Ruger Precision rifle, blowing both assailants off their feet before they are able to fire a shot.

*

Not quite in position for the synchronised attack, the third pair are sparked into action by the sound of the rifle fire. Spider opts for speed over stealth, hoping that the gunman's focus is fixed, and bounds counter clockwise up the spiral stairs. He reaches the second landing as the black hood opens fire – he launches a flying kick at the gunman, crashing his boot hard into his hip sending the AK-74's butt downwards and the stream of fire arcs up and away from the crowd. Spider loses his footing as he lands and falls hard on the metal grated floor.

Rounds snap and ricochet around them, confusing Spider, but the hood is oblivious to the Police rounds being fired by the foot patrol who have only made it as far as the back of the crowd. The gunman is only concerned with taking the fight to Spider. He swings his rifle around at him. Spider scrambles to position his feet to get up, but the heavyset man from Liverpool has pulled the AK back into his shoulder and has his finger on the trigger.

Spider looks him in the eye, sensing it is all over as a sadistic grin spreads across his face. The second volley of shots slices up and through the railings, cutting through the hoody, killing him instantly. He slumps forward, down onto Spider.

*

Jambo tries not to let the fate of his mate distract him, ignoring the sounds of shots fired behind him as he sprints through the cordoned area at the back of the stage, navigating the boxes, trolleys and cables.

As he reaches the other side a torrent of screaming teenagers flees across his path.

He runs into the stream of stampeding bodies, pushing to cross their path, he makes it through and finds himself behind the arc of view of the gunman, Hamza, who is firing wildly into what is left of the main body of the crowd.

The Police pair, engulfed by the swarm of people trying to escape towards the riverside paths, are powerless to help. Jambo has 20 metres to cover – he snarls, takes a deep breath and charges.

Jambo's sharp movement catches Hamza's peripheral vision. He turns and reasserts his vague aim at Jambo's centre of mass and pulls the trigger.

Jambo dives to the right and rolls, anticipating that the weapon, not properly supported, will lurch up and to his left.

Hamza moves to adjust, but he is too slow. He is peppered by a burst of automatic fire. He staggers backward into the shrubs of the Glass Centre car park's decorative border; his legs buckle beneath him as he drops.

From his sprawled position, Jambo looks at Hamza - dead, then across the arena to the Police, they are still embroiled. Finally, he looks up to the fire escape to see his buddy dropping the AK from the aim to give him a calm thumbs up.

Joseph Mitcham

72

Martyr

As the echoes of gunfire dissipate through the frameworks, tubes and chimneys of the plant around them, Tariq remains entranced with shock, his eyes fixed on the body of the dead man. Sharif's rounds had both entered the centre of Ger's chest. There were no long-winded theatrical death throes, he had blinked, taken one step back, then collapsed.

"It sounds like our brothers have had limited success." Sharif says with a calm glee. His young ward fails to respond. "Tariq, TARIQ." he shoves at his shoulder.

"Huh? Sorry. What?"

"It sounds as though our brothers have done their jobs, however short-lived." Sharif says with less enthusiasm.

*

"All the boys are checked in okay, just a few civilian casualties over at the campus site." John summarises from the front passenger seat as Nick speeds past the grain silos and tests the big BMW's grip as they bear east along the bottom edge of the dock.

"Where are we going?" Nick asks.

"Tatersby Chemical Plant." Alex answers from the back seat. "Follow the road to the left – the entrance is 250 metres on the right.

*

Sharif looks at his watch, 12:57 hours. He walks between Tariq and Ger's motionless body and leans back onto the high rim of the boot lid, feeling the heat of the early afternoon sun being absorbed by the thick, dark polyester of his hoody. "It makes little difference; their part was simply to attract as many emergency service workers as possible into the port." He looks into the back of the car through the parcel shelf at the laden back seat. "Do you have the car key?"

Tariq takes the key from the pocket of his tracksuit trousers and dangles it by the fob.

"Throw it over the wall." Sharif nods to the perimeter of the plant beyond the car.

Tariq looks at the key; he is hit by what this means - that there is not going to be a way out for him. He looks at the gun, still in Sharif's hand, it begins to tap on Sharif's thigh; he has a look of impatience. This is the first time that his mentor has shown any sign of anything but pleasantness towards him. Sharif rotates his neck deliberately toward the wall, and the cold North Sea beyond it.

Tariq takes one big step forward and launches the key as far as he can. It just about makes it over the wall, not past the sea defences – lost all the same.

*

Nick slows as they approach the plant entrance, keeping the revs low. A few metres short, John and Alex pop their doors open and jump out. John takes the lead and shuffles his way into the grounds, he looks across to the guard hut, but doesn't waste his time checking out the body. Alex runs over to investigate, but soon changes his mind as he gets close. He follows John, who is making good progress.

Together they move in a half-attack formation, John on the right side of the road, Alex on the left, behind on a diagonal line. Nick stays in the vehicle. "Keep a tactical bound back, Nick." John instructs.

"Roger, will do."

John sees Tariq first, he tenses, but continues, walking straight until Tariq sees him.

"Sharif." the young lad says nervily, no longer knowing what is going on. Sharif doesn't flinch, just taps his pistol against his leg.

*

John stands off at about 10 metres from Sharif. Alex stays at the far side of the road and absorbs the situation as he chooses a position - in support of John, but not giving Sharif too easy a grouping to shoot at. He feels an intense nervousness and hopes that no one else can see him quivering. He latches onto John's strength, feeds from his confidence, sheltering under his umbrella of bravado.

John breaks the silence, "That on a timer?" he gestures at the car.

Sharif smirks but says nothing. He raises his left arm and checks his watch once more, 1259 hours.

Without warning, John dips his head and charges. Sharif's reactions are quick, his right arm is up, and he fires hitting John high in the chest; he falls down to his hands and knees and rolls with his momentum onto his back.

Sharif takes his weight off the boot of the car, taking a more balanced stance and bringing his pistol back up to aim at John's head.

"You'll be lucky if a homemade IED is going to pierce that tower." Alex says loudly.

Sharif looks from John to Alex, and swings his pistol around, pointing it straight at him.

"Even a vehicle-borne IED would need to be hard up against the skin for that to work." Alex forces his point hoping to communicate it fully.

Sharif steps forward, taking a nervous look down to his right at John, but he is barely conscious. Sharif trains his aim on Alex and his arm waivers with the tension as he applies pressure to the trigger.

The roar and screech are terrifying as the BMW 4x4 lunges into Sharif's line of fire. He releases two rounds into the windscreen before Nick slams into him, skittling him back and crushing his legs into the back of the Toyota. The Yaris offers little resistance, Nick keeps his foot hard down and ploughs the Yaris into the wall, smashing the soft block bricks and crushing the car further. The mangled mess comes to rest halfway through the perimeter boundary.

Sharif screams out, trapped in the mangled wreckage by what is left of his legs. Nick shrugs off his seat belt, opens his door, and runs to help Alex pick up John. The three make it a few metres before the main charge on the back seat of the Yaris detonates; the blast wave sends them flying to the ground.

73

Tariq

Alex crawls to his knees and puts his hand on John's shoulder. "You okay, mate?" The big man is still. Nick groans and rolls over coughing violently.

"John." Alex says desperately. He puts his hands under him and hauls him over onto his back.

"Arrrrgh, fucking hell." John yelps. Alex sees the blood on his hands, he has lifted John by his wound.

"Sorry, mate." His sense of relief is acute, he chokes up a little. "Hello, anyone, we need an ambulance, John's got a gunshot wound to the chest."

"On its way." Dev replies.

John opens his eyes and looks over to the MI-5 agent. "That wasn't so nice… Nick." He is in too much shock to laugh.

Alex gets to his feet and walks over to Tariq. He stares down angrily at him, as the young man sits with his knees hunched to his chest. His head nodding faintly, he stares into nowhere with a vacant expression on his face.

"Tariq." Alex says loudly. The lad's eyes shoot to meet Alex's. "I know who you are." Alex gives a few seconds of eye contact to make his mood clear. "Not so hot with your updates this weekend." he says, hoping to stir a reaction. Tariq bows his head.

Alex pivots to look at the aftermath. The X6 has taken the brunt of the blast. The Yaris being boxed in, has been all-but destroyed. The chemical storage tower is peppered with scuffs and scratches; Alex shakes his head trying not to think about what would have happened if Nick hadn't come around the corner.

*

The road around the south of the dock runs hot with emergency vehicles for the next ten minutes as resources and personalities arrive outside the plant, which is quickly cordoned off and an incident control point is set up behind the strip of dock warehouses.

Sergeant Dan Mason jumps out the front passenger seat of a Police minibus, he slides the side door open; as a stony-faced Charlie steps down, followed by Lucy, Matt and Dev. Alex and Nick walk over from the medical tent to join them, having been given the once over for secondary blast injuries. "How was he?" she asks.

"Fine." Alex says with a smile. "He took one here," he points to the top of the right side of chest, just below his clavicle. They think he might have some lung damage, but nothing worse than he's used to."

"Good. Right - hot de-brief." Charlie says, not wasting a second. "First things first; is the investigation compromised?"

"FOOK YOUR INVESTIGATION, YOUNG LADY." booms an incensed and red-faced Councillor Crawford. He marches over with Chief Constable Chanders, who looks like he's had a good earful already.

"Because of your investigation; twelve people are dead."

Charlie doesn't give him the argument he wants; she stares at him hard, allowing his rage to subside. He shakes his head. "You people," he waggles his finger at the group, "you play your high stakes games, and it's the little people that get squashed." He shakes his head and storms off.

"Actually, it was Jhiani that got squashed." Nick says quietly.

"Nick!" Lucy squeals.

"Really 'not so nice' Nick." Alex smirks.

The Chief Inspector takes no notice, he turns to Dan, "Report on my desk 0900 hours tomorrow morning? Shall we have a coffee over it at 1000?" He winks at Charlie and strolls off after the Councillor.

"The only local compromise concern we have is Tariq." Alex says fingering the proverbial elephant in the room. Matt, Nick, nor Lucy put up a defence for him.

"Eeee, well he'll be subject to a thorough de-brief." Charlie says thoughtfully. "He's already being isolated and will be until we've had our time with him. So, we're good?"

Alex looks up from his phone, "There's been some strange activity at the safe houses. I've got lots of messages showing movement at what looks like all of them at around half an hour ago."

"About when they opened fire on the festival?" Lucy notes. Alex nods.

Epilogue

Lucy, Dev and Nick stayed on in Sunderland to support the subsequent CTU investigation into the cell's activity leading up to the festival attack, where 14 died, two more having succumbed to their injuries in the days after. The search of the Echo Building flat indicated that firearms had been present and there was a selection of other bladed and blunt-force weapons left in place.

An excuse was found to raid the Cirencester address, but no other weapons were found, not even traces. The occupant being of special needs, it was deduced that the house had merely been used as a drop off station – despite the specialist nature of the hardware, all possible leads to the Interest Group via the weapons ended there.

Charlie had crashed at her sister's place for a few days while John remained as an in-patient at Sunderland Royal Hospital but was soon recalled to face the music in London. She gave a good account of her leadership and execution of the operation, actually receiving credit for the low numbers of casualties and maintaining the integrity of the on-going investigation. She retains her bosses' support – for now.

The unusual activity at the seven regional Interest Group safe houses on the day of the festival attack resulted in all remaining Lima and Uniform targets disappearing. From the counter-surveillance techniques used, it appeared that they were exercising good drills for a timed movement, rather than deliberately trying to lose known tails, so the team still cannot be sure if they have been compromised, by Tariq or other means.

Joseph Mitcham

A major disaster averted, acceptable casualties sustained, and a cell clinically removed, the team are no closer – further away, if anything, to snaring the nucleus of the elusive Interest Group.

REVIEW?

Honest reviews help bring the attention of other readers to my books. If you've enjoyed 'Hitting Home' I would be really grateful if you'd give me a further minute of your time to leave a review (it can be as short as you like). Please go to the book's page on Amazon or on your favourite readers' website and let me and everyone else know what you think of it. Thank you so much.

Follow my Amazon Author's page for news of more in the Atrocities Book Series – search 'Joseph Mitcham' on Amazon's 'About the Author' platform.

THE AUTHOR

Joseph Mitcham served with the British military in elite and technical units for over 16 years. His Service, and life experiences since as a proud veteran, have given him a rich bank of knowledge and memories that brings his writing to life.

Having never written fiction before, the inspiration for embarking on the Atrocities Book Series project came from contemplating what might happen if a group of veterans got hold of the UK Terror Watch List. Using personal experiences from the roles that he has served in, and characteristics from some of the people that he has served with, Joseph writes with grounded authenticity, which makes his plausible plots utterly believable.

Printed in Great Britain
by Amazon